Praise for C. Toni Graham's
Crossroads and the Himalayan Crystals

"I was quickly caught up in this amazing
tale...remarkable characters."

-Readers' Favorite

"A lot of magic and mysticism...bold, well-
written and larger than life."

-Butterflies and Books

"Graham starts her YA debut with a bang; the opening scene
depicting Brigara's banishment is exhilarating. Shayna adds some
humor to the proceedings, and *'gothic Tinker Bell'* Seneca brings
in some pathos and punk flavor...portal fantasy with some fun."

-Kirkus Reviews

Winner of *Readers' Favorite* International Book
Award 2015 – Young Adult Action

Winner of *Los Angeles Book Festival* Award – Honorable Mention

CROSSROADS
AND THE DOMINION OF FOUR

C. TONI GRAHAM

BALBOA
PRESS

A DIVISION OF HAY HOUSE

This is a work of fiction. All of the characters, names, incidents, organizations, and dialogue in this novel are either the products of the author's imagination or are used fictitiously.

Balboa Press books may be ordered through booksellers or by contacting:

Balboa Press
A Division of Hay House
1663 Liberty Drive
Bloomington, IN 47403
www.balboapress.com
1 (877) 407-4847

Print information available on the last page.

ISBN: 978-1-5043-9161-0 (sc)
ISBN: 978-1-5043-9163-4 (hc)
ISBN: 978-1-5043-9162-7 (e)

Library of Congress Control Number: 2017917329

Balboa Press rev. date: 02/05/2018

Kirk, I promise to find a place for the narcoleptic troll.

*Kennedy and Parker, you inspire me to believe
in the magic of imagination.*

Amber, Thanks for reading the drafts with only a slight grimace.

CHAPTER ONE

Person of Interest

Yellow crime-scene tape surrounded the deserted high school. Brigara scowled at the absurdity of the flimsy barrier. "As if this would stop me!" She spat at the ground before stepping over the tape and then scanned the parking lot one last time. Once she was certain no one was watching, she began her march toward the administration building. She was determined to claim her belongings, and nothing in the mortal realm was going to stop her. She focused on the coveted fireproof box; it called to her from inside the principal's office.

The fire investigators had recovered it in the rubble and added it to the inventory as one of the few salvageable items. The box had no distinct markings and appeared to be a simple lockbox. After several failed attempts to open it, the police had decided it wasn't worth the hassle of pursuing a court order. They'd written in their report that it was irrelevant to their investigation and left the box with the school administration. Brigara scoffed at their ignorance in not recognizing the simple spell that kept the box securely closed. She had remained close enough to view the police and arson investigators to track the movement of the lockbox, but she was pleased when it appeared no one had shown much interest.

"What an inept assembly of simpletons!" Brigara mumbled. "So completely dense, the lot of them! They don't even know that lead box is merely a mask for holding the greatest record of power anyone has ever known."

Their priority was finding Ms. Bridget, the science teacher. She was the main person of interest in the explosion, since she'd been the last one seen leaving the science wing prior to its incineration. The entire community was on heightened alert. Brigara found the ordeal amusing. The police investigators had no idea that her position as a teacher was just a role like that of a tragic Shakespearean character—a hoax of sorts. She believed the joke was on them—all mortals. She had calculatingly assumed the name Ms. Bridget to exact her plan. She mimicked daily rituals by reciting countless lesson plans to classrooms filled with inferior adolescents and each day left the school grumbling about the pointless routine. She scoffed at the mortal students and cursed them for being oblivious to the existence of anything beyond their own dull realm. The police were among the highest of the incompetents, and she was convinced they posed no real threat. Their investigation was just a nuisance, and as a result, she was forced to wait it out in the shadows.

Brigara calmed her angst by reminding herself that her job as teacher had come to an end, along with a great portion of the school's science building. The smoldering rubble emitted a smell that was almost sweet as she fanned away the ashes that drifted past her wrinkled nose. No longer would she have to endure playing the part of the dutiful instructor for sniveling teenagers. She had only tolerated the role in order to execute her plan of returning to her true home: the Otherworld. Her attempt had failed, but she considered it a challenge. It was fuel for her rage. The setback had not thwarted her mission; instead, she fixated on fighting to the end. Her triumphant return came into being before her eyes, and she could almost hear the cheers and screams of fear.

She grimaced as the last police car drove from the parking lot and cruised out of sight.

"Finally!" she said, her voice cracking in a harsh tone. As she pulled her dusty cloak closed, she cringed from a jolt of pain that radiated through her injured shoulder.

She eased around the tree that had camouflaged her presence. Her tall, skeletal frame stalked briskly across the lawn. Her disheveled cloak fanned out and hovered in the wind like a menacing phantom as the lampposts cast her shadow eerily across the administration building. She jogged around the corner toward the side entrance, the closest door to where the fire had started.

She had only one goal: retrieve the box. Brigara had been calculatingly clever in acquiring it. Only a few knew of its existence, and no one suspected she possessed it. It was one of the essential keys needed to gain everything she sought: power, respect, and the destruction of all that stood in her way.

She maneuvered silently down the dark halls. She blended into the darkness with only the soft corridor lights giving signs of her presence. Once inside the administrative offices, she pulled down the hood of her cloak. She groaned at the flickering fluorescent lights and the effect they had on her eyes, but she resisted the urge to shatter them. Brigara squinted from the glare they cast on the highly varnished veneer-paneled walls. The place reeked of potent pine-scented cleaner, a wasted substance that only masked the true culprit and source of the germs. She scoffed at the cleaning staff. They were prone to spread the disinfectant about haphazardly and failed to actually decontaminate the common areas. After the classes let out for the day, they would incompetently wipe away the grime. "To what end?" she would grouse. The task was useless and ineffective. She had observed that the same filthy students would mindlessly pollute it again, day after day. The cleaning staff should have eliminated the root of the problem: the vile students!

She thought about the most wretched ones, those who collided haplessly into each other daily like blind mice in a maze. Their practice of passing contagions back and forth—the exaggerated hugging, the constant hand slapping, and the ridiculous action of bumping fists together—made her stomach turn. She often thought about trapping them in the school's unsanitary conditions and watching them stumble and then collapse one by one into a germ-infested heap. Thinking about that and other means for their demise was one of Brigara's favorite pastimes.

Seeing cluttered desks, mounds of papers piled across the counters, outdated articles on the bulletin board, and unopened boxes crammed in the corners reminded her of the days she'd had to bear the administration's stupidity and limited thinking. She longed to show them that she was no ordinary mortal teacher. Their pathetic ways were beneath her, and she'd only tolerated it long enough to execute her plan. Returning to a mundane classroom and teaching mediocre minds was so far beneath her that she scoffed at the mere thought, but she was not there to reminisce. There was only one purpose for being there.

She closed her dark eyes and focused on the familiar vibration she could detect when it was near. Her breathing quickened as she sensed the box's presence. She dashed to the corner office and shoved the door open with more force than needed. The doorknob smashed into the wall and created a deep divot. Plaster crumbled onto the dingy green shag carpet.

Brigara scanned the office. She slinked to the principal's old walnut desk, which was cluttered with picture frames holding nondescript photos taken at common mortal vacation destinations. She grimaced when she noticed each face had the same staged grin. With a slight swipe of her hand, she sent the frames crashing to the floor.

The bottom drawer was illuminated around the edges. She opened it and lifted the lockbox for a close examination. Though the authorities had tried their hardest to open it, the surface bore not a single scratch. She recited the charm to release the latch, and the lid opened to reveal the contents. Seeing it again, she smiled at her cleverness in its acquisition. The source of such abundant power made her heart thump with excitement. She hesitated for a moment before slowly and gently touching it with the tip of her finger. It glowed at her touch. The sensation warmed her to the core; her posture straightened, and she raised her chin. Brigara closed the box and secured it under her arm.

Shattered glass crunched under her feet as she exited the office without bothering to close the door. She paused momentarily when she saw a janitorial cart. It was left unattended in the hall, sticking out of an alcove. She heard faint whistling coming from one of the classrooms and the splash of a mop being dunked into a bucket. The scent of pine was undeniable. She cringed in irritation.

"Imbeciles!" she snapped as she drew back her cloak.

She extended her hand, allowing a blue-fire sphere to form. Without pause, she flicked it at the cart. In a mere second, the cart was entirely engulfed in flames. The smoke alarms screeched, and sprinklers hissed into action. She laughed wildly at the chain reaction of explosions. The janitor rushed into the hall, still gripping his mop tightly. He was a stout elderly man with limited mobility. He made a futile attempt to swipe the flames with the mop before realizing it was nothing more than kindling. His hand was scorched just before he let go and backed away in fear. He turned to run but found Brigara standing in his way. He was startled but realized the magnitude of the situation.

"We've got to get out of here!" he screamed. "This place is burning like crazy!"

"I can see that," she said flatly. "You should run along and get help."

"Yeah, help! Let's go!"

Brigara stepped aside to allow him to pass. She watched over her shoulder as he stumbled slightly before making his way through the door. She sneered as she watched the fire spread up the corridor walls. A wave of delight washed over her as the accelerating flames engulfed the hallway floor. She turned on her heel and headed to the exit.

"No need to worry about sanitizing after tonight!" Brigara announced when she saw the distraught janitor.

He had a cell phone pressed to his ear and shuddered when he saw her approaching. She had overheard his declaration of being positive about who had set the fire—the very teacher everyone was looking for. He walked farther away from her and continued to describe the magnitude of the flames that were swiftly consuming the administration building and all others in close proximity.

Brigara raised her hand, and a blue spark flickered at her fingertip. Her eyes narrowed, and her lips tightened. The lockbox beneath her arm rattled, and she gave it a slight pat as she realized she had other matters that needed her attention. She scampered away from the campus and vanished into the dark woods.

CHAPTER TWO

The Attack

Jake, Seneca, Conner, and Shayna were four teens trapped in the Otherworld. They'd never known the mysterious realm existed, but there they were. They had chosen the side of mythical creatures and elemental beings with a yearning to live in tranquility. Peace within the realm was not a desire shared by all. There was Brigara, a dark force looming within the human realm. She was a powerful druid who had been ousted from the Otherworld for practicing forbidden magic. She was intent on returning and terminating all who stood in her way.

"The first thing I'm going to do when we get to wherever we're going is clean off my boots," said Shayna. "They've taken a real beating." She brushed away a clump of dried leaves that clung to the heel of her leather Doc Martin boots. She flipped her thick, wavy hair over her shoulder before dusting her hands across her denim jeans. She longed for a fresh gel manicure but shook off the image. It was a luxury she was not likely to experience again.

"How we look and what we're wearing shouldn't be at the top of the list," said Jake.

"Hey, but we are the *Dominion of Four*—maybe we should look the part," said Conner. "Do you think we'll get uniforms?"

"If we do, I am most definitely going to have a say," said Shayna. "It has to fit perfectly, be the right color, and look good too!"

"Ha! You two are nuts. I seriously doubt that clothing is at the top of the list—I'm sure it's the last thing anyone is thinking about," said Jake. He wasn't sure who would be making the decision, but he'd been willing to wager that uniforms were not high on the agenda.

"What do you think?" Shayna shouted back to Seneca, who trailed several yards behind them. "Do you think we'll get matching outfits so we look authentic?"

"Costumes?" she replied. "I don't know. That seems like a bit of a waste. I think learning how to use our powers is at the top of the list."

"You're no fun, Seneca! We've got to have costumes."

"I said uniforms, not costumes!" Conner blurted out in frustration. "No way am I wearing a costume."

"Costumes, uniforms—what's the difference?" asked Jake. He shook his head at the direction the conversation was drifting. "There's so much we need to worry about, like whether or not we are going to die or something close to that."

"I say talk of costumes wins over death talk," said Shayna.

"A helluva cool cape would make the difference! No, wait—that would make it a costume," said Conner. "Glad I caught that. I need to think about this some more." He rubbed the edge of his chin as he pondered the matter.

"I'm going to mention it just as soon as we get to wherever the heck this place is," Shayna moaned. Her legs were getting tired, and she couldn't ignore the feeling of being watched. "Seneca, I think you'd look great in white with your blonde hair and complexion." She wanted to keep talking. She felt more at ease when she was breaking the eerie silence.

"White would probably get dirty. Take a look at where we are," Seneca answered.

"You're too practical!" Shayna huffed. "No fun at all."

Seneca tried picturing herself clad in white with her wings in full spread and a shimmery crest on her bodice. She liked the idea of it, but it seemed trivial. The Dominion of Four sounded way too much like a group of comic book characters. Theme songs from popular movies with superheroes played in Seneca's head. She smiled as she thought about Shayna in her boots. In her opinion, Shayna was already dressed for the part as a lead crime fighter. She giggled out loud at the image.

"What's so funny?" asked Shayna.

"You've already shown that you can kick some major butt without a fancy cape or spandex," said Seneca. "You probably don't need to worry about your ensemble." She was proud of her friend and didn't mind saying it.

"Seneca's right," replied Shayna. "I did kick some major Brigara butt! Next time I will send her into oblivion!" She beamed from the acknowledgment.

"She didn't see it coming at all! Classic fake-out." Conner snorted, punching the air to simulate a combination of boxing jabs and hook shots.

"Yup, totally clueless. I'm sure being fooled has made her even more dangerous," added Jake. He tried not to focus on what they had just experienced, but it was too fresh and ingrained in his mind to ignore.

Seneca had only caught the tail end of Jake's comment. She trotted up to close the gap between them. "I heard you say something about Brigara," she said. "She was furious! Especially when she realized we were blocking her from getting back to the Otherworld."

The image of Brigara's mangled face was seared in her mind. It was an image she would not soon forget. She was able to clearly picture Shayna's illuminated sword crashing down on the portal in perfect precision. Brigara's piercing screams rang loudly as her attempt to cross through to the Otherworld was foiled. Seneca thought about possible headlines with a full-page picture of Shayna posing in her boots. The headlines would read: "Evil Druid Stopped by Heroic Teen." Knowing someone so brave made her smile.

"We came pretty close to her busting through all right," said Jake. "I'm just glad Shayna figured out what to do in time."

He pulled Shayna close and wrapped her in a hug. Conner immediately joined in and then grabbed Seneca to force her under his arm. She felt smothered. Her head was buried in his armpit and pinned to his side, but she didn't budge. She reached out with her free arm and pulled Shayna in for a group hug.

"Thanks, guys, but this isn't a safe spot for us to stop," said Shayna. She wiggled free and smoothed her wavy dark hair. "We're surrounded by those thorny, poisonous plants we were warned about." She pointed at the menacing shrubs as she moved carefully out of reach.

"Oh yeah, the deadly blackthorns," replied Seneca. "We're surrounded by them, so we'd better stay on the trail." She recalled how she had become entangled in them before. The branches had reacted fiercely when she fell into them; they had swatted her hard in the back and sent her stumbling. She definitely wanted to avoid that again. Seneca eased into the center of the path and pulled her arms in close.

"Shayna's on alert!" Jake teased. "Help us! Please rescue us from the thorns."

"That's not funny. I just don't want to die out here," said Shayna.

"He's just kidding, you know. We're actually really stoked!" said Conner. "You know what I mean—thanks for saving us."

"Yeah, Shayna—what he said." Jake chuckled.

"Give it a rest, Jake. I'm just grateful we got away from Brigara," said Shayna.

Seneca was thankful too. Shayna had consumed the last of the enchanted Himalayan crystals, which gave her the ability to conjure a sword that obeyed her every command. She had used the light- and jewel-embellished sword to destroy the portal, thus preventing Brigara from returning to the Otherworld. However, in doing so, she had trapped the four of them there.

That had happened less than a day ago. To Seneca, it felt like years ago, as did the walk through the dark woods. She and Jake had the ability to fly, but they couldn't leave Conner and Shayna to trek through the terrain alone. It was impossible to lift them. Conner was too heavy to lift even with Jake's strength, and Seneca was so petite that managing anything other than her own weight would be futile. Walking was the only way to go. Dreya circled high overhead and was their guide to the site where they would begin their training as the Dominion of Four.

Dreya had the ability to transform her human form into various animals. So far, they had only witnessed two changes. When they'd first met her, she'd been a swan on a lake in Fiona with her daughter, Celestia. Shayna had been told that her mother had died in childbirth, but that had been a lie; Celestia was her mother. Shayna's father was mortal, making her a demi-elemental—a being of magical and non-magical descent.

Initially, Shayna had found it difficult to accept that she was related to anyone who could transform into anything other than an ATM. She had been selfishly consumed with shopping and more shopping, with small doses of window-shopping, her entire life. The word *Dad* had always been preceded by the word *more*. She had lived a life of indulgence and a superficial existence until she'd faced off with Brigara. Learning she possessed inner strength and the ability to put others' needs ahead of her own felt like discovering the missing piece. Shopping and spending were distractions, a sort of placeholders until she uncovered her true value and worth. She now knew without a doubt that she was destined to do more. She'd also become aware of an inherent ability, or, as she liked to put it, the gift of persuasion. She believed it would come in handy often. She droned on about it for quite some time with the others, especially Seneca. Seneca believed she had special gifts of her own. One was the ability to drown out Shayna's voice whenever it became too much to handle.

"I will use my persuasion superpower to get us a comfy bed tonight," said Shayna.

"Sounds like a great plan. I hope it works," replied Seneca with a snicker as she rolled her eyes.

"Oh, it will work! I will get Dreya to tell us everything she knows— no holding back."

"We have some mad skills!" said Conner.

"Most definitely," Shayna said.

"I pity the fool that tries to stop us!" Conner exclaimed in an exaggerated deep voice as he pumped out his chest.

"I guess I'm supposed to say, 'I love it when a plan comes together!'" said Jake with a hearty laugh.

"Brilliant, Jake. That's classic A-Team material!" Conner snorted.

"I guess it's an inside joke. 'Cause otherwise, it's not funny, guys," said Shayna with a shrug and a shake of her head.

"Yeah, I don't get it either," added Seneca. "Definitely falls into the guy-humor category."

"If you really want to laugh," Shayna said, "then you should have seen the horrible outfits the cheerleading squad was planning on wearing to homecoming. Someone had the awful idea that all of us should wear chartreuse. They thought it would be perfect to go with the theme of Planet Earth. I was so not wearing puke green! Now, that's what you call funny."

Listening to Shayna's ramblings reminded Seneca of how their worlds had collided. They would never have run in the same circles in the mortal realm. Fate had changed that when they discovered they had bloodlines that rooted them to the Otherworld. She was a druid and perhaps a fairy. No one had actually designated her as such, but with her newly discovered appendage of wings, she assumed classifying herself as a fairy was probably accurate. Shayna was a demi-elemental with a mother and grandmother from the Otherworld. Her grandmother had promised to reveal more once they arrived at their destination, and Seneca was determined not to let her off the hook.

Shayna eventually stopped her rants on dress lengths and straps versus strapless when no one provided any opinion. She had grown tired of listening to herself talk, but it was a way to avoid focusing on their predicament. They were all equally nervous.

"We've been walking forever," said Shayna. "I hope we aren't being led into a trap."

"It'll be great to get to wherever we're going soon," said Jake. "Having more info would be nice too."

"I'm sure Dreya will tell us what we need to know when we need to know it," said Seneca. "She seems pretty trustworthy."

"You're probably right, but just in case, I'll be prepared," whispered Shayna.

"You know, you don't have to whisper. Trust me—she's pretty tuned into what's going on down here." Seneca smiled and widened her eyes.

Shayna grimaced as they glanced up to watch Dreya cascading above them. She had transformed into an eagle with an impressive wingspan. Although she was Shayna's grandmother, she elected to communicate telepathically with Seneca—something Seneca wasn't quite used to yet. She wasn't even sure if she liked it. She'd always been a private person, keeping her thoughts to herself. Now she felt her privacy was lost forever—or at least until she could learn how to block Dreya from reading her mind.

The various changes happening to each of them made her anxious. Their abilities were multiplying, and the sooner they could begin their training, the better she would feel. There was much they had to grasp, and it was coming at them at warp speed. Harping on Dreya reading her mental ramblings was a waste of time.

Seneca took a deep breath and let her mind drift to a time when she'd felt secure and at peace. She wasn't sure where her family had been living at the time, but she was sure it had been somewhere in the southwestern part of the country. She recalled the dry, hot climate and the variety of spicy foods served for dinner. Versatility was among the positive things she appreciated about her mother. No matter where they lived, she was quick to adapt to the cuisine and local culture. She always made it a priority to fit in and ensure their family was not seen as outsiders. She would show the family the proper way to prepare and eat the food, whether with hands or utensils. Seneca looked forward to the new dishes whenever they had to relocate.

Thinking about their constant worldwide moves made her feel nostalgic; she longed for the turmoil their relocation created. What had seemed so chaotic at the time would be welcomed in the wake of what she was currently facing. At least moving at a moment's notice was familiar. She longed to be sorting, packing, and labeling boxes. No matter how mundane, she preferred those tasks to walking through the dark woods with strange, foreign, and frightening noises.

Jake, Shayna, and Conner were several yards ahead, engrossed in discussing all they had encountered since stumbling into the Otherworld. They talked mostly about the strange, dangerous, magical creatures and newly discovered family. They recalled how they had consumed a third of the crystals, which had changed them forever. They had willingly accepted this gift from the High Elder Druid Council.

They had countless questions as to what they could do with the abilities, but the answers would have to wait. They had been warned about impending danger, and getting to safety was the priority. They'd been told little about the training they would receive, which drove the discussion in another direction. They theorized about their instructor and what he or she would be like. The excitement kept them moving at a quick pace. Seneca lagged behind and avoided joining the discussion. She hadn't consumed the crystals and couldn't relate to their experiences. She was going through her own changes, which were quite different. She had discovered that she was an elemental and the child of druids.

She kept reciting over and over in her head that her seemingly normal parents were from the Otherworld. It was difficult for her to grasp how they had managed to keep that information hidden from her throughout her life. She had wings—actual appendages that could appear from her back with little effort. That was the most extreme secret. She loved having the wings, yet she felt conflicted. How such a critical aspect had been kept hidden was beyond comprehension. She didn't want to resent her parents, but their deception made her cringe with frustration. She knew they had done it for her protection, but it only made her question if there were other secrets. One of the hardest parts about being in the Otherworld was not having her parents there to fill in the blanks.

Her mind drifted to moments she had spent with her family. She searched for clues that would reveal anything about them that might help in the Otherworld. Her life had seemed ordinary. She'd assumed the oddities of her everyday life were just part of the norm. Her mother's terms of endearment, the rituals, and the frequent relocations across the globe were just their family's way of life. She'd had no idea they were actively tracking Brigara. Her family had been pursuing danger without her knowledge. She wished someone—anyone—had clued her in. Her life had now taken a swift turn from dull and mundane to hyped up and dangerous. Having to stop Brigara at the threshold between the mortal realm and the Otherworld had changed their lives forever.

"There's some odd-looking plants to your right," Jake said. "Steer clear!"

"Got it!" Seneca shouted. She glanced toward where Jake was pointing.

She spotted a protruding branch that had a thick yellowish gel dripping from its leaves. She took a wide sidestep around it and wobbled slightly while balancing on her toes. She successfully avoided stepping in a pool of the substance.

"Ew! That looks nasty!" Seneca shrieked.

"Keep up, Seneca," Conner said. "You're trailing too far behind."

"Okay, okay," she answered. She had no intention of picking up her pace. Her thoughts guided her to move slower than the others. She needed time to absorb the circumstances.

Uncovering the fact that she had wings was by far Seneca's favorite part of all she had to deal with. She had many things to wrap her head around. Every nuance baffled her yet made her heart race with excitement. The questions mounting within her demanded answers, but she forced them to wait until the four reached their destination.

They had no clue where they were going or what to expect once they arrived. Seneca hated not knowing the answers. At least when it came to schoolwork or anything involving research or problem solving, there was a method to finding the answer, even if it was difficult to get to it. This was different; the priority was to get to safety—wherever that was. Finding answers in the Otherworld seemed to be a game of avoidance. She didn't care for it at all.

"Don't you think it's odd that no one is straightforward in this place?" Seneca didn't direct her question at anyone in particular. She wasn't even sure if she spoke loudly enough for anyone to hear.

"Not odd, just annoying, if you ask me," Conner called back to her.

"Yeah, *annoying* is a better word for it."

"It's like we're in a game of guess who!" Shayna added. "Except it's not like we're going to find a dream date or anything worth having behind door number two. Door number two is always the loser—trust me."

"What?" Conner and Jake said in unison. Jake shook his head, unsure whether to attempt to decipher Shayna's comments or simply move on.

"I agree with Shayna. There's no telling who we are going to meet up with next," Seneca said.

"Is that what she said?" Conner asked, raising an eyebrow.

"Exactly! It's anyone's guess," said Shayna.

"Well, at least we know they're guessing as much as we are." Conner chuckled. "Tune in and learn all about your life in today's latest news update."

"That's funny." Jake snickered.

"Find out the latest post that you know nothing about on your personal internet profile," Conner continued. They were all enjoying his antics as he grabbed his collar and tugged it into place. "We have breaking news about the latest prophecy scroll. Only here will you find out all that you need to know before it actually happens!" said Conner, chuckling. He was convinced he sounded like an experienced newscaster. Shayna clapped, and he took a bow in acknowledgment. A cheesy smile stretched across his boyish face.

"I can't get used to everyone knowing what we're supposed to do or who we're supposed to be," Jake said. "I can't base my life on how someone thinks it's going to turn out—especially when that someone has never even met me."

"I'm certainly not going to rely on it—or them or whatever," said Seneca. She had slid in behind Jake to make sure she didn't miss any critical discussion points.

"This business of prophecies should be the first topic of discussion when we meet our new teacher," said Shayna.

"Can we please say *trainer* or *coach*?" said Conner. "The word *teacher* has left a bad taste in my mouth and makes me want to barf." He pretended to gag, and the girls squealed until he stopped.

"We'd better pick up speed. I almost lost sight of Dreya for a second," Jake said. He pointed in her direction as they stepped up their pace. He jogged ahead of the others in hopes of getting them to do the same.

"She does seem to be losing patience with us," said Seneca. "Have you noticed the nosedives she keeps doing periodically? What's up with that?"

"At first, I thought she was falling asleep up there. She is old, you know," said Conner. "She was staying really still, like wicked stealth-like. Then bam! She started flying around all spastically." Conner flailed his arms in the air.

"I noticed that too. I thought maybe she was swatting at something, but then she stopped," Seneca said. "Maybe the stress of all this is getting to her."

"At least she's not being told to go prepare for battle against the unknown," said Conner. "That's the definition of stress."

"Let's just hope she won't Brigara us," said Shayna. She was partially kidding, but she honestly didn't know anything about the family she had just met. She wanted to reserve her opinion and, more importantly, her emotional attachment until she knew more.

"Nice. Now our ex-teacher is a verb," said Jake. He had slowed when he noticed no one was keeping up with him as he'd hoped.

"Correction—an angry verb. It's a new category," said Seneca.

They all laughed, but the laughter was forced. Any mention of Brigara was a sure way to dampen the mood. They grew quiet as they thought about the teacher who had sent them to the Otherworld. She had plotted to return, and they had thwarted her attempt. She had tried to follow the prophecies that were altered without her knowledge. Those in leadership had made alternate plans, yet the idea of predicting the future was still much ingrained in the realm. Its inhabitants made it clear; they placed a lot of emphasis on prophecies.

Seneca had made up her mind that relying on old scrolls with predictions of things that were destined to happen was a waste of time and energy. She was not accustomed to having her life written about prior to experiencing it. She did concede that some of the prophecies were true, but she couldn't shake the fact that others were fabricated. If some were flawed, then the entire concept for predicting the future was unreliable. She had decided she would ignore them all. She liked not knowing what was around the next corner. An unconventional way of life was familiar. She had dealt with ambiguity and unpredictable circumstances for as long as she could remember. Accepting the unknown of where she would end up on any given day was a huge component of how she'd lived. She didn't openly embrace change, but she accepted it without fear. In her opinion, there were too many other things to be afraid of. Brigara had proven that.

Seneca froze. There was a rustling in the brush just to her right. She leaped to the middle of the trail and quickened her steps until she got closer to the others. Dreya had warned them they could not stop for anything in the woods. It was imperative they reach their training destination. All elementals were counting on the Dominion of Four to bring harmony back to the realm. The four were prominent aspects of numerous prophecies that described them as great crusaders destined to save the Otherworld from the evil Brigara. Seneca refused to accept the idea of four teens having the power to save an entire race of elementals, yet she was compelled to forge ahead. She cursed the entire concept of prophecies.

"Hey, Seneca, has Dreya told you how much farther we have to walk?" said Conner. "I swear we've been in these woods forever."

"Nope, no clue," said Seneca. "She hasn't said much for the last hour except to tell us to keep moving."

"That's not much help," groaned Conner.

"'Tis scribbled in a scroll as a prophecy, and all will be revealed in due time," Seneca chimed. "Great accent, huh?" She curtsied and pursed her lips tightly while batting her eyes.

"It's okay, but Jake does a better cluricaune impersonation," said Conner. He smiled at her attempt to make him relax. "Say something, Jake."

"As Keene Ardara would say, our fate will be known soon enough," said Jake. He garbled through the last few words to add emphasis to his portrayal. "You must know and take heed that the prophecy is the prophecy of the prophecy. Also note, I am not a leprechaun!" He scrunched his face and pantomimed holding a cane like the stout cluricaune fairy. He liked adding levity to lighten the mood.

"That's pretty funny," Shayna said with a snicker. "Although I bet Keene Ardara wouldn't think so. He'd tell you your fate will crumble because of your mockery."

"Yeah, probably—right before he made you sit in a man-eating chair," Conner said with a laugh.

"Thanks for reminding me," said Jake. "You won't think it's funny when he tells you your fate will be dusting his endless scrolls of prophecies for all eternity."

Conner laughed boisterously, and Jake chuckled along.

"He did have a lot of prophecy scrolls. I wonder if the fate of my feet is written down," Shayna said, her voice whiny. "I am seriously getting major blisters on my toes. These boots weren't made for this much walking."

"I'm sure they're not that mundane," Seneca said.

"You're calling my feet mundane?"

"The scrolls, I mean. It's probably just life-altering stuff."

"Ah, but you concede, small fairy, that fate has already been written," Conner said.

"Not exactly," replied Seneca. "I just think they write about life-altering stuff—and don't call me small!"

"As you wish." Conner snickered.

"Nothing so far makes me believe any of this is a coincidence—too many people know about us," said Shayna. "It's like they all attend these big magic folk meetings where all aspects of our lives are the premier topic."

"Yup, and the sloppy plans have already been written," added Conner.

"That might be accurate—our lives are forever changed, and maybe the prophecies are right," said Jake. "Our fate may already be known." His inflection was somber and serious.

"Let's hope that's not the case. I like creating my own drama!" replied Shayna.

The joking slowly died down, and quiet fell upon them. They began moving quicker, with Shayna taking the lead, followed by Conner. Jake glanced over his shoulder to check on Seneca, who was still in sight. He told himself not to worry as long as he had eyes on her.

Seneca made sure not to trail too far behind. Her thoughts immediately began to examine Jake's words. She had a hard time accepting a fate that was not of her own making. She had other plans for her life. Or did she? She began questioning what goals she actually had. There wasn't anything she was particularly interested in; she simply did the class assignments, earned high grades, and then moved on to the next subject. Her life had been programmed to take things one day at a time. After all, uprooting every few months and moving to Anytown, USA, wasn't giving her an ample opportunity to consider a stable future. The only thing she knew for sure was that hiking through a dark forest was not on her list of priorities. She wanted an existence that didn't include going to war in a strange world or figuring out how to use magic as a weapon. Her head began to hurt the more she dwelled on the unknown danger.

Seneca felt a surge of energy the more she thought about her purpose. It wasn't about getting the best grades or cramming for the next exam.

It was about figuring out her role in the Dominion of Four and what it meant to be an elemental. The countless houses where she had lived were just empty shells, temporary placeholders. The Otherworld was her true home, and it needed protection against someone treacherous and evil. She was determined to uncover a way to stop Brigara from destroying the realm. "So, help me, my family will return to their true home!" Seneca muttered, as though saying it out loud would make it a valid mission.

Her parents had planned ahead. They'd believed she was destined to enter the Otherworld along with the others. Part of their plan had been for her to meet Keene Ardara, a solitary cluricaune and keeper of the prophecy scrolls. He was gruff on the exterior, but her parents had entrusted the Stone of Fate to him and asked that he deliver it to her. The stone had saved her from drowning in the Northern Passages and summoned her gifts. She'd discovered her wings at that moment. She had a soft spot for Keene Ardara and longed to be nestled in one of his overstuffed sofas while sipping on one of his ambrosia concoctions. Seneca laughed when she thought back to Jake being nearly swallowed by one of his hexed chairs. She shook her head to try to refocus on the present. Getting her parents back to the Otherworld would have to wait for now. She was trailing too far behind the others.

"Hey, guys, you're walking too fast," said Seneca. She sprinted to close the gap.

"No, you're moving too slow," said Conner. "You know how I feel about the dark, and this is darker than dark." He took even larger strides in protest. He was petrified, and the sooner they got to shelter, the sooner he could relax.

"Come on! Slow down," Seneca protested. "It's not that dark."

"You know she has short legs. Petite but still short," Shayna said. "She can't walk as fast as you, Conner. Even I have to skip and jog a bit, and I'm actually taller than average."

"Whatever," Conner replied. "Hey, Seneca, I will carry you if it gets us where we're going any faster." He trotted backward and zigzagged mockingly. "Look. I will even take one foot out of the equation to give you an advantage." He hopped around on one foot, and Jake shoved him hard enough to cause him to stumble and lose balance. "Hey!" Conner snapped.

"Cut her some slack," said Jake. He smiled, knowing Conner was just easing the tension they were all feeling.

"I'm being serious, Seneca. I will carry you on my back with my eyes closed and hopping on one foot." Conner chuckled.

"No, thanks. I'll pass," said Seneca. "Hopping doesn't seem to be your best ability."

"That was Jake's fault. Come on!" Conner twisted his mouth into an overly dramatic pout. "Have it your way, but don't say I didn't offer."

"I'm good to go, but thanks for the offer." Seneca giggled.

She sped up a bit and then immediately slowed to her previous pace. She preferred trailing a few feet behind Jake so she didn't have to lead or engage in the others' conversation. They had begun debating and making guesses as to what they would learn once they arrived at their destination. They discussed how their magical gifts from the Himalayan crystals would be used to defeat Brigara. Since she hadn't taken any of the enchanted crystals, Seneca couldn't completely relate to their experience.

She felt slightly left out and wondered if she was truly part of the prophecy that everyone kept referencing. Perhaps she was just a stand-in until the absent member stepped forward and claimed his or her rightful place. If that were to happen, she could get back to her family.

She longed to see her younger brother, and she even missed her older one, who was often more of a bother than a brother. She wished she could ask him if he knew that their parents were druids and that their mother's wings had been removed for fear of detection. Her mother had worked hard to keep her daughter's wings hidden with spells and cloaking charms. Why hadn't she done the same for herself? Did she miss them? What had her father given up, if anything? Seneca wished she were able to get answers to those questions and many more. Even with more questions than answers, she knew she would forego the interrogation just to feel the comfort and warm embrace of her mother. That was what she missed the most.

Seneca didn't want to cry, and thinking of her mother's sacrifice would surely bring on the waterworks. She decided to shift her focus to the other comforts of home. She remembered she hadn't made her bed before she left for school so long ago; it felt like months ago rather than just a few days. The last morning she was home, she had been in a hurry and tried to catch a ride with her brother. He'd left without her so he could give Jake's sister a ride, which meant she'd had to walk instead.

She stopped her memory and wondered if her brother had been in on the plans as well, but she decided to save pondering that possibility for another time. She thought back to leaving the house and feeling frustrated with her brother. It was the first day she'd seen Jake up close. She had seen him moving in across the street as well as zipping around corners while riding in the car with his mother. Until he'd sat behind her during biology class, she hadn't given him much thought. That day, she had felt a surge of energy when he handed her his assignment, but she had quickly dismissed it. She now knew their parents had been working behind their backs to ensure their meeting and solidify their ultimate connection.

"That was obviously a spell," Seneca said softly, not caring that she was talking to herself. She hadn't said it loudly enough for the others to hear. "I'm glad it wasn't some love charm," she added as she smiled.

It was clear her parents and Jake's mother were involved, but she didn't know of any others. She wondered what role, if any, Conner's parents and Shayna's father had had in linking the four of them together. Seneca never had been one to buy into conspiracy theories, but she was involved in a huge one. She smiled at the irony.

"You've got to keep up, Seneca. I know this sounds familiar," Jake yelled back over his shoulder. "We should really try to stick closer together."

"When you say *we*, you really mean *me*," Seneca replied.

"If you say so. You have most definitely mastered the art of lagging behind." Jake chuckled to mask a sudden wave of anxiety. He chalked it up to exhaustion and hunger.

Seneca acknowledged she was falling too far behind again and trotted up to close the gap to within a couple steps behind Jake. He reminded her of boys she had admired when her family lived in a remote area in New Mexico. She thought about how the warm sun felt on her skin and how the dusty winds swirled about without warning. There in that dry climate, where the boys were fit, strong, and confident, there had been one particular boy who had dark hair and was tall like Jake. His name was Paul, and he'd had a way of making her laugh when she least expected it. He was kind and often bought her lunch. They would spend the entire lunch break talking and laughing so much that they rarely had time to take a bite of their food. He had gathered enough courage as he fumbled through a poorly rehearsed speech to ask her to be his date for the winter dance, and she had accepted on the spot. She'd been excited and looked forward to shopping for her first formal dress. The next day, her parents had announced they were moving. She'd never had a chance to say goodbye. That was the moment she had sworn to never get close to anyone at school again.

She wondered what Paul might be doing at that moment. She snickered and figured he'd probably be eating, since hanging out with her meant he'd missed out on a lot of food. She tried to remember the last meal they'd shared. Images of spicy southwestern food swirled around in her head, and she began to crave a crunchy chimichanga loaded with carne asada, garlic-soaked black beans, rice, and guacamole. She licked her lips as she pictured the slightly charred roasted green chilies inside. The ultimate preparation included hot and creamy habanero salsa blended with cheese that dripped across the top and down the sides. She imagined biting into the crispy tortilla and releasing the aroma. Her mouth watered as she recalled the flavor of the slow-cooked beef with a hint of a charred aftertaste and the melding of the spices. Her stomach growled in protest.

"Hey, Jake, when was the last time we ate?" asked Seneca. "I'm starving and—"

"Wait!" Jake put up his hand to signal he needed Seneca's silence. "Listen. I heard something."

Jake took a few cautious steps and then stopped. Seneca came close to bumping into him but tripped over her feet to halt her momentum. He looked around Seneca and then over his shoulders and craned his neck in search of the source of the noise.

"Maybe you just heard the rumbling in my stomach," said Seneca. "I'm starving! That's why I was asking."

"Shh! Not that. It's a faint buzzing sound. Don't you hear it?" Jake put his finger to his lips.

She complied and listened intently. "I don't hear anything," she whispered in a singsong voice.

Jake nodded as he held his breath.

"Hey, guys, what's going on?" Conner asked. He grabbed hold of Shayna to get her attention when he noticed Jake and Seneca had stopped walking.

"Jake heard some weird noise or something," replied Seneca.

"It's something coming from the air, I think," Jake said. "Like bees or wasps, except a higher pitch. More like a low hum than a buzz." He continued scanning the area, looking high and low out into the darkness, but didn't detect any movement.

"We should probably go," Conner said.

"I agree," Shayna said. "There's so much we don't know about this world that we might be the next meal for some beast or something. Let's keep moving." She didn't wait for a response as she took two long strides ahead of the pack.

"Wait just a second, okay? I'm just making sure I don't hear it anymore," said Jake.

They all stood motionless, waiting to detect anything unusual.

"I guess it's gone," said Jake with an air of disappointment in his tone. "I don't hear it anymore, but let's get going. The hairs on my neck are telling me this isn't a place to camp out."

"Maybe we scared off whatever it was," said Conner. He shook off a shiver. "Man, I hate the dark!" He kicked the dirt and created a small dust cloud.

"Let's pick up the pace. Stopping here is probably not a wise move," said Shayna as she continued forging ahead.

"Shayna's got a point, so try to stay closer together," said Jake. He stared directly at Seneca to indicate he meant her specifically. She tried to ignore his glare as she trailed behind him.

"Wait up, Shayna," Conner called as he jogged to catch up to her. She had moved well ahead of the pack. Her instincts told her to keep moving.

"We're all moving faster, Seneca. You've gotta keep up," Jake said.

"Fine. I get it—just slow down," said Seneca. She folded her arms across her chest in protest, raised her knees high, and marched hard to emphasize her dissatisfaction.

Seneca, you must listen to Jake. It is not safe where you are. You have to keep moving, Dreya said. Her voice echoed in Seneca's thoughts. She huffed in exasperation.

"I just got word from the bird above," said Seneca, making no effort to hide her sarcasm. "Dreya has weighed in and says it's not safe and that we need to get moving." Her voice was a flat monotone. She knew she was behaving badly, but she blamed it on the hunger.

"I wish I had that telepathic connection," said Shayna as she paused momentarily and allowed the others to catch up.

"Me too," Conner said.

"I'd be eavesdropping like crazy! I'd know if a salesclerk wasn't giving me the best deal or if we were going to have a pop quiz in history." Shayna beamed at the thought of being one step ahead of everyone.

"Well, if I could give you this mind-reading thing, I would," replied Seneca. "It's not as cool as you think. I'd even trade it for a burger if you had one."

"Seriously? You just don't know how to rock it to your advantage."

"Whatever!" Seneca made sure to put an exaggerated emphasis on the last syllable. She didn't care to get into a debate with Shayna, and she knew this was the one-word way to end an unwanted discussion. Shayna took the cue and dropped it.

Seneca hadn't asked for the gift to read minds or communicate nonverbally. She hated the idea of not having a say or a choice in the matter. She knew that Dreya needed to use telepathy with her, but she didn't care for that either. Dreya was quick to interrupt any thoughts whenever she deemed it necessary. Typically, she conveyed warnings, and Seneca dreaded being the bearer of bad news. She wondered if Dreya listened to her thoughts without her knowledge. She didn't like thinking about it and looked forward to discovering how to block any attempts to read her mind. Dreya had promised that knowledge would be included in her training, but until then, she had to accept that her thoughts were like open airwaves.

Seneca gazed upward at Dreya, who was circling erratically. She gave a salute to let her know she had received the message and had compliantly delivered the news. She knew it wasn't necessary, but it was a way of displaying her reluctance to be the message liaison. Just as she began to relax, her thoughts were once again disrupted.

Seneca, please listen to what I say. Dreya's thoughts were intensely clear. *Do not question what I tell you. You and the others must run north toward the hillside with the steepest incline. Do you understand? You are all in danger!*

Okay, but— Seneca tilted her head toward the sky, but she could not locate Dreya.

Seneca, it's imperative, Dreya said. *You will continue on the path until the soil is dry beneath your feet. Locate the northern mossy trail, and stay on it until you reach a gully.*

You're throwing a lot at me right now. We need to find a gully? Seneca could feel her heart racing in her chest. Dreya sounded distressed, and it frightened her.

Yes, now tell the others! Warn them before it's too late! Dreya pleaded. *Remember this. Get to the top of the hill, and then find the northern trail that leads to the gully. Only there will you find safety.*

But what am I warning them about? Seneca asked.

There's no time—they're here! Now, Seneca! Tell them now!

"Dreya, wait! I don't understand what's happening! Where are you?" Seneca yelled aloud. She spun around, searching the sky for any sign of her. She spotted her circling low.

"What's going on?" Jake asked. He followed Seneca's eyes to the sky.

"Hey, what's up with Dreya?" Conner asked. "Shayna, wait up and check this out!" He jogged back to join Jake and Seneca. "She's circling in the same spot. Does that mean we're close?"

"No, I don't think so. Something's wrong," said Seneca. "She told me to warn you guys."

"Warn us about what?" Shayna asked. She kept her gaze on Dreya as she joined the others. "She's flying all erratically. What's she doing?"

"She's circling in tighter revolutions and increasing her speed. Maybe she's trying to morph into another animal," Conner said. It was more of a question than a declaration.

"I don't think that's what's happening. She said we need to run! There's danger coming!" explained Seneca. She couldn't take her eyes off Dreya.

"What else did she say?" Jake asked. She swatted at the air and mumbled incoherently. He could tell he didn't have Seneca's full attention. He placed his hands on her shoulders and turned her to face him. "Seneca, what exactly did she say?"

"Um, she said we should—I mean..." Seneca's voice trailed off as she suddenly saw Dreya descending quickly in their direction. "Watch out!" she screamed as she covered her head and crouched down. The others reacted instinctively and ducked to avoid Dreya's charge.

"What is she doing?" Conner yelled.

"Did you see that?" Seneca shouted.

"Something's attacking her! They're like birds or giant waspy things!" Jake's voice boomed. "They're chasing her!" He rubbed his hands on his jeans. He had landed on sharp rocks when he fell to the ground in an attempt to avoid contact with Dreya.

"Not birds—they've got faces!" screamed Shayna. "There has to be at least a hundred of them going after her." Her voice trembled.

"What are we supposed to do, Seneca? What did she say?" asked Jake.

"She said run for the northern hillside. Stay on the path too. It's supposed to lead us to a safe place," Seneca said. She couldn't keep herself from shaking. "She said to find the gully—or something like that." She was sure she'd missed details, but that was all she could recall at that moment, and that was the most important part.

"You heard her. Let's go. Come on!" Jake ordered.

"What about Dreya? We can't just leave her; we have to help," said Shayna. She searched the sky but saw no sign of her. "Where'd she go? Dreya!" she screamed.

"I'm sure she was leading them away so we'd have a chance to get out of here," said Jake. "We need to move now. I don't think she would have said to run if that's not what she wanted."

"Jake's right, Shayna," said Seneca. "She told me that we had to keep going until we get to safety."

Seneca grabbed at Shayna's arm to hold her back, but Shayna wrestled away, her eyes wide with fear. "Leave then! I'm not going until I know she's okay!" Shayna snapped, trembling and unable to maintain her focus. Her eyes were full of tears that clouded her vision. She wiped them away. "I have to go after her. I just have to!"

"I get it," said Conner. "You guys go ahead, and I'll stick with Shayna. We'll catch up with you." He put his hand on her shoulder, and she raised her head in preparation. Shayna knew she didn't have a choice, and she wasn't going to try to second-guess her decision.

"Stick together, and meet up with us as soon as you can," said Jake.

Conner nodded in agreement.

"Those things looked vicious," said Seneca. "If Dreya's in trouble, then they have to be really dangerous."

"All the more reason for me to go after her and help—she's my family," said Shayna. "I have to try!" She brushed past Jake and ran in the direction of Dreya's retreat. She had decided there wasn't any time to discuss it further. She'd made up her mind.

"Like I said, I'll stay with her. Between the two of us, I'm sure we can take 'em out!" said Conner.

"Get going, you guys, and be careful because you have no idea what you're going up against," warned Seneca. "Look for the gully, and find us."

Conner stuck out his chin and gave a look of confidence followed by a thumbs-up. Jake knew it wasn't worth debating and stuck out his hand, but he was pulled in close for a tight embrace.

"Take care of Seneca, and don't let her fall behind," said Conner.

He didn't wait for a response; he turned on his heel and sprinted until he caught up to Shayna. She had just changed direction near a row of massive oak trees.

"This way, Conner. Come on!" Shayna yelled as she picked up speed.

Conner followed without question. "Man, I hate the dark," he mumbled as he jogged alongside her.

"Stop complaining, Conner. Which way did they go?" Shayna asked.

"There they are!" he shouted, pointing at a gap between two of the tallest trees. Dreya's wings were fully spread as she maneuvered and batted at the swarm. "They are really going at her!"

"Hurry!" Shayna shouted as she raced toward the attack. Conner stayed close behind and allowed her to lead.

Jake and Seneca watched Conner and Shayna as they ducked under low branches, effortlessly leaped over various hedges, and pushed away bushes that blocked their path; they moved briskly. Jake caught a glimpse of Dreya circling above, but most of whatever was happening was obscured by the dense, tall trees.

"We'll see you on the hillside," Jake called out. He was convinced they probably were unable to hear anything he said. They were running fast and didn't bother looking back or acknowledging anything he'd said.

"It's okay to let them go after her, right?" asked Seneca.

Jake watched until they disappeared completely out of sight before answering. "I'm sure they'll be fine." He sighed. He knew he didn't sound convincing.

He turned to face Seneca and was about to elaborate on his opinion, when he lunged for Seneca and tackled her to the ground. The force caused her head to hit the surface hard. The blow disoriented her momentarily, and she winced from the pain. She sat up slowly and rubbed the back of her head, feeling nauseated. The world seemed to move in slow motion as she watched Jake leap into action. She could tell he was fighting, but everything was in a fog. She wondered what he was doing as her surroundings slowly came into focus.

"We're under attack!" Jake yelled. "Get up, Seneca!"

She scrambled to her feet, but her head felt light. It slowly registered that something was flying around in the air, but she couldn't make out what it was. Her head throbbed. She squinted to clear her vision, and her sense of sound heightened; she heard loud buzzing, like a swarm of killer bees. Something thumped her in the back of the head, and she whirled around. She immediately swatted at the air but missed whatever was circling her. She wiped her face against her sleeve to clear the haze. When she opened her eyes, they widened immediately as they zeroed in on clusters of swift-flying objects. The objects were heading directly at them, and they were definitely not bees.

"Look out!" Jake shouted as he batted his arms through the air.

Seneca lunged, swung wildly, and grabbed hold of a squealing winged creature. She threw it to the ground and kicked it under a pile of leaves. She could hear it rustling and snarling in rebellion. Before she could retreat, another one rapidly approached with claws displayed.

It swerved and avoided Seneca's attempt to block it. It hastily grabbed hold of Seneca's hair. Her blonde tresses glowed in the moonlight. Her hair was a sharp contrast to the dark background of the night and an easy target.

"Let go of my hair!" Seneca screeched in a raspy voice. "I've had enough, you grungy beast!"

She grabbed it with both hands as it ripped hair from her scalp. Seneca winced and shrieked, throwing her attacker into a nearby bush. Before she turned around, another assailant scratched at her neck. She peeled it away as she felt her skin tearing beneath the creature's sharp nails. It hung on with a death grip and refused to release. Seneca clutched it hard and pulled as she let out a holler to help mask the intense pain.

"That hurt, you nasty bug!" Seneca clenched it tightly in her fist. "What's your problem?"

She shook it hard as it struggled to break free. It turned its head toward her and spit out a green substance that shot just above Seneca's shoulder and sizzled upon impact in the trunk of a young rowan tree. Seneca turned to see the mark it left. It was the size and color of a small pea. The putrid green liquid boiled as it burned a hole in the bark, leaving a mark of decay.

"Really? You were actually trying to spit that on me?" Seneca asked as she eyeballed the creature. "How rude!"

The captured fiend grimaced as it pushed hard against her hand. It growled and jerked its head back, but before it could release another lethal dose of venom, it was sent crashing into the same bush as its companion.

"That should teach you some manners," mumbled Seneca as she turned to assess the situation. Jake was skillfully defending himself.

"Jake, they're shooting some kind of green stuff!" Seneca warned. "Don't let it get on you!"

"They've already tried!" Jake yelled. "But you can stop them. You've gotta hit them before they make that noise that sounds like they're regurgitating their lunch."

"Gross!" Seneca spun around, looking for more on the approach.

"You're telling me." Jake readied himself for the next round.

He slammed two creatures into the ground, and they tumbled several yards. He circled and punched hard to send another careening sideways into a tree. It fell facedown and hit a low-hanging branch. It attempted to right itself but toppled over and landed in the dirt below, where it remained motionless.

Seneca watched Jake take several of the creatures out with multiple swings. She stared in awe as he synchronized his movements to connect hard with each approaching attacker just as they made the sound he'd described and before they could get in close. His timing was impeccable.

"Seneca, watch out!" Jake yelled.

He leaped over a fallen tree limb and spoiled the approach of a lone attacker. It was just above Seneca's head when he spotted it. He curled his hand into a tight fist and knocked it away before it could do any harm. Inadvertently, as he brushed passed Seneca, he bumped her hard enough to send her crashing to the ground. Her head hit the ground with a thump.

"Ouch!" she moaned.

"Sorry, Seneca. Are you all right?"

"I think so. Thanks. I didn't see that one." Seneca sat up and rubbed her head.

"I guessed as much."

"You can't keep knocking me down like that. I don't think my head can take it," she grumbled.

"Uh, sorry," he replied. "I didn't mean to hurt you." He smirked when he thought about how often she had hit the ground. He knew she was small, but he also knew she was tougher than she looked, even if she protested.

"I'm fine. Just give me a hand," she said.

He pulled her back to her feet. She rubbed her head in search of bumps or blood. She began wiping dust from her bottom as she looked herself over for additional injuries. "Oh my god, Jake! What the—"

"Come on, Seneca. I didn't hit you that hard," Jake protested.

"Forget about that. Look!" Seneca pointed to the approaching swarm. They had regrouped and doubled in number. They were flying directly at Jake and Seneca.

"Run, Seneca! Run!" he yelled. "Look out!"

He struck with his fists and connected with hard punches. Jake was amazed at the creatures' resilience. His blows stunned them only for a moment before they returned with another attempt. Seneca turned to help but was shocked to see how many they'd have to fight off.

"I've got this covered, Seneca. Get out of here!"

"No way," she said as she swatted one to the ground with a backhand slap.

"I'll be right behind you. Run!" Jake sent two colliding into several more on the approach. He could tell the creatures weren't going to let up, and they had to retreat, as Dreya had warned.

"Seneca, go!" he said. He was forceful.

Seneca saw in his eyes that he was not in the mood to argue. She knew he was right.

"Duck!" he shouted.

Without hesitation, Seneca lowered her head as one zipped past her ear. It made a quick turn and came back toward her to attempt another strike. Jake shoved Seneca hard in an effort to get her moving faster. She turned and took off in a fast dash toward the hillside. As she ran, she realized what was happening. They were under attack by the same flying beings that had surrounded Dreya. Her head began to throb, and she knew she'd hit the ground hard one time too many, but there was no time to focus on the pain. Her adrenaline surged as the pain subsided, and her instinct to survive kicked in. She kept running.

Jake quickly caught up to her. He stopped momentarily and swatted at the air, slapping down two that were flying parallel to each other.

He hurried to catch up to Seneca. She was losing momentum, but he admired that she hadn't stopped.

"They're angry little beasts!" said Jake.

"Yeah, and committed to being the victors!" replied Seneca, breathing hard. "Listen to them. They sound awful!"

Their attack cries were a blend of screams and high-pitched growls. While Jake found the sounds annoying, the noise wasn't what made them dangerous. He surmised that whenever they made a grotesque gurgling sound, they would release their fiery discharge. He watched them spit out the liquid repeatedly, but he had avoided contact thus far. Any surface the substance came in contact with burned or withered.

"Watch out, Jake!" Seneca screeched. She glanced over her shoulder as several closed in fast. "More are coming!"

"I've got this!" Jake hollered.

He veered to the right as he swung hard with his left fist to connect with three that flew too close together. They fell to the ground in a heap and disappeared in the tall grass. Two more attempted to scratch at his face, but he held them off by swinging wildly. They were persistent; one shifted direction and managed to claw at Jake's shoulder from behind. He grabbed hold and threw it into a nearby trench. An oversized bullfrog leaped to the spot, extended its tongue, and lapped up the dismayed creature. It was rapidly ingested.

"Bon appétit!" Jake called out, smirking with satisfaction.

He could almost swear the bullfrog winked in acknowledgment, but there was no time to dwell on the oddity of what he'd just seen. He prepared for another bout of attacks. He sprinted toward Seneca, who screamed as a creature attempted to grab hold of her hair, but she successfully shook it free and kicked it aside.

"What's with all the hair grabbing?" Seneca shouted.

"They're really annoying! Argh!" Jake shouted as he shook off one that had latched on to his shoelace.

"Ouch! Get off me!" Seneca shouted. She threw the attacker down with as much force as she could. It hissed as it went tumbling into a thick, mucky ditch.

"We have to get to the hillside! Go north!" she hollered as loudly as she could. "That's what Dreya said!"

She was winded, and her throat was dry. Her head ached, and she was beginning to see double because of the continuous spinning and dodging.

"They've retreated a bit," Jake said. "Let's outrun them before they regroup!" He ran past her. "I hope Dreya was right about heading this way."

She was thankful he took the lead. She was unable to focus on anything except hitting the attackers. Jake had been wrong; the creatures weren't retreating—they were regrouping.

"They're coming back, so watch out!" Seneca said as she vaulted into a fighting stance. "There's one!" She pointed above his head.

"I'm ready," Jake replied through gritted teeth as he spun around and slapped it squarely in the face. Its black almond-shaped eyes closed tightly as it remained suspended in the air for a brief moment before it made gagging sounds and dropped rapidly to the ground.

"Stellar!" Seneca said in astonishment. "I didn't know you had ninja reflexes like that."

"I didn't know it either. I guess we can blame it on the crystals," he said coyly.

"I wonder why that one came alone?"

"I think he was their test pilot to see if we were still in fighting mode. It kind of looks like they're in a holding pattern."

"Do you think they're giving up?"

"Not likely—just look at 'em." Jake shook his head in disbelief.

There were too many to count. They hovered in a massive swarm and moved as a unit in a slow approach. Even their growls were in sync. Seneca had a sinking feeling their numbers were increasing. They shifted into a tight formation, creating a dark mass across the sky that moved directly at them.

"Here they come!" Jake bellowed. "Hit 'em where it hurts!"

"I'll try!" she shouted. "They are relentless buggers!"

Jake knocked them down one or two at a time. They attempted to come at him from all sides. His arms crisscrossed, and he took out one after another. He swayed with ease to avoid being hit or allowing them to get too close.

Seneca watched his movements and began to imitate his rhythm. Her punches weren't as lethal, but she heard enough crying and screeching to know she was hurting them. Only a few were able to return for a second run at her, but they were unrelenting. For each one she knocked down, two more would join in to grab and scratch at her. She was quick in avoiding their razor-sharp claws. She was thankful Jake had identified how to detect when their burning venom was coming. She was able to successfully time their discharge, but she worried she wouldn't be able to keep it up much longer. Her arms felt heavy the more she swung them. Her muscles were tightening up, and the repetition made them burn. Sweat dripped from her forehead, chin, and arms. Seneca rotated her position and began grabbing the flying creatures out of midair. She threw them down, where they would meet her foot in full swing. Using a hard kick was an effective strategy. She continued booting one after another; this adjustment gave her a surge of adrenaline—so much so that she began beckoning and taunting them to come closer. Several accepted the challenge and zipped directly at her. She kicked them with such great force that they whirled into incoming flyers, knocking them down in midair. Their outcries appeared to frighten the others, and Seneca was elated when they began to scatter.

"Take that, you grimy pests!" Seneca shouted jubilantly.

"Seneca, we have a reprieve. Let's head to the hillside now," Jake said.

"I'm right behind you!" yelled Seneca. "If I'd known how powerful my kick was, I would've been using my feet much sooner."

She raced up the hill and tried her best to keep up with Jake. Her thighs burned, and her muscles tightened as she powered through and pushed her body past resistance with each stride. She was determined not to let up as they dashed up the steep terrain. Their attackers began letting up the higher they climbed.

One by one, the flying attackers backed off and withdrew to the valley below. Only one remained close, but it had a different tactic. It stayed just beyond Seneca's reach and did not attack, hovering strategically a few inches from her face. Its dark eyes were close together and extremely large for its narrow face. Its nose was thin and curled on the end, with nostrils that formed narrow slits. The mouth gaped open, allowing putrid green venom to drip to the ground below. Seneca waited for the sound she had grown accustomed to. She would know when to dodge the acidic discharge. However, it didn't growl or gurgle. It had been given a different assignment.

"Keep running, cowards! Brigara's coming for you," it said derisively in a high and grating tone. It laughed hauntingly as the green poison dripped from its mouth.

Having delivered the cryptic message, it hissed just above Seneca's head before it darted into the dark valley below. Seneca slowed briefly as she watched it retreat. She called out after it was clearly out of range.

"Yeah, you'd better get out of here, you scruffy snot!" Seneca shouted as loudly as she could.

She turned and raced up the hill and didn't stop running until she'd reached the top of the ridge. She bent over to catch her breath and thought about what she had heard. The attack had been provoked by Brigara, and it was personal.

"That was impressive!" said Jake with labored breathing.

"Which part? The running like a crazy person or the avoidance of being burned with putrid acid spit?" She massaged her ribs in an effort to ease a sharp pain.

"Well, both, I guess," he replied with a smirk. "You're tiny, but you've got spunk. Those kicks were lethal!"

"I always tell people, don't let my size fool them, or my blonde hair. I've got brains and brawn!"

Seneca ran her hands through her cropped hair and gave a satisfied nod. She had always enjoyed looking different from the rest of the girls her age, but it wasn't intentional. She had chosen to maintain a short hairstyle as a time saver, but it had the extra benefit of making her unique. Her clothing was simple, and she gravitated toward black most often, not because she was into the gothic subculture but because she didn't want to worry if the colors she wore matched. Her appearance was simple and uncomplicated, much as her life had been, until they'd stumbled into the Otherworld.

"Ha! No kidding! That last buzzing creature must have liked your hair, because it was giving you a personal escort," Jake said.

"Not funny, but you're not too far off. She was more of a personal-message deliverer."

"It talked to you?" Jake's eyes grew large, his expression serious. "What did it say?"

"Well, it was something along the lines of we're cowards and Brigara sent them."

"What? Brigara? Oh no!" Jake shoved his hands into his pockets. "What about Conner and Shayna?"

"Oh my god!" said Seneca. She looked down the side of the hill and saw no sign of them. "Do you think they were attacked too?"

"Most likely." He stared into the darkness in search of movement or anything that would let them know their friends were okay.

"But Conner's tough, and Shayna's got that sword thing going for her, right?" Seneca looked at Jake for reassurance. She saw his blank expression and grew even more concerned. She wanted and needed a positive reply to help settle herself down.

"I'm right, aren't I, Jake?"

"Yeah, you're right. They're fine. I'm sure of it."

Jake hoped they were having success in fending off the acid-spitting creatures. The fact that they hadn't seen any sign of them was bothersome. He forced himself not to conjure up any negative images.

"We have to think positive—they're fine," he said. He knew saying it out loud was for his own benefit. "They will take them down just like we did."

"I think we'd better get moving," Seneca said.

She'd rested long enough and was ready to put more distance between them and their attackers. The top of the ridge was probably not the safest place. She also could see that Jake was rattled by the idea of Conner and Shayna being in danger.

"Did you tell them about the hill, going north, and the rest of the info?" Jake asked. He wondered if he should head back down to search.

"I think so, but to be honest, I don't remember what I said," Seneca replied. She let out a deep sigh, and they strolled side by side in silence.

CHAPTER THREE

Stuck in the Mud

Seneca and Jake walked for quite a while in silence. They constantly looked over their shoulders, around hedges, and up into the trees. They were on the lookout for anything out of the ordinary. Jake finally took a deep breath and began to relax slightly. He thought it was safe to broach the topic of their intended destination. He knew in his heart that Seneca was struggling with coming to grips with their situation. He didn't know who was leading the way and feared they were wandering around aimlessly. Up until that point, he had resisted the urge to express his frustration and decided that keeping quiet was the better choice. He couldn't hold back any longer.

"Hey, Seneca, did Dreya say how long we had to walk north before we found the gully?" Jake asked.

"No, but she didn't exactly get the chance," she replied. "Plus, I'm still new at the telepathy stuff. I might have missed something or totally got it backward."

"That's not reassuring," he said. He let the words linger in the air. He was nervous that they had been walking too long without any signs of Conner, Shayna, or the gully. "Maybe it would help if you repeated it again—just to be sure."

"I've repeated it three times already!" Seneca bit her lip to calm herself. "If there were more to it, I would have said so."

"I'm just saying that it helps sometimes to review. In case you missed something," Jake said as he kicked up a clump of mud.

He noticed the ground getting softer, and much of it was muddy as they made their way through the glen with rows of mature trees along each side. It was harder to walk through, since his sneakers periodically got wedged too deep in the muck.

"Ugh! I hate this crappy mud," said Seneca. She'd noticed Jake's frustrations with it and decided it was a great way to change the subject.

"Can you imagine what Shayna would be saying about her boots about now?" asked Jake. "'Curses! My precious boots are getting so filthy!'" His voice was shrill. It wasn't a good impersonation of Shayna, and he knew it. His goal was to lighten the mood, and this was a sure way to do it.

"Yeah, she'd be complaining up a storm, but I can't imagine her sounding as silly as you." Seneca laughed. "Hey, wait a second. I just remembered something else Dreya said."

"What is it?" asked Jake. He felt a nervous surge in the pit of his stomach.

"She mentioned that we needed to follow the mossy path to the gully. Yeah, that's exactly what she said." Seneca beamed.

"Mossy path? Really?" Jake stopped and looked squarely at Seneca. "How can we see a mossy path with all of this mud?"

"I don't know. Maybe we missed it."

"Maybe?" Jake snapped. He tried to push down his anger, but his tone said it all. He sighed heavily because he knew Seneca wasn't intentionally making things difficult.

"Sorry. It's not your fault," he said with sincerity.

"No, I'm sorry. It's just that so much was happening at once," she said.

"I get it. No worries, okay? I know it's been difficult." He looked into her eyes to let her know he meant every word. She dipped her head slightly in response and wiped away a tear before it could spill over.

"Let's get out of this glen. We need to head this way. I remember seeing a path that might have had moss," Jake said. He had a sudden burst of renewed energy. He took the lead and began making his way through thicker mud.

Seneca felt a slight tingle down the center of her back. It was an itch she couldn't ignore. She knew her wings were just on the edge of emergence. She had to focus on keeping them contained. Each step she took was tentative. She didn't want to risk accidentally brushing against a tree or anything that might make a sound. She thought about the relaxation techniques her mother used whenever she felt overwhelmed. She was beginning to understand that her mother had been training her for years to control her wings and keep them hidden. She took a deep breath and exhaled slowly. She recalled the routine of repeating that step five times.

Seneca concluded the first round of the breathing exercises and began to feel the effects. She moved to the second interval and took in a deep, cleansing breath but stopped mid-exhale and froze. Not only were her wings tingling, but every hair on her body stood on end. She was all too familiar with this feeling. It was the signal for danger. She reached out to get Jake's attention. He was standing less than a foot in front of her. Before she could tap his shoulder, she was immediately stopped. Her legs collapsed, and a searing pain between her shoulder blades forced her down to the ground. She was stunned for a moment before it registered that she was trapped.

"Jake—help! Something's got me. It's holding me down!" Shayna screamed.

She had never felt anything so painful. An image of her wings being ripped from her back flashed before her eyes, but she knew it wasn't possible. They were hidden. All that she felt confirmed it, yet the pain was centered in the area where they rested.

"I think you might just be tangled in tree roots," said Jake. He assumed she was just feeling a bit on edge due to the recent attack.

"No! It's alive—I can feel it moving!" yelled Seneca. She was frantic and wrestled to break free.

"Grab my hand, Seneca! What is that?" asked Jake. "You're right. There is something moving beneath you!" He began kicking at the moving object near her legs. It burrowed into the damp soil. He slid his foot across the area and felt only mounds of mud. "Let me help you up. I think it's gone now," said Jake.

Seneca reached out to catch hold of his hand, but her arms were immediately pinned back. Jake grabbed her arms, but something pulled against his efforts and slammed her back to the ground.

"What the—" Jake's jaw dropped.

He could only make out what appeared to be a partial outline of a figure positioned beneath Seneca in the grubby dark surface. It was difficult to make out exactly what he saw. Whatever it was created a mound slightly above the surface and was covered in brush, dirt and fallen leaves. Jake stooped down to get a closer look. He touched it and realized it was an exposed root from a large silver maple tree. He saw no other movement and rationalized he was just being delusional.

He grabbed hold of Seneca's wrists and pulled. She didn't budge. Seneca screamed. Dark, mud-covered branch-like arms stretched out from beneath her and clawed at Jake's hands, drawing blood before retracting. Jake released his grip and cringed from the pain. He felt the blood trickle down his exposed skin.

"Jake, what is it?"

"I don't know. Maybe the tree's alive or something."

The muddy branches wrapped around Seneca's waist and chest, pulling her tighter into the mud.

"I can't move. It's holding me down, and I can't get away!" she cried. "It's so tight. I can't breathe!"

"Seneca, we've gotta get you on your feet!" said Jake. He tried to sound calm, but he was unable to hide his fear.

He strained to make his eyes adjust to the dark. Everything blended into the darkness. The foliage and leaves were caked in mud, making everything slippery. He lost his footing and grip each time he tugged to get her free of the entanglement. "I need to find something to wedge between you and whatever's holding you down," he said.

"I stepped on some branches," said Seneca in a weak voice. "They were on the other side of this glade." She continued to wrestle to break free. The harder she pulled, the tighter the hold became. Her ribs ached, and she strained her neck to the point it felt numb.

"Okay. Good idea!" said Jake. He jetted off in a full-out sprint.

"Hurry, Jake, please!" she shouted. She unrelentingly twisted her body to escape from her abductor. Whatever held her down was just as persistent and showed no signs of releasing her.

Jake frantically searched the ground for tree limbs or anything he could use as a wedge. The forest was thick and encircled them. It reminded him of an outdoor arena, and the clearing allowed only enough moonlight to brighten a small area. He felt as if a spotlight were on him to perform, and he was ill prepared. Everything beyond the surrounding trees was in complete darkness.

"Oh my God, Jake, it hurts. It's scraping the skin on my back! It's trying to claw out my wings!" screamed Seneca. "Stop! Let me go!" She wrestled wildly to break away. "Help!"

"I'm going to go look behind those shrubs. Hang on, Seneca!" shouted Jake. "Keep fighting. Don't stop fighting!"

He hurdled over a mound of junipers but nearly fell when his foot latched on to it. He stumbled as he attempted to get untangled before realizing he had to steer clear of a cluster of thorny bushes.

"Damn obstacle course!" he grumbled.

He cringed in pain when he realized a few thorns had pierced through his jeans and into his thigh. He brushed past two hornbeam hedges with profuse branches. Their russet-orange leaves were draped in an intricate spiderweb; its talented architect remained hidden. The sticky web traps clung to his legs, but he didn't bother to brush them away. He was desperate to find anything that could be used as a wedge.

He turned around frantically in a circle. He pushed through a thicket of shrubbery, releasing a powerful scent of fragrant red berries. The smell made him woozy, and he stumbled off balance. In frustration, he kicked up a pile of damp, rotting leaves. He was at a loss.

"Come back—don't leave me!" screeched Seneca. "I'm scared, Jake! I'm really scared."

Her voice trailed off. Saying it out loud made her panic even more. She started kicking nonstop and flailing her body to loosen the hold. The harder she fought, the more she could feel a renewed grasp on another part of her body. Dagger-sharp claws scraped at her flesh. She forced another scream, but her throat was dry, and her pleas were weakening in their intensity.

Jake realized it was a bad idea to leave her alone. He raced back to her side. Even in the dark, he could see blood soaking through her shirt. He knelt down next to her and put his palm to her cheek. Her skin was cold and clammy but warmed slightly beneath his touch. He knew the marshy ground was contributing to her drop in temperature and feared she would go into shock. He had to act quickly.

"I won't leave you. I promise," he said. His mind was racing, and panic was creeping in. He couldn't think clearly. "There's gotta be a way to get you free."

"I can't keep fighting, Jake. It hurts so much," she whimpered. "Each time I pull, I get jabbed and clawed."

"You're not giving up. Get set, Seneca. Let's do this!"

Jake began pulling at the mud-covered limbs. He moved swiftly, alternating between Seneca's arms and legs. Each time he grabbed hold and attempted to loosen her captor's grip, his hands were grazed by razor-sharp claws, causing him to release and try another spot. The cuts stung, but he continued grappling to find any place he could tug to break her free. The blood streaming onto his hands made it difficult to maintain a firm grip. Jake jerked with an uncontrollable spasm. Pain shot down his arm as a claw burrowed deep into his flesh. He snatched his hand away and stumbled backward. He scrambled on his knees to find a different angle. His hands plunged into the thick mud, grabbling with something stiff and unyielding. He pulled his hands free and wiped them against his jeans. Whatever held her down was strong and ruthless. He was intent on figuring out another tactic. He got up and backed away a few feet.

"Think, Jake. Think!" he said aloud. "This is crazy." He tilted his head back and attempted to concentrate to uncover any possible solution. He paced in a slow circle as he rubbed his bloody hands through his hair. He suddenly stopped and locked eyes with Seneca.

"Jake! No, you can't give up—don't leave me!" shrieked Seneca. Her tears stung as they rolled across open lacerations on her cheeks and created miniscule pools in the pockets of her ears.

I'm not going anywhere, but listen up, and don't question me. Seneca, when I give you the signal, you need to open your wings.

Seneca could hear his thoughts clearly, and she knew he meant well, but it was too much of a risk. "I can't Jake. I just can't," moaned Seneca.

She took a deep breath. She tried to relax and focused on keeping her wings hidden. She didn't know why Jake would make such a request. She was growing numb to the pain and stopped resisting her captor.

Seneca, you have to do it. Trust me!

He inhaled slowly and cleared his mind of all other thoughts to be sure she would not confuse his directions. She gazed into Jake's eyes, and he bobbed his head slowly. She knew that was the signal.

Without hesitation, Seneca's wings appeared spontaneously and opened in full span. In one motion, she was lifted from the ground. The force and light they illuminated caused the captor to lose its hold as she propelled herself upward Claws reached out and grappled aimlessly in the air. She was out of reach. Her wings were powerful and strong. She rocketed toward the sky, soaring higher with each thrust of her wings. She continued pushing hard to put a great distance between her and the ground below. Her wings responded instinctively, piloting her upward until she was well above the trees and suspended in the night sky. She was free.

Seneca breathed in the crisp air. Her body ached; however, she avoided checking her injuries. She didn't want to dwell on anything except her freedom. She fluttered her wings, and they replied on cue. They were intact and unharmed, which filled her with relief—for a moment. An eerie chill ran through her body. She shuddered.

Where's Jake? She suddenly realized he wasn't with her. She had been so consumed with getting away that she hadn't bothered to think about her friend.

"Jake!" yelled Seneca. "Oh no! What have I done?"

She attempted to search the ground below, but she couldn't make out anything in the darkness. The density of the trees shielded most of the view of the marsh below. She knew she had to get lower to check on Jake, but her fear kept her hovering high above the dreadful danger lurking beneath. She tried various angles to get a better view to no avail. The only consolation was the cool air, which soothed her injuries.

"Jake, can you hear me? Are you okay?" she called out. She waited for a response, but she heard only disturbing snarls and rumbling sounds echoing beneath her.

"Answer me! Please!" Seneca wept.

This time, she had no concerns about letting her tears fall. She was horrified by Jake's lack of response. Dark and gruesome images of his possible plight filled her mind. Growling and rustling sounds continued but varied in intensity. She forced away the visions of Jake being tortured and devoured. Seneca shook her head rapidly to remove the morbid images she had conjured. She called out several times, but he still did not respond. She tried to convince herself that as long as she could hear sounds, no matter how horrendous, he was still alive.

CHAPTER FOUR

Murkgoblins

J ake watched in horror as a grotesque creature sprang from the earth, jetting several feet in the air in a futile attempt to stop Seneca's escape. It landed hard and began grumbling as it crouched low to the ground. It scratched at the mud where Seneca had been held against her will. It stood erect while contorting and twisting until it faced Jake.

Jake braced for impact; he knew a battle was inevitable. They were about to embark on what was likely to be an intense brawl. He hadn't thought beyond the immediate need to save his friend. He should have bolted when he had the chance, but he had foolishly remained. He had to weigh his next move carefully. Jake expected the mud-covered creature to attack immediately, but instead, it held its position. They stood facing each other at an impasse.

Jake was curious about the filthy beast but opted not to engage verbally. He'd been wrong to think it was a vast tree holding on to Seneca. Instead, it was an Otherworld being camouflaged to blend into the brush and muddy marsh. It was atrocious from head to toe and completely covered in dried mud, leaves, sedge, and foliage. None of its facial features were symmetrical, which gave it a distorted expression. It had deep impressions on its face that resembled chiseled tree bark, with dark opaque eyes set deep in the crevices. In the center of its concave forehead was an engraved spiral marking in a dull gold hue. Its body was covered sparingly in moss and grass, and it had twisted branch-like horns extending from the top of its head. In an upright position, it was a foot shorter than Jake and extremely thin. It showed no signs of being fazed or intimidated by the height or weight variance. It was inexplicably the aggressor.

Jake held his position. He watched the tree creature move slowly around, circling him as it snarled. It surveyed him thoroughly in preparation for an attack. Its eyes widened as they peered out through the shallow cracks in its face. It growled with defiance to show its displeasure, making no attempt to hide its contempt. Its nostrils flared as it flashed ragged discolored fangs that protruded from a severe underbite that gave it a pelican-like jaw. It stomped the ground where it had trapped Seneca and growled louder. It was intent on retaliation for having lost its prey. Jake knew this to be true and knew an attack was imminent. He took in a slow breath and readied himself. The creature squatted low and hovered close to the ground. Jake took a slight step back and flexed his arms as he opened and closed his fists.

The grubby creature leaped into the air and lunged into him. The force was severe enough to knock him down. They tumbled over several times in the thick mud. The impact sent ripples of pain through Jake's spine. Before he could recover, the beast was on top of him, clawing at his face. Jake shoved it off with his forearm. His closed fist landed hard on the side of its head. It yelped in pain and scrambled away to avoid another blow. Jake quickly scrambled to his feet. He knew being on the ground would be to the advantage of the beast and meant sure death. It didn't hesitate long before resuming the attack. It charged with its head lowered. Before Jake could react, it rammed its head into his stomach, causing him to rock back on his feet and double over in pain. It didn't knock the wind out of him, but it hit hard enough to make him cringe.

Jake was angry. He turned around in circles, searching for the beast. *Where did it go?* He knew it was near, and he chastised himself for not keeping an eye on it. He could hear its heavy breathing. It blended into the surroundings like a territorial reptile. Jake turned slowly, listening for a clue to its exact location. He heard it moving, coming toward him. The sound of its feet making contact with the slushy mud gave it away.

Jake swung wildly in the air, punching and jabbing but not connecting to any flesh. He knew it was near; he felt its hot breath on his neck. The creature growled as it sprang at him. Jake sidestepped at the last second and jabbed hard with a right cross. His fist connected in a fleshy area of its midsection. The blow sent the creature tumbling into the dirt. It recovered quickly and charged with its head lowered, its horns aimed squarely at Jake's torso. He dodged at the last second and grabbed hold of a horn. It struggled to get away, flailing and clawing at its captor, but Jake held on tightly with both hands. He swung the creature around in a circle, picking up speed with each revolution. He spun around harder and faster until the scruffy creature was lifted off the ground. It was suspended parallel to the ground. Jake continued to spin and increase his speed. The beast was silent. It appeared merely as a blur as it swung through the air. Jake let go of the mangled horn, sending the monster hurtling into the trunk of a mature oak tree. He heard a loud crack upon impact. It collapsed on the ground with a thud.

Jake was out of breath and soaked in sweat. He searched the sky and zeroed in on Seneca, looking for confirmation that his plan had worked. He started to wave but flinched from excruciating pain. Something with a sharp edge pierced his skin. He tugged at his leg and felt a clawed hand wrap around it, gripping and scratching at his ankle. Just as he'd feared, there was more than one beast. He kicked with his free leg, connecting to the side of its head. The gnarly horned beast squealed and retreated a few feet away. It bared its teeth as it crouched low and rocked. It was regrouping for a return attack, but it paused. Jake heard more growls in the distance. They were getting closer. The creature was waiting for reinforcements. It was not going to attack again without help.

Jake had never felt so frightened. He swallowed hard. He didn't know which direction to run. His eyes filled with tears; he was outnumbered. He had two options: escape or fight to the death. He was desperate for a weapon. He felt a wave of nausea rising. He'd never considered himself a fighter, yet there he was, battling for survival. He could hear Seneca's faint voice overhead, but he couldn't risk losing concentration. It was best that she stay away. He hoped she wouldn't be tempted to return.

As a high school wrestler, he'd been taught to exercise discipline and to trust his instincts and utilize patience. He had also learned ways to expose an opponent's weakness. So far, he was using only instincts and reflexes. He let out a deep breath. His hands trembled from the adrenaline that pumped through him. He was exhausted. He could smell the odor rising from his armpits, but it was distinctly different from the foul smell the beasts transmitted. The closer the growls got, the more pungent the smell became. The stench consumed the fresh air, and he worried about suffocation.

Jake coughed. He stayed rooted to his spot. He focused on breathing shallowly. He tried not to open his mouth, but it was unavoidable. He was disgusted by their rancid smell and the bitter taste it left in his mouth. He spat on the ground but didn't dare shift his attention. He watched one after another of the dirty beasts surround him. He counted seventeen of them, which included the one whose eyes remained fixed on him while it clawed at its injured head.

They began growling and clicking their tongues and then made chirping sounds in unison. Jake wondered if the sound was a form of communication or a battle cry. Their sticklike legs were bent and hovered over grass-encrusted, filthy feet. They crouched lower to the ground and swayed in time. The moon gave the perfect cast of light to the clearing. Jake was able to make out the details of their marred faces; they were contorted and menacing. They had spindly arms and root-like hands with appendages that extended in multiple directions. Varying amounts of debris covered their muddy bodies. Each was a chameleon to the landscape.

"What are you waiting for—an invitation?" He goaded them rebelliously.

The mob grew quiet. Jake focused on slowing his breathing. He bent down slowly and picked up a thick maple branch. He wiped away some of the mud to get a secure grip. He noticed the wood fit firmly in his palms as he wrapped both hands around it. He pulled his arms back;

his elbows were squared to the ground. He held the branch high, just above his head, as he rotated it in small circles. He spread his feet wide apart and centered his body while he placed more of his weight on his back foot. He steadied his frame and squared his shoulders.

"Have you ever experienced baseball and the power of a designated hitter?" Jake asked, although he was not anticipating a response.

One beast slightly taller than the others stepped forward. It had numerous branchlike horns protruding from its head that curved in different directions. Instinctively, Jake was sure it was their leader. It tilted its head from one side to the other. It raised an arm and then dropped it to its side. It was a signal for war; they charged.

CHAPTER FIVE

Fairy Venom

Shayna's sword hummed as it slashed through the night air. She was winded, but she refused to let up. It was crucial that she maintain her advantage. She had no idea how many of the winged creatures were surrounding them, but she continued to swing hard with the purpose of destroying all of the attackers. She was uncharacteristically calm. Her persistence had become her protective armor. Her cheerleading training had given her agility and precision in executing effectively. She believed her athleticism gave her an edge. With each swing, she felt her confidence grow. Her arms were tired, but her reflexes would not relent.

Shayna sensed movement. She spun and wielded her sword closer to her body. The blade responded with a timely block, followed by a quick counter-maneuver into a downward thrash; her illuminated sword vibrated. She had taken three creatures out with that single strike. Her endurance was keeping her in the fight. She knew she was reacting in defense, but she still shuddered each time a combatant screamed out in agony. They were approaching from all sides without pause. Her empathy for the enemy was completely void.

She caught a glimpse of Conner, who was punching through the air with incredible speed. She knew his quickness had to be the influence of the crystals, because his movements were a blur. She could hear the sounds of the enemy meeting their demise repeatedly.

"Shayna, we need to get out of here! Head north like Seneca told us!" Conner shouted.

He took two winged beings down by slamming their heads together. He tossed them over his shoulders like a pair of dirty socks. His eyes widened as they searched the air for more.

"They've got us boxed in," said Shayna. "It's exactly what they did to Dreya."

"Run for it! I will keep them off you," said Conner.

"I'm not leaving you—no way! I'm not afraid of these nasty beasts!"

Shayna kept her sword moving. She could barely see the creatures approach until the last second. She focused on the buzzing sound they made, which gave an indication of their position in the air. It was easier to focus on the noise than to try to stay fixed on their flight patterns. They would dive in from above and below, which initially caught her by surprise. A few became tangled in her hair, but she was quick to grab hold and toss them aside. They didn't weigh much, but they were sturdy and fixated on doing harm.

"I've had enough of you crusty gnats!" said Shayna. "Take that!" She sliced the wings off its back, and it shrieked as it plummeted to the ground.

"I don't think we're going to be able to keep this up!" yelled Conner. "There's no end to them!"

He grabbed three out of the air and sent them crashing into a dry creek bed. Their bodies landed in a heap, and they remained motionless.

"I've got to keep fighting—for Dreya. I can't give up!" she shouted.

Shayna widened her stance; every muscle in her body tensed. She focused hard and screamed. It was a piercing sound that she hadn't realized she was able to make, although she wasn't surprised. She knew the root of it. Her sword grew more brilliant as it vibrated in her hands.

She raised it above her head with both hands wrapped tightly around the hilt. She flipped it over as she simultaneously changed her grip and drove it into the ground. A wave of intensely bright light shot across the vast glen. The flying creatures closest to the center of the beam fell to the ground and were unresponsive. Those out of reach resisted coming any closer and immediately retreated. Their buzzing sound diminished as they flew farther away.

Shayna pulled the sword from the ground, and its glow faded as it vanished from sight.

"What was that?" Conner asked. He rubbed away sweat from his forehead. He was hot and exhausted.

"Ha! Who knows? I guess I have some hidden talents," Shayna said. "Or maybe I was letting out some of my frustration on those flying rats!" She exhaled slowly. "Let's get out of here before they come back." The adrenaline rush caused her entire body to shake.

"I'm right behind you," said Conner. He ached and welcomed the break, even if it turned out to be short lived.

Shayna took off running without hesitation. She didn't slow down until she neared the top of the hill. She was breathing hard and could feel a cramp between her ribs. She massaged the area to relieve the ache.

"I think we're in the clear now. This is the way Seneca and Jake came, right?"

"I'm not sure. Argh!" Conner shouted. "What is this?"

Shayna turned to check on Conner. She covered her mouth to muffle a scream. He had pulled the sleeve of his shirt up to expose his skin. His forearm was completely covered in large blisters. He winced in pain as he stared down at the mound of boils and blisters. She focused on calming a jolt of queasiness.

"It burns!" Conner screamed. "It's sizzling!"

Shayna grabbed his arm, but he quickly pulled away.

"No, Shayna, don't touch me! Get back, 'cause it might get on you too. I think they're spreading!"

"Let me see it, Conner. Is it really that bad?" asked Shayna as she held her breath, and her heart tightened in anticipation. She knew the answer by the horrid look on his face. He was dripping in sweat. The blisters were throbbing and appeared to be multiplying.

"It's probably not as bad as it feels," said Conner. "Those flying devils were spitting green fire at us. Some of it must have hit me."

"I could smell something foul each time they flew by, but I had no idea what was coming out of them," said Shayna. "I was too disgusted to let them get close—their noises were nauseating."

"Each time I put my arm up to block, it seemed like they were intent on going after it." Conner groaned as he raised his arm to get a better look at his injury.

"Conner, that looks really bad. Seriously, it's not good at all," said Shayna.

"I guess I was wrong. It is as bad as it feels," moaned Conner. "My whole arm feels like it's on fire."

"What are we going to do? I don't know CPR. Where're Jake and Seneca? This is so totally out of control right now!" said Shayna.

"I'm not sure CPR would help. Probably first aid and maybe a doctor or two."

"No joking, Conner!" Shayna yelled. "You know what I mean. You need some major help. We are totally out of sync and clueless with this Otherworld."

Shayna took a step back and bumped into something hard. She turned around quickly as she readied to battle the threat, her sword illuminated in her grasp; it had appeared with a simple inhalation. She bit her bottom lip as she tilted her head upward to see bright, glowing green eyes staring down at her. She stumbled back a few steps but recovered quickly as she shifted into a defensive position.

"I did not mean to startle you. However, you ought to remain aware as to the danger that surrounds you," he said. His voice was deep and had a gruff tone.

"Are you part of this so-called danger surrounding us and attacking us too?" Shayna asked. Her eyes narrowed.

She closed both hands around the handle of the sword and eased closer to Conner. The blade's brilliance intensified as she raised it above her head. She widened her stance, arched her back, and prepared to strike.

"It is not I that you should worry about. I have taken the liberty to cast a protection charm that will shield you from detection. However, it is only temporary," he said.

Shayna remained focused on the stranger and refused to back down. She wasn't taking any chances, especially not after all she had witnessed.

"Oh—that's good, right, Shayna?" Conner whispered. He did not feel up to asking questions or putting up a fight. He felt feverish and was on the brink of vomiting.

Shayna shifted her eyes momentarily to Conner but didn't reply. She held her breath as she surveyed the tall man. She was mesmerized by his handsome face and piercing eyes. She had never seen anyone with eyes so beautiful. She noted that they were a complementary contrast to his dark skin. He was dressed in a long black cloak with elaborate gold brocades that draped over the shoulders of the garment and reflected the dim moonlight. She could tell he was extremely muscular by his broad build. She caught a glimpse of his bulging biceps. She didn't realize she was staring until he spoke.

"Your friend needs immediate treatment. If the boils turn brown, there will be no stopping the spread of the bacteria. Once it reaches that point, it will infect all major organs. Death is inevitable if he's not treated in time," said the stranger.

"Excuse me. Who are you? How do you—I mean, what are you saying?" stammered Shayna.

"He said something about dying, I think," said Conner, his voice nearly inaudible. His shirt was soaked in sweat and clung to him. He wanted desperately to discard it, but he was afraid there might be more blisters forming beneath. He didn't think he could bear seeing more.

Shayna remained transfixed by the stranger's eyes. She quickly forgot where she was, the potential danger, and Conner's need of assistance. Her brain told her not to trust the stranger, yet she knew in her heart that her instincts never betrayed her. She believed he was there to help. She lowered her sword but kept it visible as a warning.

"I am Rileau," he said. He bowed his head slightly. His expression showed no emotion, and his eyes stayed locked on Shayna's. She shifted her weight and then stepped closer to Conner.

"I'm Conner, and I'd shake your hand, dude, but I can barely raise it. This is Shayna. Are you friend or foe? Not that I could put up a fight at this point." He felt weak and light-headed as he leaned against the nearest tree.

"I am neither, but I mean you no harm. You were to be escorted to my dwelling to begin your lessons. I was made aware of the attack and came straight away," said Rileau.

"Who made you aware? And why didn't you come sooner?" Shayna asked. She flexed her fingers around the grip of her sword. She could feel it heating up in her hand, as it did each time she used it.

"I received word from Dreya. She tried to divert you away from the attack, but unfortunately, it was too late," he replied. He lowered his head slightly, causing his long dark hair to drape forward. "I am sorry for your loss."

"You know about Dreya, my grandmother, don't you? About what happened to her?" Shayna shook her head in an attempt to push away her sorrow.

"Yes," he replied. His eyes met hers as he allowed his acknowledgment to linger. He elected to say no more.

"It was awful. They just kept attacking until she tumbled over into a deep ravine. I knew she was gone. There was nothing I could do. We tried to reach her, but it was too late," Shayna said.

She trembled as she recalled the tragedy, and her mind replayed it in slow motion. She and Conner had witnessed the horror of her grandmother's death firsthand.

"Then we had to fight like crazy because those flying rats came at us," she said. "We took a lot of them out. I wanted to smash every single one of them!"

Shayna realized he was allowing her the choice to continue rambling. He made no attempt to interrupt or pry for details. That was fine with her since she didn't care to have the experience dissected. She knew she would not soon forget what she'd witnessed, and she would relive the dreadful experience repeatedly. It felt good to let her feelings out, because she hadn't had a chance to mourn or even discuss the fact that her grandmother had fought ferociously to the end.

"They killed her!" She allowed herself to say it out loud. Her tone was deadpan and sounded nothing like her. The reality of the entire ordeal washed over her. She wiped her eyes with the back of her hand. "I can't talk about this anymore!" Shayna shouted as she threw her arms into the air. Her voice carried through the trees. Slight rustling could be heard before all became quiet once again. The pain was too fresh and hurt deeply.

"Understood," he said. His eyes stayed fixed on hers.

She cast her eyes away momentarily; he made her uneasy, but she believed he could be trusted.

"Ahem! In pain here," Conner said as he slid down the side of the tree until he came to rest at the trunk. He moaned in agony.

"Reveal your injury," Rileau commanded.

He eased past Shayna to get closer to Conner. She made no attempt to stop his approach. She prayed that her instincts hadn't betrayed her. Conner stretched out his arm. He grimaced from the excruciating pain. Rileau scanned it quickly but resisted making direct contact with the damaged skin.

"Do you have other infected areas?" asked Rileau. His voice was calm and authoritative.

"No, just my arm, I think. That's enough—believe me," said Conner. He closed his eyes and pulled his arm close, cradling it against his chest. He had never experienced anything so painful. He muttered to himself as he trembled and groaned.

"He's going to be okay, isn't he?" Shayna moved in to get a closer look at the blisters.

"If we act quickly, I believe we can save his arm," Rileau said flatly.

"Save my arm? What are you saying? I could lose my arm?" Conner tried to stand up straight but remained hunched over. He stared at Rileau, who towered a good six inches above him. "Are you serious, dude? My arm?" He was panic-stricken and hoped he wasn't hearing him correctly.

"It would certainly be the first thing to go, followed by your life," Rileau replied.

His voice remained steady and serious. Conner began to feel faint. Shayna saw his eyes rolling back, and she reached out to steady him.

"Breathe, Conner—you're going to be fine," she whispered. She was careful to avoid touching his arm, for fear of causing further injury. "We'll get through this."

"He said I could lose my arm, Shayna. You know it's my pitching arm. Or army. No, I would prefer being a marine, actually," Conner said, slurring his words as his head rocked forward.

"What are you saying?" asked Shayna. She noticed he wasn't focusing on her but seemed to be drifting off to sleep. He slumped against the tree, and she guided him to a sitting position in the moist soil. "What's wrong with him?" she asked as she turned to get answers from Rileau.

"The fever is setting in. He will be quite delusional until he is treated properly."

"Eh, it's a strike for me. Betta batter up!" Conner announced. His head rocked back and forth.

"So, he's going to talk gibberish? Is that what you're saying?" Shayna asked.

"I'm not familiar with the meaning of *gibberish,* but if it implies that he will be speaking incoherently, then yes, gibberish it is." Rileau stepped away from Conner and began surveying the area.

"What are you looking for? Those flying pests are long gone. I saw to that," Shayna said. She knew she sounded smug, but she also felt it was an accurate assessment of the results.

"I am in search of something to aid Conner," he replied as he pushed back a hawthorn bush.

Shayna noticed that he was unaffected; the thorns slid across his arms like feathers. His movements were deliberate and not clumsy in the least. He was large in stature but moved with regal ease and poise. She knew she was gawking and felt the sudden need to fill the silence with conversation.

"Just to clarify, you're our trainer?" Shayna asked.

He turned toward her and smiled for the first time since they'd met. She couldn't control the blush she felt rising in her cheeks and was thankful for the darkness. She suddenly panicked as she wondered if he had the gift of mind reading. *Oh no, please, not that*, she thought over and over.

"I prefer *mentor* or *teacher*, as training implies that you are knowledgeable. From my observation, you each have much to learn in all areas of the Otherworld and your abilities," said Rileau. He was stern and direct.

Shayna didn't follow his explanation, since all she could focus on was his physique. She thought he was the most perfect man she'd ever seen. She tried to think of a comparison to a movie star, model, or famous athlete but ultimately decided he was in a class of his own. His facial features were sculpted in perfect symmetry. His skin was flawless and masculine, and he had a square jawline and full lips. *Those lips. Those eyes.* She realized she was still staring when Rileau made a low growling sound. It jarred her out of the daydream. She wondered if she had said anything out loud. She was slightly embarrassed but also a bit peeved by the interruption.

"I'm sorry. You were saying something about Conner's injuries, right?" asked Shayna. Her voice quivered an octave too high. She sounded like a small child. It was not the impression she wanted to make. She couldn't figure out what had come over her. She was not feeling like herself in that moment, but she didn't want the sensation to stop.

"Conner needs assistance. We cannot delay much longer. Do you comprehend, Shayna?" asked Rileau.

He leaned in, inches from her face, and she nodded multiple times. Her mind flashed an image of her as a desktop bobblehead doll. She huffed in disgust.

"Sure, I understand, but—" She stopped.

Shayna didn't really understand the situation, but she resisted talking more. All she knew was that she felt an unexplainable urge to know more about the handsome stranger, their teacher and mentor.

"Good. Now I must locate the others before they perish," said Rileau.

"You mean they might die?" Shayna asked. She hoped she had misunderstood what she had heard.

"The murkgoblins are uncompromising and vicious. They will not show mercy, as the fairies of the Terrain did. Once the fairies strike, they have a tendency to retreat. They are confident and acutely aware of their venom's potency. That is not the case with the murkgoblins," he explained. "They prey on anything that is pure when it crosses their path in the night."

"Murkgoblins," Shayna repeated. "The name alone sounds awful."

"We defeated them in the bottom of the ninth, right?" Conner mumbled. He faced the tree as he continued his ramblings. "It's gonna be a no-hitter for you, son, and no noise from the peanut gallery, eh? Do you hear me talking to you?"

"It's okay, Conner. No more noise from the gallery. Just sit down, and lean on that tree," said Shayna as calmly as she could manage.

"Okeydokey artichokie," Conner replied as he slid his back down the side of the tree and collapsed on the ground. "Hello, tree."

Shayna smiled as she turned her attention back to Rileau. It was a serious situation, and she really needed to concentrate.

"You were saying something about murkgoblins," Shayna said. "They sound nasty."

"Yes, they are quite nasty, as they are creatures of filth. Presently, they are attacking your friends, and they will fight to the death," said Rileau.

"Murkgoblins are inherently vicious and reside as the Otherworld's scavengers. They have no regard for life and are void of remorse."

"Are they like the things that came after us? Tiny little vicious gnats!"

"Not in slightest," he replied. "They are as big as men and are night dwellers that stay hidden by burrowing deep in the dampest areas of the earth and blending into the landscape. They can go undetected by even the most observant elementals, and they will emerge and attack without warning. This gives them an advantage to the dismay of their prey."

"Prey? They think that Seneca and Jake are their prey?" asked Shayna. "What are we waiting for? Let's help them! Where do we go?" She was riddled with concern. Fighting off the flying fairies was bad enough, but this sounded much worse.

"You must remain here with Conner, as he does not have much time," said Rileau. "He has been exposed to the fairies' deadly venom. I would surmise they targeted his arm in retaliation for the injury you inflicted upon Brigara."

"C'mon! She did that to herself. We didn't tell her to try to jump across the threshold," said Conner. He whistled a few notes and then shut his eyes.

"He's making sense now, and he's right. She asked for it!" Shayna bellowed.

"Ouch! This hurts seriously—no joke!" Conner cried. "Don't poke at the blo—" He screamed out in distress and pain.

His body shook violently. Several boils appeared on his arm, bubbling and throbbing as they spread unrestricted across exposed skin. The infected area began emitting an odor that prompted Conner to pull the top of his shirt over his nose and mouth in disgust. He moved to a fetal position and whimpered.

"Oh, Conner," said Shayna softly. "This is terrible. I'm sorry. Please try to calm down."

"It is futile to discuss the particulars of the murkgoblins or Brigara at this moment. Shayna, retract your sword. You must grab a handful of leaves from the black currant bush just behind you," instructed Rileau.

"Hopefully they help with this major stench," said Conner. "It is stinky, stinky. Oh yeah, so ooh la-la stinky." He sang melodically. He lowered his shirt from his mouth slightly before quickly raising it again.

"The evidence of a foul smell is the final stage prior to eruption," said Rileau. "Shayna, your sword. You must disengage and gather the leaves now!"

"Yeah, okay—fine!" she snapped.

Shayna knew she was overreacting, but her response was an automatic reflex since she disliked taking orders from anyone. She hadn't realized she was still in a battle stance with her sword drawn. She looked down at the sword, and it vanished. She was still not accustomed to having such an ability, and she couldn't resist smirking in satisfaction. She lost focus momentarily as she recalled the first time she had used the sword to stop Brigara from crossing the threshold. She had never felt that much power in her life. Although she had a knack for always getting her way, she had never felt quite in control. Commanding the sword was different. It was a connection like no other. It made her feel grounded and secure.

"Earth to Shayna. Time to log back in," said Conner. He cleared his throat to draw her attention. "I believe it is suppertime, and then it's off with his head!"

"No, he has a rather nice head. Let's leave it intact," she said with a smirk.

Conner whined slightly and shrugged. His face was absent of any color. Shayna was afraid he was close to dying. He was her friend, and she felt a surge of determination. She was not about to lose another person that evening—or ever again, if she could help it. She knelt down next to him and looked into his eyes.

"Conner, you're going to be okay. I promise," she said as she smoothed his drenched hair away from his brow.

She jumped to her feet and turned toward Rileau. He was looking down at her with a scowl. She hadn't anticipated that reaction, and it caught her off guard.

"Excuse me. Uh, I'm sorry. For some reason, it's really hard for me to focus right now. You want me to pull leaves because…" Shayna stammered.

"The leaves of the black currant will slow down the progression of the boils. They must not form any pus or change shades. Avoid any leaves that are showing signs of mildew or those absent of berries," said Rileau flatly. He huffed and shook his head. "You are wasting time for everyone!"

Suddenly, Rileau jerked around and stared off into the distance. Shayna had heard it too—the sound of loud screaming. It radiated above the trees. Without question, it was Seneca. It was a shriek that signaled she was under a dangerous attack. Each audible word that followed the screams had Jake's name attached to it. There was no mistake; they were together and in the midst of battling something fearful. The hairs on Shayna's arms stood on end.

She reached out to Rileau but stopped before making contact and withdrew her hand. She thought she saw smoke escaping from his nostrils, but she quickly dismissed it. She assumed her eyes were playing some sort of trick on her.

"That's Seneca! We need to help her—and Jake!" she yelled.

"It's not for you to intervene. You shall do as I say and tend to Conner," he snapped. "You have not followed through with the directive you've already been assigned. How can you expect to take on more?"

Shayna knew she needed to give Conner her attention and not question Rileau's command. She frantically tore off leaves from the branches.

"Is this enough?" She held up two handfuls of the leaves and shook them inches from his face. Her arms trembled.

"That should be sufficient. Now place them on Conner's arm, and hold them firmly. Do not release your grasp," Rileau said. "You are to continue applying pressure no matter what happens next. You must not release until I return. Is that understood?"

Rileau didn't wait for a response. He turned and ran toward the distant screams. Shayna watched him skillfully move through the brush

and effortlessly leap over fallen branches and tree stumps. She felt hopeful that he would be able to defeat whatever was attacking the others. As long as she could hear Seneca's screams, she knew Seneca was still alive. She wished she knew for sure if Jake and Seneca were fighting off the poison-spitting faeries or murkgoblins. She felt guilty that she wasn't there to help fight.

"Snap out of it, Shayna! Put those leaves on already—one of the pimply things is turning colors," Conner said hoarsely. He gawked at his arm and then closed his eyes.

"Okay, just hold still. Rileau said I have to keep pressure on your arm," Shayna whispered as she pressed down hard with several layers of leaves.

"Thanks," he muttered.

"Funny how you're suddenly coherent enough to boss me around," she said flatly.

She pressed the leaves directly on the raised boils. Green pus secreted from beneath the compress and rolled down his arm. It dripped into the dirt and sizzled upon contact. Shayna scrunched her noise. The smell was rancid.

"That is some funky stuff. Ick!" she said as she turned her head away. She wished for a free hand to hold her nose or fan the air.

Conner howled in pain, which made her quickly dismiss her own discomfort.

"Sorry about that. I guess I've smelled worse—like fur-lined boots that have been worn without socks. Now, that is pretty foul and—"

"Get them off! Take them off now! It burns!" shrieked Conner. He attempted to jerk away, but Shayna held on tightly.

"I can't, Conner. You heard what Rileau said. I just can't!"

"It hurts really bad, like so unbelievably bad," he whined.

"It's going to be okay," she whispered repeatedly.

Shayna began humming and cooing to him as if he were a small child. She tried hard to block out his moans and focused on rocking him as she held the wad of leaves firmly on the blisters. She knew her friend was in pain, but she would not risk losing him, especially when she realized she could no longer hear Seneca screaming. The only sounds she heard came from Conner as he whimpered quietly next to her. She felt warm tears rolling down her cheeks, but she didn't dare wipe them, as she refused to lessen the pressure on the leaf compress.

CHAPTER SIX

The Mentor

Seneca knew she had to return. Jake needed her, so there was no other choice. She couldn't abandon him. She didn't know how she could possibly help, but she had to try. She could feel the blood still trickling from the gashes beneath her wings. She cringed at the thought of her wings being shredded—she knew that had been the creatures' intent. She didn't want the fear to consume her, but she was dreadfully afraid. She inhaled deeply and whispered, "You can do this, Seneca. Get a grip. Just do something—anything!"

Gradually, she began to relax. Her hand found the opening of her pocket. She slid her hand inside and felt the warmth of the stone beneath her fingertips. She clasped it and raised it to her face. It had saved her in the cavern from nearly drowning and had revealed her wings for the first time. Could the stone be the answer she sought? She wondered if it could somehow help rescue Jake. Without warning, a deep and booming voice called up to her from below.

"Seneca, do not use the Stone of Fate! Put it away, and stay put until I call for you!"

"Who said that?" she whispered, searching the ground below. It was too dark to make out anything other than the trees. She saw no obvious movement as she circled in hopes of finding the source.

I am here to help. Jake is in grave danger. Do not intervene! he commanded in a bellowing tone.

Seneca's head ached; his presence was forceful. He had shifted to communicating telepathically. *Great, yet another mind reader,* she thought. She realized the intruder in her thoughts would likely pick up on her disgruntled attitude. She shifted her attention to his message.

"Who are you?" she shouted into the night air. She knew it wasn't necessary to speak out loud, but she felt compelled.

I am Rileau, and I am your mentor. We will be acquainted soon enough. You must not return to this battle. I will address it, he said sternly. *You are not prepared to handle this! Do not speak aloud again—it is too dangerous.*

"But—" She decided to remain quiet. He had already chastised her, and she didn't want to make things worse. She knew he was speaking the truth. Her ability to help was grim at best. She had suffered too much and was traumatized. Seneca began circling over the battleground below, and although she couldn't see anything, she suddenly felt hopeful. She focused on the notion that Jake would survive with the help of their mentor. The more she thought about it, the better she felt. She was confident he would emerge as the victor. She refused to let any doubt vanquish that belief. The skirmish beneath her suddenly grew louder. She rationalized that Rileau had arrived, and a fierce fight was under way.

"Help him, Rileau," she pleaded softly. She hoped her voice carried to his ears below, since she didn't dare shout. She resisted the urge to fly closer.

Rileau entered the glen undetected. He determined it would be detrimental to address Jake before engaging in battle. The murkgoblins had Jake's arms pinned to a large beech tree; its canopy covered most of the area around it.

Jake had endured countless hits and tears to his torso, but the way they restrained him was agonizing. They pulled his arms tightly around the base of the tree. He felt ligaments being stretched away from his shoulder sockets. It took every ounce of his fading strength not to scream. He refused to give them the satisfaction. He wondered if they used the beech tree specifically for dismembering enemies. Jake knew his time was short. He would not be able to hold on much longer. The pain was overwhelming.

Rileau surveyed the bodies spread about; they remained motionless in various positions. It was evident Jake had put up a great fight and had successfully tussled several of them into submission. Those that took on the task of restraining him were also engaged in taunting. The others clawed at his exposed skin and intermittently kicked and punched at his midsection.

Rileau eased in closer, and the murkgoblins snapped their heads around upon sensing his approach. The two that were inflicting most of the clawing turned and faced him. They hissed and snarled in preparation to protect their captive prey. The remaining two tightened their grip around Jake. Jake swallowed hard to suppress a scream.

"Jake, you are fixed to the elements that are inherent to you. You must use your natural powers of protection now!" Rileau commanded.

"But how?" Jake moaned. He could feel himself drifting into unconsciousness. His knees were weak, and he slumped. The murkgoblins held him fixed to the tree; they did not allow him to fall. They took turns pummeling him in his chest and stomach. The others did an effective job of not allowing Rileau to get close enough to rescue him. They swung at him with their bark-like arms, threatening each approach with their jagged claws.

"It is within you!" Rileau bellowed as he grabbed the horns of an advancing murkgoblin that came within his reach. "Concentrate, Jake!"

Rileau tossed the creature high into a tree. It hit and broke several limbs as it came crashing down and landed on a wide branch. It was there that the murkgoblin found its final resting place. It didn't move from the straddled position as its arms and legs hung lifelessly over the sides of the branch. Rileau readied for any subsequent attacks.

"Come on, Jake!" he yelled.

"I can't," Jake moaned, and then he blacked out as a blow connected to his right temple.

His captors released their hold and allowed him to collapse into the slush beneath his feet. Considering him no longer a threat, the murkgoblins turned their attention to Rileau. He beckoned them to approach, and they complied by rushing him from all sides with claws extended. He withdrew a staff from beneath his cloak and grasped it with both hands. He advanced on the closest murkgoblin and knocked it off its feet. It scrambled to regain its footing just in time to meet the rod with the side of its face. It crawled away instead of attempting another attack. Each assault was met with a dose of excruciating pain.

The murkgoblins were unwavering in their raid against Rileau, but each one was made to suffer. With succinct timing, he struck them down hard one after another. Each one either retreated or lay injured in the spot they were hit with no ability to recover. The murkgoblins' leader remained on the sideline as it witnessed each of its minions being slaughtered. It snarled with condemnation for their failure and then moved into the fray to take on Rileau. It lowered its head and charged with its horns aimed at Rileau's torso.

Rileau did not move; he held his position. A split second before the moment of impact, he swiftly pulled his staff high above his head. Simultaneously, with his other hand, he reached out and grabbed the horns of the unsuspecting attacker. With a swift swing, he severed the horns from the beast's head and held the horns high in the air. It crumpled to the ground and whimpered in defeat.

He turned in a slow rotation to display the twisted horns of the defeated leader. He dropped them and then smashed them beneath his boot. There was no retaliation from the underlings and no debate as to who was the victor. Rileau smirked as the few remaining murkgoblins scurried away. He made sure there were no deceptive ones hiding in the brush before making his way to Jake's mangled body.

"I suppose it was too much to ask for you to just use your powers, eh?" Rileau whispered. He picked up Jake and tossed him over his shoulder. Jake was motionless and barely breathing.

"We need to get to Seneca before I revive you," Rileau said. He was aware that Jake was unresponsive, but he was also aware that Seneca was now attuned to what was transpiring. His words were meant more for her than Jake. "I've got him. Meet us in the clearing," he called up to her.

Seneca let out a heavy sigh. She abided and immediately descended just as Rileau stepped away from Jake. He had placed him on a mound of soft moss.

"Is he okay? Jake, are you all right?" she called out as she ran over and sat beside him. He groaned slightly but didn't open his eyes. "What's wrong with him? Is he going to be okay?" Seneca scrambled to find the words she dreaded speaking. "Is he going to die?" she asked as she looked up into the stranger's eyes. Had she been mistaken to put her faith in someone she didn't know? Had he gotten there too late? She pleaded with her eyes for answers.

"He will be fine. He just needs a bit of recovery time," said Rileau. "He suffered greatly, as they intended, but it appears the crystals may have aided him."

"Do Himalayan crystals have healing elements?" Seneca asked as she tried wiping some dirt and blood away from Jake's face.

"I am told that no one knows the extent of the powers that may evolve from their consumption," he said. "I was able to assist mildly, but there are other factors that may counter my intervention."

"What exactly are you saying?" Seneca asked.

"It is unimportant. He will heal, and that is all that matters," Rileau replied.

"I thought he was—I mean, I was hoping he wasn't, you know. I was just scared." Seneca struggled to make sense of it all. Who was this stranger, and was he to be trusted?

"You should adjust your thinking. Death is not to be feared," Rileau said. He pulled his shoulders back and held his chin up.

Seneca realized she hadn't introduced herself. She didn't know what to make of this person who had just swooped in and saved Jake. She stood up to get a better look at him. The sky was clear, and the moon cascaded brightly across the open glen.

"As you already know, I'm Seneca," she said, extending her delicate hand out to him, and he bowed in response and smiled. "I feel like we've met before, but I guess that's impossible."

"Indeed, Lady Seneca, your arrival has been anticipated," he said. "However, I have not made your acquaintance. I would have recalled such an encounter."

"My understanding is that it's all about the prophecies." She made no attempt to hide her disapproval.

"That is certainly a factor," he replied. "We must join the others as soon as Jake is stable enough for travel."

"So then, you know where Conner and Shayna are?" she asked anxiously. "Are they okay?" She feared the worst and bit her lip in preparation of hearing bad news.

"They are not without strife, as they met with the misfortune of not escaping the fairies of the Terrain," he said. "Conner is being tended to by Shayna, but they are not in a safe place."

"Conner's hurt?" asked Seneca. "How bad is it?" Her eyes widened.

She could feel her heart racing. There was too much happening around her to keep calm. She commanded herself to breathe. She shook and flexed her hands feverishly to get the feeling back. Her fingers were completely numb.

"If Shayna complies with what I charged her to do, then he will survive," he said impassively.

"Shayna's not hurt?"

"No, she is quite well in spite of her loss," he replied. "Regretfully, Dreya did not survive the attack."

Before the gravity of his declaration could set in, Seneca realized Jake was standing beside her. He had taken her hand and held it firmly. His expression let her know he had heard it all. He allowed her to lean into his chest as she wept quietly. He put his arms around her and closed his eyes in contemplation. They stood there for a few moments without exchanging any words.

"I'm glad you're okay," she whispered. "I was so scared you wouldn't survive."

"Well, to be honest, I wasn't sure either," Jake said.

He knew the stranger standing a few feet away had saved him. He didn't recall much, but he was sure he wouldn't have survived if the man had not arrived when he had. Seneca resisted the urge to hug him, as it was clear he was in a lot of pain. She released his hand and touched his cheek. It was one of the only areas that hadn't been marred.

Jake tried to smile as he rubbed the area where his ribs ached. He cringed when he inadvertently touched an exposed wound. His shirt had been ripped to shreds and was caked in blood and mud. While he was battered and bruised, he felt a sense of relief. He had been saved.

"Thanks for showing up when you did. I'm Jake, by the way," he said, extending his hand. Rileau shook it with a firm grip and grabbed Jake's forearm as well. It caused him to wince slightly, but he didn't complain.

"It is my honor to meet you, Jake. I am Rileau." His voice was deep, and he spoke in a formal tone.

"He's our mentor," Seneca said.

"Mentor? Well, thanks again for helping me out. What were those things?" Jake asked. He was thankful he was beginning to feel steady on his feet. His movements were not as painful, and he could breathe without discomfort.

"They are murkgoblins. They are absent of admiration by all elementals—at least by those that are not interested in doing Brigara's bidding."

"Brigara told them to attack us?" Seneca said. She wiped her tears, and her angst turned quickly to rage.

"It is highly probable," Rileau answered with a furrowed brow. "Although I emphasize that it does not take much to provoke an attack from a murkgoblin."

"But, it's plausible. Brigara could have made them go after us," Jake said. "Just like those acid-spitting gnats!"

"It is evident that she has already begun to use her influence and is likely to continue," said Rileau.

"She's not wasting time—that's for sure!" said Seneca.

"Which means we must do the same," he said. "Jake, are you fit enough to travel?"

"Sure—I think so. I feel kind of weird, but I'm fine." He looked down at his multiple abrasions and lacerations. "My skin seems to be healing really fast."

"That is to be expected. We need to move now," said Rileau. "The castle is not too far from here, but we must take the terrain that is less occupied. It is highly probable that the direct route is being watched. We must avoid any further battle engagement before you are ready."

No one questioned that tactic. They were injured, exhausted, and frightened. Thinking about what else could possibly be lurking in the dark and preparing to attack on Brigara's command was overwhelming.

"You don't need to convince me. Just show the way," said Shayna.

Rileau took the lead, and they fell in line behind him. They were determined to stay close with their senses tuned to high alert.

CHAPTER SEVEN

Castles and Dragons

The castle was finally in sight. It stood tall against the clear backdrop of the star-filled sky. The glow from the full moon highlighted the majestic architecture. It was positioned on high ground with rivers on either side. It had high crenellated walls, each adorned with limestone fleur-de-lis finials affixed on top of the solid sections. The main tower was an impressive rotunda. It was elevated well above several less superior ones and was nestled in the center. A cobblestone bridge extended from the mouth of the forest to a grand front entrance. The walkway was flanked by stone walls on each side, with the adjoined rivers flowing beneath it. It led to the main entrance, which was nestled beneath a large ivy-framed archway. The heavily gilded iron door was as high as it was wide.

"That must be it! We're almost there. I'm so excited!" Shayna squealed.

"Me too!" Seneca said in an equally high-pitched voice.

In Jake's opinion, the girls were acting foolish and uncharacteristically giddy. He frowned and fought back the words he knew would sting. He couldn't figure out the right approach to let them know their behavior was ludicrous. He questioned why they were fawning over the guy. Every few feet, they talked about his walk, talk, and skin and other topics he found annoying.

"He smells like warm apple pie with just the right amount of cinnamon," said Shayna.

"No, I think it's more like fresh lavender," Seneca said. She closed her eyes and sighed.

"Whatever. I just know he smells sweet," Shayna gushed.

"You've both lost it!" Jake grumbled. He folded his arms tight across his chest in protest. He figured Rileau's scent was some sort of magical enchantment, because he couldn't smell anything other than the dampness and sulfur.

"I kind of think he smells like extra crispy bacon. Not bad, actually, since I love bacon," Conner said.

Jake shoved him hard and picked up his pace to put distance between them.

"What's wrong with bacon?" Conner called out.

Seneca giggled and batted her eyes admiringly at Rileau. Jake knew his temper was rising to the brink. He could feel his ears burning, and it made him uncomfortable. He straightened his posture, pushed out his chest, and stretched his neck in a futile attempt to appear taller. He felt the need to get control of the situation before it worsened. He wanted an ally, and he hoped Conner would share his opinion of their mentor. So far, that wasn't the case, but he wasn't ready to give up on converting him. Jake slowed down to let the girls pass. He wanted to make another attempt to commiserate with Conner. He cringed when he noticed Shayna and Seneca were doing more skipping than walking.

"Ever since we met up with you and Shayna, the girls have been acting really odd," said Jake. "I just don't get it. We just met this guy, and they act as if they've known him their entire lives."

"Maybe it's just because of what we all just went through. They're probably feeling safe. I know I am. That guy is huge!" said Conner. "Maybe they like that."

"What's the big deal? So what...he's maybe three inches taller than I am and has ridiculously massive shoulders and biceps, but other than that, I don't get the attraction," said Jake.

Conner muttered in agreement but was more focused on his own arm. He nodded and shrugged as Jake continued berating Rileau. He was pleased to see the blisters were healing rapidly, and the pain had subsided to a mild discomfort. He had shoved a few of the healing leaves into his pocket as a precaution.

"Keep up, and do not lag behind!" Rileau called out over his shoulder. "We must arrive before daylight."

He pounded his staff into the ground every few feet. He was taking long strides and moving at an exceptionally quick pace. Seneca and Shayna followed eagerly. They alternated between a fast walk and an intermittent jog to keep up. Jake and Conner lagged behind in silent protest but kept sight of Rileau and the girls as they maneuvered through the overgrown vegetation.

"Come on, Jake. They're getting too far ahead. We need to pick up the pace," said Conner. He tugged at Jake's sleeve to pull him along.

"What's so special about this guy? I don't get it. Why are Shayna and Seneca drooling all over him?"

"Who knows? Maybe it's the tail," replied Conner. He laughed rowdily.

"Tail? What tail? What do you mean a tail?" Jake stopped midstride and pulled Conner to a stop.

"Dude, you can't tell me you haven't seen it. It sticks out from the bottom of his cloak," said Conner.

"You're joking, right?" Jake rubbed his fingers through his sweat-drenched hair.

"No joke. He has a tail! I'm totally sure—no doubts. Now, come on. They're getting too far ahead," said Conner. He took off in a full sprint with Jake trailing close behind.

They soon closed in on where Rileau, Shayna, and Seneca were waiting. Just out of earshot, Conner whispered, "See? Right there—

check it out." He pointed to the tip of a tail poking out of the split back of Rileau's cloak.

Jake's mouth dropped open, and he wondered how he hadn't noticed it before. "Are you sure it's a tail?" he asked.

"Uh, yeah, what else could it be?" Conner replied.

"I knew there was something about him that I didn't like. That tail might be the reason, and I bet the girls haven't even noticed." He also wondered if Rileau was attempting to hide it from view.

"I think Shayna and Seneca have checked him out from head to toe, and it's kind of hard to miss that tail. It's huge. Hey, I'm surprised you missed it. You're usually on top of it, dude!" Conner laughed. "Maybe those murkgoblins banged your head a little too hard."

"I'll bang your head if you don't back off," Jake snapped in response.

"Settle down. You're getting too worked up over nothing," said Conner. "Sheesh!"

"You might think it's nothing, but I don't trust that guy. There's something off about him."

"He saved us both—all of us, actually. If he hadn't come along when he did, those blisters would have been the end of me," said Conner. He rubbed his hand along his arm, and the skin felt nearly smooth.

"I guess you're right, but for some reason, I just don't trust him," Jake protested.

"Well, until he proves otherwise, tail or no tail, he's good in my book," Conner retorted.

He ran ahead and left Jake behind kicking at twigs and rocks. Jake knew he had to find out more about Rileau. Their lives were in his hands, and unlike the others, he was determined to have more information before following him blindly. He decided once they arrived at their destination, he would find out all he could in regard to their mentor. He trotted ahead and closed the distance between him and the others. He remained quiet and lost in his thoughts. He felt slightly feverish, but he decided the brisk walk and angst were making him feel overheated.

"This place is beautiful! I can't wait to get inside," said Shayna excitedly.

"How will the castle protect us from attacks?" Seneca asked. While she agreed with Shayna on the impressive exterior of the castle, she was more concerned about their safety.

"You pose an interesting question," Rileau replied. "It is the Castle of Lorcan. The exterior is indestructible. As such, it will block attacks from dark magic. Brigara and her followers cannot breach the walls of Lorcan. These walls were forged with the magic found only in Arcadrom, the source of all pure magic." Confidence was infused in each word he spoke. He picked up his pace as they reached the bridge that led to the entrance. His tail swept back and forth across the cobblestones.

"What's Arcadrom?" Conner asked.

"It is a realm, untouchable by all, that stores the purest of magic—the source of it and the power that wills it," explained Rileau.

"Yet another realm? I don't know if I can get used to this," Conner muttered.

"You're sure that not even Brigara could get to us inside the castle?" Seneca said. Since he was willing to reveal information, she saw it as an opportunity to get more details.

"Lorcan has charms of protection that were woven in every fiber of the very stones and bricks used to build it. The magic of protection extends to the surrounding waters and grounds. As I have stated, dark magic will not ever breach it."

"If someone created a spell, say of dark magic, that was meant to break through, could it be done then?" asked Seneca.

"Lorcan was created using the purest of magic—from the very source of magic. It was built of the purest of light magic. Dark magic will only be absorbed. Please be at peace with this."

"What you're saying is that the castle's a great hideout!" said Conner.

"'Tis not a dwelling to hide in. It is a place where you will learn to use your magic and realize your gifts. Its purpose is to prepare you for what you must face outside of these walls. You are charged with bringing balance to the Otherworld, not becoming cowards within these walls," Rileau said.

"I didn't mean it like that," Conner muttered. He shoved his hands in his pockets. He looked to Jake for a response but only received a raised eyebrow.

Rileau pushed the iron door open and held it to allow Shayna, Seneca, and Conner to enter. Jake hung back. He examined the stonework of the archway that framed the door. The details of the carvings fascinated him.

"You have noticed the engravings that are visible only to some," said Rileau. "That is quite telling of your gifts. The fata morgana is an enchantment used to disguise elements."

"Why would you want to disguise the engravings?" Jake asked, his curiosity piqued.

"It is not an attempt to deceive, if that is your concern," Rileau said. "The engravings are forms of blessings, messages of goodwill and healing. The enchantment was used so that all who enter the castle may receive the blessings without exception."

"Can you tell me what the large engraving in the center of the archway means? It caught my attention more than the others," Jake said.

"That is my favorite as well. It means that whoever shall enter through this door shall be one who masters the marvels of magic and shall control elements of the sea," said Rileau. "That particular one was created by a fairy who had the gift of foretelling the future. She has authored many of the most telling prophecies."

"Are you guys coming or what?" Shayna said as she danced about in the doorway. A smile was plastered across her face as she swung her arm to invite them inside. "You've gotta see this place, Jake!"

Jake would have preferred to discuss more of the carvings, but he reluctantly followed Shayna's prompting to go inside. He assumed no one else was interested, so he shrugged it off. The emotions that invaded his thoughts were confusing. One moment, he felt that Rileau was completely trustworthy. He would then be jarred to believe the opposite; he couldn't shake off his suspicions. To make matters worse, he didn't feel completely stable on his feet. His surface wounds from the murkgoblin attack had completely healed and weren't causing discomfort, but his head was pounding like a bass drum, causing him to sway slightly. In addition, he felt exceedingly hot.

"Isn't this place totally magnificent?" Shayna beamed. "I can't wait to see the entire layout."

She spun around and began giving a guided tour of the foyer and adjoining rooms on either side of it. She discussed the tapestry, the marble floors, the large picture windows, and all of the other fineries. She felt grounded and comfortable; she hadn't felt that way since their arrival in the Otherworld.

"I haven't gone beyond this point, because that would be rude. At least that's what Seneca keeps telling me," said Shayna as she scrunched her nose in protest.

Seneca frowned and shook her head. She agreed with Shayna on the impressive decor and remarkable architecture of the castle, but she didn't think they should wander about and explore without Rileau's approval.

"Jake and I did not intend to keep you waiting," said Rileau. He waited for Jake to reply, but when Jake simply shuffled his feet, he continued. "We will have a brief tour. Then we shall begin with the foundation of your training. Nightfall is the perfect time to begin, as I am a nocturnal elemental. Many dragons are, after all."

"A dragon!" Shayna and Seneca screamed.

"A dragon?" Conner asked as he jerked his head back. He hadn't expected that, but it made sense. He looked at Rileau's tail as it moved across the floor, and he was convinced.

"That's utterly amazing," said Shayna as she smiled widely. "By the way, so is this castle! Can we get on with the tour now? I can't wait to see the other rooms."

She didn't bother waiting for Rileau to decide on their route as she skipped ahead to lead the way. Jake grabbed Conner's arm to hold him back. Seneca and Rileau trailed behind Shayna as she made her way down the wide corridor. She poked her head into various rooms before deciding which to enter. Jake waited until they disappeared inside before he spoke.

"I can't believe it. A dragon?" Jake said. His tone was brash, and he spoke through gritted teeth. "He could have claimed to be anything else, but he's no dragon. Trust me."

Conner didn't want to engage in Jake's banter. He felt caught between siding with Jake and trusting Rileau. Rileau was the one who had told Shayna how to treat his blisters. He'd saved his life, yet Jake had to be suspicious for a reason. He didn't know what to believe or whom to trust at the moment.

"C'mon, dude! The girls don't seem to have a problem with him being a dragon or whatever," said Conner. "Me either, really—I think it's cool. You need to give him a chance. That's all."

"He's not a dragon! Let's be clear about that," retorted Jake. "It has to be something he's secreting or throwing off in the air that has them acting like that."

"Secreting? What does that mean? That sounds gross!" said Conner. He winced and shuddered at the thought of it.

"You know what I mean—like pheromones. Something that's released from the body and attracts the opposite sex."

"That doesn't sound so bad." Conner smirked and cocked his head to the side. "That might come in handy."

"Forget it!" Jake huffed. He was frustrated that Conner wasn't joining him on the put-down-the-dragon bandwagon. He started down the hall to join the others.

"I think you need to relax," said Conner. "This guy is the one who's supposed to teach us how to cover our butts in an attack. We would be dead if he hadn't come along."

"I know. It's just that—oh, never mind! Just drop it. You don't get it." Jake grimaced.

"Great idea. Let's drop it," said Conner. He was relieved and hoped it was the end of the discussion. He glanced over at Jake; from his expression, it was clear the subject was not closed, not even close. He sighed.

"I hear them coming out of that room on the right. C'mon. I don't want to miss anything," said Conner. He strutted ahead to join the others. Jake was barely able to contain his reaction as he grumbled to himself.

"I'm so fascinated with dragons," said Shayna, wide-eyed with the expression of a star-struck groupie. "What else can you tell us?"

"I realize most mortals think dragons are either benign, extinct or, better yet, ferocious creatures of mythology. I actually don't mind the references, as they are quite humorous," said Rileau. "A scaling of dragons that swarm in and make away with unmarried maidens is beyond asinine."

"Many people have written stories about dragons and how dangerous they are," said Seneca. She smiled, as she was enjoying the discussion.

"I have heard many exaggerated tales of stealing children and women and then hiding them away in towers and caves. All falsehoods!" Rileau said. His voice grew slightly louder, but his demeanor remained calm. "I find the notion insulting, as it is baseless and bears not a pinch of truth."

"It's kind of hard to dismiss what others have said for centuries just on your word alone," Jake said as he twisted his face into a look of disdain.

"Regardless of your previous ignorance, you can now see that I am a dragon." Rileau raised his tail and slammed it hard against the slate floor, leaving a scorch mark in the aged limestone.

"How is it possible that everything we know about dragons is, for the most part, consistent? They are always portrayed as oversized fire-breathing reptiles," Jake said with a scowl.

"That sort of sounds like an insult, Jake. You're really crossing the line," whispered Conner.

"I don't think I was talking to you," Jake snapped.

"Well, I'm talking to you, and this has gone on long enough. If he says he's a dragon, then who are we to question it?" Conner replied.

Jake wasn't bothered by Conner's attempt to intervene. He had no intention of backing down. He could feel sweat dripping down his back, and his breathing was labored. He had no desire to let up; he was just getting started.

"Except for the tail, you seem more like an ordinary man," Jake said. "Granted, having a tail is different. I will give you that, but it doesn't make you a dragon."

Conner shook his head in disbelief. Seneca gasped, and Shayna was furious. She wanted to react, but she knew it wasn't her fight, and Rileau was handling Jake fairly well on his own.

"You are correct. It is not my tail that makes me who I am. Without it, I am still a dragon," Rileau said. He grinned widely, and Jake pretended not to notice.

"Actually, I'm just not that easily convinced, but hey, if you say you're a dragon, then I guess we'll just have to take your word for it. It's not like we can prove you're not." Jake tightened his lips and crossed his arms across his chest.

"It appears that Jake has been misinformed in all things relating to dragons, and as such, he believes without merit." Rileau sighed and shook his head.

"Me and millions of others," Jake snapped.

"Since you have obviously done some studying, I trust you are thoroughly aware of the Greek astronomer Ptolemy. Mortals once put all of their faith into his theories," said Rileau. "We thought it humorous that you believed him. His baseless teachings of Earth as motionless and the center of the universe were just proof that mortals were too young of a species to accept more."

"Sure, but over time, he was proven wrong!" Jake shouted. He knew he sounded defensive; however, he wasn't going to accept a condemnation of mortals without a fight.

"You are correct. We waited for about a thousand of your years and then realized you might finally be able to handle the truth. Frankly, it wasn't funny any longer either. It was pathetic," Rileau said.

Jake knew that was an indirect jab at him, especially since the dragon's green eyes were locked on his.

"What happened next?" Shayna asked. She was fascinated by the story. Rileau began pacing as he continued.

"There was a young, promising lad who was mentored by a druid named Gabriel. Gabriel assisted him throughout his life with inspiration and education and comforted him after the loss of his parents," said Rileau. "He taught him tolerance while living with his demanding and narrow-minded uncle. The young man endured countless distractions, such as religion and medical studies, but he was eventually led to the truth about Earth. As planned, and with well-executed magical intervention, he did prevail." He turned toward Jake to wait for a reaction. He shrugged when Jake remained quiet. "Questions?" Rileau asked.

"You're not talking about Nicolaus Copernicus, are you? I did a report about him last year." Seneca got excited, and her head began filling up with all the facts she had learned on the subject.

"Indeed, that is precisely whom I reference. He was quite receptive to the teachings."

"Awesome!" Seneca beamed.

"It's good to see you have knowledge of him," replied Rileau. His green eyes shifted toward her, and he tilted his head slightly. "Continue, Seneca."

"I was interested in his story because he discovered so much without the telescope and physics. He figured out that the sun was the center of our universe and that Earth rotated on an axis. His theory wasn't proven to be right until after he died. Galileo figured it out," Seneca said. "Hardly anyone gives credit to Copernicus.

"Brilliant! He did indeed open the door for Galileo. We elementals were able to pull back since the mortals were then on the right track," replied Rileau. He bowed his head, and Seneca basked in the acknowledgment.

Seneca felt the heat of anger intensifying from Jake. She knew his rage was rooted in jealousy, but she also knew that nothing short of a dousing of water was going to calm him.

"And what's your point?" Jake asked. His tone was icy.

"My point is that initial beliefs are not always accurate and that an open mind to unlimited possibilities may prove that previous notions are actually false," said Rileau. "In this case, your facts on dragons are erroneous!" His voice echoed thunderously, causing the windows to rattle.

"Argh!" Jake growled through gritted teeth. "Come on!"

"Jake, calm down already," said Seneca. She tried to reach out toward him, but she decided to pull back. She looked at the expression on his face as he locked eyes with Rileau. She didn't want to shift his anger toward her.

"You have much to learn, Jake. Much to experience and even more to accept," said Rileau. "There will come a time when you will be required to accept all that is presented to you. You will have no choice."

"That sounds ominous and like a way to dismiss the topic," snapped Jake.

Rileau turned away and began walking the perimeter of the room. His tail crashed hard every few feet. Each time, a new scorch mark was stamped into the stone. Seneca sensed he was growing inpatient. She didn't dare attempt to read his thoughts. She had learned she wasn't adept at shielding to avoid detection. Her shortcoming was what had caused Brigara to discover that she was a druid. Still, she wondered about the knowledge he possessed. The mystery made him even more attractive in her assessment.

Seneca said, "Excuse me, but can you tell us more about Gabriel and—"

Jake interrupted. "Why didn't Gabriel come set things right if we were so wrong about dragons?" asked Jake. He believed he had new ammunition to challenge Rileau's claims.

"Jake, you must listen closely, as your obstinacy is most certainly your constraint," Rileau said. "You shall wisely concede that you do not know of what you speak. Or is it that your beliefs are rooted solely in what you've been taught up until this moment? Is there no option to expand your intellect to other possibilities?" Rileau paused to allow a response.

Jake refused to reply and remained quiet in protest. Shayna was thankful Jake wasn't able to create a sword or any other weapon; she had a feeling the ability would have been used at that precise moment. Rileau did not appear fazed by Jake's attitude and continued with what was undoubtedly turning into their first lesson.

"Your beliefs are based on false tales that were intentionally spread to your realm. Many rumors began and took on lives of their own," explained Rileau. "As I have attempted to explain, we have been falsely portrayed as wild beasts and pillagers that steal women and lock them away in towers. It took many eons to earn back trust of dragons in the Otherworld. What mortals were led to believe was not our concern."

"Why would anyone start ugly rumors like that?" Shayna asked.

"Maybe because they were true," said Jake. He smirked and looked for consensus from Conner. Instead, he received a disapproving head shake in response.

"As many conflicts begin, it involved a highly desired pollen sprite and a jilted fairy lover who wanted revenge," said Rileau.

"Wow! Are pollen sprites really beautiful?" In Shayna's observation, the story was just getting to the juicy part.

"Most definitely beautiful—much like you," Rileau said, smiling.

Shayna was accustomed to compliments and was typically not moved. She knew this time it was different, and she looked away bashfully.

"Can we hear the rest of the story?" Conner asked.

"The issues arose when the pollen sprite let it be known that she preferred a dragon over the fairy. This was the spark that initiated the lies and treachery," said Rileau. He grimaced and shook his head. "It was the beginning of the defamation of all dragons."

"That's so typical of guys," Shayna said. Seneca nodded in agreement.

"Sure, blame the guy—I mean fairy. It's never the girl's fault," Conner said in a sarcastic tone.

"Exactly!" said Shayna. "Most of the time, it's the guy."

"She probably led the fairy on or something like that," said Jake.

"Exactly!" replied Conner mockingly.

Jake felt compelled to side with the fairy. He realized he didn't know much about matters of the heart or anything else involved, but he had decided that dragons were not on his list of those to side with.

"You're saying the fairy started spreading lies about the dragon just because the sprite fell in love with someone else?" asked Shayna. She wanted to get back on track with the story. She rolled her eyes at Jake and then smiled broadly at Rileau.

Jake resisted saying anything. He didn't understand his feelings, but he began to relate to what the fairy most likely had been experiencing.

"The pollen sprite was part of the noble heritage of Brill, and it had been prophesied that she would wed the fairy. This would serve to unite the beings to bring greater harmony. She embraced her destiny until she met the dragon that won her heart upon first glance," said Rileau.

"Sounds a bit far-fetched," Jake said.

"Sounds romantic," Shayna countered.

"Sounds like another case of a prophecy gone wrong." Conner snickered.

"I'd like to meet this wannabe author in charge of the prophecies and demand a rewrite!" Jake sneered. "There's something seriously wrong with the plot."

"Please continue, and just ignore him," Seneca said.

"The dragon returned her feelings of love without compromise. The pollen sprite knew she was obligated to inform the fairy of her true heart. When she confessed that her love was meant for another, the fairy went into a jealous rage and vowed revenge," Rileau said.

"Did they fight or have a duel or something?" Shayna asked. She was jubilant and loved the drama of the tale. She hung on each word and was completely absorbed in the details of the story.

"The fairy had a plan that would go beyond this particular dragon," said Rileau. "He wanted to punish all dragons that had ever lived and all those that would follow. He cast a spell that caused all elementals to fear and loathe all dragons."

"That sounds like a really powerful spell," said Seneca. She was intrigued that anyone could be so angry over a broken heart.

"Indeed, quite powerful. His spell was weaved with dark magic that caused all to question the intentions of dragons and to categorize them as evil creatures that could not be trusted," he said.

"Appears pretty accurate to me," Jake said. From the looks he received from the others, he knew he had probably pushed things too far. He cringed and shrugged in response.

"That is not cool, Jake," Seneca said. She stared at him until he looked away.

"Sorry, Rileau. Please excuse Jake. Maybe the murkgoblins ate part of his brain or something," said Shayna.

"No, Shayna, wrong again. That would be *zombies* that eat brains," Jake chided.

"Calm down, Jake. That's enough!" said Conner. He was becoming frustrated with the snide comments.

Shayna was ready to pounce on Jake as well. She was glad to see that Conner wasn't teaming up with him. It disturbed her that he was being intentionally rude.

"I know that you trust Keene Ardara. Is this correct, Jake?" asked Rileau. Before he could respond, Seneca chimed in.

"We all do. We trust him enormously," she said.

"Well, I'm confident that within his possession are the very scrolls that chronicle the event of which I speak," said Rileau. "The battle of the fairy and dragon, as well as the breaking of the prophesied matrimony, was well documented. Such battles do not end well."

"Was there an actual battle over the girl—I mean pollen sprite?" asked Shayna.

"Ah, indeed," replied Rileau. "Love is a powerful force. It is like no other, and it can drive even the most civilized and harmonious of beings to do the unthinkable." He paused for a moment and looked at each of their faces before continuing. "Never take its power lightly— never. Love fills one with pure, divine light, but when tampered with by the elements of rage, envy, or other dark matters, it can turn deadly. Remember this always."

"And the fairy let his jealousy turn his love into a dark spell?" Seneca asked as she paid close attention to the details of the story.

"It was believed to be an essential part of why he wanted to punish the dragon."

"But why all dragons and not just the one who stole the girlfriend?" Conner asked.

"Why indeed. It would take much speculation and a lot more time to delve into that, so let's save that for another time," replied Rileau. "I will tell you this much. The spell was not as powerful as the fairy had intended. There were flaws."

"Okay, so there was a spell, and it was broken, blah, blah. You didn't mention the fairy casting a spell that changed what people thought a dragon looked like," said Jake. He didn't attempt to hide a hint of condescension.

"That is accurate, and yet, rumors do take on lives of their own," Rileau said. He offered no other explanation.

Jake was not satisfied, and he questioned why Rileau did not continue with the story. "Mostly the physical characteristics vary, but dragons are always portrayed as animals, like serpents and reptilian-type creatures," said Jake. "Why would a beautiful pollen sprite want to be associated with that?"

"Aren't we all animals?" Rileau replied. He made no attempt to hide his sarcasm.

"Some more than others," Jake snapped as he waited for Rileau to engage in more one-liner banter, but instead, he only received a smirk in response. "Are you also able to fly and breathe underwater?" Jake asked. He raised his brow to display his skepticism.

"My current form would not allow such feats—" Rileau stopped midsentence and then decided not to continue. "I actually try to avoid water. It acts as a base surge. Much like the reaction of volcanic lava."

"That sounds more like what I've read on dragons," said Seneca.

"Again, how we've been painted in your books is not how we actually appear. However, there may be some truth weaved in. Our actions seem to be the most blatant of the falsehoods," said Rileau. He looked down his prominent nose at Jake in anticipation of a rebuttal.

Jake tightened his lips. Sweat rolled down his back.

"I see that you still have comments that are weighing on your tongue. What is it that you need to know?" asked Rileau. "Speak up, Jake!"

Rileau's tail came crashing down hard. Shayna and Seneca moved close together. Conner was ready to intervene in what appeared to be the escalation of an inevitable fight. A thin cascade of dark smoke seeped out from beneath Rileau's tail. Jake fanned it away and stepped closer to Rileau. Conner put out his arm to stop any further advance.

"Calm down, dude!"

"You are clearly more man than a so-called dragon. All you have is a tail, and I'm not even sure it resembles a dragon tail at all. You being a dragon just doesn't seem plausible," said Jake. He pushed Conner's arm away but made no attempt to engage in a physical altercation. Conner remained on alert.

"Jake, what difference does it make? Why are you harping on this?" Seneca asked.

She began pleading with him telepathically to stop and let the matter go, but she couldn't detect if he heard her. If he did, he made no attempt to acknowledge her.

Jake wished he could back down or shift the topic of discussion, especially since he stood alone in distrusting Rileau. He knew Seneca had a great point. It didn't matter if Rileau was a dragon or not. He was not a dragon expert, but he still believed he had cause to challenge the legitimacy of Rileau's claim. He also felt as if something were driving him to be skeptical, something beyond the norm. He wasn't typically confrontational, but his anger ran deep. He wanted to question his behavior, but he seemed blocked from doing so. He suddenly realized that Rileau was still talking, and he was missing his words.

"Jake, you seem to think that an all-knowing and all-powerful creator would be incapable of designing life-forms such as me, a dragon. Have you forgotten that you are in the Otherworld?" asked Rileau. "Until recently, you considered this realm unfathomable. Is this not correct?" He was visibility irritated. His brow furrowed, and his large hands formed tight fists.

"Hmm," Jake said softly. His head throbbed, and his eyes burned.

"Are you listening?" Rileau asked.

Jake realized he was staring blankly at the wall. He wanted to stay focused, but his muscles ached. He realized he hadn't eaten in quite a while, and fatigue was probably setting in. He wondered if the feeling had anything to do with his mood or if the murkgoblins had hurt him more than he realized.

"I was just taking in what you were saying," said Jake. "It's just that it doesn't exactly make sense that you are a dragon. Explain how you can breathe fire and not set yourself on fire."

He knew he was grasping at anything to throw out as a question. The relevancy of his queries was beginning to wane. He didn't know why he felt the need to stand up to Rileau, but something drove him to desire a chance to knock him down a notch or two. He opened and closed his fist repeatedly. His head was throbbing, and he squinted from the pain.

"You presume to know more about dragons than I," said Rileau. "Such hubris is rather disturbing."

"Hu-what? Are you calling me arrogant?" said Jake. "You don't like to be questioned or something?" His nostrils flared, and the veins in his neck protruded. His eyes began to sting, and he squinted to fight back the burning sensation. He had never felt such rage.

"He's right, Jake. I'm sure he's more of an expert," said Shayna. She smiled widely and tilted her head in admiration. "Just calm down. He knows what he's talking about."

"I'm not so sure about that," said Jake. He huffed and shoved his hands deep into his pants pockets. "He hasn't exactly explained anything. It's like smoke and mirrors."

"I will address this once—and only once—in an attempt to satisfy your curiosity, but afterward, I will not entertain this foolishness," Rileau said.

He crossed the room and retrieved one of the many silver jars that lined the shelf. He opened the lid and held out the jar for them to survey the contents. It held a fine deep red powdery substance.

"What is that?" Seneca asked. She moved in close to get a better view.

"It is platinum blood. It is blood of the dragon." Rileau replaced the lid and returned the jar to the shelf.

"I always thought platinum was silver. Red is my favorite color, so I'd love some platinum-red earrings," Shayna said. She smiled and was impressed with Rileau's explanation.

"You keep your blood in jars?" Conner asked. He leaned in to get a better view.

"Might you have a better suggestion for storage?" Rileau asked. Conner decided a head shake was a good enough reply.

"Why do you need to keep your blood in storage?" asked Seneca. She was mesmerized by Rileau and was pleased that he was revealing so much. She considered it their first lesson.

"Many ages ago, during a dark time in the Otherworld, our kind was taught by the elder druid the methods to harness our platinum blood," said Rileau.

"Was it Garbhan?" asked Seneca. "We met him before he passed away, and he only told us about the Dominion of Four stuff."

"No, it was not Garbhan, although he was a superior elder. This was long before his time and that of the elder before him. Would you like me to continue?"

"Yes!" Conner and Shayna said, and their voices echoed off the walls. Seneca nodded obediently.

"The elder druid that I speak of uncovered properties in the blood that would enhance a dragon's strength during battle," said Rileau. "He preserved the blood with anointed power derived from the purest noir kristilum."

"What's that?" asked Conner.

"Noir kristilum in the purest form comes from the dander of an arion," replied Rileau.

"My cat allergies feel like they're kicking in just from the mention of dander," said Shayna. "I hate hives. My skin just gets all—oops. Sorry. I know. Shut up, Shayna." She smirked as she made eye contact with Seneca. She shook her head to clear the image of inflamed, itchy skin. "Sorry. Please continue, Rileau."

"Once it is ingested, a dragon's abilities are unmatched," said Rileau.

"It doesn't seem wise to give one being so much power," said Jake. "It would be an unfair advantage. It's sort of like cheating."

"Yeah, I have to agree with Jake. It sounds like cheating to me too," said Conner. "The dragons wouldn't get away with that if they were playing sports in our realm."

"I assure you that what we faced in the dark times was not sport," Rileau replied. "It is only used when required. Abuse is not tolerated."

"It just sounds like it does the same thing that steroids and other enhancements claim to do," said Jake. "The stuff is created all the time to get athletes to beat their opponents and—ouch! What the—" Jake grabbed his arm away from Seneca's grasp. She had pinched his skin just above his elbow. "Why did you do that?" asked Jake.

"Just let him finish, and stop interrupting!" said Seneca.

"Fine. Just lay off the pinching—sheesh," he said with an exaggerated sound of angst.

Seneca gave him a raise of an eyebrow to indicate she meant business and returned her attention to Rileau. She knew that whatever their mentor had to say would probably explain the exact use and purpose of the platinum blood. Rileau smiled slightly and gave a nod toward

Seneca. She could feel her cheeks flush. She closed her eyes and exhaled slowly to regain her composure.

Jake rubbed his arm and decided it wasn't a good idea to continue his probing. He'd hold his comments and mounting concerns a bit longer. He rubbed the back of his neck and whisked away beads of sweat. He felt a chill wash over him. He zipped his hoodie and shoved his hands into his pockets.

"Tell us more about the platinum blood, please," Shayna said. She smiled and flipped her wavy dark hair behind her back as she tucked one side behind her ear.

"The platinum blood is superior to what may have been created by mortals. It cannot be duplicated, as it has properties that are only found within dragons and from a realm that is out of reach," said Rileau. "It is harvested to maintain a dragon's ability to manifest fire for extended periods of time. It is kept in reserve for battle." He directed his attention solely at Jake in anticipation of a rebuttal.

"And that's it? You use it, and—poof—there's fire?" Jake asked. "Your enemy is extinguished, and the fight is over?" He knew he sounded childish, but he was unable to control his reactions. Jake was adamant about maintaining his belief that Rileau couldn't be trusted. He no longer felt any chill at all. Instead, he was overheating and boiling inside. He wondered how he could shift to such extremes in a matter of seconds.

"Not exactly, Jake. Once placed in my mouth, it acts as a catalyst. When combined with hydrogen, it combusts, thus producing a more potent fire. Also, as a point of clarification, a dragon does not breathe fire. We expel it," Rileau sneered.

"I'm curious. You mentioned an elder druid, the one who showed dragons how to harvest their blood. Why did he think it was necessary?" asked Seneca.

"As I mentioned, the Otherworld went through dark times. Much has changed in how we now live and what type of magic we are allowed to use," said Rileau. "At one time, there were those who wanted to have power over all beings. The desire to harness the source of magic in its purest form was the objective."

"My guess is protecting this magic source was the mission for the elder druid," said Jake.

"Yes, Jake," replied Rileau. "The elder druid knew he could not allow corrupt forces to disrupt the balance of our realm. To allow anyone this level of power would potentially destroy our entire existence. This was the essence of the conflict."

"Blocking the bad guys from getting to the source seems like the right move. But doesn't that just mean that someone else has to be in charge of it?" asked Jake. "Who's to say that person wouldn't get sucked into a power trip too?"

"It is prudent to never allow an individual such an offering, as there is always a risk of corruption. As a result, safeguards were put in place, and the pure source is no longer accessible to those within the Otherworld," Rileau said. "The temptation was removed to establish a new balance."

"There are always the greedy, power-hungry ones who ruin everything," said Conner.

"So that was the reason for war?" asked Seneca.

"A war indeed. It caused much destruction and disruption to our Otherworld," said Rileau. "Those who were neutral in such matters were forced to choose sides. Dragons, arions, and elves were most sought as allies to the opposing sides."

"We haven't met any elves yet," said Shayna. "Are they good guys or bad ones?"

"*Good* and *bad* are relative terms," replied Rileau. "Things cannot be divvied up so simply."

"What you're saying is that dragons can be on Brigara's side?" asked Jake.

"We all have free will to choose our alliances," said Rileau. "Since the beginning of time, dragons have never strayed from the light of righteousness."

"But it's possible," Jake replied.

"All things are possible, Jake. As you know, even you may become corrupt or have your integrity questioned," said Rileau. "Aye, while remote, it is quite possible." He bowed to Jake. Seneca stepped in front of Jake to end the showdown.

"Not again!" Conner rubbed his head in disbelief.

"Tell us more about the elder druid. I'm curious about him or her," said Seneca. She knew it was a perfect time to change the subject. She stomped on Jake's toe. "Cut it out!" she grumbled through tight lips.

Jake fought back a yelp. He allowed his silence to be his response.

"His name was Merlin, and he was a druid like no other before or after," Rileau said.

"Merlin? Like *the* Merlin?" Conner asked. "Merlin the mighty wizard from King Arthur's Round Table kind of Merlin?" His jaw hung down with his mouth gaped wide open.

"I don't know of this Merlin you speak of," said Rileau. "Merlin the elder druid kept the balance of harmony among those in the Otherworld."

"Can druids also be wizards?" asked Shayna.

"I have never encountered wizards. Are they a type of mortal?" asked Rileau.

"Not quite," Seneca said. "There are a lot of stories about the wizard Merlin, mostly about him doing magic and protecting King Arthur in a place called Camelot."

"They go through a huge battle, and it's a classic clash of good versus evil right on the battlefield. With dragons and magic," said Conner. "Well, not like your kind of dragon. You know, the big kind, with wings and horns and—"

"Maybe they're just stories that were made up," said Seneca. She wanted to cut Conner off before he continued rambling.

"Yeah, good movies and books, though—on King Arthur and Merlin, I mean," said Conner.

"In the mortal realm, the truth has a tendency to become legend when astounding acts cannot be explained rationally," said Rileau. "Perhaps this Merlin that you speak of did exist, and the stories are simply flawed."

"Great coincidence, though," said Jake. "The Merlin we know about had a thing for dragons."

"Perhaps there are similarities. Merlin the elder druid did have a fondness for our kind, as he did for all elementals," said Rileau. "He was a true believer that we are all connected. We arise from the same light and source of all life's beginning. Maybe they are one and the same."

"When he showed dragons how to use their own blood, did it end the war?" Conner asked.

"It changed the course of the conflict. The dark forces were driven into hiding by the dragons. The balance of power was restored," Rileau said. "This was not without consequence. The Otherworld was changed forever."

"Changed in a good way?" asked Seneca.

"Change is what you make of it. There are those who adapt and evolve, while others reject and rebel," said Rileau. "My existence began after the change. I only know what we are now, and I know of no other way."

"I bet Brigara is one of those who can't stand change," said Conner. He felt a chill run down his spine and shook in response.

"You said something about consequences. What happened?" asked Jake.

"It is a story for another time. Its relevance will be revealed much later. I request your patience," said Rileau.

"Sounds like more avoidance to me," griped Jake.

Rileau did not respond. For him, the topic was closed. Jake knew it was useless to push further, since he believed Rileau wouldn't reveal more.

"The platinum blood sounds really powerful if it changed the outcome of the war," said Seneca. She wanted to redirect the focus back to the mysterious element in the jars. "Did you use that before you came to help us?"

"Yes, as it was necessary," replied Rileau.

"I didn't see you expel, cough, or spit any fire on the murkgoblins," said Jake. "How does it work anyway?"

"It increases my physical strength, enabling me to withstand attacks and increase my stamina," said Rileau. "As for your question, Jake, I have the ability to burn my enemy internally if I so choose. It is not always an external discharge."

"Like a microwave—cooked from the inside. Ew!" Shayna shrieked. "Uh, what I meant to say is it sounds totally gross but also totally cool. At least I think it's cool." She vacillated on her opinion and wasn't sure how unsettling it actually was.

"Shouldn't you catch on fire? Your skin or your insides, I mean. You know, from the fire?" Conner asked. He was fascinated by Rileau's explanation.

"Exactly. That's the point I was trying to make. Explain that one!" Jake shouted. He wiped sweat from his forehead as he shifted his weight and swayed back and forth.

Shayna and Seneca exchanged a look of embarrassment at Jake's behavior. Shayna thought he appeared to be on the verge of passing out.

"It is quite simple—my skin is impervious to fire," snapped Rileau. "It would be like you suffering injury from your own saliva. I release smoke from my nostrils, as this cools my core after expelling flames of any magnitude."

"How can you make someone burn in the inside?" asked Jake.

"How does Shayna create a sword? How do you fly? I could go on, Jake." Rileau allowed his words to hang in the air without continuing. His glare zeroed in on Jake.

"Sounds good to me. What about you, Jake?" asked Conner.

Rileau locked eyes with Jake. A wisp of smoke escaped from the dragon's right nostril and quickly dissipated into the air. He was growing impatient and snapped his tail hard against the floor. Seneca felt the situation was sure to continue escalating. She slid next to Jake.

"Well, I think that about covers all we need to know. Right, Jake?" asked Seneca. She nudged him hard in the ribcage. He jerked in reaction but kept his eyes on Rileau.

"Great—a staring contest," said Shayna in a monotone.

"Come on, Jake. Let's move on. Enough already," said Seneca. Her plea was more of a whine than a forceful demand. She was losing her patience, as were Conner and Shayna.

Jake refused to acknowledge them. His mind was racing to find something—anything—that would discredit the dragon. He felt ill. Perhaps the injuries he'd sustained had affected his emotions or, worse, his judgment. There was something definitely wrong, but he couldn't dwell on it. He concentrated on coming up with more questions.

"Is she correct, Jake?" Rileau asked. "Can we move on, or do you need to know about how my somatic and autonomic nervous systems function in parallel to produce the accelerant for controlling the speed, distance, and direction the flames are dispersed?"

"Aha! You admit it. You do shoot out fire!" Jake shouted. His body was rigid and drenched in sweat. He was confused; he struggled against the pull to be rational and levelheaded.

"You are accurate. As with you, there are a multitude of abilities I possess. I do expel flames when I so choose. It's an advantage to having a third lung that ignites the flame," said Rileau. "Do you desire a personal demonstration?" He stepped forward to within inches of Jake.

Rileau's sarcasm was undeniable. Seneca reached up and gave Jake a gentle rub on the shoulder. She massaged deep into the tissue between his shoulder blades. She stood on her toes and eased her hands up to his shoulders. She pressed her thumbs and index fingers into the muscles across his back. She had no idea why she felt compelled to massage him, but she continued. Jake made no attempt to remove her hands. Her touch had a calming effect. He felt the heat he was experiencing diminish. The sensation of a cool breeze washed over him. He inhaled deeply. He thought he saw smoke coming from his mouth and drifting into the air. It disappeared from sight before he got a better glimpse. He waved his hands through the air, trying to capture it.

Seneca assumed he was shooing her away. She abruptly stopped her massage and let her arms drop. Jake wanted to ask her to continue but resisted.

"Is this now a closed topic?" Rileau asked. His voice was controlled. He backed away from Jake.

It made Seneca uncomfortable to see that Jake was not relenting and was intent on holding his ground. She also observed that Rileau's stature appeared to expand each second Jake delayed in responding. She feared the stalemate would not end well. "Jake, are you going to answer him?" Seneca asked. She nudged his shoulder.

"I am so not in the mood to smell you getting barbecued," said Shayna. She was concerned the situation was escalating beyond control.

"Huh? What do you mean?" Jake replied.

His focus was not on the conversation; it was on a noticeable drop in his body temperature. He felt a chill and shivered. His body relaxed as the tension he had been experiencing dissolved. He was calm.

"What I mean is that we're all perfectly satisfied. No need for any more questions—right, Jake?" said Seneca. She cleared her throat and pulled down hard on his shirttail. "Right?" she repeated.

"Sure, yeah—whatever," he said.

He didn't have a clue what he was agreeing to, but he sensed it was the right thing to do. Jake knew she wasn't going to let up until he conceded. He shifted his focus to Seneca. He looked into her eyes for only a second, but it was just long enough for her to catch a glimpse of the pain in his eyes. He knew she was reading him, and he turned away. She recognized the signs of jealousy but didn't understand why Jake was feeling insecure. It was unlike him. He brushed her aside and folded his arms across his chest. It wasn't jealousy, she surmised. There was something else driving him. She wished she knew what it was, but she decided not to intrude into his thoughts. After all, she would have wanted the same consideration if the roles had been reversed.

"Well then, it's settled!" Shayna snapped. "Let's move on." Her voice was cheerier than the situation called for, and she knew it. She had no idea if Rileau had a short temper or not, but she wasn't interested in testing any theories.

"Now that we've had our lesson on platinum blood, what's next on the syllabus?" asked Seneca. She wanted to allow Jake additional time to simmer down, but she was also anxious to learn more.

"Actually, there's one more element I need to explain about the platinum blood," said Rileau. "It has medicinal components. There is no need to discuss this in depth, but know that the rage Jake is experiencing is due to his exposure. It should resolve soon."

"Excuse me? Exposure?" said Shayna. "He's been exposed to something?"

"Are you saying he has a disease now?" said Conner.

"I don't think that's what he means," said Jake. "Is that why I recovered so quickly from the murkgoblins' attack? You treated me with your platinum blood?"

"That is correct. Your injuries were mostly superficial, but there were severe internal issues," said Rileau. "Your ability to recover is admirable. You must be in top form for what you are about to face."

Jake raised his shirt and rubbed his hand down his ribs. He had noticed the pain had subsided, and now he knew why. He was sure he had sustained at least two cracked ribs, yet his breathing wasn't labored, and except for slight bruising, there were no signs of injury.

"Your blood did this? I mean, the platinum blood healed me?" Jake asked.

"I think what you meant to say was thank you," said Shayna. Her raised eyebrows and a well-placed hand on her left hip emphasized that her words were more of a scolding than a correction.

"Yeah, you're right. Thanks," replied Jake. He was in awe. The healing had transpired without him noticing. He'd been so consumed with berating Rileau that he hadn't thought about his injuries or about his near-death encounter with the murkgoblin beasts.

"Your blood could have killed him, right?" said Seneca.

"Healing properties and those that do harm have a close alignment, as do most elements in nature," said Rileau. "There are always opposing sides. You can't have darkness without the light, good without evil, and so forth."

"That makes sense. It's like when I use my sword. I swear it does exactly what I want," said Shayna.

"That is true, Shayna. It is about focusing your intention. My blood is what makes the platinum elixir, and therefore, its purpose is directed by me," said Rileau. "My intent was to heal. It was the desired purpose."

"You mean the side effects make you act like a jackass?" asked Conner.

Seneca and Shayna couldn't resist laughing. Seneca caught a slight grin on Rileau's face as well. It was quickly replaced with a scowl.

"Hey, what's up with that?" Jake asked. He turned to face Conner.

"No offense, Jake, but he's right," said Shayna. "You've been totally out of control. Am I right, Seneca?"

"Well, how should I put this? It's like this—you've been a catastrophic jerk since we met Rileau," Seneca said. "Hey, but at least we know there's an explanation." She was reluctant to chime in; however, she felt compelled to address the issue.

"I guess knowing it was the dragon blood that made me difficult does help," said Jake.

"No, I'm fairly sure Seneca said 'catastrophic jerk.' I want to be clear on the epic scale you've hit today," said Shayna. She smiled widely, and Seneca laughed.

"My mistake—I got it!" Jake chuckled. "Rileau, is there more I should know?"

"The rate at which you heal will improve. That is a benefit that should serve you well in battle," said Rileau.

"Excuse me. I have a question," said Shayna. "Is there a time limit here?"

"In other words, how much longer will he be acting like a you-know-what?" Seneca asked, cringing.

"What they're saying is, will Jake be a jackass much longer?" Conner said with a huff, crossing his arms over his chest.

"If you're speaking of the aggression, then the effects will taper off over time," Rileau replied. "I am convinced it is happening already."

"Thank goodness. I'm not sure how much more I can take," said Shayna.

"Hey! I'm right here," said Jake. He knew he hadn't been acting like himself, but he was relieved there was an explanation.

"Only the healing qualities will remain. Once Jake's body has healed, no remnants of the platinum will be evident," said Rileau. "He will resume his previous state of being."

"Splendid! I kind of prefer the old Jake to this new model," said Shayna.

"I've gotta second that one," said Conner. He gave Shayna a fisted knuckle bump. They simulated the action of a hand-explosion gesture with perfect synchronization.

"Me three!" said Seneca. She danced around Jake as she made various faces to mock his mood with alternating pouts and grimaces.

Jake laughed. "You know you look psychotic, right?"

"It worked! Hey, you can say whatever you want, but I got you to laugh," said Seneca. She giggled and wrapped her arms around him. "I missed you. Welcome back."

"Thanks. I guess," said Jake.

"Great. You're back to your dull self!" Conner laughed. He gave Jake a shove that set him off balance and made him stumble a few feet.

Jake didn't protest. He worried about the damage he'd done to his friendships and his standing with Rileau. Since there was a clear explanation, he hoped all would be forgiven.

"Rileau, when Seneca touched my shoulder, it felt like she calmed me down. It really helped—I mean majorly," said Jake.

He smiled at Seneca, who was taken aback since she hadn't been aware of the effect of the massage. The revelation made her just as curious. She forced back a tinge of embarrassment. Having the focus shift to her was uncomfortable.

"I did that? I calmed you down?" she asked.

"It is possible she expedited the platinum's effect. The massage quickened the rate of absorption. It would seem your friend is not just a druid but also a healer of sorts," replied Rileau. "Not at all common, I acknowledge. I will look into assimilating this into your training."

Rileau cleared his throat and motioned for them to gather closer. They complied without hesitation. Conner gave Jake another shove to keep the mood light. He knew Jake was becoming a great friend, and having him in the Otherworld helped to relieve some of his own anxiety. He had been more worried about Jake's mood swings than he'd realized.

"I need you all to know that you have much to learn. I will not be able to explain all aspects of your lessons. You must find a way to trust me, or it will be useless to continue," said Rileau. He addressed the entire group, but they knew his comment was meant for Jake.

"Trust is a tough one," said Shayna. She'd discovered that she had been lied to her entire life. The truth that her mother was alive and living in the magical realm was still shocking. She hadn't come to grips with her mother's ability to change forms or the fact that her mother was Brigara's sister. Trusting others was not high on her list of must-dos.

"You must understand that we've been dealing with a lot," said Seneca. "The Otherworld is so different from where we came from."

"Even our parents lied to us," said Jake. "About some major stuff too. Like who my real parents are."

"The primary difference between our Otherworld and the mortal realm is the absence of acceptance. Mortals are raised with skepticism and doubt in all they do not understand," Rileau said.

"That's no excuse—they could've made us understand!" Shayna protested as she scrunched her nose and tightened her lips.

"I'm sure your parents did what was best for you," Rileau replied. "Can you imagine telling your mortal friends about this realm? Do you think they would believe you?"

"No, but that's not the point," said Shayna. "Look, the stuff we're dealing with is so foreign. It's like those care instructions on the label of your favorite sweater that have symbols instead of words. Hello—is it dry-clean only or what? I'm always thinking, *Do you wash it by hand and lay it flat to dry?* Is it too much to ask to make it clear and simple? I don't think so."

"Shayna! We get it," Seneca said abruptly. She hadn't meant to yell, but she sensed that it was highly unlikely there would be a break in the ranting anytime soon. "Nothing's clear, but hopefully Rileau's going to help with this. Am I right?"

"If you mean, will I assist in your quest to master your abilities, then the answer is yes," Rileau said. "However, I will not be addressing the caretaking of sweaters."

"Fine, but it's going to be something I will be looking into as soon as we get back to our realm," Shayna huffed.

"*If* we get back," Seneca said. She had attempted to say it under her breath, but she knew Jake heard her. She appreciated his nonresponse.

"Maybe this is bad timing, but can we get something to eat?" Conner moaned. "I'm hungry-hippo starving!" He drummed on his stomach. "It's echoing in there it's so empty."

"I have to agree with Conner. I'm barely functioning right now," said Seneca.

"Then you shall dine," replied Rileau. "Come along this way."

Chapter Eight

It's a Feast

Rileau led the famished foursome down a wide corridor until they came to a long, narrow, poorly lit hallway. His broad shoulders barely cleared the walls, but he continued without pause until they reached a spiral staircase. The center column, handrail, and treads were a majestic polished brass and showed no signs of dust or wear. The banister had flecks of gold that sparkled and reflected light.

"This is an impressive stairway," Shayna said as she slid her finger along the smooth rail.

"Thank you for your kindness. Your meal has been prepared and waits at the top," said Rileau. He bowed his head and extended his arm to allow her to pass.

"Maybe someone else should lead the way," Shayna said. She was too apprehensive. She slid behind Seneca and nudged her forward.

"That's a lot of stairs to climb, and I'm guessing there's no elevator," Seneca said flatly. She estimated it had to be at least six hundred or more steps to the top.

"No lift will get you to your destination other than your haunches and stamina," said Rileau. "Follow me." He began walking up the stairs without further discussion.

"What are haunches, and do they have a motor attached?" asked Conner.

"He means move your butt, so let's go," said Jake. "We've come this far, and we need to eat."

"Come on, Shayna—I'm right behind you," said Seneca. She returned the gesture of pushing her forward, causing Shayna to stumble a few steps.

"Fine. Let's do this already," said Shayna with a huff and a toss of her hair. She intentionally made sure to swing it directly across Seneca's face.

Seneca scoffed, brushed Shayna's hair away, and then spit out a few remaining strands that clung to her lips.

"Whoops, sorry about that." Shayna laughed.

"Real mature, Shayna," groaned Seneca. "Move your *haunch* before I kick it."

Shayna smirked as she followed Rileau up the stairs; the others trailed close behind. They continued up several flights with no sign of the stairs coming to an end. The gold shimmers in the handrails provided intermittent gleams of light in an otherwise hazy stairwell. It was only made brighter when they passed the occasional lit lantern set deep in the stone wall.

"Are we there yet?" asked Conner as he tilted his head back to get a better view of the winding stairs.

"We shall arrive shortly," Rileau called out as he whipped around and continued to climb.

He took long strides and periodically skipped several stairs. Shayna intentionally stayed a few steps behind to allow room for his tail to clear before she proceeded. She had a sudden image of stepping on it. She grimaced at the thought of him screaming in pain.

They scaled higher and higher up the narrow flight of stairs while engaging in minor conversation.

"We must be in one of the towers," said Seneca. She was out of breath, and her legs ached. "I bet we've walked more stairs than the ones in the Eiffel Tower."

"I'm getting sort of claustrophobic," said Jake.

"Me too! And I'm a bit light-headed," added Shayna. She placed the back of her hand across her forehead. "I think I'm running a fever too."

"Really? You're just sweating—that's all!" snapped Seneca. "As foreign as it might be for you, it's what happens when you exert yourself."

"So, you're saying I'm not the only one?" Shayna asked with a tone of sarcasm.

"Nope, not just you. We're all sweaty. I'm just hoping the food is worth this workout," said Seneca. "If I weren't so hungry, I would have given up already. My thighs are on fire!"

"You're going to have to come with me to my elite cycling spin class when we get back," said Conner. "That will whip you both into shape. It's all about the cardio."

"You do spinning?" Seneca and Shayna asked simultaneously. They burst into laughter from the mental image they shared.

"Oh yeah! It's improved my stamina," Conner declared as he puffed out his chest. "Move over, and let me take the lead. You two are moving like snails."

They stepped out of the way to allow him to ease past them. He trotted higher until he was only a few steps behind Rileau.

"I should tell him to watch out for the tail, but he deserves to get swiped, being that close," grumbled Seneca.

"Impressive, Conner!" said Shayna.

"This is really steep," Jake said as he craned his neck over the side and looked down the stairs. "I can't even see the bottom anymore."

"I think we're nearly there. Can you smell it?" asked Conner as he licked his lips.

"Oh yeah—let's go!" Jake shouted.

He pushed past the girls and moved just behind Conner. They jogged the last flight of stairs until they reached the top. The landing was connected to a vast and well-lit open space. The room was a perfect circle, with etched windows that went from floor to ceiling. Shayna eased into the room. She wiped moisture from her brow and gazed out the window. She stood motionless as she examined the panoramic view. She knew in the daylight she would be able to see the mountains and forest on one side and the ocean on the other. The moon was still high and reflected on the water below, but the rest of the landscape was cloaked in darkness.

"You can probably see so much from up here," Shayna said softly. Her mind drifted to Dreya, and she tried to focus on the area she believed to be her final resting place. "Bye, Grandmother."

She turned to join the others, who were gawking over the lavish feast set out on a large round wooden table. Positioned around the table were high-backed mahogany chairs upholstered in garnet tapestry, with ornate carvings along the armrests. The decor in the rest of the room was simple yet elegant. The table had been set with gold chargers and matching flatware, along with goblets filled with a lime-green beverage with clusters of blackberries set along the rims. There were several large serving dishes filled to the brim with stew, potatoes, and fresh vegetables. There was a platter of sliced meat, bowls of ripe fruit, and several breadbaskets; the aroma of the fresh-baked bread filled the room.

"Amazing!" Conner beamed as he rubbed his stomach. "This is a truckload of food. Wow!"

"And it smells great!" Jake said as he swallowed hard in an attempt to control his salivating response.

"I am glad you're pleased. You must try the Cornish pastry and the scrumptious cock-a-leekie," said Rileau.

"The what-a-leekie?" Conner asked. He wasn't sure if it was something alive or something to be feared, but he was willing to try just about anything to satisfy his hunger pangs.

"It is a soup. I will leave you to dine and then return to discuss sleeping arrangements and other matters," Rileau replied.

"You're not joining us?" Seneca asked.

"I will not," he replied. He turned swiftly on his heel. An iron door located at the end opposite where they had entered swung open. It closed silently behind him.

"You can't tell me that guy doesn't have something to hide—that was really strange," said Jake. While no one else acknowledged it, he knew from their expressions that they agreed.

"Hmm, yeah, well, we can talk about Rileau at some other time. Let's eat!" Conner exclaimed.

"You don't have to tell me twice," Seneca said. "I wanna cram this whole thing into my face!" Her smile extended ear to ear as she held out a large loaf of bread.

"You're kidding, right?" Shayna asked.

"Oh no, I'm not joking. Stand back because this is not gonna be pretty," Seneca mumbled after she bit down on the bread.

Crumbs tumbled down the front of her shirt. She brushed a few crumbs away and took another generous bite. She climbed into a seat and grabbed a bowl. She ladled in a generous heaping of stew and carelessly dripped some onto the table and down the sides of the bowl. She grappled through the basket of bread, pulled out a sizeable yeast loaf, and ripped it apart. She sloshed one end in the broth and then chomped down. She chewed quickly as she spooned a chuck of meat onto the remaining portion of bread and jammed it into her wide-open mouth. Jake looked at Shayna for a reaction, and she shrugged as she watched in awe.

"Your cheeks look like a chipmunk preparing for winter," said Shayna. She frowned and walked away slowly while shaking her head. She strolled to the window and glanced out at the darkness.

"Humph. Who cares?" Seneca snapped as she swallowed hard and then reached for another slice of bread to repeat the process.

"I get it. I'm with Seneca. Pass the bread," said Conner as he slid into the chair beside her. "Let's see if I've got it down. Bread, dip, meat, and chomp."

"There ya go!" she said jubilantly, but the food muffled most of her words.

Seneca never looked up as she slid the basket of bread in his direction. She dipped a sizeable hunk of sourdough into the remaining broth in her bowl and swirled it around until she'd collected all traces of the stew. She savored the flavors as she chewed each bite. She looked around briefly to the other offerings but decided to continue with her original choice and scooped up another serving of stew. She regained her vigorous meal consumption without pause.

"I guess we'd better hurry up and join them if we expect to get anything to eat." Jake laughed.

He navigated around the table and chose the seat across from Conner. He couldn't take his eyes off Seneca as he watched her with astonishment. He was sure she wasn't bothering to chew half the time before she reached for more bread. He looked at Conner, who was doing a fairly good job of emulating her. He piled more meat on top of a piece of bread before jamming it into his awaiting mouth, but otherwise, he was following her methods.

"Slow down, you guys!" Jake chuckled as he surveyed the other offerings on the table.

He decided on a hearty slice of beef from the roast just to his right and added garlic-seasoned red potatoes to his plate. He scooped up a slice of a meat pie that was prepared in a semicircle. It had bits of steak, potato, and large pieces of onion and turnip beneath the flaky dough. After one bite of the tender pepper-seasoned beef, he chewed and swallowed quickly and then gorged on it.

"This is the best—no joke!" Jake proclaimed. "I'm gonna get some more of this. It's so good."

He took two slices of bread, made a sandwich out of the sliced beef, and added various other items from the table. He smashed it down enough to fit into his awaiting mouth and took a generous bite. "I'm not kidding—this is the best!" he said as he wiped the drippings from his lips.

"It's about time you recognize it!" Conner bellowed. He leaned across the table, pulled the platter of beef over, and piled several slices onto his plate. "A sandwich is a great idea!"

Seneca nodded in agreement. She nestled into her seat and closed her eyes. She had consumed enough food to keep her satisfied. She sipped the green beverage and realized it tasted familiar. It was similar to the tea her mother made on warm days. She let her body relax as she enjoyed the sensation of being full. She patted her slightly bloated stomach and grinned. She looked around and noticed Shayna wasn't seated. She was standing at the window, staring off into the distance. Seneca pushed her chair away from the table and made her way across the room. She could see Shayna's eyes were filled with tears.

"Hey, there's plenty of food. Come sit down and eat," said Seneca. She stroked Shayna's arm softly and slid her hand into hers.

"It's just so hard to accept all of this," Shayna said. Her voice was airy and soft. "It's just not fair that I never got to know her."

"I know it isn't fair," Seneca said. "None of it is. We're all feeling lost."

"I didn't even have a chance to ask where she lived or her favorite things to do. I don't even know what she wanted me to call her—Dreya or Grams or maybe something else," Shayna said softly. She wiped away the tears that were now flowing steadily.

"I'm sure that whatever name you came up with would have been fine," Seneca replied. She knew her words were just filling the silence and not offering much comfort. She didn't know what else she could do. She had never met her own grandparents or lost anyone close.

"Do you think Celestia knows?" asked Shayna. Her eyes were glassy and wide as she turned toward Seneca. "Do you think they attacked her too?"

"I'm sure she's fine, and the way word gets around in the Otherworld, I bet she knows about it."

"Probably, and I'm sure that hag Brigara knows too," Shayna sneered. "I can't wait to make her pay for what she's done. No way is she getting away with it."

"And her evil minions are going down too," Seneca added.

"That's good to hear. However, you will need to have more than just your raw emotions if you are to defeat her," Rileau said abruptly.

Shayna and Seneca jerked around and eyed their mentor. He had entered the room and overheard their conversation without detection.

"Oh, hi—I mean, we didn't hear you come in," said Shayna. She was startled, and the heat on her neck rose to her cheeks; she felt embarrassed. "I hope I didn't say anything wrong."

"Stating your intentions is encouraged in these surroundings," he said. "You do not have to be on guard or mince your words here."

"You're saying I have permission to rage?" asked Shayna.

"It is just one facet of your complexity and is just as much a part of you as your laughter or sorrow," he replied.

"Well, you can scratch laughter off the list—that's nowhere near what I feel for Brigara," Shayna said adamantly.

"If you insist, but humor can be off-putting for those who do not expect it. It can be a divisive maneuver when dealing with an adversary," Rileau said. He smiled at Shayna. "Be prepared to use all your talents, even those that are dormant."

"Oh yeah, like the powers of persuasion? That didn't do me much good when we had to fight off those acid-spitting fairies," Shayna said with a scowl as she twisted her lips into a pout.

"Knowing when and how to use your powers to your advantage will be mastered soon," he said.

"I can't wait to figure out some mumbo-jumbo hex-popping stuff. Then I can kick some major Brigara butt!" she grumbled.

"Excuse me, but she can't do that on an empty stomach, right?" Seneca said. She could see that Shayna was overwhelmed, and the grief of losing her grandmother was the only fuel she was living on. Her loss was turning to pure anger. Seneca surmised that a good meal would probably settle her down, at least temporarily.

"Yes, this is true. Please take a moment to eat," said Rileau. "We have much to cover when the sun rises, and you will need your strength."

"Fine. I will eat—if there's anything left," Shayna said. She exchanged a forced smile with Seneca as Rileau led her across the room.

"I know you think I've eaten enough for the both of us." Seneca laughed.

"I am pretty sure you've eaten enough for all of us!" Shayna retorted.

Conner nearly choked on a nugget of beef as he laughed. "You're right on point with that one. Even I'm having a tough time keeping up with her."

"I'm just packing it away for battle," said Seneca. She sighed and patted her slightly protruding belly. "I'm good to go!"

"That's a relief! I can finally slow down. I thought I had to keep up," said Conner.

"I gave up as soon as I saw her practically inhale that whole loaf of bread!" said Jake. He laughed boisterously until his sides ached.

Seneca tried hard not to laugh, until she couldn't hold back any longer. She glanced at Shayna to see if she'd jump in too, but she merely shook her head and smirked slightly. She was not in the mood to engage in the frolicking. Seneca watched Shayna's expression change and had an urge to push further to read her thoughts. Insinuating herself into her mind would be easy but also a violation of privacy; she knew she should resist. She bit down on her bottom lip and concentrated on the pain to shift her focus.

Rileau pulled out Shayna's chair and filled her bowl with stew.

"Thank you," she said softly. She stirred the oversized spoon slowly as she took a whiff of the comforting smell. She inhaled the aroma before scooping up a generous portion. She liked the warmth of the food as it slid down her throat. It was what she needed at that moment. She wiped away the streaming tears as she listened to Jake and Conner debate which dessert had the most chocolate.

"These are called hermit cookies," Jake said. "My mother baked them all of the time."

"No way! They're spiced raisin cookies!" Conner retorted. "My grandmother practically invented them."

"Who cares? Just eat them already, and pass three my way!" Seneca said, and they turned and stared blankly in astonishment. "What? Did I say something wrong?" She reached across the table, slid the tray to within reach, and grabbed a handful before plopping down in her seat. She bit into the warm cookies and closed her eyes to savor the various flavors.

"You have a bottomless stomach," said Jake. He was only partially kidding. He was amazed that someone so small could wolf down that much food.

"Hey, I just feed the hunger." Seneca smiled and closed her eyes again.

They continued light banter and kept the conversation flowing without further mention of their surroundings or the mission that awaited them. They were careful to keep the mood calm. Although it was unspoken, they knew a tumultuous storm was brewing, and the levity of that moment would likely be their last. Evil was waiting for them outside the castle walls.

Rileau remained fairly quiet, but his presence was felt and contributed to why they kept the conversations generic. He stood at the far end of the room. He had taken Shayna's place at the window and stared off into the distance.

"Do you think he can see in the dark?" whispered Conner near Jake's ear. He gestured to Rileau and finished off his last bite of dessert.

"If he really is a dragon, you'd better believe he can," said Jake.

CHAPTER NINE

The Perplex

The room was brightly lit and alive with laughter. The dining room had the smell of warm cinnamon rolls. The breakfast offerings were simplistic, but the flavors and amounts served weren't compromised. They all had consumed several helpings and were feeling content.

Rileau entered the room, allowing the door to slam behind him. The conversations in the room came to an immediate halt. They sat up in their seats with discipline. Their eyes were fixed on him. No one was surprised by his arrival, but they hadn't anticipated his entrance to be so alarming. Conner gulped down the last of his breakfast without chewing. He wheezed slightly but resisted reaching for his drink.

"I hope your sleeping quarters were satisfactory and that you have found the morning meal to be suitable," said Rileau flatly as he patrolled the table. He resembled a drill captain conducting an inspection.

"The food here is totally excellent!" Seneca howled as she wiped her mouth and tucked her napkin beneath her empty plate. She sat up straight and grinned. Before he had entered the dining room, she'd been preparing to confiscate a stack of bannocks; there were only a few remaining, and she was eager to drench them in honey. She sighed heavily. She knew the meal was over.

"My bed was heavenly." Shayna beamed. She thought about the large beds that were raised on platforms well above the floor. Stepstools were placed bedside to assist, but even with the added boost, she still had to climb to get in. She and Seneca shared quarters, as did Jake and Conner at the other end of the hall. She had pulled the thick down-stuffed quilt up to her chin and nestled her head into the fluffy feather pillow. Unable to relax, her mind had raced through all they had encountered. She'd tried to imagine what they would face in the coming days, but that had caused her even more anxiety. Her body had been exhausted, and she'd been mentally drained. She had looked across the room and noticed that Seneca had dozed off fairly quickly. She'd listened and heard a whisper of a snore. Shayna had found it comforting, and she'd focused on the soft rhythm of Seneca's breathing, which eventually had lulled her to sleep. Her dreams had carried her to places she'd never seen and encounters with people she'd never met. When she'd finally awakened to Seneca's chattering about the morning's cuisine, she'd felt as if she had only been asleep for a few minutes. She had somehow made it down to breakfast before Seneca and Conner devoured every morsel of food, but she had barely taken a bite, when Rileau made his entrance. She tried to muffle a yawn, but she caught him glaring and adjusted her posture to show she was attentive.

Rileau cleared his throat and moved farther into the room. He was wearing formal battle attire beneath his hooded cape. His tail fanned across the floor as he moved past each of them. He stopped once he reached Seneca.

"Have you enjoyed your morning thus far?" he asked.

"Yeah, it's been great. We really should thank your staff, but we haven't met anyone yet," said Seneca. "Are there a lot of people here?" She had been wondering who roamed the halls and kept the castle cleaned and stocked.

"That discussion is for another time. There are greater issues at hand."

"Okay," said Seneca softly.

"The four of you have not formed the necessary bond to secure the dominion," said Rileau. "To enhance the properties of the elements you have consumed, your energy must be weaved."

"That makes sense," said Jake. "We need to be cohesive like any team if we're going to win." He pushed his plate aside and leaned across the table.

"That sounds like something a coach would say," said Conner excitedly. "I'm on board with teamwork." He reached for the platter of cinnamon rolls and shoved two into his mouth. He licked sticky frosting from his fingers.

"As long as you don't expect me to be cheerleader," said Seneca defiantly. "I draw the line with the rah-rah stuff."

"Hey, cheerleaders are a team too!" said Shayna. "Besides, you're so tiny; you'd make a great flier from the top of the pyramid. Or maybe a mascot."

"A mascot! Not in this realm or any other," snarled Seneca. She rolled her eyes and balled her fists.

"Enough! I demand your attention," Rileau snapped. "We must proceed. Come along."

His green eyes glowed. Without hesitation, they followed him to the stairwell at the end of the corridor. They climbed down the winding stairs. After only a few flights, they stopped at a gilded iron door. Jake stared at it; he hadn't noticed it on their climb to the dining room. He wondered how he had missed it but rationalized it had likely been cloaked from detection.

"What we will need is in the solar room," said Rileau as he pushed open the door.

The space was small yet large enough for them to sit comfortably. A fire was lit in a small fireplace. It flickered and crackled. The room smelled of chamomile and was decorated with aged colorful tapestry. The furniture was sparse. The few pieces were spaced close together, making a comfortable arrangement for conversations. Two cabinets made of thick oak painted in bright reds and greens lined the walls. The chairs were covered in heavy velvet with heraldic designs coordinated to the design on the heavy rug that took up most of the floor space. The room was lit with well-placed oil lamps, but most of the lighting came from the wide window at the end of the room. Shayna sat on the window seat and looked out to the garden below. She exhaled slowly and took in the majestic beauty.

The garden was a mix of blood red roses and lilies. Perfectly manicured and maintained. Shayna wondered if they were kept pristine by magic or a skillful groundskeeper. Rileau hadn't addressed Seneca's question about the staff or others that lived in the castle. She wondered if he had reason to keep secrets about who prepared their meals, dusted the tapestry and swept the floors. Surely, there had to be others.

"Shayna––are you paying attention?" Rileau asked, snapping her from her daydream. His voice resonated loudly in the tight quarters.

"Yes, I am." She decided to keep her response simple.

"We are about to discuss what will be needed to strengthen the bond you share," he said. "Please join us." He smiled slightly and gestured for her to come closer.

Shayna sat in the chair next to Seneca. Rileau crossed the room and opened one of the cabinets. It was filled with gold goblets and various vials and canisters. Jake locked eyes on Seneca and she shook her head in response. Rileau selected one of the vials and emptied the glowing onyx contents into one of the goblets. He took long strides until he reached the window. He raised the goblet to the light and waved his hand across the opening. Sparks shot silently into the air and cascaded over the goblet before dissolving.

"It's like the fourth of July, except without the kaboom and finale," whispered Conner. Jake nodded in agreement.

"What I hold before you is the Oil of Animation Perplexity. It is enchanted to create a primitive perplex," said Rileau as he looked into the cup with admiration. "It is in its purest state for consumption."

"Consumption? You mean like for drinking?" asked Shayna.

"Yes, and I believe you are the one who should indulge," he said. Rileau extended the goblet toward her.

She put up her hands in protest and leaned back in her chair. "Why do you think I should drink it?" she asked with fear and confusion.

"It was you who destroyed the portal and prohibited Brigara from returning to the Otherworld. You chose to pursue the fairies that brought down Dreya. You took watch over Conner when he needed vital assistance. Therefore, I ask, why not you?"

"Maybe if you told us what it is and what it does first," said Jake. He stood next to her chair in a protective stance.

"Yeah, I think Jake's got a point. What does it do?" asked Shayna as she slid closer to Seneca and gripped her hand.

"The perplex is a vortex of mystic energy that allows one to be suspended between realms. It does not sustain a living entity for extended periods of time," said Rileau. "It is the closest charm to banishment." He spoke calmly, as if it were an everyday occurrence. He did not retract his hand as he held the goblet steady and within Shayna's reach.

"Well, if you can banish people with it, does that mean it's dark magic?" asked Seneca.

"It is not dark magic. And banishment is not its purpose," he said. "In the purest form, it is intended as a temporary suspension in an animated state. The elder druids have used it to enhance their abilities and strengthen their connections with other druids."

"Is it like the spell they used when they tried to send Brigara to the Inbetween?" Jake asked.

"No, it is not of the same properties. The spell they chose had origins from ancient charms. Their attempt was thwarted because of interference," replied Rileau. Smoke escaped his nostrils and made a small cloud at chest level before evaporating.

"That's what Keene Ardara was trying to explain too. We found out that Shayna's mom helped her escape—no offense, Shayna," said Jake.

"None taken. I'm sure Celestia—I mean my mother—was doing what she thought was right," said Shayna.

"The heart can be used as a weapon, and Brigara is an expert at seeking weaknesses," said Rileau grimly. "Now let us continue with the perplex."

"What happens if we have trouble getting Shayna back?" Jake asked.

"If the entity is not retrieved, then the perplex will discard it."

"Entity? You mean me?" said Shayna. "It will discard me?"

"Throw her away? Like last week's smelly trash?" said Conner. When he saw the glares cast his way, he pantomimed zipping his lips and tossing away the key.

"Does that mean Shayna will come back on her own—you know, if we can't get her out?" Seneca asked.

Shayna felt suddenly ill. She could hear her heart booming in her chest.

"The perplex will discard her in any realm it chooses. There is no control over this," he said. "For her to return to the Otherworld, she must be released here. Otherwise, there is no guarantee or way of tracking her expulsion."

"Did you just say *explosion*? Seriously, can I explode?" Shayna said. She leaped up, grabbed hold of Conner's arm, and gripped it tightly. "You're not blowing me up!"

Jake shook his head and pinched the bridge of his nose. Seneca wanted to laugh, but she had her own concerns based on what Rileau had actually said. She took a deep breath and waited to hear more.

"That's not what I said. Your emergence will be unpredictable in terms of the realm in which you are released unless it is directed with the right intention," he explained.

"Oh, sorry. I guess I misunderstood. I swear I heard something different, but never mind," said Shayna. "It still sounds like a gamble, though; maybe this isn't such a great idea. The mention of discarding me sounds awful."

"I don't know about this, you guys," said Shayna warily.

"I have to agree with Shayna on this one," said Conner as he peeled Shayna's nails away from his arm. "Seems like too big of a risk."

"Indeed. You will have to choose whether or not you are willing to take it," replied Rileau. "The four of you are not connected energetically. In traditional circumstances, this happens naturally over time. Time is not something we have in abundance. We must force the bond due to the impending war."

"You really think putting me in the perplex will do it—will bond us together?" asked Shayna meekly. She felt a surge of anxiety rush through her core.

"That is the intention," said Rileau. "It is an acceleration of sorts."

"How does it work?" asked Seneca. "I'm still not clear."

"It acts as a prompt to intertwine your connection. If you succeed, your magic and powers will be elevated. The perplex will bridge the energy of the dominion."

Jake exchanged a look with Seneca. He could tell she was nervous. She shrugged in response.

"As of now, your powers are intensifying independently—outside of the dominion. While it is a necessity for you to strengthen your powers, it is even more important for them to be entwined as the dominion. The bond must occur. You cannot defeat Brigara as individuals."

"I get it. The perplex is a jumpstart to making us the Dominion of Four," said Jake.

"You are only repeating what I have already articulated," said Rileau gruffly.

"Yeah, but sometimes I've gotta hear things in my own words for it to sink in," replied Jake.

"The way Jake says it makes sense to me too," Conner said. "Brigara's trying to stop us before we bond. I can feel it."

"And we're already behind," added Seneca.

"Again, it is why I chose the perplex. It will quicken the process," Rileau said. "It is imperative that you mesh your magic, gifts, and will together as soon as possible. Otherwise, Brigara will be the victor."

"Sounds like we've gotta do it," said Shayna in a whisper. She turned to face Rileau and lifted her chin. "We need to come at her with everything we've got."

"It is crucial," Rileau said.

"Well, I think we have our answer then. Let's get this party started!" Shayna said with a smile that twisted into a grim expression. "I can do this—we can do this."

"Are you okay with this, Shayna?" Jake asked.

She smiled and nodded slightly as she fought back tears. "I just need a hug."

She didn't have to ask twice. Conner and Jake were the first to offer embraces. Seneca waited until they were done and then wrapped her arms around Shayna's waist. She hugged her tightly, released, and grabbed hold again.

"You can do this, Shayna. You can't leave me with these two for long," said Seneca with a smirk.

Shayna hugged her again and rearranged Seneca's hair away from her face. "There. That looks better." She smiled. "Okay, Rileau, I'm ready."

Rileau stirred the contents and raised the goblet to the light before handing it to Shayna. She peered inside and rubbed her nose when she got a whiff of the odor. She held the cup out at arm's length.

"It smells rancid!" she griped as she waved her hand to dissipate the aroma rising toward her face. "What am I supposed to do with this stinky stuff?"

"Drink the elixir. It will accelerate the process to activate the perplex," Rileau said.

Shayna lifted the goblet slowly to her lips and sipped a sampling. She spewed it out immediately, nearly spraying Rileau in the face. He slid just out of the projectile range and avoided contact.

"Gross! That's awful! There's no way I'm going to drink that. Yuck!" Shayna protested. She wiped her mouth and shook her head.

"You've done what is required," Rileau said as he removed the offending goblet from her grasp. "Only your palate needed to be exposed to elixir for the perplex to be activated. There is no need to drink more."

"That's disgusting! I'm never going to get this taste out of my mouth." Shayna's eyes watered, and her nose began to burn. She suddenly felt her face numbing, and she started rubbing her cheeks to relieve the sensation. "I feel funny."

She looked out at the faces staring back. She felt a burst of cool wind, followed by the sensation of spinning. The furniture in the room blurred; she reached out to take hold of a chair but grasped at air. The room before her faded into darkness.

"She's gone!" Conner said as he waved his arms through the air where Shayna had stood seconds before.

"Now the three of you must go retrieve her," Rileau commanded.

"Retrieve her how exactly? You haven't gone over that part," said Jake.

"Aren't you coming to help us?" Seneca asked with wide eyes. She could feel her stomach twisting in knots.

"I will not. It is up to the three of you to bring her from the perplex. I thought I made that clear," said Rileau. "You must increase your connection. Use what is in your heart of hearts to pull her from the perplex."

"How are we supposed to do that? I guess I dozed off, because I don't remember this at all," said Jake. He tried to hide his terror, but he was trembling. "What you've said is as clear as mud!"

"Pardon me. I must remember that what is obvious to me is not so for you," Rileau said with only a slightly condescending tone.

Jake could tell Rileau was distracted. He hadn't known him long, but there was something different about his behavior. He was tense.

"Are things okay, Rileau? I mean, are you okay?" Seneca asked.

"I was wondering the same thing," said Jake. "You're acting a little different."

"Given the lack of knowledge you possess of the Otherworld, you cannot expect to master all things at a swift pace. Time is your adversary, not my demeanor."

"I get that, but—"

"Stop seeking what is irrelevant. Instead, focus on the quest, as you must be the victor."

"I just have a quick question," Conner said.

"Enough! It is not favorable to spend this much time on frippery," Rileau said gruffly.

His thick tail slammed the floor. Conner jumped, and his eyes widened. Jake shot a glance at Seneca. He didn't want to press further. He was convinced that something was wrong. He had to remind himself that Shayna was the priority. He couldn't be distracted. They needed as much information as possible. Even if he had to drag it out of Rileau, he was determined to get it. Jake liked the image he conjured of the highly unlikely altercation.

"Retrieve Shayna. The fate of the Otherworld depends on it," said Rileau.

"Okay, so what do we do first?" Seneca asked calmly.

"You must bring her from the perplex while near water. It cannot be done here. The protective charms surrounding the castle will not allow her entry," said Rileau.

"The water that surrounds the castle won't work either then," Jake surmised.

He was determined not to let Rileau's lack of focus disrupt his efforts to find Shayna. He could feel his inner clock ticking down the time they had remaining. He felt time whizzing by, and his clock ticked louder with each second they wasted.

"Where's the nearest lake or pond?" Seneca asked.

"There's a large pond not far from here. Once you see the grove of mature ash trees, you will be near it. You must hurry, as nightfall will mean the end of Shayna's time in the perplex," Rileau said.

"Once we get there, what do we do?" Seneca asked. "Is there a spell or potion or something we need to put in the water? I understand you want us to do this, but why can't you be there to make sure we do it right? I demand a reason for this." She sounded frantic, but she didn't care. She felt guilty since Shayna was the one in jeopardy, and the guilt was fueling her emotions. She knew it was irrational. It made sense for Shayna to be in the perplex, but it didn't take the feeling away.

"You must remain focused, Seneca. You will be met by a trusted elemental to aid you in this quest. She will be your guide and lead you," replied Rileau. "I will not accompany you. This is a task you must undertake in my absence. You will need to rely on others within the Otherworld, as I cannot be your only alliance. It is all the reason I will provide you."

"But you said we could lose Shayna to another realm. Won't we be in danger if we don't get her back?" Jake asked in a raised but controlled tone.

"Yeah, there would be no dominion without her," said Conner.

"Trust what I say. You will be provided the assistance needed," said Rileau.

He explained in detail the location of the pond and the paths to take as well as those to avoid. He told them of the skillful elemental who would join them. Together they would extract Shayna from the perplex, which would reunite them as a stronger unit. He explained how they should prepare for the acceleration of their powers.

"Be aware. While Shayna is in the perplex, she too may experience tremendous alterations in her gifts. I will await your return. You must go now. Seek out the elemental who shall be trusted. Concentrate only on releasing Shayna from the perplex, and prepare for the binding of your connection." Rileau turned and left them standing in silence.

"Hey, wait!" said Jake.

"Nope—stop! Don't say another word. Let's go!" said Seneca in a growl.

She took hold of Jake's arm and rushed him toward the door. He did little to resist as she shoved him into the hall and pulled him along through the corridor. She looked over her shoulder and was satisfied that Conner trailed close behind. Jake's mind was racing as he allowed Seneca to lead him out into the bright sunshine. The circumstances were worrisome to Seneca, but she elected not to address her fears. Shayna's safety was her greatest concern.

Jake tried to piece Rileau's last words together to determine their meaning. Multiple questions swirled around his head as he was led across the stone bridge and onto the path. He intensified his pace once he spied the woods. Seneca and Conner trotted behind him. He found it strange that Rileau had refused to supervise such an important task, especially since it was obvious he considered them inept. He wondered if Rileau secretly wanted them to fail.

CHAPTER TEN

Elf Encounter

A cool wind skimmed across the surface of the water and carried a fine mist that settled across the mossy embankment. The breeze directed a kaleidoscope of magnolia butterflies to flutter near Seneca. She watched as they looped and soared carelessly toward a cluster of wildflowers. She wondered if she would ever have the chance to fly without worry or purpose.

"Did you hear something?" Conner asked. He sensed movement in the trees and craned his neck to get a better look.

"Nope, I didn't hear anything," said Jake.

"We're always hearing something, but as long as it stays hidden, I'm good," replied Seneca dryly. She sat down on a mound of soft grass and pulled her knees in close.

"At least we're out here in the daylight. Let's get this done before it gets dark," said Conner. "This place is great right now, but I'd hate to see what's lurking behind those trees on the other side of this massive pond."

"Or what's beneath the surface. It reminds me of thick split-pea soup," said Jake.

"What do we do now?" Conner asked as he plopped down next to Seneca.

"We can review what Rileau *didn't* say about the perplex," said Jake.

"I agree with that plan," Seneca moaned.

"You must release her before dusk, or her essence will be reduced to dust," Conner recited in his best impersonation of Rileau.

"That's not what he said," Jake replied. "But it's about as doom and gloom as his real statements."

"If we don't release her from the perplex, then she could be lost to who knows what or where for eternity," Seneca said. It was the mantra she had repeated as they trekked through the woods. She buried her face from view. Tears were on the brink of spilling over. Her heart sank at the thought of Shayna being lost to them forever. It seemed more like a cruel joke than a lesson in battling evil. She pictured Brigara's thin lips twisted tightly, mocking them for their failure. Her ears burned from the anger rising in her at the thought of the cruel woman winning.

"Sounds just like what I said to me." Conner chuckled.

"Let's get serious and focus, you guys," said Jake. "Are you okay, Seneca?" He plopped down next to her on the damp mound of grass and leaned in.

"Yup, just peachy!" Her sarcasm was heavy. Jake and Conner exchange a worried expression.

Seneca scrambled to her feet. Her face was flushed, and she almost tripped over Conner as she stomped around in protest. The wind rustled a few of the bushes, and she jumped. Searching frantically for the source of the movement, she sighed as she realized it was merely the breeze. Her nerves were shot. "Maybe I need to take Conner's lead. Hey, a little comic relief might help since we aren't any closer to getting Shayna back," Seneca moaned.

There was no holding back the tears, and they flowed heavily. Conner ran over and joined Jake in wrapping her in their arms. They hugged her tiny frame between them.

"Mmmf, lut muh go. Can't breathe." She pushed them away to get much-needed air. "Seriously, you two are overgrown bears, and a shower wouldn't hurt either of you!"

"You're okay then?" Jake asked. "We're gonna get Shayna back."

"I know. I'm just worried. I'm allowed to freak out once in a while!" she scoffed. "It just seems like something is off."

She didn't understand why Rileau would have selected such a place. She couldn't shake the feeling they were being watched. Since emerging from the woods, they were out in the open and vulnerable to attack from multiple directions. There were too many places the enemy could be lurking.

"It's too quiet here," said Jake. "Say something, Conner."

"My grandmother was always reciting oddball words of wisdom," said Conner. "May you live on beyond your youth and die old and rich with at least one good tooth."

"That's a funny one. Random, but funny," Seneca said. She smiled and tried to recite it in her head.

"She had tons of them for just about every situation," said Conner.

"We could use some of that limerick stuff right now," said Jake. "Shayna will only be released if we solve the perplex."

"Jake, it's not like a real test, you know," Seneca said as she folded her arms across her chest and tapped her foot. "Rileau's sending us an elemental to help."

"Let's hope he told the elemental that it's same-day delivery, 'cause I'm already tired of waiting," Conner complained.

"If we don't get this right, we won't stand a chance of countering Brigara's hexes," Jake said. His nostrils flared as he huffed in frustration. "Her fire spheres will take us down in a heartbeat. We'd better make this connection work."

"Chill, dude! We're going to have an uber-ridiculous strong bond like none of them have prophesied. They're gonna get writer's cramp trying to keep up with the Dominion of Four. You can quote me on that too—if they ask," Conner said. He made fist pumps in the air and raised his hands above his head, as if he were receiving a standing ovation for his feats.

Seneca covered her mouth to muffle her laugh.

"Don't be a chicken; you've gotta go at this with confidence," said Conner. He made a mocking motion of a squawking chicken behind Jake but in clear view of Seneca. She laughed.

"Hey, knock it off!" Jake turned quickly around just as Conner was attempting another gesture. Jake shook his fist inches away from Conner's nose as Conner raised his hands to surrender.

"Oh, just settle down! You need to relax before you pop a vein." Conner snickered. He found Jake's reaction to be over the top. Continuing the taunting probably wasn't wise, but he couldn't resist.

"How 'bout I pop you? Then we can all see how tough you really are—or not!" Jake attempted to shove him, but he didn't have much success. Conner stayed rooted to the spot, which only served to infuriate him.

"You were saying?" Conner laughed. "You wanna try that again?"

"Maybe I'll try a different tactic," said Jake as he pulled back his fist.

"Seriously, Jake?" Seneca stepped in and pulled his arm down. "We need to work together to figure this out. Let's just go over all of it from the beginning—before Rileau's friend gets here."

"Tell him to stop fooling around, and maybe we can get this right," Jake retorted.

"All right, no more goofing," said Conner as he stretched out each syllable to sound robotic.

Jake shook his head and threw his arms in the air in exasperation. As he glanced out across the emerald pond, he wondered if a fairy lurked beneath the surface. His thoughts shifted to the time when he'd almost drowned. He'd encountered an overprotective fairy who dwelled in the lake near Kryt na nOg. Just as his mind began to replay the experience of his body being thrashed around by powerful waves, he saw something moving in the corner of his eye. He turned and saw what appeared to be a haze of low blue fog just above the surface of the water. It headed in their direction as it separated into four parts. As it drew closer, it became clear that it wasn't fog. They were beings of some sort.

"Check that out. What are they?" asked Jake in a low voice.

"What's what?" Conner asked.

"Those four things coming at us—right there skimming along the water," said Jake. He turned to make sure they were looking at the same place.

"I don't know what you're talking about. I don't see anything on the water," said Seneca as she stepped forward and squinted.

Jake moved behind her and directed her shoulders to the area where he had spotted them. "Right there—those wispy translucent things over the huge cluster of lily pads. It's like they're floating right on top of the water," he said. "Tell me you see them hovering and heading this way."

"What does *translucent* mean?" asked Conner. He scanned the area but shrugged when he didn't see anything out of the ordinary. "I see nothin', dude."

"Nope, I don't see it or them either," replied Seneca. "Where exactly are they?"

"Come on, you guys!" Jake shouted in frustration. "See over there? Look at them now—they've changed direction and are heading toward the cluster of dense trees over there."

"Now they're by the trees?" asked Conner. "I thought you said they were over the water."

"They were a second ago, but they're moving fast!" Jake yelled. He ran to the edge of the pond and skidded into the slimy embankment. "The last one just went around those cypress trees. Didn't you see them?"

"They had to be crazy-wicked fast, 'cause I saw zip, nada, zero!" said Conner. "Like blink-and-they're-not-even-there kind of speed."

"Cut it out, Conner. There's no way you didn't see them!" said Jake. "There were four of them going across the pond. They passed the trees and then drifted into the woods." He looked at Seneca for acknowledgment, hoping she'd caught a glimpse of them.

"Sorry, but we didn't see anything, and we're right beside you," said Seneca. She shrugged. "Maybe you're just imagining it or something."

"Listen! I'm telling you exactly what I saw!" he yelled. "I don't know why you guys didn't see them."

He ran to the edge of the pond and looked out across the water. He slumped back up the embankment when he realized they had vanished.

"Describe exactly what you saw," said Seneca softly to ease his anxiety.

"Okay. There were four of them; they all looked the same. They had nearly transparent skin. Maybe it was actually blue or a bit of indigo—a really pale color, but it sparkled," said Jake.

"Like when we consumed the Himalayan crystals?" Seneca asked. She was fascinated by his description.

"Yeah, a little—maybe." He pondered his experience of flying and having his body glisten from the effects of the crystals. "It was really shimmery on their wings."

"They had wings? Were they like mine?" Seneca couldn't hide her excitement.

"Actually, no, they were nothing like yours. As a matter of fact, I'm calling them wings because I don't know what else they could be. They were more like long streamers of really delicate wings, but without cartilage. They sort of draped down and trailed behind them as they glided along," replied Jake.

"Humph. Those don't sound like wings at all." Seneca snorted and folded her arms.

"What stood out the most were their enormous almond-shaped eyes. I think they were either a really pale blue or silver—I couldn't tell," said Jake. "They didn't get close enough."

"Anything else?" asked Conner. "So far, they sound harmless."

"They were all wispy looking and moving in sync—not exactly flying, but they weren't walking either. They were magnificent." Jake's voice trailed off when he realized he probably sounded as if he were losing his mind. The scene was so vivid for him. He wanted his description to paint a picture for them. He shook his head in frustration.

"They were in the air but not flying?" Conner asked with a raised eyebrow.

"Yeah, not flying. More like hovering or floating, I guess. It seemed effortless. They moved around like schools of jellyfish. They moved with a pulsating motion as they glided along. They were upright and had super skinny legs. They sort of bowed out as they moved."

"And they weren't actually touching the ground or water?" Seneca asked.

"No, not at all. They weren't small either," Jake said. "They were as tall as I am, with really broad shoulders and extremely narrow torsos. Odd but beautiful in a way. They were awkward looking but graceful at the same time." He paused to think about what he'd just said and bobbed his head in confirmation. He felt he had summed up their description accurately.

"Amazing. Sounds like an epic event. Wish I had seen it." Conner tried to sound empathetic, but he knew it wasn't working from the expression on Jake's face.

"Look, I don't know what to tell you—they were there." Jake let out a loud sigh.

"Let's just say you're right—and I'm not saying you are," said Seneca. "If they appear and move in such a way that Conner and I can't see them, you know what it means, don't you?"

Her eyes grew wide as she stared intently at Jake. He returned a glare but didn't reply as he stroked his fingers through his hair.

"Great!" Jake moaned.

"What does it mean? I'm confused," said Conner. "You guys have gotta fill me in here."

"She's saying it's a power I've picked up from the crystals," said Jake.

"Exactly," replied Seneca. "You have a new ability."

"That's cool, I guess, but—" Conner stopped in midsentence and decided to keep his opinion to himself. He knew Jake was on edge, so criticizing his newfound ability was probably not wise.

"But what?" Jake asked.

"Never mind—just forget I said anything," said Conner.

"Tell me. I can take it," said Jake.

"Okay, here it goes," said Conner. "I just don't know how that ability is going to help us defeat Brigara. Don't get me wrong. I think it's fierce and all, but having the power to make those fire spheres would be better."

"Oh, is that all? Yeah, you've got a point there," said Jake. "Fireballs would be astounding!"

"You two are kidding, right?" Seneca said. She couldn't believe what she was hearing. "You mean to tell me that being able to see things that no one else can see isn't awesome?"

Jake and Conner exchanged looks of puzzlement, shrugged, and then shook their heads.

"Come on! You saw those wispy things, and we didn't even know they were around. You totally warned us," said Seneca. "What if they were evil or wanted to attack? We'd be dead meat right now."

"Hmm. Nah, I still vote for the fireballs," said Conner.

"I kind of have to agree with him," said Jake.

"You two are so dense! Anyone can make a fire sphere. Rileau told me," she said. "I really doubt that anyone can be taught to see what can't be seen with the naked eye."

"Well, you have a good point there, but I'm not sure how it will come in handy when we have to square off with our bio teacher," said Jake.

"Oh, wow, I just realized something," said Seneca.

"What—that we're right?" asked Conner. "And that a flaming fire sphere trumps seeing better than anyone?"

"No, don't be ridiculous. And no, you're not right," said Seneca as she glared at him in frustration. "Jake, don't you remember what happened with Leander?"

"Yeah, I think so. You mean the cuffs I saw?" asked Jake.

"Cuffs? What cuffs? You never said what you saw," said Seneca. "You never even mentioned you actually saw anything."

"I know. I was confused, and we were focused on getting the portal. I didn't think it was worth talking about," said Jake.

"Well, we're going to talk about it all right! I'm sure it's super important, and we should probably tell Rileau about it as soon as we get back," said Seneca with authority. She stood up and shook her finger an inch away from Jake's nose. "I mean it—tell him!"

"Settle down, Seneca—it's nothing," he groaned. "I'll talk to him."

"You can't hold out on stuff. It might be significant to saving all of us."

"Calm down. I said I'd tell him. Just chill already!" Jake huffed.

Her wings suddenly flashed in a full spread. She thrust them hard to create a swell of wind. Jake was lifted off his feet and blown into Conner. The impact sent them stumbling with legs entangled. They hit the ground hard and tumbled over into a heap.

"Okay, that came out of nowhere," said Conner as he pushed Jake off his chest and got back on his feet.

"Whoa! When did you learn that?" Jake asked as he winced. He'd hit the ground hard, and a sharp pain shot through his shoulder. "Now who's keeping stuff a secret?"

"Cool, huh?" Seneca replied. She smirked in satisfaction. "That felt really good, actually. Sort of a cathartic release, I'd say."

"Well, as long as you feel better," replied Jake as he stood and dusted his pants off.

"I do, so thank you!"

"Okay, I agree with you. You can stop the badgering. I'll tell Rileau about what I saw when we were at Leander," said Jake with a huff. He knew she was right, but he didn't care for her tactics in making her point.

"I thought Shayna had the gift of persuasion. That was unexpected and impressive." Conner snorted as he braced for another blast.

Seneca smirked. She thought it was a funny comparison. She preferred the direct approach to getting her way. "And, Jake, don't leave out the part about what you saw today. Conner and I didn't, so you have to." She acknowledged his slow nod as enough of an agreement.

"I'm getting tired of waiting. The sooner we get Shayna, the better. It's time we learn how to use our powers. If this perplex is supposed to bond us together, then we need to make it happen already," Jake grumbled.

"Maybe we're in the wrong place, or Rileau's friend is a no-show," said Conner.

"This looks like the place he described," said Jake. "There's the fir tree with the swirl carved in the trunk right next to the pond."

He slowly scanned the area and started to shrug but paused. He saw movement in the corner of his eye. He looked up just as a body dropped from the trees and landed right in front of them. He leaped back and startled Conner, causing him to let out a loud squeal. Conner stumbled awkwardly into Jake and stepped squarely on Jake's instep.

"Ouch!" Jake cried, and he shoved Conner aside.

"Sorry," Conner said sheepishly. He stared blankly. He was baffled by the sudden appearance. Seneca grabbed his arm, and he instinctively pushed her behind him.

"Did she just come out of the trees?" Seneca said quietly.

"Yeah, I think she did," said Conner as he surveyed the mesmerizing girl poised before them.

Jake readied and widened his stance in anticipation of an attack. "Who are you?" he asked sternly. His voice bellowed deeply.

She smirked but did not reply. It was obvious she was waiting for them to take in her presence as she began moving slowly in a circle, making eye contact with each of them. She held her gaze beyond the uncomfortable point. She looked over her shoulder briefly and then drove her staff into the ground. She showed no signs of intimidation as she adjusted the long bronze sash slung low across her middle. She turned down the tops of her thigh-high snakeskin boots and positioned them just below her knees. She placed her hands on her hips, turned to face them, and glared but didn't utter a word.

"I bet Shayna would have boot envy if she saw those," whispered Seneca as she moved out into the open but remained close to Conner. He was too mesmerized to respond.

"H-hello," said Jake. It sounded more like a question than he'd intended. His voice raised an octave. He scowled at how uncomfortable he felt when talking to girls.

"Hello," she replied. She made eye contact with Jake for a brief moment before she acknowledged Conner and Seneca. "I am Wren." Her voice was pleasant, and her expression was serious.

"I'm Seneca." She felt extremely small and made an attempt to adjust her posture by raising her chin to add a bit of height.

"Hi. I'm Conner." His tongue stuck to the roof of his dry mouth. An involuntary clicking sound followed. He resisted saying more.

Jake shot a look at him, but all he could do was shake his head in disbelief. He knew they were all taken aback by her presence, so he couldn't fault Conner for his reaction.

She was a statuesque beauty adorned in a dark emerald full-length velvet cloak that draped loosely around her. She pushed back the oversized hood, revealing long, thick ringlets of scarlet hair that cascaded down her bodice and well beyond her waist. Her hair was held in place by a delicate, intricately detailed antique gold and jeweled headdress. It came to a point and rested between her perfectly arched brows. Her rich caramel skin was the perfect canvas for her large, vibrant hazel eyes. She smiled slightly for a moment, but her expression returned to its previous stern glare. She held her shoulders back with an air of confidence.

"Why aren't you more aware of your surroundings?" she asked sternly. "Surely you have been warned of the danger that seeks you."

"You just came out of nowhere—bam! Ambush, you know," Conner said.

"We all come from somewhere. What an odd sentiment you have stated," she said as she stepped closer.

"You just caught us off guard. That's all," said Jake.

"Certainly, you were told of my arrival. Otherwise, you wouldn't be here, correct?"

"Sure, we were told to expect you, so we weren't completely thrown off," said

Jake. "Just didn't know you'd appear out of the trees."

"Strange way to make an entrance, if you ask me," added Conner. "Rileau didn't mention we were training with a ninja."

"Nor did he inform me you were slug-witted," she replied flatly.

"Do you really think insults are the best way to start out when you first meet someone?" asked Seneca. She could feel her wings tingling, but she was mastering her control and kept them relaxed.

"You might only be insulted if you believe the sentiment to bear truth," Wren snapped in response. "Your actions will determine what the mouth may or may not reveal."

"Well, aren't you the bearer of positivity?" said Seneca sarcastically. "Rileau didn't tell us you were so warm and friendly. Remind me to share the greeting we've received."

She felt accosted by Wren and her demeaning remarks. Wren eyed her and seemed to measure her response before speaking. Seneca was pleased that her grumbling wasn't lost on her.

"It would seem Rileau most certainly has had his hands full in dealing with the lot of you," she scoffed as she unlatched the clasp of her cloak and removed it. "I am here as he requested and will do all I have promised."

They kept their eyes on her as she stalked slowly to a row of moss-covered tree stumps of varying sizes. She considered a few options before deciding to toss her cloak and a gold leather satchel atop the largest of them. Jake caught a glimpse of the satchel and could tell it was stuffed with something lumpy. He was curious and made a note to inquire if she didn't reveal its contents at some point.

"You must focus on the unexpected. Consider all possibilities of an attack—even ninja." She looked squarely at Conner with a raised eyebrow.

"Well, that should come in handy." Conner laughed. "Defense against ninja invasions is at the top of my list."

He knew her comment was targeted as a jab, but he had dealt with harsher verbal squabbles from his siblings and teammates. He believed making light of the situation helped to diffuse matters. She tilted her head and examined Conner from head to toe, but she didn't reply. Instead, she began tightening the laces of her gloves. She used her teeth as an anchor as she tied and knotted the excess laces around her wrists. She flexed her hands and seemed pleased with the feel of the gloves as she stroked them in admiration. Jake and Conner watched her in silence. Seneca observed them watching the ritual and rolled her eyes.

"Dense as mushrooms!" Wren muttered under her breath.

Jake was unaffected by Wren's insult. He was distracted by the elaborate crest on her iron breastplate. It was composed of a symbol with three interlocked fish set in a raised position at the center of a gold shield. He figured the symbol represented something important since it was also on her gold-armored wrist and forearm bands. She was a warrior from head to toe. He found her staff to be the most impressive. He was enamored by the intertwined roan-colored wood. It was just a few inches taller than she. It had gouges and scrapes in various places. He deduced it had likely been involved in a multitude of battles. The topper was a crystal amethyst globe held in place by four gilded supporting prongs. It had a hazy glow, and he sensed it had magical elements; he was convinced it was powerful.

"How long were you up in that tree anyway?" Conner asked.

"Long enough to grow irritated with your endless gibbering," said Wren. "I thought dragons droned on."

"Now that you mention it, Rileau does talk an awful lot," replied Conner. "Gets a bit annoying."

"Quite," said Wren.

"Dude, she's saying we talk more than him!" Jake said.

"Oh, right. Yeah, I know," said Conner.

"Are we going to learn to use weapons to take Brigara and her minions out?" Seneca asked in an attempt to get the topic back on their mission.

"Do you believe you are equipped to battle the likes of Brigara?" asked Wren. "Give it ample thought before you spew out any answer."

"My answer is that we are not equipped," said Jake.

Seneca shot a look at Jake. She did not care for his jumping in before she had a chance to reply, although she did agree that they were not equipped.

"Then why are you in the Otherworld? This is a waste of my time! I could be off with the others and preparing for her return," Wren said. Her face was flushed as she jabbed her staff into the ground. Jake instinctively looked at the crystal, but there was no change.

"A waste of your time? Are you kidding me?" asked Jake.

"You lack skills, awareness, and training!" said Wren.

"Why are you so angry?" Seneca asked. "I thought that's what we're here for—you know, to get training on how to get Shayna back."

"Yeah, what gives?" said Jake. "Rileau told us you would help with the perplex."

"If you do not believe that you are equipped to put an end to Brigara, then there is nothing I can do," she said. Her anger was still present as she glared at them. "You must consider that your companion Shayna will surely be lost to another realm. You cannot have doubts as we face this war. Brigara will capitalize on this weakness, as you wear it so prominently."

"How the heck are we supposed to have confidence in something we've never done before?" Jake asked.

"Do you not possess any esteem at all? Do you not walk in the belief of limitless possibilities? Rileau did not inform me of your simple minds," she said.

"Excuse me! Why are you acting so rude? You're supposed to be here to help. Stop giving us your sermon on how we are beneath you!" Seneca yelled.

Seneca was livid. Her wings expanded and flashed brighter than Jake had ever witnessed. He felt an instant wave of heat. The tips of her wings glowed as she pulled them back and spread them wide. Conner stumbled back from the turbulent force they created.

"Whoa!" said Conner. "I seriously didn't see that coming."

"Me neither," said Jake. He knew it was time to step in to deescalate the tension. "Obviously, we need your help, and you're either going to give it to us, or you're not. Let's calm down and talk this out—please be reasonable."

Wren did not acknowledge Jake's plea, as she was fixated on Seneca. Her eyes locked in a stare-down with Seneca. He worried it was potentially the beginning of a magical brawl.

"Look, we're all supposed to be on the same team. It's us against Brigara, right?" asked Jake. "Maybe we can call a time-out, maybe a truce or something."

Wren and Seneca remained unmoved and silent. Jake was startled but pretended not to notice the edges of Seneca's wings turning a brilliant cobalt blue. Sparks flickered at the tips. He could feel his heart beating hard and fast. He knew that was not a good sign. He prayed they weren't about to erupt into an all-out knockout fest. He held his breath when Seneca moved several steps closer to Wren. He had experienced a small glimpse of how gutsy she was, but he thought she was taking it a bit too far.

"Hold up, Seneca!" he shouted to no avail.

She was on a mission of confrontation, and he feared there was nothing he could do to stop her. As if she sensed his fear, she took in a deep breath and shifted her stance slightly. She looked at Jake, and he read her expression to mean she wasn't going to do anything foolish. He tried to relax but couldn't.

"I'm sure slander by a trainer ranks somewhere on the list of not-to-dos," said Seneca. "It comes down to this, plain and simple. You either help us figure out this perplex thing and get our friend back, or you can just go climb back in your tree. In either case, you need to stop with the putdowns."

"Get ready for a blast from the wings!" Conner said. He was only moderately kidding as he stepped back a few feet. He identified an old oak tree to dive behind if needed.

"I seem to have lit a much-needed fire under you," said Wren. "Your surge of spirit will serve you well in battle. Restrain it, or your anger will cloud your judgment." She stopped suddenly, and her body became rigid.

Something or someone had caught her attention. Wren grabbed her staff and gestured for the threesome to follow her. Seneca felt her body tremble. She rarely felt such rage, and shutting it down wasn't easy; she took a deep breath in an effort to refocus. She counted slowly to ten. Her wings relaxed, and she opened her hands. She had balled them so tightly that nail imprints were embedded in her palms.

"Remind me to stay on your good side," Conner whispered to Seneca.

She huffed in response and walked ahead of him to create distance. Wren led the way to the edge of the pond. She pointed her staff in the direction of a lone bullfrog. Its wide body was perched on a partially submerged log.

"It is time," she said. Her voice was airy and light.

"Is she talking to that fat frog or us?" asked Conner.

"I guess we wait and see," said Jake.

"I can hear you. While you may find it unbearable, remain silent, please," said Wren as she closed her eyes. "You must always become tuned into your surroundings—that bullfrog is an emissary and has gathered much from our encounter."

"The frog is working for Brigara?" asked Conner as he lowered his voice and craned his neck to get a closer look.

"Things are not always as they appear on the surface—you must heed this belief at all times," said Wren as she pointed her staff in direct alignment to the frog.

The illuminated amethyst orb brightened. The bullfrog's yellow throat expanded. It sensed danger and let out a deep baritone croak. Wren aimed the staff directly at it. The frog pushed off with its hind legs and leaped high while stretching its wide body to full length. It was attempting to escape. The globe emitted a charge of light and shot across the water. The beam hit the target in midair just as it transformed into a squatty, scruffy black-bearded man. His eyes closed, and his mouth gaped open before he exploded into a barrage of sparks and ash. Fragments of what remained spread across the water's surface.

"Wow. Did that just happen?" Conner said softly. "You just took him out like a mosquito. I didn't see that coming."

Wren lowered her staff and turned to the threesome. They stood motionless as they gawked at the water, searching for any sign or remains of the frog man.

"That's a powerful weapon you're holding there," said Jake. "Are you sure it was necessary to obliterate him completely?"

"I am quite sure. His task was to do the same to us," said Wren. "That was Scarge from the forest of Praves. He was infused with dark magic and would have killed us all."

"It's good you were here, because I sure didn't have a clue," said Conner. "He just looked like any ordinary bullfrog—enormous but otherwise just a regular frog."

"How did you know?" asked Seneca.

"An ordinary frog would not pass up the tempting dragonflies that meandered within reach of its tongue," said Wren. "Frogs have a voracious appetite. He was quite inadequate in adapting to his elected form."

"The crazy thing is that I could swear I heard it giggle just before it was zapped into dust," said Jake.

"Me too!" shouted Seneca. "I thought I was just imagining it."

"Here's an even stranger thought," said Jake. "I may have crossed paths with it before. It happened when Seneca and I were fighting those nasty acid puking fairies."

"Seriously?" asked Conner.

"I fed it one of the fairies. At the time, I didn't think it reacted right, but I just brushed it off as another strange thing in the Otherworld," said Jake.

"That is not a good sign," said Wren sternly. "He is known as a skilled tracker."

"Have you dealt with him before?" asked Seneca.

"Yes, I have. He led the attack on the fairies of Fionia two moons ago. He escaped and was the lone survivor," said Wren. "I knew we would cross paths again, as his kind will always resurface."

"As in the Lake of Fionia, where Celestia's from?" asked Jake. "Is she okay?"

"There were no casualties of fairies," said Wren. "They are fierce and wield great magic. Celestia is quite safe." Her tone reflected a sense of pride.

"Are you a fairy?" asked Seneca. "You haven't really told us anything about yourself or where you're from."

"I am an elemental, as are many in the Otherworld," said Wren. "I am an elf, to be precise. I am from the clan of Evan."

"An elf? I totally pictured elves as roly-poly, short guys with pointed ears," said Conner.

"I think what Conner is trying to say is that, uh, you know, you're quite unique," said Jake. He felt like kicking himself for stumbling over his words.

"More like extraordinary," said Conner. His flushed cheeks framed a wide grin.

"Actually, I'm not," she snapped, and she took a long pause before continuing. She calmed her tone and spoke with controlled authority. "It is you who have qualities like no others before you. Be thankful of your inherent gifts as well as those bestowed upon you. Not all elementals are allowed to experience the gifts of magic, as they are born into this world without it. Only a few have lives precisely charted in prophecies. Do not focus on outer appearances, as they can be lures for cruel deceptions."

Jake could feel the heat rushing to his ears. He caught a glimpse of a snobbish expression just before Wren turned away. She was not pleased. He hadn't intended to anger her and prayed that he wouldn't be the next target for her staff.

"Sorry if I said something wrong," he mumbled as he shifted his weight and cast his eyes downward.

"Guess you blew that one, huh?" Conner whispered. "You're not at all smooth with the ladies."

"Hey! You've gotta be kidding—you suck at it too!" Jake tried to keep his voice down but had an uneasy feeling he was overheard. He decided to drop the topic before getting even more embarrassed.

"I'd like to learn more about the different kinds of elementals. Each time we turn around, we're being told about another type," said Seneca. "It's like there's this endless list in the Otherworld. Can you tell us about elves?"

"There is truth in what you say, Seneca," Wren replied flatly. "I will say this much: to be of the elf clan means to be strong. We are warriors and are aligned with the ancient ways of the forest. Our gifts are rooted in nature and, as such, are unpredictable. Now, let us proceed with the vanquishing of the perplex."

"You do realize that's sort of a cliffhanger you just threw at us, don't you?" asked Conner.

"I do not understand what you imply," said Wren. Her brow furrowed as she glared at him. "We must prepare for the release of your friend. The time is nearly upon us."

"I have a question. It's probably not relevant to the perplex, but if you wouldn't mind answering, it could really help," Seneca said meekly as she shot Jake a look.

"What is your question?" Wren asked without any attempt to disguise her impatience.

"Seneca, don't!" Jake protested, but he knew it was pointless. He started to reach for her but thought better of it. He shoved his hands deep into his pockets. He grunted under his breath and winced as Seneca cleared her throat.

"Jake claims to have seen some floating things—some kind of beings. He saw them floating over the lake. Conner and I didn't see them," said Seneca. She could feel Jake's eyes burning a hole in the back of her head. She resisted communicating telepathically. She refused to be distracted from getting an answer. Instead, she did something impulsive and regretted it the instant it happened: she looked over her shoulder, stuck her tongue out, and rolled her eyes before whipping her head back around to Wren.

"Did she just—"

"Let it go, Conner!" Jake snapped.

"I said we could talk about it with Rileau," Jake grumbled.

He knew it was a weak rebuttal. He wasn't completely against bringing up the idea with Wren, but seeing things no one else could wasn't something he wanted to discuss. What if she thought he was delusional? He let out a heavy sigh. Conner instinctively gave him a comforting pat on the shoulder.

"Is there a question coming, or can we move on with our preparation?" asked Wren dryly.

"What I wanted to ask is about what Jake thinks he saw," Seneca said through clenched teeth. "Do you know if it's real?"

"I cannot say. What specifically did you see, Jake?" Wren's eyes narrowed as she jabbed her staff deep into a mound of dirt and placed her hands on her slender hips.

"These wispy things—maybe I just imagined them," he muttered while looking at the ground.

"Tell me more!" she commanded.

She was skilled at exerting an aura of intimidation. Jake knew it was useless to resist. He sighed heavily.

"There were four of them, I think—right there over the water." He pointed to the area where he'd last seen them. Immediately, his finger began to shake. "They're back! Do you see them?" He pushed Wren toward the edge of the pond. He was anxious for any confirmation of his sanity.

"Uh, nope," Conner replied as he shook his head.

"I'm talking to Wren! Can you see them? They're coming this way. I'm telling you—they're right there hovering or gliding!" Jake said.

He was frantic and searched for any sign of confirmation from Wren. He couldn't tell from her expression if she believed him or not. She remained quiet and just looked out across the water.

"Sheesh! You've gotta be kidding me. Am I just imagining this?" Jake ran his fingers through his hair. It was damp with perspiration.

"Wren, do you see what Jake's talking about?" asked Seneca as she eased next to him.

"No, but he is correct. The Glactra are approaching," she said slowly.

"Glactra, huh? So I'm not seeing things. There is something out there—Glactra," Jake said. He was relieved. He felt even more nervous at the realization that there was something out there as he wiped a stream of sweat from his brow.

"How do you know it's the, um, Glactra things if you can't see them?" asked Conner.

"See the ripples in the water? They're uniform and moving in the opposite direction of the water's natural state," replied Wren. "It's a clear sign they're moving and heading in this direction."

"Are they another Brigara nightmare ready to pounce?" Seneca asked as she flared her wings. The tips flashed a shade of electric blue.

"They are not our enemy. Glactra are neutral during strife and usually act as observers," Wren explained.

"Usually?" Jake said. "Can you clarify that?"

"They do not enter battles unless they deem it necessary."

"Does that mean they might choose to take the side of evil?" asked Seneca.

"That is not what I've stated. Glactra are neutral. If elected, they will resolve the divergence until it is neutralized," said Wren. She lowered herself to one knee and examined the water's movement.

"They won't harm us?" asked Conner. "Are you sure?"

"They will do what is necessary to stabilize conflict," Wren replied.

"That's not the answer I was hoping for." Conner scratched his head. "Hard to fight something you can't even see."

"If it were your fate for the Glactra to be involved, you would be unable to fight, even if they were in your direct line of sight."

"They sound dangerous. Why am I the only one seeing them?" asked Jake. "Are they coming for me?"

"I do not understand why you have been given this gift. It is rare," said Wren. "I suggest you speak up. Ask of their presence and why they have remained for you to see."

"Talk to them? Seriously?" he said nervously.

Jake backed away from the water. He was afraid to blink as he watched them steadily glide in his direction. Their pace remained slow and steady. Jake tried to focus on their delicate details; he wanted to relay what he saw accurately. They continued to move closer, and he sensed they were not changing their course.

"Aye, Jake. You must speak," Wren said stiffly.

"I should ask them—you think I should actually talk to them?"

"Why not? Fear is your only limitation. Why let it control your fate?" Wren asked.

"Uh, what do I say? I mean, what should I ask them?" Jake asked as he turned to Seneca and Conner. "Any suggestions? They're getting pretty close."

"How about asking them what they want and why we can't see them too," said Conner.

"That's brilliant, Conner. I agree. Ask them that," said Seneca.

Jake searched for confirmation from Wren, but she remained transfixed on the water.

"They're moving this way—straight for us. Do I ask now or wait for them to get really close?" asked Jake. His voice cracked as he tried to settle his nerves.

"I am positive they have heard all we have discussed," said Wren flatly. She retrieved her staff and ushered Jake to the edge of the pond. "Pose your questions."

"Will they answer?"

"I do not know. You should be aware that they serve another purpose," said Wren as she watched the ripples in the pond.

"What is it?" Seneca asked anxiously.

"They keep track of elemental gifts. They are known to reveal themselves to the young. I recall seeing them once as a small child. I was first learning about my gifts of agility. I can climb the tallest of trees without much effort," she replied proudly.

"Yeah, and hide in them too," Conner muttered.

"Do you think that's why they're here—to record our gifts?" Jake asked.

"Perhaps, but not likely," said Wren. "You will not know their purpose unless you ask. They have revealed themselves only to you."

Jake stood motionless as he gathered his thoughts. It was alarming to know he was the only one able to see them. Their ethereal presence appeared fragile, but he reminded himself that he shouldn't be fooled by that. He looked across the water and saw their movement was slow but deliberate. There was no mistaking their intent. They were coming for him. He braced himself as he let out a slow exhalation.

"You can do this, Jake," Seneca whispered. She was nervous and tried to hide it. She didn't want to add to his noticeable anxiety. She maneuvered next to him on his right, and Conner eased in on his left.

"You've got this, man." Conner gave him a hardy slap on the back.

"Hello. I'm Jake," he said more softly than intended. He cleared the phlegm gathering in his throat. "I was—I mean, we are wondering if we can ask you a few questions."

Wren pointed to the water. Seneca saw it too. The murky green water was as still as glass. Not even the slightest ripple could be detected.

"Are they gone?" Seneca whispered as she grabbed Jake's hand.

"No, they're just dangling in midair. They stopped moving," he said quietly.

For the first time since he had caught a glimpse of them, the Glactra's movement came to a halt. Their airy transparent forms were suspended. Even the gentle breeze causing the tall grass and flowers to sway had no effect on them.

"I don't know what happened, but they're just—I don't know— frozen or something. They aren't moving at all," said Jake as he looked to Wren for some guidance. "What did I do?"

"Ask your question again," she replied. "This time, only represent yourself. Do not include us."

"If you say so, but I doubt that's the problem. Maybe we're not supposed to talk to them."

"We are not. It is you who is conversing," said Wren.

Jake stared at the Glactra and thought how out of place they looked. The image of a possum rolling over to play dead flashed in his head. He wondered if their response was a defense mechanism. Then he remembered what Wren had said about their power, and he rationalized there had to be another explanation. Either way, he was curious about his ability to see them as much as their reaction to it.

"Excuse me. I would like to talk to you, if you don't mind," Jake said. "I am able to see you clearly, while others cannot. Is there a reason for this?"

Before he could exhale, one of the Glactra zipped to within inches of his face. Jake's head jerked back in response. He didn't dare run, even though every brain cell in his head was screaming, telling him that was exactly what he should be doing. He felt Seneca tighten her grip. He could tell she was reading his thoughts. In a strange way, that allowed him to relax a bit. The being didn't move. It hovered with its ice-blue eyes transfixed on Jake's. It opened its mouth wide, forming an elongated oval almost as large as its head. Jake was startled, but he didn't move.

"You have returned, yet you did not retrieve what is yours." It spoke with the voice of many. It transmitted high and low tones. The voices were a blend of both male and female as well as what sounded like a young child. The voices blended together but were slightly out of sync. Some words finished with an echo of others. The mouth did not open and close or move with the words; it remained open in the same position as a syphon for the sounds.

"We will not interfere unless you refuse to claim what is yours," the Glactra said, using a lower register of tones. Jake couldn't detect the child's voice and found himself waiting to hear it. Somehow, hearing a child speak helped to create a safe zone. He pushed the thought out of his head immediately and concentrated on the message.

"What am I supposed to claim? We've accepted that we're the dominion that's supposed to stop Brigara—is that what you mean?"

"Are they talking to you, Jake?" asked Conner.

"Quiet! Do not disturb him!" Wren grumbled.

Jake resisted answering and waited for clarification.

"You and only you must retrieve what belongs to you. They must not be left, as she will find them and disrupt the balance."

The voice rattled loudly. The other Glactra in waiting hummed on cue like a well-rehearsed choir. Jake assumed it was their way of agreeing. Upon completion, the lone Glactra returned to the others.

They remained unmoving momentarily before gliding in concert to the far side of the pond. He tried hard not to blink until he could no longer see any sign of them. He released his hand from Seneca's and paced around in a circle.

"Well, I'm sure you caught all of that, right, Seneca?"

"Caught what? I tried to read your mind, but it was all blocked off. I got worried. That's why I was gripping your hand. That's it."

"What did they say?" Conner asked. "Did they tell you why you can see them?"

"Uh, actually, they didn't, and now they're gone."

"What did they say?" asked Seneca.

"Actually, only one spoke, but it was like it was talking for all of them. It had a lot of voices—hard to explain," Jake replied.

"Never mind that. What did they say?" Seneca asked.

"It—or they—said I have to get what belongs to me or something like that. I have to retrieve what I left behind. It really didn't give much detail. To be honest, it was creepy."

"Do you know what she was referencing?" asked Wren. "Do you know what you must retrieve?"

"How do you know it was a she?" Jake replied.

"It is the way it has always been. Do you know the reference of her directive?" Wren's voice was forceful.

"I might have a clue," Seneca said. She raised an eyebrow as she glared at Jake.

"Yeah, I'm guessing the same thing. We should tell Rileau about this so we can figure out what we need to do," he said.

"Can somebody clue me in?" asked Conner.

"Later!" Seneca snapped. "We've got to focus on Shayna."

"I am curious, but I agree—it must wait. Our mission is to release Shayna from the perplex," Wren said sternly. "We must move quickly, as this area has been exposed to the enemy."

"What do we do?" asked Seneca.

"Follow me is what you do!" snapped Wren.

Seneca sensed Wren wasn't happy because they weren't forthcoming about what they suspected. She felt Jake was right in not divulging too much information. They needed to talk to Rileau, the one they trusted the most to guide them, especially if it meant another trip to Leander.

"Let's get to higher ground," said Wren.

Conner trailed a little too close and nearly stumbled into Wren more than once. Seneca watched Jake's eyes drift off into the distance. She wondered if the Glactra were still lurking in the distance or if he was hoping for their return. She followed Wren without disturbing him. She knew he would join them without prompting. Jake turned and watched Seneca walk away. He had hoped she would offer some solace. He took a deep breath and sauntered quietly behind her. They listened as Wren began explaining how to free Shayna from the perplex.

"The way to break a perplex is to feed it," Wren said. "You must provide the answers to release the hold."

"How do you feed magic?" asked Seneca. "Provide answers? Do we even know the question?"

"You must give it exactly what it needs. To strengthen the dominion bond, you must provide the answers to prove your connection is true and pure," said Wren. "Once you do, the perplex charm is broken."

"If we answer correctly, then—poof—Shayna's back?" Conner asked. "That's it?"

"There is always a balance with magic. There is give and take. Once you feed the perplex, it gives back what it is holding on to—Shayna. It is magic of light, so it will respond in a positive way if fed correctly."

"Does that happen with all magic?" Jake asked as he wedged between Seneca and Conner.

"Not exactly. However, there's always a counter to any curse with an origin of dark magic," said Wren. "The crux is finding a counter-spell by detecting the seam of light. It's always there, as there cannot be darkness without it."

"Just to be clear, you're saying dark magic can't be done without light or good magic?" Seneca asked.

"Dark magic has no origin of its own. All magic starts out as that of light, as its essence is to bring harmony," said Wren. "It is only through corruption that light magic succumbs to darkness."

"So that's why you say there's a seam of light—it's like a coat over the good magic," said Jake. "We find the crack in the dark magic, and we're golden!"

"If we are done with the questions, then let us begin," said Wren.

"Right. I'm sure Shayna is complaining that we're taking way too long," said Jake.

"Perplexes exist with the notion that you will solve one question," said Wren. "The question is always the same. You must feed it by knowing the captive one's greatest love."

"Well, that's easy," said Conner. "It's gotta be those boots she's always going on about."

"She's not that shallow!" Seneca snapped. She frowned at Conner and shook her head with discontent. "It's her family. Shayna loves her family—that's her greatest love."

"I have to agree with Seneca on this one," said Jake. "She was pretty torn up when Dreya died, and she'd only known her for like a second."

"She pretends like she's detached, but she really loves her family," added Seneca.

"Whatever. I still say it's the boots, but if you guys say family, then we can go with it," said Conner.

"It is love of family?" asked Wren.

"Yes, family," said Seneca. She looked to Jake and Conner for confirmation, and they both nodded in agreement. Conner mumbled something inaudible and then grunted before folding his arms in protest.

"You must now use the power of projection to disengage the charm by tapping in on the love for her family," said Wren.

"The power of projection?" Jake repeated.

"How are we supposed to do that?" asked Seneca. "It sounds complicated."

"Only the first time, and then it becomes easier," said Wren. "The important thing is not to doubt your intentions, as the perplex will only allow one try."

"Excuse me. One try?" Jake asked. "What happens if we have it wrong—if her family isn't her greatest love?"

"Then she will be enveloped in the perplex for eternity or be released to a realm unknown," said Wren. Her tone was even, and there was no change in the inflection in her voice.

"Hold on a minute—this is just a drill, though, like a training exercise. Shayna's not really in danger, right?" asked Seneca. "Or is she?"

"Magic is not a game. The perplex is pure. As such, there is a possibility Shayna will not be released to us," said Wren. "Did Rileau not make this clear?"

"Rileau did make it clear," said Jake. "I'm just hoping Shayna's not in any danger."

"The perplex is the closest charm to banishing one to the Inbetween," replied Wren.

"He said that too," Seneca said flatly. "He explained it wasn't the same as what happened to Brigara but that she could end up in another realm."

"No, it is not the same. You must be aware that Brigara is skilled at conjuring a perplex and may use it to neutralize threats as retribution. As you have discovered, you do not need a triad to cast it," she said.

"So that's why Rileau decided on it. Makes sense, I guess," Jake said inaudibly as he thought about the logic behind the strategy.

"It serves two purposes: first to bond the dominion tighter and second to warn that Brigara might use it against us," said Seneca. "Yeah, Rileau left that second part out."

"It would seem so," said Wren. "No need to dwell on what you cannot change."

"She's safe, right?" asked Conner.

"Within the perplex, Shayna is safe. If our attempt to release her fails, then she might be released beyond our reach. She would remain there until her time ends," said Wren.

"We should have asked more questions!" shouted Seneca. She pulled at her hair and spun around in a circle. "This is so frustrating!"

"Talk about fine-print disclaimers. We definitely shouldn't have signed on for this one," added Conner.

"How much time do we have?" asked Seneca frantically.

"Not nearly enough for you to vacillate. You must not wrestle with fear, as you will never persevere," said Wren.

"You're acting as if we're making an easy decision here. This is our friend we're talking about," Seneca grumbled.

"Then you must do whatever it takes to save her. You must not hesitate or deliberate. You have to act now," said Wren. "Do you think you will have time to weigh your options if you are being thrashed with killing spells?"

Wren turned away from Seneca and swiftly moved to inches from Jake. He could feel her icy breath on his face.

"What is your decision?" she asked firmly. Her eyes were fixed on his, and he resisted blinking.

"We get Shayna out of the perplex—now!" he replied. He felt the urge to salute, but he resisted.

"Let's do this. Shayna needs us!" Conner shouted.

"What's next, Wren?" asked Seneca. Her wings fluttered quickly. She wiped her damp hands on her jeans. She felt exhausted and nervous. She knew they didn't have a clue what they were doing.

"Trust your instincts. They are your greatest guide and weapon," said Wren. "Know it to be true—beyond doubt, fear, and vision."

"Got it. What do we have to do?" asked Seneca.

"You have declared her greatest love to be family," said Wren. "You must be sure, as there is no second chance. Is it now clear to all of you?"

"Maybe we need to discuss this some more," said Conner. "What if we get it wrong?"

"We're doing it, Conner. Get a grip!" said Jake. "You're sure, right, Seneca?"

"I think so. I know it's a risk, but I truly believe Shayna loves her family. There's no greater love for her," said Seneca. "And before you say anything, Conner, it's not the boots."

"If you say so," replied Conner. "Family it is. I'm on board."

"Okay, Wren. We're ready," said Jake. He draped his arm around Seneca's shoulders.

He was shaking, but she pretended not to notice. She reached for Conner's hand, and it almost slid away with the amount of perspiration pooling in his palm. She gripped it hard, and he gave a gentle squeeze in return.

"We need to get Shayna back, so we're sticking with it. Family has to be the answer. I trust—I mean, we trust Seneca," said Jake.

He smiled down at her and could hear her words being planted in his thoughts. He grabbed hold of her hand and gave it a gentle pat before pressing her fingers to interlock with his.

Thank you, Jake. We'll get her back.

"I only need one of you to recite what I tell you. It will be you, Seneca," said Wren. Her voice was a flat monotone.

"Got it."

"Seneca, Jake, and Conner, you must each pay close attention. Keep your hands joined, and do not release—no matter what happens. You must maintain your connection. Let us begin. Do exactly as I instruct."

Wren stretched out her arms with her palms facing up. Seneca and Jake watched her actions as Conner closed his eyes. Jake noticed and shook his hand to get his attention.

"What? Huh?" Conner muttered.

"Pay attention!" snapped Jake.

Seneca took a deep breath and held it. She could feel her palms perspiring, but she tightened her grip on Jake's hand to ensure a secure hold.

"Recite after me," said Wren. "Eadrom sos fidjum."

Seneca complied. She felt her body begin to warm as she repeated the charm.

"Love of family shall be the twine that breaks the bind," said Wren. "Now you, Seneca."

"Love of family shall be the twine that breaks the vine—uh, I mean bind," said Seneca as she glared down at her hands. They were a vibrant scarlet, yet the heat they generated was tolerable. She glanced down to see Jake's and Conner's were the same hue. She clutched harder.

"We are done," said Wren. "You may release your hold."

Wren lowered her arms and picked up her staff. She walked to a nearby tree stump draped in moss. She sat down and crossed her legs. Seneca followed her with Conner and Jake trailing close behind.

"What's next?" asked Seneca. "Are we done?" Her voice was brittle.

"Did it work?" asked Jake. "I felt some major heat, but I thought there'd be more to it."

"Magic can be a mere flicker or nothing visible at all," she said in a matter-of-fact tone. "Do not underestimate subtleties of a spell." She closed her eyes and stretched her arms. "There is definitely magic in the air."

"Do we have to wait long?" Conner asked anxiously.

"We shall soon see," said Wren. "It should not take long to determine if you were successful."

"And if I wasn't?" asked Jake.

"We will know that as well," said Wren.

CHAPTER ELEVEN

The Reflectoire

W ren's lack of empathy disturbed Jake, but he decided not to dwell on it. He was concerned only for his friend. He spun around when he heard the sound of crackling dry leaves crunching beneath quick-moving footsteps. They all heard the sounds. Unmistakably, someone was coming toward them. Through a tapered path separating rows of fragrant and majestic eucalyptus trees emerged Shayna. She was sprinting toward them.

There were no flashing lights, smoke, or transparent thresholds to step through. It was simply Shayna, with her hair blowing behind her in the breeze. A broad smile stretched across her excited face. Seneca squealed and ran to meet her with Conner close behind. He scooped her up and twirled her around with her feet parallel to the ground before placing her down. Before Jake could take it all in and comment on Shayna's transformation, he had joined them as they danced around in an entangled embrace. The laughter and cheers were of pure joy and relief. They'd done it. They had saved their friend.

"I guess you missed me. How long was I gone?" Shayna asked as she pulled away from Conner's lingering embrace. "Did anything go wrong?" She was out of breath as she fanned her face with both hands to keep the tears from streaming down her face.

"A few hours, I think—maybe less. It's so hard to track time here," said Seneca. "I'm not really sure." She turned to Jake and Conner for support, but they stared blankly at Shayna and remained mute. "Thanks, guys," she mumbled with more disappointment than the intended sarcasm.

"What do you mean? What happened?" Shayna asked. The euphoria was instantly washed away, and her smile disappeared. "Does it have something to do with her?" She looked at Wren.

"No, she's fine; she works with Rileau. Wren's the one who showed us how to break you out of the perplex," said Seneca. "It's, um, well, it's something else, actually." She bit her bottom lip and wasn't sure how to explain what she'd seen. She looked to Jake for some sign or signal, but he looked dumbfounded.

"Hi, Wren. Thanks for your help in getting me out of the perplex thing," said Shayna.

"You are quite welcome," replied Wren as she bowed her head slightly. She extended her hand and smiled.

Seneca took a deep breath and turned Shayna around to face her. "Shayna, you have to listen. What I was trying to say is—well, uh, I mean it's that, it's like…" Seneca fumbled with finding the exact words to break the news.

"What? Spit it out already," said Shayna. "You're babbling. What are you trying to say?"

"What Seneca is trying to tell you is that you've got something on your forehead," said Conner. He pointed to the spot where their gaze was transfixed.

Shayna swept her hand across her face. "What is it? I can't feel anything," she said. "What does it look like?"

"It looks like you've got a diamond in your forehead," said Conner. "I think it looks—"

"A diamond? What the heck are you talking about?" Shayna rubbed her forehead roughly, and her hand moved in a frenzy. "Is it gone? Did I get it off?"

"No, and rubbing it all crazily like that isn't working," said Conner.

She huffed as she brushed him aside and grabbed Seneca by the shoulders. "Is it gone, Seneca?" she yelled.

"No—sorry, but it's still there," said Seneca. She peeled Shayna's hands from her shoulders and held them in hers.

"I don't think it's coming off. It really looks like it belongs there, because it's blending in pretty well with the skin around it," added Jake.

"That can't be right. There has to be a way for it to come off!" Shayna said. She spun around to face Wren. "Do you know anything about this thing they say is on my face?"

"Yes, I do. It is a *reflectoire*," said Wren. "It is quite rare, actually."

"A reflect-a-what?" asked Shayna as she moved closer to Wren. "Just spit it out! What is it?"

"A reflectoire becomes a part of your being, just as any other appendage or organ," Wren replied. Her tone was nonchalant. "You are entirely lucky in its placement. It is quite impressive."

"Lucky! Hello? Somebody please tell me she didn't just say I'm lucky," said Shayna. She looked around and noticed the others were staring in awe.

"Maybe it's not that bad," said Seneca. She knew she was treading on volatile territory, but she wanted to calm her friend down. "If Wren say's it's lucky, maybe we should find out more. We could really use some luck right now." She forced an ineffective smile.

Shayna rolled her eyes and turned to Jake as the voice of reason. "Jake, what do you think?" she asked, wide-eyed.

"I think it's cool—different, but it works for you, and it looks great," said Jake. He hadn't planned what he was going to say, but he spoke the truth. The more he thought about it, the bigger his smile became.

"Yeah, I like it too," agreed Conner. "Makes you stand out—not that you need it, but you know what I mean."

Shayna didn't react to their flattery; she wanted answers. She had just come through an experience that she hadn't had time to download to the others, and now she was feeling overwhelmed. "Rileau said nothing of the perplex having side effects—maybe he can reverse it," she said. The panic in her voice made it evident that Shayna was on the verge of a meltdown.

Seneca scrambled to grab hold of her hand. It felt cold and a bit clammy as she squeezed gently and patted her arm. Seneca glanced at the color fading from Shayna's cheeks.

"I'm sure I don't have to stay like this. Or do I? It's temporary, right?"

"It cannot be reversed, as it belongs only to you. Would you reverse your ability to have sight or the rhythm of your heart?" asked Wren. "It is as much a part of you as the other facets you value."

"I need to catch my breath," said Shayna. "This is entirely unfair. Why is this happening to me?" She wanted to cry, but the tears wouldn't come.

"Your perspective is misplaced," said Wren. "A reflectoire is bestowed upon only a few. I've never seen it granted for a demi-elemental."

"How do you know that I'm a demi-elemental?" asked Shayna. "Oh, never mind—I'm sure it's posted all over the *Prophecy Daily News*." She closed her eyes to gather her thoughts.

"That's actually funny," said Conner. "Maybe that's the side effect of having a diamond embedded in your forehead."

Shayna whipped her head around and stared at him with contempt. Seneca readied herself to intervene as she tugged her hand out of Shayna's death grip.

"Too soon?" he asked meekly. From her expression, he had his answer. "Sorry."

"Well, I think it looks more iridescent and less like a diamond. It's perfectly brilliant and beautiful," said Seneca. She hoped Shayna picked up on her sincerity and didn't view her remark as just an attempt to defuse the tension.

"Beauty isn't the most important thing. I know that. However, it would've been great to know this was a potential. It's not like this kind of thing just pops up every day. I mean, come on. Look—dead center on my forehead!" Shayna complained, pointing at her new feature.

"If anyone can relate to having appendages that suddenly appear out of nowhere, I'm your girl," said Seneca. She fluttered her wings for emphasis.

"True, but at least you can hide your wings," groaned Shayna. "Wren, is it possible to hide this reflectoire?"

"Shayna, wait!" shouted Seneca. "Don't you think you should find out more before you make it disappear?"

"Like what?" Shayna asked. "Should I figure out what color earrings to coordinate with it? Or test it out to see if I light up a room when I walk in?"

"That'd be a stellar benefit, if you ask me," said Conner as he nodded with satisfaction.

"No one asked," grumbled Jake.

"Hey, you guys know how I feel about the dark," he said. "A handy flashlight whenever you need it!"

"You're not helping, Conner!" Seneca growled.

"I'm just saying it could help a guy out, you know," Conner said just as Jake grabbed his collar and yanked him backward. He gagged slightly as his shirt tightened around his throat.

"We're not talking about you and your issues, dude. Let them handle this," said Jake sternly as he pulled him several feet away.

"Okay, got it," Conner moaned.

Jake believed that Shayna just needed time to adjust to her new facial feature. He stared at the glistening stone and its perfect placement. He thought it made her look even more exotic than when he'd first laid eyes on her. His mind flashed to the day when his mother had nearly plowed her down with their minivan. It seemed so long ago, but at that precise moment, they'd been unknowingly swept up in a spell; it was the enchantment to bind them as partners in the dominion. Upon reflection, he realized he had no regrets. He was sure he was on the right path in figuring out his life's purpose. He knew from the sudden quickening of his heart that Shayna was an essential part of it. The sensation made him smile, but the smile disappeared quickly as his instincts for providing protection rose to the surface.

"Maybe we should listen to this, Conner," Jake said. "You need to stop the crazy talk! She's freaked out enough without you trying to make her a human flashlight."

"You're right. We need to zero in and get the real down-low info," said Conner.

They quickly joined the others. Shayna paced with her hands on her hips. Her thoughts were all over the place. She was having difficulty accepting that the reflectoire was a permanent feature. She had flashes of what she'd experienced while in the perplex, but she pushed the images away. She wanted to know why she had been branded without her permission.

"Wren, why do some people get the reflectoire, and others don't?" asked Seneca. She sensed that Shayna would rather ignore it. She was sure it impacted all of them, and the more they knew, the better.

"What difference does it really make why I got it? At least we know I don't have to display it for the world to see," Shayna said before Wren could respond.

"I do not have an answer as to why you were chosen," said Wren. "I do know that having a reflectoire means you have the ability to absorb dark magic and return it to its originator."

"Are you freakin' kidding me?" Conner shouted. "That is hella awesomeness at a peak! Ricochet power!" He jumped high in the air and simulated a slam dunk. Wren watched the exhibition unmoved.

"Ignore him. Just spill it," said Shayna. "Because now you've got me interested." Her attitude flipped from outrage to intrigue. She wanted to stay composed, but she was having a hard time containing her excitement. "How does it work?"

"As I have stated, a reflectoire is rare. I am not versed in all facets," said Wren. "I do know that it is like other senses, yet it is like no other. It will react when required."

"Do you think Rileau will know more?" asked Jake.

"Perhaps," replied Wren. "He may anoint you with the guidance you will need."

"Maybe you can answer this," said Shayna. "Let's just say, for example, that I want to hide it from view—sort of use it as a surprise attack. Can I do that?"

"It is possible," said Wren. "Mastery in projecting the reflectoire into your shadow should bestow this."

"Projecting it into the shadows sounds intriguing," said Shayna. "Do you know how I do it? Can you show me?" She grinned broadly, and her eyes widened.

"No."

"No? Are you saying you don't know how, or you won't show me?"

"I will not discuss this further—I have said enough. I deplore such endless questioning," said Wren. "Direct your queries to Rileau. He may elect to teach you if he believes it to be useful in battle." Her voice quickened as she readied herself. She gathered her cloak and reattached the satchel to her belt. She gazed into the globe of her staff, and her lips tightened. "We must leave this place now, as it is not safe!"

"Seems to me you're avoiding what you obviously know something about," Shayna said with a raised eyebrow.

"The only thing I am avoiding is being attacked in the open," snapped Wren. "Our location was breached when I obliterated Scarge. We must make haste to the castle before we are besieged."

"Lead the way," said Jake. "I really want to talk to Rileau about the Glactra."

"Scarge? What's a Scarge? Is it contagious?" asked Shayna. "And who or what in the heck is Glactra? OMG you guys, how long was I gone?" She latched on to Seneca's shoulders and shook her. She could feel the panic setting in. She closed her eyes to relieve a sudden wave of dizziness. She dug her nails into Seneca's shoulder to steady herself.

"Ouch! That's a bit rough," said Seneca. She cringed as she pried Shayna's fingers away. She knew bruises were sure to follow.

"Sorry. This is just a lot to take in right now. I'm feeling off balance and out of control. I feel like I just stepped off a boat," said Shayna.

Seneca caught a glimpse of the others making their way to the path with the row of ash trees. "I know, and I get it. I'll explain on the way, but we've gotta go," Seneca insisted.

"Fine, but I'm getting some answers from somebody," Shayna said sternly as she followed closely behind Seneca. "When we get back to Rileau's, remind me to tell you what I saw in the perplex. It's not good."

"Okay. Let's wait until we're safe," replied Seneca. She was intrigued and wanted details but resisted. They dashed up the embankment and caught up to the others.

They raced through the woods in virtual silence, with Shayna falling uncharacteristically behind the others. She knew they weren't far from the castle once they reached a picturesque glen filled with a dense blanket of heavily scented wildflowers.

She slowed down to take it all in: the smells, the sounds, and what she'd experienced. She was aware there'd been a chance of her not making it out of the perplex, and the idea of dying young and alone was an awakening. It was also a reminder of how important it was to stop Brigara. She sighed. Seeing the familiar arched stone bridge outside of Rileau's castle was a relief. She raced to it and ran her fingers along the cold wall. She loved the feel of the smooth square stones beneath her feet. She knew it wasn't home, but the feelings of security and comfort were good enough.

Rileau had assured them the castle was cloaked under the most sacred of magic, making it invincible and unlikely to be breached by intruders. Even the grounds outside of the walls were charmed under the same protection. The water that encircled the castle was the first line of defense, since it was enchanted to repel even the darkest of spells. Shayna liked knowing that the more dark spells it encountered, the stronger it grew. She gazed into the calm water. She hoped to see the reflectoire in her reflection, but the water was too dark. She hadn't noticed before, but the water was actually black. She stood on her toes and leaned over the aged limestone wall to get a better look. The water was eerily still. She wondered about its depth and the source that caused the water to be so black. *How odd*, she thought.

"Must have something to do with the protection spell," Shayna said aloud as she walked through the massive iron doors and rushed to join the others inside.

CHAPTER TWELVE

Intentions Revealed

Returning to the safety of the castle was a relief. Their rooms had been cleaned, and fresh changes of clothes had been set out. Shayna collapsed on the large poster bed nearest the window. She wanted to sink into the stuffed feather mattress and sleep until she awoke in her own bed in the mortal realm. It was a thought she didn't allow to linger, for fear of getting too nostalgic and forgetting her purpose. She pulled herself up and joined Seneca in getting changed for dinner.

"I've got something for you," Seneca said. Her voice was uncharacteristically cheery. She was anxiously waiting for Shayna, and her excitement was out of character.

"Oh, do you?" Shayna said with suspicion.

"I think you'll like it. Actually, I'm pretty sure you're going to love it." Seneca laughed.

"Okay, you're scaring me now."

"Ta-dah!" Seneca shouted. She smirked when she noticed Shayna had closed her eyes tightly.

"What is it? Just tell me! You're freaking me out." She was now positive she wasn't going to like anything that caused Seneca to sound so upbeat.

"Open your eyes, and check it out for yourself."

"Check what out? I dunno about that. I'm pretty sure I don't want to see whatever it is you're trying to show me." Shayna shut her eyelids tighter.

"Oh, I think you're gonna wanna see this—trust me," Seneca said in a singsong voice.

Shayna shook her head, braced herself, and opened her eyes slowly. She batted her eyes several times to regain focus as she leaned forward. Seneca held an ornate mirror right at eye level. Shayna finally saw what the others had seen: the reflectoire was exquisite. She raised her fingers to it, and it warmed to a sapphire blue. As she lowered her hand, it faded to the previous hue.

"Thank you, Seneca. I thought it would be, you know—"

"Ugly? Hideous? Grotesque?" Seneca teased. "Perhaps disfiguring?"

"Hey, excuse me! I was going to say 'more obvious,'" snapped Shayna.

"I don't get it." Seneca frowned.

"I thought it would look out of place, like a wart or a growth, but it doesn't."

"That's what we've been trying to tell you. I knew you wouldn't believe it until you saw it for yourself," replied Seneca. "It's really beautiful."

"Thank you. I have to agree with you. I think I might not want to hide it after all." She sighed. "I was afraid, and I still am a little. So much is changing, and we have no control over it."

"True, but it doesn't have to be a bad thing," said Seneca. "Maybe if we try embracing some of the change, it won't be so scary."

"I like that idea. Plus, something this gorgeous couldn't be that bad," said Shayna while tilting her head toward the light.

"I kind of knew you'd feel that way once you got a look at it," Seneca said. "Come on! The guys are already up in the dining room, gobbling up everything for sure."

"Seneca, be honest. Would it be weird if I held on to this mirror a bit longer?" Shayna rotated her head as she looked at her image from every conceivable angle. She twisted her face and pursed her lips to resemble a duck's bill. She raised her eyebrows up and down repeatedly while alternating between smiling and snarling. She batted her eyelashes with each new pose.

"I think it'll be fine." Seneca giggled.

"You're sure no one will mind?"

"Nah, Conner and Jake were making bets that you'd probably bring it with you to dinner," said Seneca as she headed for the stairwell and skipped up the steep stairs.

"A bet, eh?" Shayna spoke aloud, but her mind was on admiring her image in the mirror.

Seneca decided not to reveal that she had initiated the wager. She was tempted to let Shayna know the loser not only would have to pay but also would have the challenge of prying the mirror from her clutches. She snickered at the images that flashed in her mind as they sauntered into the dimly lit dining room. The table was adorned with a buffet of delicacies for their enjoyment.

"I don't think I'll ever get used to this," said Seneca as she looked at Conner and Jake.

They were working their way through piles of food they had heaped on their plates. Jake looked up but barely nodded as Shayna and Seneca sat down.

"Thanks for waiting for us. Pass the zucchini bread before Conner inhales the entire loaf," said Seneca as she climbed into the oversized chair and sat on her knees.

She was petite but felt even smaller each time they ate at the massive table. Jake complied without looking up from the sandwich tower he was creating. Shayna made her way to the opposite end of the long table.

She tilted her head to see how the reflectoire looked from various angles with the change in lighting. She was thankful for the mirror and began to relax about her new appearance.

"Conner, why's all of the food bunched up around you? Are you seriously planning to eat everything on the table?" Seneca grumbled.

"Yuh aw hmm feishyee mem yor mungry." Conner attempted to speak with a mouthful of mutton. He pushed a tray of sliced lamb in her direction.

"What are you saying?" Seneca asked as she caught a familiar scent. Her eyes searched the table to find its location.

"He said you're feisty when you're hungry," Jake said, translating. "And that he owes me five bucks!" He watched Shayna take a long glance at her reflection in the mirror. Jake smirked in satisfaction as he elbowed Conner, who was focused on shoving boiled potatoes into the pockets of his cheeks. Conner bobbed his head in response, oblivious to losing the bet.

"Thanks—I think," Seneca muttered. She was not fully paying attention. Her eyes searched the offerings on the table. She had spied what she desired most. It was just out of her reach, and her taste buds were screaming in anticipation. She licked her lips as she reached as far as her arms could stretch. The table was wide, but she refused to give up until she got what she wanted. She skillfully scooped a generous amount of the creamy white bean, potato, and carrot soup from the large crock. She filled her bowl to the brim without spilling a drop. She took in a full whiff of the aroma and smiled. It reminded her of home. It was the soup her mother made on cold nights. The broth was thick, with loads of garlic—just the way she liked it.

"Seneca! How are you doing that?" shrieked Shayna.

"Doing what? I like potato-and-bean soup. Don't you?"

Jake bumped Conner's shoulder just as he was biting into a five-decker sandwich and sent it flying out of his hands. It landed with a thud, and the smorgasbord of ingredients spewed across the floor.

"Hey—" Conner stopped as he realized why he'd lost his great sandwich creation. He joined Jake and Shayna in gawking at Seneca.

"What are you staring at?" Seneca asked as she reached for two sourdough rolls.

"Uh, you're hovering over the table!" Shayna shouted.

"I'm what?" Seneca looked down and realized she was suspended about a foot over the table. "Wow! Cool, huh?"

"How are you doing that?" asked Jake. "Your wings aren't even out."

"I have no idea. I just knew I couldn't reach the soup, and I wanted it so badly," Seneca replied as she spooned the steamy soup into a wide-open mouth. "It's so good!"

"That's the trick! Starve the girl, and she will perform any feat," Jake said.

"You can float around all you want. Just don't take all the rolls," Conner joked. "I'm starting over on my mega sandwich." Seneca, Jake, and Shayna laughed as he began stacking meat, potatoes, and wedges of cheese on a jumbo-size baguette.

"I'm sure hovering over the food is probably in the *What-Not-to-Do Dining Etiquette* book," said Seneca as she lowered herself into the chair.

"There's probably an entire chapter dedicated to it with Seneca's picture as an illustration," Shayna said loudly. She found her comment to be hilarious and was dismayed that no one else found her remark funny. She started to protest, but as she looked around, it became apparent why the lighthearted mood had suddenly ceased. The expressions of Conner, Jake, and Seneca said it all. She followed their gaze to Rileau and Wren, who stood silently at the far end of the dining room. Their eyes locked on Shayna. Rileau stepped forward and began walking toward her. She shifted in her seat and wondered if she was supposed to stand or remain seated. Wren followed close behind and did not acknowledge the others, who watched in anticipation.

"It appears you have found the food enjoyable this evening. It would seem you have elected to leave a great deal of it on the floor," said Rileau dryly.

"Sorry about that," said Conner. "It sort of got away from me." He scooped up the sandwich remains quickly and folded them into a napkin.

"The time you spend here is to be dedicated to the expansion and development of your gifts. If it is not what you choose, speak now!" Rileau's voice echoed against the stone walls.

No one replied. Barely a moment passed where they didn't realize the importance of their situation or the weight of their responsibility. Finally having time to laugh was something they needed.

"We apologize if it appears we're not taking this seriously," said Jake. "We were just horsing around. We know what's at stake."

"Do you?" Rileau asked as he scanned their faces.

They all nodded in confirmation.

"It's probably my fault that we were, uh, sort of distracted," said Seneca timidly.

"If you mean your ability to manipulate flight without wings, I witnessed as much when I arrived," said Rileau. "As evidenced by your continuous lack of awareness, you did not notice Wren and I observing."

"Eh, so you saw her?" Conner asked. "Awesome, huh?"

"It is impressive. We shall explore this further, as well as your other druid abilities. We will begin at first light," replied Rileau.

Seneca smiled and tried to relax. She stirred what remained of her soup. Her appetite had waned due to the knots in her stomach. Her parents were druids, and the idea of learning more was comforting but also frightening. She hadn't the slightest clue what it meant to be a druid.

"What about me? Notice anything different since I broke out of the perplex?" Shayna asked, beaming as she leaned forward. She hoped for a positive response and held her breath. She fought back the urge to point out the obvious change. She wiggled in her chair with nervous anticipation.

"Yes. I am quite aware of the emergence of your reflectoire. It suits you well," replied Rileau. He smiled and tipped his head slightly.

"Thanks. I like it too," said Shayna.

"Wren told me that you have not been made aware of its intention. Was it not revealed to you within the perplex?"

"Not that I know of. What could it be?"

"You said something happened that you needed to talk about," Seneca reminded her.

"Oh yeah, that stuff," said Shayna. Her smile faded as she thought back to her time in the perplex. "First, before I tell you, let's not do the perplex thing again, okay, Rileau?"

"It will not be necessary. The energy of your bond was present upon your arrival," said Rileau. "The Dominion of Four is sealed, as it should be."

"Excellent!" Conner blurted out. He turned to fist-bump Jake but only received a dismissive grimace. "Thanks for keeping me hanging."

Jake shoved a dinner roll in his mouth and returned his attention to Rileau.

"Shayna, please tell us of your experience within the perplex," said Rileau.

"Great! Okay, where do I begin? First, you've gotta know that it was really strange. It wasn't exactly like a dream but not like I was actually there either. It's hard to explain." Shayna took a big breath. "The entire experience was super odd. I kept bouncing around to all these different places that I used to go to when I was a kid. I would start to look around, and then...Kaboom! I would bounce to somewhere else."

"What do you mean when you speak of this bouncing?" asked Rileau.

"I was like hopping from place to place, you know? Never stayed long before—poof! —I was somewhere else I knew," Shayna explained. She jumped out of her chair and used animated hand gestures. "Two seconds there, and boom! Off to another place I would go."

"Please continue." Rileau was careful in masking his frustration, but Jake could see a small stream of smoke swirling from his left nostril.

"Get to the point, Shayna, and tell us what you saw," Seneca said.

"Well, at first, I was at my ballet class. I haven't been back to that dance studio since I was about twelve. I was standing right by the old out-of-tune piano," Shayna said. "Then, just as I was about to touch it, I left. Next thing you know, I was standing by the huge oak tree in my neighbor's backyard. I loved that tree until I fell out of it and broke my arm. I kept going to places like that. It was like a bad sitcom that tried to be a reality-TV thing. I was waiting for someone to jump out and reveal hidden cameras."

"I'm not sure how I'd react to seeing my past," said Jake. "Pretty mundane stuff."

"Except it wasn't really the past. That's the strange part," said Shayna. "What I mean is that the tree was so much larger, and that old piano was shoved in the corner. It was replaced by a new fancier one. It was like how things are now. I know it sounds weird."

"You're right; it does," said Conner. "Bizarro world if you ask me."

"I agree. Especially since there's no way I would know the studio got a new piano. I haven't been to that school since they gave Katie Winston the lead in *Grease*. Sandy does not have to be a blonde. Plus, I'd look good in a wig and poodle skirt." Shayna gibbered on.

"Rileau, what does this have to do with her reflectoire?" Seneca asked. She was accustomed to Shayna going off topic and decided to seize the opportunity to get back on track.

"Yeah, what does it all mean?" asked Jake.

"I believe Shayna has revealed the intention of her reflectoire," Rileau replied.

"I have? I don't understand. What did I reveal?"

"Your reflectoire is the means for traveling from one place to another by way of magic," Rileau said. "That is the intention."

"Whoa! Do you mean like… Are you saying as in tele—" Shayna's mouth opened wide. She turned to the others, who were wide-eyed at the revelation. They all understood what Rileau was saying. No one had words as they stared at her in disbelief and shock.

"Did you hear what he just said, you guys?" Shayna screamed. "Teleportation! I'm going to master this like a boss!"

Conner, Jake, and Seneca exchanged surprised and excited looks. They had needed to hear it aloud for it to sink in. The room erupted into screams and cheers. They were out of their seats, exchanging hugs, high fives and improvised dancing.

"You're serious that I can actually teleport?" Shayna asked, nearly out of breath. "That's totally sci-fi super coolio!"

"Indeed, that is quite the situation. It appears the visits to familiar places created the intention of your reflectoire," said Rileau as he moved to the table and pulled out a chair.

Wren followed his lead and sat down to observe the celebration. Jake thought they appeared to be eerily calm and seemingly unaffected.

"This is really good news, right?" Jake asked. "We've got nothing to worry about, right?"

"It would not be prudent for me to respond, as I do not know. I am unaware of any reflectoire that has been tuned with the intention of teleportation. It could prove to be useful if perfected," replied Rileau. "Is there anything else, Shayna, that you care to reveal?"

"There was something else I saw when I was teleporting," Shayna said, panting heavily. She could feel her heart racing wildly. She focused on calming down, since she was about to reveal the most disturbing aspect of her experience. "Just give me a second. I want to be sure I get the details right," she said.

"Is this what you tried to tell me?" asked Seneca. She swallowed hard in anticipation.

"Yes, it is. I saw our high school, and it had been destroyed. I mean completely destroyed. Nothing was there," she said somberly. "It was just a pile of rocks and dust. Broken glass, crumbled blocks of concrete walls, and broken beams were all that was left. Everything was charred and smoldering, and I could smell the smoke fumes too. I'm telling you—the entire place was decimated. It was definitely a huge fire or explosion or something catastrophic."

Seneca gasped. She shuddered at the thought of the school's destruction. She felt a sudden drop in body temperature and trembled. She hoped Shayna was exaggerating, but she let go of that notion. Jake stared blankly as his thoughts flashed to images of the school he'd only experienced for a day. He struggled with his emotions and wasn't sure how he felt.

"What happened?" Conner asked. "Did you see who did it?"

"Not exactly. It had already happened, but I know who did it," replied Shayna. "I looked around really super-fast, because like I said, I never stayed in any of the places long. I didn't know if or when I'd pop to another place. But anyway, I saw her. Well, I mean, I saw the back of her. She was moving all creepily through the trees. She was heading toward the woods."

"You saw the back of *her*. You mean Brigara, don't you?" said Seneca.

Shayna's expression said it all; there was no need for her to say more. They knew exactly who'd destroyed their high school. Seneca felt sick to her stomach and sat down. Jake ran his hands through his hair and then punched the air hard before plopping down into his chair.

"Is there more?" asked Rileau in a low voice. He stood up, and his tail thumped the floor.

"She was carrying something—a box, I think," replied Shayna. "It was dark, but there was a glow around it. It was the last spark of light I saw just before I bounced to the woods. That's where I met up with everybody, near that pond."

"Your emergence from the perplex was quite timely. If Brigara had become aware of your presence, then things may have ended differently," said Rileau. "Fortunately, you were never within her reach."

"It felt like I was there. Plus, all of the smells and sounds—they seemed real."

"They were indeed. You were within the perplex and not physically within her grasp. My guess is that you were also hidden from sight and that your movements were not audible. Were you able to touch anything or anyone?" Rileau asked.

"Well, no. But you said that things could have ended differently if Brigara had seen me," said Shayna. "What could she have done?"

"If the perplex had revealed you, then she would have attacked without hesitation. Her hatred for the four of you runs deep. Isolating you from the others would work to her advantage. But why speculate?" said Rileau.

"This is remarkably telling," said Wren. It was the first time she had said anything since arriving. "You were able to see from within the perplex, and you crossed to the mortal realm. I've never heard of such an event."

"I agree," said Rileau. "It means that in addition to teleportation, you have the gift of farseeing. While you may have felt as if you were present in each of these locations, you were not. This is why your senses were active but you could not touch or feel your surroundings. You were not physically there. Only your mind was in those locations."

"Being able to project your reflectoire to the mortal realm may serve us in determining where and when Brigara will return. More importantly, it will be useful in tracking her movements within the Otherworld," said Wren. Her excitement was evident in her voice and demeanor.

"That sounds really great in theory, but I don't know how it works," said Shayna. "I was bouncing around like a rubber ball and had no choice of where I ended up. I had no control at all."

"Controlling this gift is vital. Mastering your reflectoire is a top priority," said Rileau. "You will begin training with me upon first daylight. Conner and Jake, you will join us. They must understand how it works and how their powers shall complement it."

"What about me?" Seneca asked nervously. "Don't I need to get involved in this too?"

"No. You are a druid, and as such, all magic is inherited within you to utilize at will. Linking to the others is natural," said Rileau. "Has this not been explained to you?" He turned to Wren, who remained silent and only a raised an eyebrow to indicate she was listening.

"I haven't been told much of anything about being a druid. My parents never taught me," she said softly.

"They were fools to leave you ill prepared and leave so much unsaid," Rileau grumbled. "Then that must be remedied. I shall attempt to remember that you are all ignorant to our way of life and our Otherworld."

Seneca knew Rileau was insulting them, but she agreed. Her parents should have trusted her enough to tell her about where they were from. In her heart, she knew they'd done what they believed to be best. The Elder Druid Council had selflessly given up their elemental gifts to form the dominion. Her mother had even shaved her wings for the cause.

"We all know I'm behind, so how do I learn the Druid 101 thing at this point?" Seneca's fiery spirit was sparked, and while she wasn't up to speed on all things druid, she was not a slacker.

"I will lead Seneca through her training," said Wren. "I will show you the ways of the druid."

"Thanks."

Seneca tried to force a smile in acknowledgment, but she'd hoped Rileau would help her with the druid aspects. After all, Wren was an elf, so what did she know about being a druid? Admittedly, Seneca didn't know what being an elf meant either. For all she knew, elves might be experts on druids, fairies, and other elementals. Seneca began to think that being trained by Wren might not be so bad. She didn't care much for her, but Rileau appeared to trust her.

"Okay, so it's Wren and me tomorrow," she said with a forced smile.

"We shall meet in the interior garden at first light of morning," said Wren.

"It is settled. Please finish your meal, and turn in early. We have much to do upon your awakening," said Rileau. He turned and exited the dining room. Wren trailed closely behind him.

The room was silent for quite some time. They were lost in their own thoughts. Seneca gazed across the table at Jake, who was distracted with crumbling a blueberry scone onto his plate. Shayna had resumed admiring her perplex in the mirror, and Conner had returned to assembling another sandwich.

"Jake, you didn't tell them about the Glactra or that you were able to see them," said Seneca. "Why didn't you say anything?"

"I didn't know how to bring it up. Besides, it was the Shayna show. I didn't want to interrupt. I'm sure Wren told him about it," said Jake. "It's probably not that important, or he would have said something."

"I don't know about that, Jake," said Seneca.

"What about what it said to you?" Conner asked. "That sounded important to me, dude."

"Yeah, maybe. I'll tell him tomorrow. I just don't think it's that big of a deal right now. Shayna and Seneca are the priority anyway. Didn't you see how the plans got shuffled once they realized what Shayna's reflectoire can do?"

"It does seem like the strategy changed—not that we knew what it was anyway, so I wouldn't even know the difference," replied Seneca. "And after all the talk about sticking together like glue, I get stuck with Wren."

"I wouldn't mind sticking to her a bit," Conner hooted.

"Ew, gross!" Shayna said.

"Just ignore him," said Seneca. "He can't focus when Wren's around."

"Speaking of focus, why aren't we focused on how we're going to stop Brigara?" asked Jake. "Her minions have already attacked all of us, and we haven't learned anything yet."

"Maybe it's because our powers keep changing and evolving, and they don't know what to do with us," said Conner. His new sandwich was complete, and he took a large bite. He smiled, bobbed his head in satisfaction, and gave a thumbs-up.

"I can't believe you're still eating," Shayna said. She had lost her appetite. All she could think about was Brigara. "Can you believe what she did to our school?"

"She's a maniac!" Seneca snapped.

"What do you think is in the box she was carrying? Did you notice that Rileau and Wren said nothing about it?" Jake said.

"Yes, I did, and I also noticed they were holding back on telling us more," said Shayna.

"Maybe they don't want us freaking out," said Seneca.

"Too late!" Conner sputtered and spewed food across his plate. "Sorry." He gulped down what remained of his sandwich. "I think they're freaking out for sure and are just not letting us know. They probably think it's best."

"You might be right. I can't wait to see what happens tomorrow," said Jake.

"Hey, Seneca, you could do your mojo and read their minds," Conner said before loudly slurping what little remained in his mug.

"What?" Seneca squeaked, her nose wrinkling.

"You know, that mojo, funny woojoo mind-meld stuff you do. Find out what's going on by reading Rileau's mind."

"Maybe you could find out what's in the box," Shayna added.

"No, that's probably not a good idea," said Jake.

"It could backfire," Seneca said, "like with Brigara. He would totally catch me."

"Well, I'm just saying you could probably at least snag something before you get caught," said Conner. "Come on!"

"Nope, no way. I'm not doing it."

"Leave her alone. Just drop it, Conner!" Jake snapped.

"Whatever! What good is a power like that if you can't even use it?" Conner grumbled.

"Change of subject," Shayna said. She cleared her throat. "You get to learn about being a druid tomorrow. How exciting!"

"Yippee. Learning all things druid. Can't wait," said Seneca sarcastically. "I'm heading to bed. I hate cold soup."

"Wait for me. I'm coming too," said Shayna. "This knot forming in my stomach tells me that I need to be well rested to face whatever is happening tomorrow."

CHAPTER THIRTEEN

Mastering the Gift

"This thingamajig isn't working right," said Shayna. She was as frustrated as she was disappointed. When she'd awakened that morning, she'd been excited about mastering her new ability, but now she wasn't so sure.

"Your reflectoire will respond to you once it calibrates and clears," said Rileau. "Typically, this happens over time. However, that is not a luxury we possess. We must continue to accelerate the alignment."

"Accelerate, you say? Didn't you see how fast I was running? Those sheep weren't exactly thrilled with me interrupting their lunch!" Shayna snapped.

"The need to move this along expeditiously should not be made light of," Rileau sneered.

"Fine, but I need some better direction here. You told me to go to the room with the wool tapestry, and all I could think about was how itchy it would be, and the next thing you know, I'm face-to-face with Mary's flock," said Shayna.

She was distraught and took a whiff of her sleeve while turning up her nose in protest. Conner resisted the urge to chime in with a timely quip as he exchanged a smirk with Jake.

"They could use a bath too!" she said, adding to her protest.

Rileau ignored her complaints and elected to forge ahead with the lesson.

"And they're mean little snots."

He rubbed his chin in contemplation. "We must take a different approach. What room in the castle are you most familiar with and comfortable in? Perhaps being inside will be easier for mastery."

"I agree with that. Let's see. As I'm sure you're aware, most of this place is a bit drab and not really my taste, but there's the library," Shayna said as her face lit up. "It reminds me of my dad's study. It has lots of books, and there are really comfy places to flop down."

"Flop down?" Rileau asked dryly.

"Yeah, you know, just chill and snooze. Anyway, that's my favorite room."

"It is a pretty awesome room," said Jake, nodding in agreement.

"Very well. Then you must use your mind's eye and imagine the room. All elements within must be seen in the utmost detail. Do you comprehend this, Shayna?" Rileau asked. He leaned in close, and she could feel his hot breath on her forehead.

"I'm all about details, and I know that room like the back of my hand," she said.

"Then proceed. Do not move your hand across the reflectoire until you have the room clearly in your mind."

"I've got it this time. Don't worry," she said. Her confidence was anything but solid. Shayna closed her eyes and shook out her legs and arms. She followed those movements with a slow head roll. "I'm ready."

"Wait!" Jake said. "How about if Conner, Rileau, and I head to the library first? That way, we're there to congratulate you when you pop in."

"Oh, I like that idea!" Shayna beamed. "I don't think I pop, though."

She welcomed the support. The tension was thickening and becoming overwhelming with the multiple failures. The situation with the sheep was just one of many unsuccessful attempts, and she knew Rileau was growing impatient.

"That's fine. We will leave you here and will await your arrival in the library," replied Rileau.

He turned to exit the corral, and the sheep parted to allow him to ease by. Jake and Conner shuffled close behind. Shayna attempted to follow but had to dodge a rogue sheep charging at her. She hurdled over the gate to avoid being struck and landed gracefully. She turned and shook her fist at the dismayed sheep. "Better luck next time!" she sneered before jogging ahead to join the others. She caught up with them as they entered the castle.

"We shall try a more simplistic approach," said Rileau. "Think about the elements of your destination in layers. Focus on the foundation of it, and then build the details upon it. Imagine the colors and smells. Your reflectoire is tuned to your emotions as well as thoughts, but it is literal and will obey as such. The slightest alteration will shift your teleportation."

"I will try," she said softly.

Shayna was beginning to understand that the key to teleportation was in the minute details. The more she thought about it, selecting the library was the best solution. She closed her eyes, and she could see the room. The elaborate draperies were pulled back with a braided velveteen sash that surrounded the large window, which provided the only natural light in that part of the castle. Beyond that window was a lush garden filled with marigolds and rainbows of tulips and lilies in full bloom. She shook her head to clear the image.

"Not the garden, Shayna! Come on. Focus!" she said, chastising herself.

"Focus, Shayna!" Jake said. "You can do this. We will meet you in the library."

"Okay, I've got it," she said.

"Just be careful," Conner added. He followed Jake out of the room and headed down the corridor.

Rileau placed his hand on Shayna's shoulder. She looked into his serious eyes. She didn't want to disappoint him.

"You have the gift, so use it," he said sternly.

"Okay, I can do this. I know I can. The library is the answer."

"Then we shall await your arrival." He turned and left her standing alone.

Shayna took a deep breath and exhaled slowly. She was feeling the pressure but also the anticipation of getting the teleportation right, which steadied her.

"What's in the library? The furniture. Yeah, that's it. Gotta picture the chairs. Oh yeah, I've got this," she whispered.

She closed her eyes and swiped her hand across the reflectoire. It glowed in response. Her eyes popped open just as she faded away from where she stood, leaving behind only slight impressions from her boot heels in the rug.

Shayna appeared suddenly with a flash of light. She crashed directly into a large bookcase filled with volumes of books. She hit the stone floor hard as nearly all the books crammed into the shelves tumbled down on top of her. She was nearly buried completely before Conner rushed over and pulled her out from under them. She barely escaped before an entire shelf of books crashed down in the spot where she'd landed.

"Are you kidding me? What happened?" she muttered as she checked her head, face, and arms for injuries.

"You did not follow my instructions is what happened," Rileau said.

"Huh? I'm in the library, so I had to be close, right?" Her head was feeling the impact of her crash. She tried to steady herself in an attempt to look unfazed. She resisted the urge to sit down. "You did say the library, right?"

"The mind can be quite literal. If your image is of books, then you are likely to end up exactly where a book is located," Rileau said dryly.

"You obviously thought of cooking when you ended up in the kitchen. I can only presume that hay was on your mind when you frightened the mares. Should we review each of your less-than-stellar results?"

"I don't think that's necessary. I know I haven't done it right," replied Shayna.

"That is an understatement but at least accurate," Rileau said.

"I did what you said. I focused on something I remembered from the room. At first, I was thinking of the really huge ottoman and how nice it is to sit there. Then my mind shifted to the bookcase and how it really needed dusting," Shayna explained. "I think the dusting became my focus, but I had already swiped by then."

"It looks like you took care of that problem!" Conner snorted.

"Shut up, Conner!" Shayna retorted. "I'm sure you'd end up much worse off."

"Only if you think sinking in a pile of doughnuts is worse than dusting a bookcase with your face. Splat!" He laughed.

"Dude, that's harsh," said Jake, muffling a laugh.

"Yet you didn't say I wasn't right. I'd think about doughnuts all day long—chocolate glazed with sprinkles, powdered, jelly filled. Oh, that'd be the life indeed!"

"You have to imagine a real place!" Shayna shouted as she crossed her arms tightly. "You're such a clown!"

"Who says it's not real?" Conner said. "You didn't think the Otherworld existed not too long ago—maybe there's a doughnut realm nearby."

"Oh, forget it!"

"Just sayin'," Conner teased.

"That's enough for today and perhaps permanently," said Rileau as a ring of smoke escaped from his nostrils.

Conner's eyes followed the smoke until it dissipated. He shifted his gaze after realizing the dragon was glaring with displeasure. "Oh, sorry."

"Your banter seems to have captured more of your interest, as well as other matters of no relevance," Rileau said gruffly.

"But I can try again. I will focus better," pleaded Shayna. "I promise—I can do this!"

"Your progress is not at all impressive. We have devoted much of the day to this, and you are no better than when you began. You must devote time to your other gifts. There is little time remaining to master the skill of teleportation."

Shayna didn't reply. She knew it was useless to argue with him.

"Jake, your training begins at daylight in the center courtyard. Do not keep me waiting," said Rileau.

"Okay," Jake replied. He resisted the sudden urge to salute as he stood with his eyes forward and his arms plastered to his sides in a military stance.

"Conner, you will join us."

"I'll be there! I can't wait to perfect my body-slam techniques."

Rileau snapped his tail against the floor and sneered. Conner took the hint and followed Jake's lead by mimicking his demeanor.

"I must check on Seneca's progress. I suggest you work together and return this room to its previous state." Rileau turned on his heel and left with a trail of smoke billowing behind him.

"I didn't mean to make him mad," Shayna whispered. Her head was pounding, and she could feel bruises making their presence known. She moaned in agony.

"Are you okay, Shayna?" Jake asked.

"Sure. Just banged up a bit," she replied.

"You know I was just kidding, right?" Conner asked.

"Yup." Shayna stopped short of adding anything else. She knew she would be reacting out of frustration, and she was the only one to blame for not mastering teleporting.

"At least you finally got into the targeted room this time. He could've given you credit for that," said Conner. He was hoping to cheer her up. He felt bad that he had likely turned a bad situation into a disaster with his remarks.

"Close isn't good enough in his eyes," said Jake. "You can tell he's losing confidence in us. We keep screwing things up. No offense, Shayna."

"None taken," she said flatly. "I agree with Conner, though. A little credit for not breaking my neck or getting stuck in the wall would have been nice." She smirked.

"What does it feel like when you're actually teleporting?" Jake asked.

"It's like you're floating for a second, and then boom!" Shayna shouted. "Realty sets in, and you're buried beneath a pile of heavy, dusty books. It wasn't as bad as knocking down the pots and pans in the kitchen or nearly being trampled by a herd of sheep, but it was definitely the most painful."

"Sounds surreal," said Jake.

He was hoping for more information but decided not to push. She had teleported to practically all areas of the castle in an attempt to get to the library. Each failure had been followed by a growl, puff of smoke, or slam of the tail by Rileau.

"Surreal, huh? Yeah, that's not how I would describe it," Shayna sneered.

Jake hated watching Shayna roll her eyes. He was at a loss for words, and that had been the best he could come up with. He started picking up books and putting them back on the shelf in an effort to deescalate the situation. He didn't want to add to her humiliation, but it was important for Shayna to master teleportation. The more extensive an arsenal they had to face Brigara, the better, although he had to admit he was worried Shayna might injure herself.

"Shayna, I was thinking about a tactic you might try next time. You know, just to minimize hurting yourself," said Jake.

"If there's a next time, you mean," Shayna said.

"Listen, what if you focus on all aspects of the place you want to go, even the tiniest details? Do a complete picture in your head before you swipe your reflectoire. Maybe you'll have better luck," said Jake.

"Use all five senses, and really picture yourself there," added Conner.

"I thought I was doing that, but he said the brain is literal—whatever that means," said Shayna. She sighed and examined her bruises. A purple one was swelling and pulsating on her forearm. She rubbed it and then winced in pain. "Do you think Keene Ardara's chocolate will help these bumps and bruises?" she asked.

"Chocolate is a cure for whatever ails you!" Conner said as he joined them in returning the books to the shelf. "I have plenty of it in my room. I'll get it when we're done here."

"Thank you," she said.

Shayna stepped away and allowed the boys to finish replacing the books. She climbed onto the incredibly comfortable overstuffed ottoman. She tried to lie down in the least painful position, but she realized she ached all over, including her heart. She was exhausted and homesick. She missed her father. She closed her eyes and tried to picture his face as she imagined what he would be doing at that moment. She wondered how he'd reacted when told his daughter was in the Otherworld. Images of his smile, his brown eyes, and what she always considered to be a bad haircut came into focus. She longed to reach for his face and wipe the smudges from his glasses. It was a habit for him to constantly touch the lens of his glasses, and she would make a fuss each time she removed them for cleaning. He was always patient and tolerated her high energy, which was the opposite of his calm and steady demeanor. She wondered what had caused the separation of her parents and why he had lied about her mother dying in childbirth. Growing up without a mother was a void in her life that could never be filled. She rehearsed what she would say if she got the chance to confront him. Each imaginary conversation ended the same way. She couldn't fathom a different ending that would give her the satisfaction she craved.

CHAPTER FOURTEEN

Training Day

"Why do I get the feeling this is going to be a long day?" Seneca mumbled to herself as she waited for Wren's arrival.

She had awakened well before dawn. She'd had a restless night and tossed about for the majority of it. *Exhaustion* couldn't begin to describe how tired she felt. She'd grown used to sleeping in unfamiliar places, so she knew that wasn't the cause of her sleep deprivation. The anxious news of learning what it meant to be druid was what created her angst. She had skipped breakfast and gone straight to the garden well before sunrise.

The garden was oval shaped and nestled in the center of a grove of trees. It was peacefully quiet. The only sounds were from a family of birds that rustled about in the trees. Seneca wondered how the lessons were progressing with Shayna. She'd really wanted to be included in the teleporting lesson. She sighed heavily and plopped down on a small bench. She whipped her head around when she heard the snap of a twig. Wren stood mere inches from her.

"You are prompt—nice quality in a druid," said Wren.

How had Seneca not sensed her approach? *It must be an elf trait*, she thought. "Uh, hi. I didn't hear you walk up," said Seneca as she stood and looked up. Wren was at least a foot taller.

Wren cast her eyes down but never tilted her head, keeping her chin raised as if to emphasize her superior height. "It appears you must adjust your sensitivity. It is familiarity with your surroundings that will yield you protection as well as opportunity."

"It sounds like the lessons have begun," said Seneca.

"And so they have. What about your wings? Have you learned their capacity for attack? Or perhaps the magic they possess?"

"Well, I'm not sure. I know they're strong enough to create a force to knock a couple of teenage boys on their butt," she said, beaming with pride. "They glow brightly when I'm angry."

"That doesn't seem useful. Have you used them in battle—other than putting boys on their bottoms, I mean?" Wren asked.

She's all business, and this is going to be a long day, Seneca thought. Wren seemed fixated on interrogating her. She knew her wings could probably do more, but she'd thought the lesson was supposed to be about being a druid and learning to fight.

"No, only to get away," she said. "You know, like fly out of their reach."

"You're not using your wings at all, it would seem. What a waste," Wren scoffed. "This is definitely going to be like placing petals back on a spring bloom upon the emergence of autumn."

"You're basically calling me hopeless or a waste of time?" Seneca asked, fuming. "Not cool, Wren!"

"I am just reciting the obvious. If you're not curious enough to delve into your gifts, then why should I waste my time? It appears your motivation is lacking when it comes to exploring your capabilities."

"Look, I thought you were going to teach me about being a druid, but if you're not up for it, I can talk to Rileau, or we can just call the whole thing off," snapped Seneca. "I really don't need your sarcasm, and to get things straight, I am not a waste!"

Seneca's wings appeared in full spread. The tips vibrated blue, which was a perfect contrast to her red cheeks. She raged inside. Wren's expression caught her by surprise. It was smug and content. It was obvious Wren had been trying to get a reaction that would force Seneca to expose her wings. Seneca wondered if it had been a test and if she'd passed.

"You are quite testy to be so demure," said Wren. "Perhaps you might actually have the makings of a suitable druid. It seems you have a bit of a temper, though. You must learn to control that. You wouldn't want it used against you." She smirked and then turned away to retrieve her staff.

Seneca let out a huge exhalation. She hadn't realized she'd been holding her breath.

"Glad you did that," Wren said. She glanced over her shoulder with the same smirk still present. "Breathing is quite important. It keeps your stamina during long battles. You can anticipate that your battles will take you to your limit, and Brigara will know exactly what that is. It's highly probable you will not be able to keep pace."

The unmoved smirk was hard to dismiss. Seneca mocked the expression and glared as Wren's snide smile slowly faded to become more of a grimace. *Why is she so rude?* Seneca wondered. If Wren didn't believe in their abilities, then why was Rileau trusting her to help? Seneca had more questions than answers.

"Wren, I'm willing to do whatever it takes to stop Brigara, and it's obvious you know more about her then I do. Can we just focus on whatever it is I need to know?" Seneca asked.

"You must first realize that I can only teach you basic skills. Your natural gifts will need to be used when you deal with her. You will need to use your wings and push them to their limit. Do you understand what I am telling you?" asked Wren. Her face twisted into a snarl that distorted her otherwise beautiful features.

"Yeah, I get it. But are my wings really a weapon?" Seneca asked. "They don't seem like they should be used for that purpose. Seriously, they're wings."

"You underestimate so much. Know that an elemental's gifts, such as your wings, are the arc of your magic. They are what ground you when calling on magic. They act as a beacon for spells and charms," said Wren. "Surely you must know this."

"There's a lot I don't know. I'm not scared to admit it either. I can tell you this much, though: I went my entire life not even knowing I came from this place or that my parents and I were druids. Heck, I didn't even know what a druid was until I got to the Otherworld. Excuse me if I'm not all-knowing about all things magic like you! You even said that not all elementals have magic, so I'm sort of like them in a way. I've gone my entire life without knowing anything about my gifts. I trust you when you say my wings are important, but that's it. It ends there. I don't know how to make them my beacon. Don't you get it? I need your guidance." Seneca was out of breath. "Great. Now I'm rambling on like Shayna."

"So be it. We shall begin with expanding your mind to embrace the nature of your elders. It is a long tale, and your attention cannot waver," said Wren.

Seneca sat in the tall grass and folded her legs beneath her. "Please tell me what you know."

Wren's expression softened. She tilted her head and nodded slowly. She circled Seneca and then came to rest on a mound of earth that served perfectly as a stool. She told stories of the Otherworld, explaining the strife and the harmony of the elementals in great detail. She showed her pride whenever she spoke of the elves. She explained that they and the druids were kindred leaders. She told of the fate of magic and how most were born with some degree of it, while others were completely without. Seneca could tell from the change in her tone that this was a delicate subject. Seneca asked questions periodically and asked for demonstrations of some of the magic Wren possessed. The time went by slowly, and the information was vast. Seneca was about to ask about the signs for identifying animals that could speak, when Wren abruptly stopped speaking and jumped to her feet. The action startled Seneca, and she searched around for the possible cause.

Wren folded her arms across her chest and began to hum a tune that first began slowly and then stopped in the middle of a note. Seneca was confused and started to interject but remained silent as Wren reached behind her back and untied a slender tubular-shaped object attached to her belt. It was bronze and approximately eight inches in length. Seneca wondered why she hadn't noticed it before. On one end, it curved slightly in an L shape, while the other end was a sculpted head of a bird. She didn't know many species of birds, so she couldn't make an accurate guess on the type. Wren rotated it several times in her hand. She took hold of her shirttail and began polishing it. She raised the L-shaped tip to her lips and blew. It was a musical instrument that made sounds like no other horn Seneca could recall, yet the melody was familiar. It took several more notes before she recognized it. It was a song that her mother often sang at bedtime, a lullaby she'd heard during her entire childhood.

The words and sound of her mother's voice filled her head. Seneca began to sing softly, at first missing a few of the words and humming in the spots where she couldn't remember any. The more she sang, the more she remembered, and her volume increased. Wren played the song again without pause, keeping her eyes closed as she swayed slightly to the melody she created effortlessly. By the third round, Seneca sang along without hesitation.

To be strong is to be subtle, and to weep is to bend.
The trees will ever sway, protecting you till the end.
To be brave is to be true, and to forgive is our blight.
The birds will ever soar, giving warning in their flight.
Our life's blessing is to be true; our promises we must keep.
With the moonlit sky, my dear one, it is time for all to sleep.
Upon rising, the day will be anew; the sun shall be our guide.
Until then, my dear one, 'tis our sweet dreams we must now abide.

Wren wiped the instrument with her shirt and then slipped it around her belt, where she secured it. She remained quiet. Seneca could tell she wanted to discuss what had just happened, but it was the last thing Seneca wanted. If she dared to utter a word, it would likely end in disaster. She was on the brink of tears that would surely turn into a loss of all composure and obnoxiously loud sobs. Too many memories were wrapped in that song. She couldn't recall the last time she'd heard it, but she knew it was one of her mother's favorites. She gulped hard and took a deep breath. She blew the air out slowly until her shoulders relaxed.

"Wren, I'm guessing you figured I would know that song. Why did you play it?" Seneca asked. Her voice quivered as she fought back tears.

"It is a song that is sung to lull the young to sleep or to put to rest any fear they may have encountered. It is a song the elders find pleasure in passing along. It is also a song that druids and elves share. We are quite similar—elves and druids, that is. We are especially aligned in our place in the Otherworld. We seek balance among all elementals," Wren said. "It is why Rileau believed I should be the one to teach you the ways of the druid. As I am an elf, I may teach you only so much, but it is better than no teachings at all. Would you not agree?"

"I suppose," said Seneca hesitantly. She desperately wanted to know more.

"Why do you not ask what you have been carrying in your heart? It is best that you do not sit on thoughts that interfere with the rhythm that beats in your chest," Wren said flatly.

Seneca thought she detected a hint of compassion, but it was so slight she couldn't be sure. "I was just wondering ... Well, I mean, I wanted to ask if you know my parents."

"Ah, that is a fascinating question. I am pleased and honored to respond. I have known of your parents since I was quite young. They are prominent in the prophecies of our teachings. The ways and actions of those who impact our way of life in the Otherworld are passed along to all elementals. Your parents sacrificed their gifts to protect our way of life. Do I know your parents? I have never met them to share greetings, but I know of them in my heart," said Wren. "They are why I chose to help you and the others. You are vital to restoring peace. Druids are necessary to maintain the balance of power. You are needed, Seneca."

"I didn't know. Thanks for telling me. It helps to know that you feel that way about them—and me," said Seneca softly. "Thanks for the song too. It brought back great memories."

Seneca wiped a tear away before it spilled over. She wanted to know more about how the Otherworld viewed her parents and their infamous sacrifice. She suddenly got a surge of determination to focus on her mission. She wanted to make them proud and not regret all they had given up. She and the others were there to bring peace and restore balance. She couldn't lose sight of that.

"I thought the song would be a nice distraction. Your focus was waning," said Wren.

"I'm good to go now. Teach me what I need to know," replied Seneca. "What's next?"

"I will tell you more about the ways of the druid," said Wren.

Wren stood back, examined Seneca for a moment, and then shook her head and frowned. She adjusted her headpiece and pushed her long ringlets of hair away from her shoulders so they cascaded down her back. As she moved, a medallion on her breastplate caught the sunlight and cast a beam of amber light that sparkled at Seneca's feet. She watched it as curiously as a cat until she realized its origin. The medallion's engraving was similar to the smooth stone in her pocket. It was the Stone of Fate. Seneca resisted inquiring about it, as she had been told to keep the stone guarded. She felt it linked them together in such a way that made her feel connected, not just to Wren but also to the Otherworld. It was the elusive home she had longed for her entire life.

"Druids are born with distinct gifts. These gifts involve the primal senses," said Wren. "These gifts are those of touch for healing or sight for visions of events that have not yet occurred, which is quite rare. There is hearing of thoughts, and that happens to be quite common." Her brow furrowed as she waited for a reaction.

Seneca was unable to contain her feelings as her mouth stretched into a thin line, but she refused to reply. Wren smirked and then regained her staunch composure.

"There are druids who control elements in nature. Only a rare few. Finally, there is the common gift of being endowed with wings," said Wren flatly.

"Really? I can control things like wind and fire?" Seneca asked excitedly. She elected to ignore the snide remark about her wings.

"I said usually. I haven't seen any sign of you being endowed with these gifts," scoffed Wren.

"If you say so. I'm not sure I've mastered anything, but thanks for telling me about being a druid," said Seneca. "I was hoping to learn how to use my gifts, but it seems today was more about a history lesson. I guess you know best."

She was frustrated, but she was committed to learning as much as she could. Survival in the Otherworld was her first priority, and bringing down Brigara was a close second. She didn't want to derail the progress she was making by complaining.

"You remind me of someone close. I am hard on her as well. I must remember this in future teachings. Of course, you may have complaints, as you are new to our Otherworld. You are not to blame for your parents' deceit or poor judgment in preparing you. Gifts are not to be wasted. Surely, they should have been wise to this," said Wren.

"Add *judgmental* to that list too. You certainly aren't shy about expressing your opinions of others," snapped Seneca. "Sometimes it's best to keep your thoughts to yourself."

"I am told that my opinion is worn like a helmet strapped too tightly on the crumpet. It is placed there for protection, but removal will be painful," replied Wren. "I say, it is useless to waste time on placing flowers on the truth! If there are thorns on the stems, then surely they will be exposed eventually."

"I think I'm keeping up with your analogies, but being tactful never hurt anyone. Try it once in a while," retorted Seneca. "Anyway, let's get on with this. Are you training me or what?"

"I have told you what it means to be a druid. Your gifts must be brought forward by you. You cannot be a sook or a lost fawn. You must be brave; there is no other path for you. You are expecting me to train you in what should be as natural as breathing. You cannot master your gifts or intertwine them with magic if you do not use them."

"I may be small, but I am not timid. I am strong. I just need guidance. I believe that's why you've been asked to help," said Seneca. She focused on keeping her wings in check and keeping her composure.

"You are not even aware that the stone in your pocket has been humming to be used? Brigara will find you like a hawk to a mouse if you cannot silence it. Your senses are mute! You may as well accept your passing if you are too afraid to accept your destiny," said Wren.

"Wow! That is really harsh," said Seneca. She was stunned by the elf's brash attitude.

"Perhaps we should confer with Rileau before we continue."

"You've made it clear that you think I'm clueless with my gifts. Well, you're right. How about we take a different approach. Instead of running off to Rileau, what do you think about including Shayna in the training? We're all here to figure out how to take Brigara down, and getting us to work as a team is probably the best approach," said Seneca. She tried her best not to sound desperate. "What do you think?"

She prayed her confidence would return with Shayna by her side. Druids were needed in the Otherworld to restore and keep the balance, and she had to remember that the responsibility rested on her petite shoulders.

"That is a brilliant idea. I believe Rileau will agree. Certainly, you and Shayna should train together," replied Wren. "You must exert your opinions more often. Perhaps you will feel the constraint of the helmet too."

"Maybe you can tell me how to quiet my stone," Seneca said as she winced. She anticipated Wren's snide rebuttal.

"That I can do. It is quite simple, actually. Tell it to remain quiet until you ask for its assistance," she replied. She raised her eyebrows and nodded to Seneca. "It will respond to you."

"Like programming it? Okay, stay quiet until I need you," Seneca said skeptically. She patted her pocket, and a cold jolt of energy shot down her leg. She wiggled slightly but felt the change instantly. The warm sensation she had experienced from the stone was gone.

"It is done," said Wren. "That is how you use your magic. You command, and it shall reply."

Wren didn't bother to wait for a reaction as she slipped away and dashed into the castle without any fanfare. Seneca pulled at her hair and kicked a mound of grass in frustration. Several beetles scrambled away in search of safety. She laughed at the irony of being threatening enough to chase away bugs, but when it came to handling the magic or growing conflict in the Otherworld, she was the one who wanted to scurry to a safe place. She tried hard to push away the fear. She wished she had gone with Wren to see Rileau's reaction. She didn't want to come across as weak, but she wanted backup, and being around Shayna always seemed to keep her on her toes. She raised her head to see Shayna dashing toward her. Seneca could see that she wasn't happy. Her stomach tightened in anticipation of hearing bad news. She opened her mouth to speak but was cut off immediately as Shayna raised her hand to halt her from talking.

"Seneca, it was terrible!" Shayna blurted out as she worked to catch her breath.

"What are you talking about?" Seneca asked.

"I'm a blunder when it comes to this reflectoire," Shayna said as she dropped to the ground and leaned into Seneca.

"I'm sure it wasn't that bad," Seneca said consolingly.

"Sure, if you don't count me nearly being killed by a shelf full of dusty, moldy books!" said Shayna. "I can't wait to do some combat training. That I know I can handle after years of kickboxing and tae kwon do." She jumped to her feet and began demonstrating a sequence of kicks, punches, and simulated strikes in the air. When she was done, she took a bow and smiled.

"Are we doing combat training? I thought we were going to learn spells," said Seneca. "You're confusing me. What are you talking about?"

"I'm talking about my forms, or *Poomsae*, as they say in Korean," she said, slightly winded. "That was Olympic-level form too!"

"You studied martial arts?" asked Seneca, trying to make sense of what Shayna was saying. "Let me get this straight. We're going to learn how to fight and not learn spells and charms?"

"Correction. You're going to learn how to fight. I've got that part handled." She grinned. "As for the magic stuff, we both have to learn that. We have to use spells and our powers when we're fighting. At least that's the way Rileau was explaining it earlier. I think it was when I almost knocked him down, or maybe it was when I bounced into Jake and almost bloodied his nose. I can't actually recall, but anyway, we definitely have to use magic when we fight in the Otherworld. You can't do one without the other. Not if we want to win anyway."

"Okay, Shayna. I've got it—I think," said Seneca wearily.

She couldn't imagine anything more contrary than Shayna doing martial arts. She tried to picture her battling anyone in the standard *gi* robe. A gi was shapeless and plain, and on top of that, it was what everyone else wore. It was nothing like the designer and original flare of her trendy outfits. Seneca smirked because she knew that aspect alone was probably enough to stop Shayna from being a real expert. "Are you good with martial arts?"

"Oh yeah! I've studied tae kwon do since I was four. My dad would take me each Saturday. It was something we did together, and it's a big reason why I got into cheerleading," said Shayna.

"What does one have to do with the other? You in a short skirt—I get it. But a gi with a sash just seems totally not you," said Seneca. She had blurted it out without thinking. She knew Shayna was not as shallow as she could sometimes appear.

"Get it straight. You wear a gi in karate. I wear a *dobok*, and it's so much cuter," replied Shayna. "Tae kwon do teaches you speed, flexibility, and balance. I have to use all of that with cheer. I think I'm good at using the sword because of my years of training. Hey, I hadn't thought about that before."

"You are full of surprises, Shayna," said Seneca as she shook her head in disbelief. "By the way, where's Wren?"

"She wanted to chat with Rileau a bit. I decided not to wait and just rushed down. As I was saying, this reflectoire is giving me fits! I'm really having a tough time getting it to work right. I could tell Rileau was losing his patience. You and Wren had perfect timing."

"I wonder what they have to talk about. I'd like to get on with this training," said Seneca.

"Whatever it is, it's intense," replied Shayna.

"What do you mean?"

"Well, when I was trying to focus on trying to teleport again, I overheard raised voices. Conner and Jake were blabbing too loudly, so I couldn't make out the exact words. It was heated, though—more like Wren was the one upset."

"She was probably complaining about me being a total washout with the magic and druid-mastering stuff," Seneca said.

"Maybe, but I don't think so." Shayna explained that she'd been in the process of keeping her eyes shut while attempting to fight off a yawn, but the involuntary response had won. She had wiped her eyes and shaken her head.

"And then?" Seneca said through gritted teeth. It was difficult not to show her impatience with Shayna's way of telling a story. The need to fill in every detail was frustrating, but she was getting used to it.

"Well, of course, falling asleep was not an option. So that's when I decided to do a few jumping jacks—you know, to shake off the need for sleep."

"So you did jumping jacks?"

"No, of course not!" Shayna said. "That's when I got distracted by the voices coming from the other side of the door. It was Wren and Rileau. And from Wren's tone, she was definitely upset."

"Did you hear anything about what she was upset about?"

"I tried to get close, because Jake and Conner were getting all worked up in their silly discussion, but just when I got close to the door, it swung open. I had to leap out of the way to keep from getting smacked in the face!"

"So that's it? You didn't hear anything at all?"

"All I can say is that Rileau was definitely agitated. He was puffing smoke like crazy. Wren was all flushed and was wiping away tears. I asked if everything was okay, and then Rileau jumped in before she could answer me," Shayna explained with animated and exaggerated hand motions. "They practically pushed me out the door before I could say two words. They told me to come here to train with you in combat and incantations." Shayna sighed. "Rileau did his deep-voice bellowing and said I'd be instrumental in helping you draw out and embrace your druid skills."

"Is Wren coming back? I sure don't know what we're supposed to do," Seneca whined.

"I'm assuming so, but I bolted out of there so fast. I needed the break and didn't ask questions."

"What about Jake and Conner? What are they doing?"

"My guess is they're probably still arguing about the things that dwell in the water that surrounds the castle. Rileau will likely put them to work, because so far, all they've done is watch me slam into walls and sheep."

Seneca muffled a laugh as she pictured what was likely painful for Shayna but humorous to witness. She encouraged her to describe the various mishaps and helped her find the humor in each one. They stretched out in the overgrown grass and picked dandelions. They blew the delicate petals into the wind as they stared up into the billowing clouds above.

"Seneca, we could be heroes," said Shayna. "Have you thought about that?"

"No, that's not even close to what's been going through my head. I'm so scared about all of this. Aren't you?"

"I think I'm more afraid of the unknown. I can feel in my gut that this is where I'm supposed to be. You know, like it was inevitable. I just know there's going to be a showdown of some kind—like all heroes have to face."

"If you believe in fate, then yeah, maybe we are meant to do this. But right now, it's everyone else telling us we have to do this. I honestly don't know if this is what I'm supposed to do. I keep waiting for a sign, a feeling or something that says this is the right thing," said Seneca.

"I get what you're saying. For me, it's the idea of saving the elementals in the Otherworld. Thinking that Brigara wants to destroy it all twists my stomach into knots. I know we can do it. We have to!" Shayna sat up and looked around. "Look how peaceful it is here. To think that evil woman wants to destroy it makes me so angry! It's up to us—you, me, Conner, and Jake—to stop her."

"I know. I get it," said Seneca. "Maybe I'm expecting too much, looking for that flashing sign and all."

"I'm telling you, Seneca. Even though you don't see it yet, this is our fate, our destiny, and all of those other words that say we are meant to do this."

"Being a hero, though—that's a lot of pressure. Maybe that's what scares me the most. Everyone's depending on us to bring her down. What if we can't?"

"You can't think like that. Once you say that c-word, then we are all doomed. Erase and delete that from your mind!"

"Got it." Seneca laughed and sat up. She watched Shayna braid a few of the dandelion stems and decided to join her. "You know, we might end up being here forever—like never seeing our families or our homes again. Maybe that's what's really bothering me. It's hard for me to focus on the dominion when I'm missing my family. Wren sang a song that my mother used to sing, and I almost lost it." Seneca sighed heavily.

"I miss my dad and, believe it or not, school," said Shayna. "But being here feels right. I feel like it's what I've been preparing for my whole life. I didn't know it at first, but I do now. I know I will see my family again, but for now, I have to make sure my family here has a safe home."

"I agree with you on that. If we can do that, then maybe my family can come here too. I have to remember that the Otherworld is their home," said Seneca softly. "Maybe that's how I have to look at this: I'm doing this for them. Even if we're clueless without any chance of winning."

"There's no way prophecies would exist about us if we didn't stand a chance. Plus, think about the constant attacks to stop us. If we didn't have something special, no one would bother with us. I'm confident we can do this, and you should be too," Shayna said boisterously.

Seneca looked closely into Shayna's eyes. It was obvious Shayna believed completely in what she was saying, but she felt a sudden urge to change the topic. "Tell me more about your tae kwon do stuff," said Seneca.

Shayna began explaining the various kicks, throws, and open-handed strikes. Seneca was impressed with her knowledge and felt slightly guilty for prejudging her. Just as the conversation began to die down, Wren appeared. From her sour expression, it was obvious she was not in a pleasant mood.

"Why are the two of you sitting about as if you're sloths on a holiday? Let's get started!" Wren bellowed.

Her cheeks were flushed, and her eyes were bloodshot. It was clear she had been crying, but they knew better than to push for an explanation. Seneca and Shayna exchanged a quick glance and quickly scrambled to their feet. Wren didn't bother with pleasantries as she brushed past them and discarded her belongings.

"It is time to make you into the dominion that has been foretold. You will obey me without hesitation as you learn the ways of magic in our Otherworld," said Wren. Her voice quivered slightly, but she showed no other signs of being distraught. "As an elemental and a demi-elemental, you will harness the magic that is in your blood, but as the color of your hair is different, so will be your gifts."

They listened intently as Wren explained about manipulation magic and how to use it in battles. She demonstrated basic spells, advanced incantations, and complicated charms. She drilled them in hand-to-hand combat laced with magic. Shayna proved to be efficient in her footwork and guiding her sword to absorb weak spells in midair. Seneca excelled at learning strategic counter-spells and quickly gained comfort in weaving charms with the shielding light from her wings.

Wren showed only small elements of what was needed to defeat Brigara. She spent the majority of the time enlightening them on various tactics Brigara's dangerous followers were likely to use. Some of the potential methods she described were simple to follow and didn't need much explanation. The more difficult or elusive maneuvers were expounded upon in great detail. She pressed heavily on the notion of instinct.

"You must learn to trust and not question," Wren said. "Magic follows what you feel. If you are fuzzy with your instincts or allow doubt to interfere, then your spells will be formless. They shall dwindle like the petals of a daisy in a drought."

Wren retrieved her staff and pulled a handful of leaves from the nearest tree. She threw them into the air and aimed her staff. A blue orb of light surrounded the leaves, keeping them suspended as they rotated. Wren said a short incantation, and the light of the orb turned black. The leaves transformed into a slew of black crows. They circled above her head and then flew directly at Shayna, who ducked and tumbled head over heels to avoid being hit. The angry birds reversed their direction to attempt another attack. Shayna scrambled to her feet and slashed her sword through the air but missed. They circled and made another advance in a tighter formation. Their cries were harsh and grating as they aimed directly at her.

"Dilagna wivnoro!" Shayna screamed the defensive spell she had just learned.

She lunged with her sword. It vibrated beneath her grip, and she grasped tighter to remain in control. She swung repeatedly, fatally striking the enchanted crows. Each bird crumpled to the ground and faded into a pile of dry leaves. A small gust of wind lifted and carried them away. Shayna let out a slow sigh of relief and watched until they were completely out of sight.

"That was impressive. You expressed the spell like you knew what you were doing," said Seneca. Her words sounded more like a question than a statement.

"Thanks. It felt right," said Shayna.

"It is what you both must do. Stop thinking about your next move, and just act," said Wren dryly.

"I used my sword, but that was really about the spell—about magic. Do we rely on magic more than fighting with our fists?" Shayna asked as she wiped away beads of sweat from her cheeks.

"Hand-to-hand combat combined with magic is by far the most used in the Otherworld. Having the skills necessary to climb, jump, and punch is essential," Wren said. "Since both of you are feeble in all areas of combat, you must work even harder to disarm and overpower your attackers."

"Well, Shayna's an expert in tae kwon do, and I'm sure—"

Wren raised her hand to indicate silence, and Seneca reluctantly obeyed. "What you have learned or think you've mastered as expert, as you say, will mean absolutely nothing here in our Otherworld. Do not convince yourself that the knowledge you have gained in the mortal realm can compare to what you must know to survive here. Keep this in mind always. I am teaching you to arm yourself with enchantments and defend yourself with lethal combat skills intertwined with magic," Wren said sternly.

"Sorry, Shayna," Seneca said softly.

"No worries. I'm up for whatever she's ready to throw at us," Shayna mumbled, her cheeks flushed.

"Let us begin," said Wren.

Seneca and Shayna exchanged glares as they readied themselves. Wren launched into the most aggressive training demonstration they had seen so far. She focused on every aspect of their bodies. She was precise and focused on each nuance of the various maneuvers. She focused on their balance and recovery.

"I keep hesitating, even though it's identical to the last spell, and I don't know why," said Shayna, breathing heavily as she bent over in exhaustion.

"You must be comfortable in being the attacker. Do not wait for the enemy's advance, as such tactics will be your end," Wren said. "Seneca is beating you each time because you are not precise in your attack. Now, do it again."

Just as they got comfortable with one movement or tactic, Wren would change things up. They were impressed with her ability to contort into a multitude of positions to avoid injury. She stressed the importance of mastering charms for protection. The session went on for hours, and each time they faltered, she would force them to repeat the movement or spell until it was mastered. Once they became comfortable, she would add even more difficult maneuvers and incantations.

The spells came fairly easily to Seneca, as she had an innate sense of rhythm in the words, although she thought most of them sounded like gibberish. She believed it was like a language that had been dormant in her subconscious. Shayna was a natural with the physical elements and excited whenever there was a combination that included charms and the use of her sword. Her sword responded with little effort, even when she forgot a word or two in the spells.

"This is exhausting! Can we take a break? I am not grasping what you're doing with the elbow armlock move at all," said Shayna. She leaned forward to catch her breath. She enjoyed a rigorous workout, but what Wren was putting them through was well beyond the norm. Her knees were ready to give out, and she tried her best to steady them.

"There is no time for rest. Your foe will not take time for leisure, and neither shall you!" Wren snapped. She had barely broken a sweat, and her attitude was just as dry.

"I agree with Shayna. We've been going at this a really long time, and the sun is about to go down. It's getting more difficult to see,"

Seneca complained, her voice hoarse. She was drenched in sweat, and her clothes stuck to her as if she'd gone for a plunge in the lake.

"What are you quibbling about?" asked Wren. Her nose twitched in irritation.

"There isn't much light hitting this side of the castle. Maybe we can pick this up again in the morning," said Shayna. Her throat was dry, and she could feel the dead skin forming on her chapped lips. Her back had a dull ache from the wrenching she had endured when Seneca had clumsily tried to duplicate Wren's attack technique at her expense.

"If you are both going to whine like kids of a goat, then I have no desire to waste more moments with the likes of you," Wren huffed.

It was evident Wren had grown frustrated with their less-than-stellar progress. She had resorted to snapping twigs between her thumb and forefinger each time they needed to repeat a failed hold, punch, or spell. As the hours had ticked by, she'd advanced from twigs to sticks and, finally, fallen branches. Both Shayna and Seneca had noticed but did not dare to comment. They tried to keep their focus as they sparred and attempted to incorporate each incantation or move they had been taught.

When Seneca misjudged a countermove that included multiple combinations of complicated charms, bobbing, and weaving, she was thrown off balance and went tumbling backward into the mud. Shayna couldn't hold back and broke into a hearty laugh. Seneca joined in when she realized how ridiculous she must have looked. Wren was livid and screamed at a raging pitch. She snatched a sizable branch and swung it hard into the trunk of a helpless hawthorn tree. The tree shook from the repetitive bashing it was forced to endure. A family of birds that had gathered on the highest branches took flight. They found refuge in a nearby ash tree, where they chirped angrily in a disgruntled chorus. The abundant branches were no match for Wren's attack. Several large limbs with clusters of small light green leaves broke away from the tree and came crashing down. Shayna dodged to avoid being clobbered by one. The remains scattered in bits at her feet.

Wren spun around and faced the girls; she still had a firm grip on what remained of the branch. Several splinters were lodged in her palm.

Blood trickled down her hand and seeped between her fingers. Her face was ridged, and although she was beautiful, her expression was distorted from its natural form. Seneca and Shayna were speechless as they witnessed the elf's temper tantrum. They watched with as much fear as fascination. Wren kept her eyes locked on them as she skillfully twisted, snapped, and crumpled the branch into a heap with seemingly little effort.

Seneca didn't know if she should be concerned or impressed, although neither seemed to be the correct reaction. She realized she was actually confused. In her opinion, Wren's behavior was an overreaction. It must have stemmed from something other than her blunder with the sparring.

"Look, Wren, I know exactly how I messed up, and we can start again," said Seneca. "There's no reason to take it out on the trees."

"Yeah, I'm tired, but I can probably go another round," added Shayna. She knew she didn't sound convincing, but she was too drained of energy to care.

Wren glared momentarily but did not reply. She turned her back to them and began to gather her belongings. She strapped on her belt and fastened a flask and a satchel to it. She snatched her cloak, paused, and then dropped everything in a heap. She took a deep breath and slowly turned to face them. Her face was etched with anger.

"I am done with the two of you! You are becoming more tentative with each passing phase of the sun. You are weak and lack focus." Wren berated them without pause. "Just because you are sisters within the dominion, you must not hold back from advancing your attacks. If you are strategic in your counter technique, you will avoid injury. You must not hesitate or relent in your advance. Do you not grasp this simplistic action?"

"Let me get this straight," Shayna said as she placed a hand on her hip. The other hand held firmly to her vibrating sword, which she had summoned unknowingly. "You want us to actually try to hurt each other? Wait! Before you answer, just know that's ludicrous!" Shayna yelled.

The birds echoed her sentiment with a resounding screech from the ash tree.

"I agree with her—these are supposed to be drills," said Seneca. "I'm not about to hurt Shayna."

"As if you could," snapped Shayna with a roll of her eyes as she shifted her weight to lean more into her hip stance.

Wren stayed silent as she looked at Seneca for the anticipated rebuttal.

Seneca's ears grew red, and she pressed her lips tightly together. "Look, Shayna, you might have a sword, but that's all you've got! With my wings, let's just say there'd be no contest—trust me!"

"Flash your little wings, and let's test your theory, blondie!" Shayna shouted as she wrapped both hands around her sword. The blade glowed brightly as she raised it above her head and locked her elbows. She was positioned to strike. "Come on! What are you waiting for?"

Seneca was unmoved and simply smiled. She turned to Wren and was not surprised to see the gleam in her eyes and the smirk plastered across her face. "Is this what you wanted, Wren?" Seneca asked with a tone of sarcasm. "You wanted us angry enough to be willing to attack each other without cause?"

"What?" Shayna asked in confusion as she lowered her sword. She noticed it felt heavier than she had ever experienced. Her shoulders ached as she let her arms drop to her sides and allowed the sword to vanish.

"Don't you see? She's been provoking us all day, and we wouldn't react the way she wanted. In other words, she wanted us to turn on each other. My question is, why? Why are you doing this?" Seneca asked.

"You are being ridiculous," replied Wren.

"What's ridiculous is you thinking I would ever hurt Seneca!" said Shayna. She walked closer to Seneca and put an arm around her shoulders. She eyed Wren with contempt.

"As I've said before, we should call it for the day and begin again at daybreak," said Wren. "I am pleased with your progress."

"Excuse me—are you kidding me?" Seneca huffed.

"Tomorrow will prove to be a day to remember! Your instincts are a testament to your druid nature. I was beginning to believe your attunement was out of sorts. Rileau will be pleased to learn that you are quite skilled as a druid."

"What do you mean by my attunement being 'out of sorts'?" Seneca asked.

"It simply means I thought you were not connecting to your true nature, and as such, you were somehow blocking or disconnecting from being a true druid. You are damn jammy is what you are! Mark my words: you are surely trapped in the muck that's cluttering your abilities, but you will be able to overcome that. I'm quite positive," said Wren. She smirked and nodded, as she was pleased with her assessment.

"What?" Seneca asked with a wrinkled nose.

"No need to bother with this now. We can discuss more when we meet again."

"Let me get this straight—you got all that from me not wanting to fight Shayna?" Seneca asked suspiciously.

"That was a significant aspect of it, yes," said Wren. "I don't care to tussle with this now, but know this: druids look for balance in all things. They disarm to find peace and stay calm while others are unfocused. These are essential in being a druid. As I said, we are done for now. You must report back to Rileau." She proceeded to gather her discarded belongings and made no attempt to address the confused looks etched on Shayna's and Seneca's faces.

"And you actually want us to do this again tomorrow?" asked Shayna. "Seriously?" She was dumbfounded by the turn of events and Wren's turnabout in attitude.

"Absolutely. You have both handled this day to perfection," said Wren. Her voice was uncharacteristically charming and light.

Seneca turned to look at Shayna, who was slowly shaking her head. They watched as Wren picked up her cloak, adjusted her boots, and repositioned her armbands in preparation to leave. She picked up her staff before returning her attention to them. She cocked her head and twisted her lips into a tight pucker, as though she were preparing to scrutinize them further. She shook her head dismissively and sighed before approaching them. They hadn't moved the slightest bit.

"I have decided that we shall continue your training at first light but not here. There are far too many distractions. We will meet at my dwelling on the fairest side of the forest, where the flowers bloom only in pale shades and the water from the brooks runs clear. We shall have a meal together and then continue our training. The lighting cascades evenly through the canopy of trees. It will be most ideal for advancing your training," Wren said.

"You want us to come to your house?" Shayna asked as she watched Wren remove something from her pocket.

"Here is a map to guide you. Arrive before the dew is absorbed by the daylight."

She handed a tattered scroll of parchment to Seneca, who tentatively accepted it. The map showed Rileau's castle circled in black. There were several other landmarks, etchings of trees, clusters of forests, trails, and waterways. Wren's home was clearly identified.

"You will know you're close when you pass a fairy arch covered in fragrant orchids," said Wren.

"It looks pretty easy to find," Seneca mumbled. She looked into Wren's eyes and was tempted to read her thoughts but fought back the urge.

Shayna leaned in to examine the map and decided she wanted to hold on to it, so she slid it out of Seneca's hand. "I'll hold on to it," Shayna declared.

"Fine, go ahead," replied Seneca dryly.

"I must see my clan this nightfall. They dislike any delays. As you awake for a new day, you shall meet high challenges. Eat hearty this night, and sleep deeply, as you shall need your strength," said Wren.

She turned on her heel and sprinted toward the woods, picking up speed with each stride. They observed her move silently and skillfully through the terrain, watching until she could no longer be seen.

Annoyed that Shayna had confiscated the map, Seneca snatched it away and examined it closely. She wondered if there was more to the map than it appeared. She scanned it closely for anything unusual but saw nothing out of the ordinary, so she rolled it up and shoved it in her back pocket.

"Are you sure I shouldn't hold on to that?" asked Shayna.

"It's safe with me," said Seneca.

"Whatever. Hey, what was the sudden stage-left exit all about?"

"She was acting strange all day," replied Seneca with a shrug.

"Yeah, but she's off to see her clan? She hasn't mentioned anything about meeting with anyone before. That is one crazy elf!" said Shayna. "I can't believe she was taunting us to fight. What's up with that?"

"And you fell for it!" Seneca snapped. "You were actually going to come at me!"

"No, I wasn't. Well, only if you came at me first! I'd never strike you unless you gave me a darn good reason," replied Shayna. "After all, you wouldn't last two seconds once I made a move. It wouldn't be an even match."

"Ha! In your dreams!" Seneca laughed. "Thank goodness we both know we'll never have to put any of this to a real test. But it makes me wonder."

"Wonder about what?"

"Why Wren was trying to provoke us into actually fighting. We'd done drills and sparred all day, but something snapped. And I'm not talking about half the tree limbs in the forest. Didn't you see that look in her eyes when she thought we were going to really fight?" asked Seneca.

"Yeah, she was practically licking her lips and chomping at the bit. She was like a hard-core fan in a front-row seat for the brawl of the century, just waiting for blood!" said Shayna. "She said it was basically about testing you and your attunement. I'm still not clear on what that's all about."

"Precisely. I know she supposedly knows more about being a druid because she's an elf and whatever, but there's no way that confrontation between us had anything to do with whether or not I was acting like a true druid or not," said Seneca. Her head was spinning, and she didn't like questioning Wren's motives, but she felt something was off.

"On the other hand, maybe she's just high-strung. You know, like she's coiled too tightly. She's all business, and we weren't up to her level of expectation. She's probably just feeling the pressure of trying to prep two newbies for a war against a barrage of magical creatures and who knows what else," Shayna replied.

"I think it's more than that," said Seneca. "There was something off about her."

"All I'm saying is that you could be reading too much into it. We were both getting tired, and maybe we just need to regroup," said Shayna. "I doubt Rileau would have her training you on being a druid if he didn't trust her."

"I'm not sure Rileau knows her tactics. To push us to the point where we might attack each other? Come on! I bet she went way off the grid with that one," replied Seneca.

"Maybe," said Shayna. She knew Seneca was suspicious, and she didn't care to fuel her suspicion by pushing the conversation further. "Anyway, we should probably get back inside. I'm starving."

Seneca knew it was Shayna's way of dropping the topic. She reluctantly agreed, knowing she should be hungry as well, but instead, she felt slightly queasy from exhaustion. Seneca allowed Shayna to take the lead and trailed close behind. Her thoughts shifted to Wren's methods as she recited some of the complicated spells in a whisper. They started the long climb up the spiral staircase that led to the dining room.

A wonderful aroma lingered in the air as they reached the top. Seneca and Shayna were lost in their own thoughts and exchanged little conversation as they reached for their plates and began piling on the offerings. Jake and Conner were in the midst of a debate as to who had devoured the last slice of chocolate cake. They paid little attention as the girls reached around them to claim the small portions of what remained from the obviously lavish dinner spread.

Seneca felt an uneasiness wash over her. Something was not right; she sensed there was something brewing. She glanced at her forearms; they were covered in goose bumps. The fine blonde hairs that covered her arms were raised, and she shivered in reaction. She rubbed and cupped her hands together and then raised them to her mouth. She puffed hot air into the hollow opening and continued to rub them together in an attempt to counter the sudden drop in her temperature.

"You okay, Seneca?" Conner asked with his cheeks puckering from the mounds of food he was quickly devouring. "You don't look so good. I left you plenty of beef. Don't pout!"

Seneca forced a smile and nodded slowly. She picked up a slice of rye bread and nibbled the thick crust. She realized it was the only thing she had managed to put on her plate; it alone was overwhelming. Her stomach rebelled in reaction as she took a deep breath to keep from vomiting. There was definitely something wrong, but she had no way of proving it.

CHAPTER FIFTEEN

The Dupelene

Seneca cradled her head in her hands. She couldn't figure out how to breathe. She was choking on her own oxygen. It was a classic panic attack. She had experienced enough of them to recognize the signs, but this one was different. She could feel the salt forming beneath the cold beads of sweat above her lip. She wanted to lick it away, but her tongue was paralyzed. Her mouth was open, yet she could neither exhale nor inhale. Her arms flailed wildly to maintain her balance. A sense of vertigo had kicked in, and she felt the room spinning as nausea began to build. There was a voice screaming inside her head that she tried hard to focus on. The intensity of her efforts sent a shooting pain that pierced through her temples as her head rocked back. "Just breathe. Come on. Do it—now!" She gasped and then coughed hard.

Tears rolled down her face, and she blinked hard to regain focus. At some point, she had fallen to her knees; she jumped to her feet quickly and spun around. Through the blur, she spotted Brigara with an outstretched hand. It took merely a second to register what was happening as she saw the flash of light from a fast-spinning sphere. It was heading directly toward her. Seneca lifted her arm to cover her face; her wings wrapped around her and enveloped her entire body. She was completely covered in a cocoon of light. She felt the impact but knew she was protected.

"You may have inherited the power of your mother's wings, but she will know precisely what to do about that!" Brigara yelled.

Who will know? thought Seneca as she braced for impact. Brigara sent two flaming spheres hurling at her. The impact slammed Seneca into the wall, but her wings remained fixed. Another set of spheres appeared; they hovered and spun quickly, ready for launch. Seneca closed her eyes tightly. The overwhelming fear blocked her from reacting. She focused on slowing her breathing, but being wrapped in her wings was like a sauna and was causing her to hyperventilate. What had Wren said to do? Her mind was blank. She released a dreadful scream and braced for impact.

"Back off, you raggedy skank!" shouted Shayna as she stormed across the room. Her eyes were fixed on Brigara. "Get away from her!"

Shayna was winded, but she allowed her adrenaline to propel her into action. She raised her sword in preparation. Just as she began the magic chant to increase her sword's power, an excruciating blow plowed into her lower back. She was stunned and crumpled to the floor. Before it registered what had happened, the attacker straddled her and started pounding on her chest. Shayna knocked it off with an elbow shot to its head and scrambled to her feet. Before she could get her balance, she was knocked down again. This time, she was prepared and countered by kicking it squarely in the shin. Shayna leaped high and came down hard with the hilt of her sword. It landed solidly between the attacker's eyes, rocking it back on its heels until it collapsed at Shayna's feet. Her sword hummed beneath her firm grasp.

Slightly disoriented, Shayna spun around until she spotted Brigara. She was dragging Seneca by her wings through a doorway. "Stop! let her go!"

Shayna darted across the room. It was too late. The door vanished just as the trailing tip of Seneca's wings crossed the threshold. It was now a blank wall with aged water stains and peeling plaster. Shayna rubbed her hand against the wall, although she knew it had been a portal that only magic could reopen.

"No!" she screamed as she banged her fist against the wall.

Sensing movement, she quickly turned toward the enemy left behind. It was charging directly at her, its sword drawn and aimed directly at her. Shayna didn't hesitate; she closed her eyes, crouched low, and swung as hard as she could. She shouted the incantation Wren had drilled into her head.

"Strikata escapto novatum!"

She felt the impact as the blade slashed through flesh. She timed her maneuver with precision to avoid injury while striking the exposed area of the assailant. She knew it was a lethal assault. She opened her eyes to survey the results. The attacker, with labored breathing, lay at her feet.

It was the first time Shayna noticed that her attacker was female. The fight had been moving so fast that it hadn't registered. Shayna swallowed hard as she looked down on the fallen enemy. She had thick waist-length auburn hair. It was matted and twisted in clumps throughout, and the style appeared intentional. Each twisted section was wrapped in gold thread and decorative bands of maroon and black. She was taller than average but extremely gaunt. Shayna figured she was most likely an elf since she resembled Wren slightly. Her ears had the same angular pointed tips, and the clothing was similar. Her eyes might have been just as vibrant at an earlier time, but now they were bloodshot and filled with rage.

The elf held her side, just above her pelvic bone, with both hands. The injury was major. Blood flowed steadily and drenched her clothing. Shayna watched motionlessly. She had never seen so much blood. She needed to contemplate the situation.

Shayna flexed her fingers and tightened her hold around the grip of her sword. The ice-blue blade vibrated in acknowledgment. She positioned the edge a fraction of a millimeter from the elf's throat. She steadied her hands and looked directly into her enemy's eyes. "You will tell me where Brigara has taken Seneca, or I will put an end to your wretched existence!" Her voice quivered slightly, but her stance remained fierce.

"I'm passing from this world soon enough," she groaned. "Your threats are meaningless."

Although her coloring was deep, her face was somewhat pale, except for the eyelids. They had turned a dark shade of purple and were nearly swollen shut. Shayna assumed the hits to the bridge of her nose and head were the cause.

"You're not going anywhere until I get some answers!" Shayna raged.

"You may strike at will, as my fate cannot be altered," she replied. The elf gasped for breath and cringed. "I will be passing soon." Her eyelids fluttered, and her dark hazel eyes had a cloudy haze across them. She closed them tightly as her body arched slightly, and she muffled a cry of pain. The elf released her grip on the wound and let out a soft sigh.

Shayna slowly realized the full extent of the damage her sword had yielded. Her chest tightened, and her throat was too dry to swallow. She took in a deep breath and positioned the sword above her head as she pulled her shoulders back. She was ready to strike. She looked down at the dying elf, and her eyes filled with tears. *There's no room for pity*, she thought. *I must find Seneca, no matter what.*

"You can die slowly and in pain, or I can offer you mercy with a swift end to your suffering," said Shayna sternly. She focused on not allowing her tears to flow and sniffed hard to keep them at bay. She wanted to sound convincing, although she was merely quoting a famous line from an action movie she had seen several times.

"You would grant this to me?" her enemy asked. Her voice was barely audible.

The confusion on the elf's face caught Shayna by surprise. The elf's eyes locked on hers briefly; the lids fluttered and then closed.

"Well, yeah, I mean, isn't that the noble thing to do in these situations?" said Shayna.

Her confidence in being able to kill was waning, as was her adrenaline. It was different when the battle was active. It didn't help that her enemy was trying to have a conversation.

"Look, just tell me where Brigara took Seneca. Then we can figure out the terms of my offer and all that later." Shayna lowered her sword but kept both hands firmly around the hilt.

"She is not who you believe her to be. She is not…Brigara does not have—"

"Brigara does not have what?" She raised her sword again in a threat to strike. "Spit it out! She doesn't have Seneca? Is that what you're trying to say? Huh? Tell me!"

It was too late for any reply. Shayna's mouth hung open as she watched the elf take her last breath. She resisted the urge to grab hold and shake her. She wanted to scream at the top of her lungs, but she didn't have the strength. *What did she mean? What was she trying to say?* The words kept swirling around in her head. *"She is not who you believe her to be."* If Brigara doesn't have her, who does?

"I've got to get back to Rileau," she mumbled. "He can get Seneca back."

It had taken them hours to get to there. She needed help now. Shayna knew that teleporting was risky. She'd only tried it in and around the castle. Picturing the dining room or the bedrooms was tough enough. She could still feel the bruises from slamming into the bookcase. Ending up with the sheep wasn't desirable either, but at least she'd be close.

"Think, Shayna!" she yelled. "Get your butt into gear and do this!"

She closed her eyes and attempted to see the details of the flowers that lined the edge of the stone bridge leading to the castle. She imagined the lavender scent that wisped through the breeze and the feeling of it tickling her nose. She recalled the sensation of touching the cool stone wall. She thought of the dark and mysterious water beneath the bridge and the massive archway that framed the entrance to the castle. She was ready. She held her breath. Squeezing her eyelids shut tightly, she swiped a hand across the reflectoire. The familiar vibration and dizziness came in a sudden wave, as before, but something was wrong. It was too late to stop, so she braced herself for impact.

She instinctively held her breath. The dark water was too dense to make out anything around her. Shayna kicked hard and pushed her way until her head bobbed above the surface. The water was surprisingly warm and calm. She swam effortlessly to the closest bank and crawled into the thick grass that lined the water's edge. It hadn't been her target, but she was close enough. She stood and looked out at the familiar bridge that led into Rileau's castle. A brisk wind blew leaves across her soaked boots. She gazed up at the sky to see a mass of ominous dark clouds looming.

"A storm is definitely brewing. I've gotta work on this teleporting thing," she said aloud as she ran as fast as her legs would propel her. She rushed to the massive door and pushed hard. "Brigara's got Seneca! Help! She's got Seneca!"

Rileau rounded the corner and nearly crashed into Shayna before putting his arms out to avoid impact. "What are you saying? How is that possible?" he asked skeptically.

"What's going on?" asked Jake, who had heard the yelling. He and Conner had followed Rileau to the foyer.

"Brigara's here, and she's got Seneca!" Shayna shouted as she brushed past Rileau and grabbed on to Jake before quickly pulling away. Her mind was racing, and the words weren't forming as clearly as she wanted. She was shivering and circled frantically as she tried to slow down and tell them all she knew. "She came without warning, and she wasn't alone. An elf was helping her."

It took every ounce of strength she had to stay steady and not collapse. Saying the words out loud gave them truth. She felt sick each time her mind tried to paint a picture of what could potentially be happening to Seneca. It was unbearable.

"Brigara has Seneca? How? What happened? I'll destroy her!" Conner fumed. He pounded his fist into the palm of his hand.

"Where is she?" Jake asked "What are we waiting for? Let's get her back!"

"She's gone. Brigara took her," said Shayna faintly. Tears rolled down her cheeks as she covered her face.

"Tell me all. Do not forego any detail!" said Rileau as he motioned for Shayna to sit down.

Shayna hesitated as she wrung her hands. She was too keyed up to sit, but she decided not to protest. Her thoughts were jumbled, and she wondered if it was a residual effect from teleporting. She felt a little nauseated and decided that sitting was probably a good idea. She swallowed hard in an attempt to keep anything from rising up. She took a deep breath and wiped her tears. "I can tell you what I know, but I don't know if it will help any," she said.

"I can't believe this. How did she do it?" asked Jake anxiously. He circled around like a caged animal. He feared the worst.

"Let her speak," said Rileau. His large hand waved through the air to motion for silence.

Jake didn't argue as he sat down and eased in next to Shayna. Conner hung back. His mind went blank as he mumbled incoherently.

"Are you okay? Did you sustain any injuries?" Rileau asked in a low, steady voice.

"I'm fine," replied Shayna. She knew she wasn't, but it was her knee-jerk response. She started to change her answer before Conner bounded across the room like a young kangaroo.

"Really? You look like you're soaking wet!" said Conner. "Maybe she used some kind of water spell on you—like zap! Hocus-pocus—you're a sponge!" He wiggled his fingers in the air to simulate casting a spell.

"Shut up, Conner! Pay attention for once. Seneca's in danger. Don't you get it?" Jake roared.

"Who cares if I'm fine? She's not! For your information, when I tried to teleport here, I ended up in the water outside the castle," said Shayna. "There. I said it. Are you satisfied?" She ran her hands through her hair and whisked away the excess water. She created a small puddle that was quickly absorbed into the area rug.

"What you're saying is that you have bad aim, and that's why you're dripping?" asked Conner.

"Enough! Conner, you must hold your tongue and let her explain what has become of Seneca," snapped Rileau. His eyes glowed a deep green.

"Brigara disappeared through some kind of portal with Seneca!" Shayna yelled. Her cheeks flushed red as she glared at Conner. He took the hint and stepped back a few feet while eyeing her closely.

"Brigara..." Jake's voice trailed off. He hadn't thought they needed to be prepared to battle her already. They were still learning. "What do we do, Rileau?"

They turned to Rileau and searched his face for a reaction and a signal that he had a game plan. He didn't respond. Instead, he strolled slowly to the window and gazed out into the distance. A swirling cloud of smoke encircled his head and momentarily obscured his face.

"You heard me, right? Brigara took Seneca!" yelled Shayna. "Say something!" She leaped to her feet, ready to charge, and Jake pulled her back to keep her from pouncing. "What are we going to do?" she screamed.

"We've got to get her back. Are you listening?" Jake said. He loosened his grip on Shayna as she wrestled free.

"Yeah, I hear you both. Now, tell me exactly what happened, Shayna," said Rileau as he turned to face them. "I must know the specific details if we are to get her back."

"If," Conner muttered to himself.

Rileau fanned the continuous streams of smoke that escaped his flared nostrils. The smoke was filling the room quickly, and Conner joined him in swiping at the air.

"Please sit down, Shayna. Speak of all that happened," Rileau said sternly. "Time is of the essence. If Brigara has her, it is not likely she will survive for long." He paced in front of her but kept his head turned in her direction.

Shayna slid to the edge of the enormous velvet upholstered chair. She smoothed a few strands of drenched hair away from her face and tucked them behind her ears. She took a deep breath and began to recount each aspect of the attack. She included as much detail as possible. She described how the elf had looked, the sword she'd used in the attack, and how her nose had been broken in the battle. She tried to be vague about the fatal blow that had ended the elf's life, but she gave enough details so that they surmised it had been brutal but necessary. Shayna never revealed the incantation she'd cast. She was aware that it was the magic that had ended a life. It was hard for her to fathom the new reality of her life.

"You said this elf you combatted was the one who took Seneca, right? Was it not Brigara?" asked Rileau.

"Not exactly. Well, maybe, sure, but you've gotta understand. The elf was dying and mumbling a lot," replied Shayna. Her mind flashed to the blood that had pooled around the elf. She shook her head to erase the image. "It seemed like she was trying hard to tell me that it wasn't Brigara, but then again, I can't be totally positive."

"But you said you saw her! So, was it or was it not Brigara who took Seneca?" Jake said.

He had made himself a part of the interrogation, although he knew Rileau wouldn't welcome or tolerate it. Jake heard a low growl as he met Rileau's eyes. He took a small step sideways as a precaution.

"Allow me to put forth the questions," said Rileau firmly. Another burst of smoke filled the air. He returned his attention to Shayna.

Shayna was beginning to feel the chill from her damp clothes. She pulled a heavily embroidered wool blanket from the back of the chair and draped it around her shoulders. She pulled her knees to her chest and wrapped the blanket around her shivering body until she was completely covered; only her face remained exposed. "Indeed, it was Brigara. I saw her! And did I mention those fireball things she was hurling at Seneca? Seneca, by the way, did an awesome job protecting herself with her wings. She has some mighty powerful feathers. I guess they're not really feathers though. I wonder what they're made of."

"Shayna! You must focus," Rileau said. "Tell me if she spoke. Did Brigara actually say anything?" They all watched the stream of smoke jet from his flared nostrils and dissipate in the air above his head. His tail raised and then smacked the ground like thunder. The room shook as they kept all eyes on him.

"Yes. She did talk. Ah, but you know how she's always ranting. She said something about Seneca's wings—when those big ole flaming fireballs didn't hurt her," said Shayna. Her voice trembled slightly. An image flashed through her head of being clobbered by Rileau's tail, and it made her shudder. She blinked hard to erase the disturbing picture in her mind. She didn't want to provide false information, so she concentrated hard to recount all she had witnessed.

"What were the specific words she spoke?" asked Rileau as he released more smoke. It rose slowly and twisted upward before it dissipated high above his head.

Jake followed the trail upward and watched it swirl and evaporate. He was fascinated by the idea of generating smoke from within. He realized that like a steam engine, Rileau needed to release a bit of it as a way to maintain his composure. It made him wonder what would happen if Rileau's anger reached its peak. He'd been vague about how powerful he was when consuming the platinum elixir. Jake realized he actually wanted to see Rileau rage and reveal his full capabilities. He didn't know if it would ever come to that, but now that Brigara had Seneca, perhaps under the circumstances, his hopes would be realized.

"Okay, give me a second," said Shayna, closing her eyes to focus. "She said something like 'She will know what to do about those wings.'"

"She? Who was she talking about? Who is she?" asked Jake. "Is Brigara working with someone else?"

"I believe the elf was being truthful when she declared that it was not Brigara," said Rileau abruptly. He rubbed his chin and tilted his head upward. "It was not Brigara. Curious circumstances. I must reflect upon this." He repeated his last statement several times aloud as he nodded slowly.

Jake stared at the continuous chain of smoke that escaped his nostrils. Shayna decided to remain silent before adding anything else. Conner waited patiently without whispering a word. They were all interested in whatever Rileau was thinking.

"You are quite sure about the elf's last words?" Rileau asked. It was clear he'd already made up his mind but sought a final confirmation just the same.

"Yeah. But I saw her, you guys! Trust me—the same stringy hair and bony fingers and that pitifully bad outfit. It was her. I'm telling you!" Shayna said with exasperation. She was frightened. She tried not to think about what Brigara would be doing to Seneca. It was sickening to imagine the torture and suffering Seneca was probably enduring. She recalled how Seneca had used her wings to block the fireballs being thrust at her, but she knew it was probably only a matter of time before the wings would no longer be an effective defense. She looked at Rileau with tears welling in her eyes. "We've got to save Seneca from Brigara. We just have to," she pleaded.

"It was not Brigara!" Rileau said adamantly. "However, I do suspect the encounter was with a dubious follower. A *dupelene*, to be exact. Had it actually been Brigara, it is likely you would not be seated before us. Nor would I have hopes for Seneca's survival. She is quite clever in her deceit, however. That is also quite telling."

"What do you mean it wasn't her?" asked Shayna. She hiccupped slightly and was reminded of her parched throat. "Then who the heck was she?"

"Obviously, it's someone clever enough to fool people," said Jake. "Fireballs and all! That's some powerful magic to have going for this dupelene person."

"Yes, it is quite disturbing," Rileau said gravely. "It will take much to disarm such a power. The wrong attempt could be fatal."

Shayna's jaw dropped. She hadn't learned to defend against fire spheres. Seneca had her wings for defense, but what did she have? She had a feeling she would be facing the fake Brigara soon, but stopping that kind of attack was beyond her abilities. She bit her bottom lip in contemplation.

"Whoa! Our crazy teacher has a look-alike roaming around?" asked Conner. "An actual Brigara evil twin?"

"Not exactly, but we are dealing with someone who has been in Brigara's close proximity," said Rileau. "It would seem Brigara has lured a rare dupelene to be under her control. Their gifts are not merely to look like another but to replicate mannerisms and basic magical abilities," he explained. "Changing the outer appearance is a simple enchantment for a dupelene, but to mimic one's gifts is a bit more involved. In order for them to duplicate gifts of another, the gifts must first be revealed and then used. Only then can they be mimicked."

"Holy horse droppings! This dupelene thing can do all that?" asked Conner.

"Indeed, and far more. They are a rare talent in our Otherworld," said Rileau.

"And you're sure that's who grabbed Seneca? A dupelene who took on the form of Brigara? Are we going to have to face a lot of them?" Jake asked.

"They are quite rare elementals. I was led to believe they were all removed from this realm since their powers can be corrupted. Their natural state is one of trust and innocence. This makes them vulnerable, and they may easily be misled or manipulated."

"That sounds sad," said Shayna. "Being controlled by Brigara must suck."

"It is most unfortunate; however, you must not pity them, as they are quite dangerous."

"How dangerous?" Jake asked. He felt his stomach tightening. The more Rileau spoke, the more anxious he was becoming.

"They come into existence as mimics, and as such, they are able to duplicate the magic they witness. Brigara obviously displayed her gifts for this particular dupelene. She is using it for her own gain," said Rileau.

"And this dupelene is mimicking dark magic," said Jake. "Like Brigara's fireballs and making portals."

"Precisely," said Rileau.

"Let me get this straight. If she has to see it to copy it, then does that mean Brigara is here in the Otherworld?" asked Jake. He felt his heart jump in his chest.

"I am not convinced of that. The dupelene is likely to have held on to the mimic of Brigara until the time was right."

"But it's possible—Brigara could be back?" asked Jake.

"It is in the realm of possibilities," said Rileau. "However, I do not believe she has returned. Her ego would not allow another to stand in her place. She craves the attention to boast of her conquests. It is most definitely a dupelene."

"But she looks, sounds, and acts just like her," said Shayna. "That's creepy to be able to look like someone else, especially someone as hideous as Brigara."

"Yes, that is essential to their mimic. It must be a complete transformation," replied Rileau. "You must understand—do not confuse the dupelene with Brigara. It is not her, and you must accept this."

"She definitely fooled me—I swear it was so much like her," said Shayna. "I'm positive Seneca will think so too."

"Well, she convinced you," said Conner. "I'm freaking out, and I haven't even seen her yet."

"How long can the mimic last?" asked Jake. "Is there a time limit?"

"Excellent question. The mimic is temporary and can only be sustained for short bursts. The more complicated the magic, such as the fireball orbs, the shorter it lasts. My guess is that time may affect the results as well," said Rileau.

"Since she was hurling so many fireballs and also opened a portal, do you think she's lost the ability to produce Brigara's power?" Jake asked.

"We should be prepared for the possibility that whatever power she is able to mimic might still be lethal," replied Rileau.

Shayna gasped. The thought of two dangerous people looking alike and having the same powers was incomprehensible. "Do you suppose the dupelene's torturing Seneca right now?" she asked.

"It is most probable that Seneca is highly uncomfortable," said Rileau. "I surmise that she is being held until Brigara's return."

"We've gotta get Seneca back!" Shayna said as she threw off the blanket and leaped to her feet. "If the two of them team up, there's no telling what they might do."

"I concur. It is my hope that Seneca can prompt her to attack, thus diminishing the velocity of the orbs. It should not be too difficult to provoke such actions, as dupelenes are not known for their patience. They have quite a temper. The more orbs the dupelene creates, the better Seneca's chances for survival," said Rileau.

"How much time do you think we have?" asked Conner. He made no attempt to hide his worry.

"I hate thinking about Seneca having to deal with this alone. She's probably scared out of her mind," Shayna said softly.

"From what I know of the dupelenes, they must reduplicate continuously to maintain the magic they have mimicked. Otherwise, they return to their natural state," said Rileau. "I am hopeful she has expended what magic she replicated from Brigara. It will be Seneca's best chance to survive."

"The worst-case scenario: she reaches Brigara before we get to Seneca," Jake said. His mind raced quickly in an attempt to come up with a strategy. He knew they had to take action without further delay.

"I do share your thoughts, Jake. We must not allow the dupelene to reach Brigara by any means to strengthen or replenish her mimic," replied Rileau.

"No way are we letting that happen! We've got to find Seneca!" Jake shouted.

"Hopefully retaliate with a vengeance!" said Shayna. "I know Seneca learned some powerful stuff from Wren. So that poor imitation Brigara thingy had better watch out!" She could feel the warmth returning to her body. She was determined to find her friend, her sister, no matter the cost.

"Let's get going!" Conner shouted. He balled one hand into a fist and punched the palm of his other. He yelled an incoherent battle cry and stomped several times in place as the others looked on. "I'm pumped!"

"What do we do? How do we find them?" Shayna asked. She was ready to take action. Witnessing Conner's display of emotion made her heart race with even more urgency.

"Tell us what to do and where to go!" Jake said. He trembled from the surge of adrenaline rushing through his veins.

"It would seem you are ready; this is good," said Rileau. "Very good."

He extended his hand to Shayna and did a slight bow. She placed her hand atop his. She looked into his mesmerizing eyes as he raised his head momentarily and then looked down at her. She felt slightly feverish as she bit her bottom lip and scrunched her nose in anticipation of his response.

"Now is the time to put some good use to your reflectoire," he said. "The truest use of this gift is to act as a guide for you and the others."

"I'm getting better. I got back here, didn't I?"

"Yeah, but you're a bit soggy," said Conner. "Before you go ballistic on me, I'm not teasing you this time. You should probably put on something dry."

"You're right—I'll be back!"

Shayna ran in the direction of the stairwell and bounded up the steep stairs, skipping several steps at a time. Although she was brave, she longed to find a bed to crawl into where she could pull a warm comforter over her head and forget the danger they were about to face. Falling back into the routine she'd left behind in the mortal realm would be a snap.

She envisioned her bedroom and the condition in which she'd left it on the morning she'd gone off to school. She hadn't thought about cheer practice, her father, or the multitude of social events she'd missed for quite some time. Thinking about what she'd left behind seemed trivial. Her life had meaning and purpose. It was much more than pep rallies, high kicks, and sticking dismounts. She was becoming a warrior. She pushed the door to her room open and immediately disrobed and tossed her wet clothes onto the floor.

Jake had waited until he was sure Shayna was out of listening range. He knew she was worked up, and the pressure was mounting. They were all relying on her to get them to Seneca. He worried how she would handle it if she fell short in her efforts.

"Rileau, we didn't choose to be involved in this war, and look what's happened. Seneca's in danger, and we don't know how much. And now we're expecting Shayna to find her?" Jake's face flushed red.

"Actually, you chose to be in this war. You all did," replied Rileau. "Specifically, you, Jake. You have always known your destiny. Your ego would not allow you to accept it."

"But—"

"You've always had an unquenchable thirst to be better than ordinary. You've never been satisfied because you've always sensed that you were meant to do more, to be more. You are like your father and his father before him," said Rileau.

"My father? What are you talking about? What do you know about my father?"

"I know that the man who reared you is not your natural father. You have been made aware of this. Am I correct?"

Jake shrugged and didn't respond. He knew Rileau spoke the truth. He was accurate in his assessment. Jake did believe he was meant to do more than the norm. He'd never quite fit in. He gathered it was because he was from the Otherworld, but he had little else to go on. He cast his eyes to his feet and focused on his mud-caked cross-trainers. He recalled buying them with the father he'd grown up with. He had been excited that day; he was getting a top-of-the-line pair of shoes just before starting the new school. It had been a rare outing they'd made together, and he remembered enjoying the one-on-one time. He wondered if the father who'd raised him knew that he was the offspring of someone else. His heart fluttered momentarily, but he regrouped and pushed the sentimental memory away. He had to focus on the present.

"You're right. We do have a choice in this war. And I want to end it without any of us getting hurt," said Jake somberly. He didn't want another verbal sparring match, so conceding was the best option.

"That is an admirable goal. Let's see if we can accomplish it," said Rileau.

They all looked up as Shayna came charging into the room. Her hair was brushed and barely damp, and a change of clothes draped her lean frame perfectly. Her favorite boots were strapped tightly and polished to perfection.

"Let's get going—we need to bring Seneca back like a Chanel vintage handbag!"

"Oh yeah!" shouted Conner with a fist pump over his head.

"Are you ready to use your reflectoire as it is intended? It will mean that you must embrace the connection of the dominion. By doing so, you will propel the three of you to Seneca's location," said Rileau. "Your time in the perplex will now be tested."

"This is major! What if she transports us into the middle of the sea or to the edge of a cliff?" said Conner. "Or in front of an oncoming wrecking ball? Ouch!"

"Conner's got a point. Shayna hasn't exactly mastered the teleporting yet," said Jake as he grimaced and shot a worried look at her. "You know what I'm saying, right?"

"Look, you guys, I might not be perfect, but I didn't get appointed cheer captain just because I wanted it. I'm fierce, and I know I can do this!" said Shayna. She swung one hand above her head and snapped while placing the other hand on her hip for emphasis.

"*Fierce* is a good way to describe you. Also, well, there is that gift-of-persuasion thing you've got going on and maybe—" Conner smirked, getting a glimpse of Shayna's expression, which he took to mean he'd better stop talking.

"No, it's determination! I refuse to fail!" said Shayna. "Seneca's counting on us to get to her, and we will. If using my reflectoire is the way, then it's happening. Unless one of you has some other negative thing to say—actually, scratch that. Don't talk! Swallow it, and let's do this. Got it?"

Jake and Conner exchanged looks and decided to remain silent. She was right, and they were not about to argue or protest. Jake smiled, and she flashed a wide grin in return.

"You just might be the dominion that has been prophesied," said Rileau. His expression was one of pride and satisfaction.

"I believe we're ready, Rileau," said Shayna. "Let's get our Seneca back!"

"Shayna, join hands with Conner and Jake. No matter what happens, you must not let go. You must follow my instructions precisely and without hesitation," he said.

"What do we do once we get there and find her?" asked Jake.

"You return here at your first opportunity," said Rileau. "That means all four of you."

"Understood!" Jake said as he grabbed Shayna's hand, and she looked at him and smiled. "We can do this. I trust you, Shayna."

He gave her hand a firm squeeze. Shayna tried to squeeze back, but his hand was too heavy. It was uncomfortable, and she wanted to resist complaining, but her fingers were going numb. She decided it was better to speak up than risk losing all circulation to her hand.

"Loosen your grip just a bit, please," whispered Shayna.

"Ah, yeah, sorry," muttered Jake. "I just wanted to be sure I kept up with you, but I do trust you."

"Me too. I'm with you one hundred percent. Go big, or go home!" Conner said as he slid his hand into Shayna's. "I don't mean literally to go home, you know. What I meant to say is, we've got this, Shayna. No doubts!"

"I understand. Okay. It looks like we're ready, Rileau. Let's do it," said Shayna.

"Listen to my voice, and do not activate your reflectoire until everything I say is precise. You must not let go of the image or sensation that will propel you to Seneca," said Rileau. "Seneca has a connection to each of you, and together you must bridge that bond. Her voice is unique. Listen, and hear it speak to you. Her wings have touched each of you. Feel them. Her hair, her eyes, and the light that shines from them see you. Now you must see her."

Shayna closed her eyes. She felt the now familiar sensation; it was somewhat similar to what she experienced when she commanded her sword. The reflectoire was finally beginning to feel as if it were truly a part of her. She relaxed into the confidence of knowing she could channel the power it generated. She was no longer afraid of failure. She tightened her grip on Conner's and Jake's hands.

"Get ready for an adventure like no other you've ever experienced," she whispered.

Jake held his breath, and Conner bit down on his lower lip. He closed his eyes right at the moment a light breeze blew across his face. They were in motion, and he could no longer feel the floor beneath his feet. He focused on his hand, and suddenly, his grip slipped away. He opened his eyes in search of Shayna's hands just as he stumbled forward. He fell in a heap on top of Jake, who had already landed on Shayna. She had ended up at the bottom of the pile.

"Get off me," she muttered. She pushed and crawled out of the entanglement.

"Where are we?" Jake whispered. "Did we make it?"

"I'm not sure. We're somewhere near Seneca. I can hear her—listen!" Shayna said softly.

Conner remained quiet as he sat up on the floor. He felt disoriented. They were in a dark room, and he was terrified. He wasn't sure what lurked in the darkness, and staying still was his first instinct. The only light was a beam that seeped in from beneath a door. As their eyes adjusted, it was clear they were in some type of dwelling. The room had a bed but little else. The light was coming from another room, from which they could distinctly hear Seneca speaking to someone.

"Seneca's in there for sure," said Shayna. "Can you make out what they're saying?"

"It sounds like Seneca is doing all of the talking. I'm not sure, but the other voice sort of sounds familiar."

"I was thinking the same thing," said Shayna. "Conner, do you hear them?"

"Um, maybe," he moaned.

"What's wrong with you? Did you hit your head?" asked Jake. He tried to keep his voice just above a whisper.

"No, it's just really dark in here. You know what I think about being somewhere I can't see," said Conner.

"Look, we've gotta have a game plan," said Jake. "I don't think just pouncing in there is the right tactic."

"I think the surprise attack is our best bet. We go in, grab Seneca, and get out," said Shayna. She leaned in close. "Who knows if the dupelene can still make the fireballs or not, but I think the sooner we get in there, the better. You can tell from Seneca's voice that she's really upset."

"You're right. Let's go over to the door and see if we can hear what they're saying," said Jake.

"Come on, Conner. There's light on the other side of the door. We might need you to break it down if it's locked," said Shayna. She gave a tug on his shirt and got to her feet.

She flexed her hand, and the sword appeared, casting a warm light across the room. Conner relaxed when he saw there was nothing lurking in the dark corners. Shayna smiled at her mastery of the weapon. Her confidence in handling it grew each time she called upon it. She dimmed the beam and then swept it through the air several times. Jake crept quietly across the room. Shayna eased in just behind him. They eased closer to the door and leaned in with their ears against it. Conner remained a few feet back and readied for an attack.

"Did you hear that? She's talking to herself," whispered Shayna. Jake nodded in response.

"What's wrong with her?" asked Conner. His voice cracked in his attempt to keep quiet. He felt uneasy but resisted asking Shayna to make her sword brighter. Instead, he moved closer to the low light it cast at their feet.

"Probably some spell has gone wrong. She's yelling one second and then calm, almost pleading, the next," replied Shayna as she struggled to keep her voice quiet. "I don't like it—she's being tortured or something. We need to get in there."

The sounds from the other room immediately stopped. Shayna exchanged a look with Jake; they knew they'd been overheard. They stepped back from the door in anticipation of an attack. A minute passed, but no one came crashing in. Conner sighed in relief. He wasn't looking forward to battling anything that could look like Brigara, especially in the dark.

"Maybe they didn't hear you," said Jake. "Listen. I think Seneca's talking again."

They crept back to the door as Jake motioned for Shayna to remain quiet. She reluctantly nodded in agreement and placed her ear to the door.

"Something's not right," Jake whispered. His muscles were stiffening in anticipation.

"We've gotta get in there," Shayna said, making sure to speak as quietly as possible. She could hear Jake's breathing intensify, and it caused her to tense up.

"Not yet—just wait a second. We need to know what we're walking into," he said through gritted teeth. He tried to remain calm, since it was apparent they were both getting anxious.

"I wasn't planning on just walking. It would be more like a furiously fierce runway strut!" Shayna snapped.

Jake turned and looked at her in confusion. He knew the moment wasn't right to burst out laughing, and he struggled to hold back the laughter. His body shook from the restraint. The image of her walking the catwalk with a sword in hand was humorous. He believed if anyone could pull it off, it was Shayna. He covered his mouth to muffle a snort.

"What?" Shayna asked. "Why aren't you saying anything? Are you actually laughing?" she said in a huff.

"No, I'm sure you'd be unforgettable."

"I'm just saying I don't like casual entrances. They don't get the desired reaction; they never go viral."

"Got it. Now, keep your voice down, and listen. Did you catch that? Seneca sounds really agitated," he said in a low, flat voice.

"Do you think she's hurt?" whispered Conner. He had moved just behind Shayna and attempted to hear the commotion coming from the other room.

"I don't know, but they're at it again," Jake said quietly.

"What do you mean *they*?" asked Conner, being sure to keep his voice low. "It sounds like just Seneca—but she's arguing with herself."

"Yeah, I don't know about that. I can only hear Seneca," said Shayna.

"Shh. Listen," said Jake. "I think there's someone with her."

"I think you're right. It's probably the psycho shape-shifting copycat thing," said Conner.

"Quiet—I'm trying to make out what they're saying," said Jake.

"I will kill you without a second thought if you don't give me what I desire!"

"I'm not going to do it, so you might as well do what you keep threatening to do. I'm tired of looking at you!"

"You will reveal them fully to me now or die!"

A piercing scream penetrated the walls, followed by noises of furniture being overturned, shattering glass, and a loud thud against the wall.

"Okay, that scream was bad. It's obvious we need to get in there, like, now!" said Shayna as quietly as she could.

"Why is Seneca threatening herself?" asked Conner.

"I don't know, but I'm not waiting for her to make good on it!" Shayna's sword shook in her hand as she aimed it at the door. Jake jumped out of the way just as she carved an opening around the doorframe in a single swiping motion. Without hesitation, she leaped through the enflamed entryway. Conner and Jake immediately followed. Once they crossed the threshold, they stopped. They stood motionless in the room and exchanged horrified expressions at the scene before them.

Shayna gripped Jake's arm, and he flinched when her nails dug into his flesh. In the center of the room was Seneca, her right wing charred, shriveled, and mangled beyond recognition. The one on the left was drab and void of color. It was limp and lifeless, resembling a dragonfly whose wings had been frayed out of cruelty. Seneca turned her head slowly and looked at them with vacant eyes. Her skin was blotchy, and she appeared to be on the brink of death. Jake wondered if she was doing this to herself or if the cause was an enchantment. Whatever the situation, she clearly needed help.

She was surrounded by broken glass that covered most of the floor. Four windows lined one wall, and they were all shattered. There was little to no glass remaining in any of them. The entire room was in disarray, with chairs overturned and wooden tables reduced to kindling. The room was chilly, and a foul stench of burned flesh lingered in the air.

Jake started to rush over to her but stopped short. He promptly held out his arm to halt Shayna's approach; she started to protest but resisted. She realized his reaction was justified. Their eyes locked on Seneca's hand. She had an orb—not of fire, as Brigara had used, but one that resembled a glowing ball of snow. It glistened and hovered above her palm with icy streams of mist rising and revolving around it.

"Seneca, it's okay. We're here now," said Jake soothingly.

"We're going to take you back to Rileau. I'm sure he can fix you right up and put some color back in those cheeks," said Shayna in an attempt to sound reassuring. She avoided mentioning anything about the wings, since she saw them as a complete loss. She felt a wave of sadness. Seeing what had once been so beautiful reduced to a tragedy beyond repair was heartbreaking.

Seneca stared back at them blankly as she tilted her head in contemplation. She opened her mouth slightly, but no words came out. Jake followed her glance and realized she was only looking at Shayna. He noticed her sword was still illuminated.

"Shayna," Jake said calmly.

"What? Why isn't she saying anything?" Shayna said in a low voice as she resisted looking at Jake directly.

"She might be threatened by your sword. Maybe you should put it down," he whispered.

"Maybe if she put that ice-ball thing away, I'd consider it," said Shayna with exaggerated sarcasm. She made no attempt to keep her voice down. "Otherwise, not a chance!"

"Perhaps you'd like a demonstration of my power to make you reconsider," Seneca replied in a monotone. She raised her arm to display the icy orb still swirling above her palm. Her eyes were lifeless, and her expression was stern.

"I don't think she's kidding," Shayna mumbled. She raised her sword in a countermove.

"I think you're right," Jake said in a surprised voice. "Hold steady."

"Guys, wait!" yelled Conner. "Hold on! Get over here."

Shayna refused to acknowledge the interruption. She was more concerned with the threat just three feet in front of her. Her friend was now a foe. It was clear to Shayna that Seneca wasn't acting like herself. Whatever had happened had made her almost unrecognizable.

"Jake, see what Conner's yelping about. I'm going to keep my eyes and sword on Miss Teen Frosty here," said Shayna in a growl. "You've gotta snap out of this, Seneca!"

Jake spun around toward Conner, prepared to be annoyed by something less important than witnessing Shayna and Seneca on the brink of a showdown. His jaw dropped. In the far corner of the room was a slumped figure lying in the fetal position. His first thought was that Seneca must have wounded the dupelene, but that assumption was quickly erased when he saw Conner's expression. He stood motionless and watched in horror. His mind went blank. He couldn't comprehend what he was witnessing. Something was wrong, and it wasn't completely registering. He watched Conner lift her up in his arms and cradle her small body as her arms dangled freely. She wasn't moving.

"Conner, wait—" He stopped midsentence and rushed across the room.

"Look at her, Jake," said Conner somberly. Tears rolled down his cheeks as he held the limp body close.

"Seneca?" Jake said sympathetically. "What happened to her?"

Jake brushed her hair from her eyes. Her face was cold to the touch. For the first time, he noticed how frigid the room felt. It was extremely cold. Each breath he exhaled let out a cloud of mist. Jake fought back his tears. He was angry, and he charged toward the look-alike Seneca. She had no chance to respond as he shoved her square in the chest. She fell hard and slid across the shards of glass that blanketed the floor. The ice orb she'd been taunting Shayna with rolled from her fingers and crashed into the wall, leaving a seared mark where it connected. She screamed in agony as she crawled to her feet. Blood rolled down her legs. She frantically attempted to scrape away slivers of glass that protruded from her pale skin. She rocked back on her heels and willed another icy orb into her hands. She smirked as she backed away to create distance from her attackers.

"Jake!" Shayna screamed. "What are you doing? She's hurt. Why would you do that to Seneca?"

"It's not Seneca. It's the dupelene! She's the one who did that!" Jake shouted as he pointed to Conner, who looked as if he would topple over at any second.

"Seneca?" Shayna said inaudibly. She didn't move—she couldn't. "Is she all right?"

"She's really cold—her lips are blue, and she's not responding at all," said Conner. "The cold is coming off her like an uber Arctic blast!" He was shaking from the cold she was emitting, but he didn't dare let go.

He shivered involuntarily as he focused on keeping Seneca warm by rubbing her arms and shoulders.

"Yes, she is cold—she's actually freezing!" said the ghastly, disfigured dupelene. "And she will die unless she reveals her wings and gifts to me." She leaned against a wall and smiled, displaying a row of rotting teeth.

"If she dies, you won't be around to see it, because you're going out first!" Shayna shrieked and raised her sword. The vibration was too intense to manage with one hand. She adjusted her grip to accommodate both hands. She positioned the blade high above her head. She started to charge but was stopped as Jake intervened. He wrapped his arm around Shayna's waist and nearly lifted her off the ground. He had to duck to miss being struck by her flailing sword-wielding arms.

"Let go of me! What are you doing? Let me go!" she shouted as she wrestled free. Her eyes were wild with anger and confusion.

"We need to focus on Seneca. Just look at her! That dupelene's no threat to anyone looking like that," said Jake. "Seneca already did a number on her. Leave her to suffer on her own."

"Jake's right," said Conner. "We need to help Seneca." His teeth chattered, and he shook uncontrollably.

"We need to get her back to the castle," said Jake. "That means you, Shayna!"

Shayna looked at the dupelene, who was now on the floor with her eyes closed. Jake was right that she wasn't a threat. Whatever had been done was obviously more than the dupelene could handle. Shayna repositioned her sword and contemplated all she had experienced. She had already battled several of Brigara's followers, and it was clear this would not be the last she had to face. The war had become personal after her grandmother Dreya was taken. Now her friend's life was in jeopardy. The burden of failure loomed. They weren't winning in the magical war thus far, and the absence of success was weighing heavily. For each ounce of confidence she gained, she felt as if Brigara figured out ways to tear it away. She felt bitter as a wave of doubt washed over her.

"I can't do it. It's too risky," said Shayna. Her voice was soft. She relaxed, and her sword dematerialized. She turned and slumped away from the dupelene. She brushed her hand gently along the outer edge of Seneca's cheek. "She's so cold."

"That's why we need to get her back to Rileau," said Conner as he adjusted Seneca in his arms and pulled her in close.

"I just can't take the chance."

The hairs on the back of Shayna's neck sprang erect. She whipped her body around. Her sword reappeared before she could blink. The dupelene had produced two icy orbs, and they were flying directly at them. Shayna lunged with her sword fully extended. She swiped one out of the air, catching it with the tip of her blade. The orb exploded upon impact in a shower of icicle daggers. Shayna dodged to avoid being hit, but in doing so, she couldn't maintain her balance. She lost her footing and slipped on a chunk of ice. She slammed into the ground hard and slid across the slick floor. Her head banged against a table leg. She lay motionless.

The second orb hit Conner directly in his shoulder blade. He had shifted his body to protect Seneca, the intended target. He fell to one knee and yelled out in pain. He rocked unsteadily, placing Seneca down gently, before collapsing onto the floor.

Jake readied himself as two more orbs slowly began to take form. The dupelene's eyes met his. She smirked smugly in triumph.

"I thought you were the mighty dominion, but look what I've accomplished." She cackled. "Brigara will be quite pleased." She glanced down at the slowly swirling orbs in her hand. Their intensity faded as they flickered feebly and then vanished. Frustration was etched on her pallid face. She grumbled and cursed under her breath.

Jake closed his eyes and took a deep breath. He stretched his arms out to his sides. The floor began to shake beneath his feet. In front of where he stood, a hole opened in the floor. At first, it was about the size of a large coin, exposing a miniature pool of water. As it swirled, it grew in diameter and speed. It expanded until it extended three feet wide, forming a rapid spinning whirlpool of water. The whirlpool sped up and got faster with each revolution.

"What is that? What are you doing?" she shrieked. She backed farther away. "This is impossible." She attempted to run, but there was no escape route. No doors or windows were reachable without going past him. She fumbled as she tried to create an orb. A few fleeting sparks appeared and then instantly flickered out like a lighter low on butane.

Jake's eyes opened wide. He lowered his arms, pulled back, and then thrust them in her direction. She crossed her arms in front of her face and screamed. The enchanted water followed his command. It rose from the swirling pool and plunged into her like the force of the ocean against a rocky shoreline at high tide. There was no relenting. The velocity lifted her high above the floor. She was thrust against the wall. The momentum of the crash was enough to break completely through the entire partition. A large beam swung precariously above by a single bolt and hinge, threatening to pull away with little effort. A partial area of the roof was exposed through a large hole; roof tiles had been ripped off and washed away. Broken planks of wood were blasted in all directions, leaving splintered remains of what was once the bearing wall to the home. The dupelene's spindly flailing body was forcibly expunged from the room and out into the open air. She tumbled and thrashed about like a stuffed doll. The rushing water swept her down the rocky hillside, forcing her over the jagged cliff, and dumped her into the open sea below.

Jake watched in awe. He lowered his hands slowly and looked at the massive damage. Having completed its mission, the pool of water evaporated, leaving no trace, as if it had never existed. He eased closer to the opening and scanned the grounds. The only sign capturing what had just occurred was the gigantic gaping hole in the damaged wall. Shreds of splintered wood framed the outdoors like a 3-D landscape. Even the spot on the floor where the pool of water had originated had vanished. He looked down at his hands and caught a quick glimpse of shimmer before it too disappeared.

"Wow! Did you guys see that?" Jake turned quickly in anticipation of a reaction. The room was silent. He had been so caught up in the moment that he'd forgotten the state his friends were in. He rushed to Shayna. He could hear her moaning from beneath the table. Only her boots were exposed. He knelt down to get a better look and assess her injuries. "Are you okay? I think you hit your head," he said.

"Ya think? Where is she?" Shayna pushed herself out from beneath the table. She got to her feet quickly and looked around, dazed. "What happened? Where did she go? We gotta get after her, Jake," she said, rubbing her head. It throbbed, and she squinted from the pain.

"She's gone now. There's no need to worry about her any longer. We've gotta check on Seneca and Conner."

"Conner? What happened to Conner? What else did I miss?" she moaned as she trailed slowly behind Jake.

He looked over at Conner momentarily but decided to examine Seneca. She was still abnormally cold to the touch. He noticed that her hair seemed more platinum, an almost silver color, especially on her spiky tips. He looked around for something that could be used to warm her up. The room was dank and absent of anything resembling a blanket. The house was deserted; its previous occupants had removed all of the furnishings. All that remained were a few wooden stools and a small table with severe dry-rot damage.

Shayna felt a breeze whip through her hair and turned to see the large exposed hole in the wall. The wind had carried a mound of dry leaves inside and sprayed them about the room.

"Jake, where did that big hole come from?" Shayna asked. She felt disoriented and wondered how long she had been unconscious.

"I'll tell you later. Seneca's still freezing," he said. "We don't have time to waste, Shayna. Her breathing is really shallow."

"Okay, what do we do?" she asked. She tried hard to concentrate on what Jake was telling her. Her head was drumming loudly. She rubbed her head and detected a lump that had formed; it hurt when she touched it. "What about Conner? Did you check on him?" she moaned as she sat on the floor beside him.

"Not yet. I think he's going to be okay, even though he took a hard hit," said Jake. "You should have seen him. He was glowing and shimmering just as that ice orb hit him. He protected Seneca until he went down."

"I'm sure it was the Himalayan crystals at work," said Shayna.

Conner's arm was extended toward Seneca, and his hand rested just inches from her. Shayna shook his shoulders a few times to revive him, but she was unsuccessful. She placed her hand on his chest and felt it rise and fall.

"He's breathing, but he's out. That cold orb did a number on him. He's really cold too," she said sadly. "I couldn't stop both of the orbs, but I tried."

"I know you did. Right now, you need to get us all back to the castle," Jake said.

"My head hurts—I don't think that's a good idea," she said. "I probably have a concussion, you know. Plus, there's no telling what might pop in my head."

"That's always a risk," said Jake. "The way you think never tracks like anybody else."

"I'm guessing that's not a good thing," she said with a raised eyebrow. "But I have to agree with you—that's why I can't be trusted to get us back."

"You have to try, Shayna. Look at them!"

"I know, I know. I just don't want to make things worse," she said.

"They're going to die. It can't get worse than that! Don't you get it?"

Jake jumped to his feet and shook his fists in the air. He could feel panic rising to the surface. He pulled at his hair and looked down at Seneca. Her body was eerily still. Conner stood by stiffly with a look of extreme pain on his face. Jake could feel his heart beating out of his chest. He knew Shayna was hurt too, but he had to push.

"Come on, Shayna. Use your reflectoire. Get us out of here!"

"You don't get it!" she screamed. "What if I screw up?"

Tears rolled down her flushed cheeks. Images of Brigara taunting her flashed through her mind. She wanted to scream from the frustration. She hated feeling so doubtful about her abilities, but she feared failure even more.

"This is not one of your soap operas or sitcoms with a wrapped-up-tight, formulaic ending! It's all happening now in unscripted reality!" Jake yelled.

"I get it, but you need to listen to me. I really don't know if I can get us back. Not on solid ground anyway. To be honest, I keep envisioning a warm bath because I'm so cold," she said.

"That's probably okay. It really is if you could just try to picture the bath being inside Rileau's castle," Jake replied. He struggled to keep his voice even and not sound condescending. When he saw her lips twist into a tight knot, he knew he hadn't succeeded. He cringed slightly. "Shayna, you're strong in more ways than I can explain. You can do it! If we have to take a bath, then so be it!"

Shayna dried her tears and gazed at Seneca. She cringed at seeing her so helpless. The tears began to flow again. "Fine! No one had better complain about the water temperature." She sniffed, took a deep breath, and then mumbled a few swear words inaudibly.

"No complaints from me." He grimaced. He tried hard not to show his angst. "Let's get them close and join hands. And I know you're in pain, but I also know you're strong."

"Got it. Now, hold on tight. We are going to do this!" exclaimed Shayna. "As Rachel Platten sings, ''Cause I've still got a lot of fight left in me.'"

Her voice was beautiful as she sang each note in perfect tune. Jake looked at her with admiration but remained quiet. He thought back to their first meeting. She was the cheerleader who didn't give him a second thought. She was brazen and confident, exactly what they needed at that moment if they were going to survive. He grabbed on to Seneca and Conner. "Let's go, Shayna," he said softly as he closed his eyes.

Shayna smiled. She let her mind visualize the beautifully sculpted marble tub adjacent to her bedroom in the castle. She imagined submerging her toes into the steaming water. She saw herself sliding into the tub until the bubbles rested beneath her chin. "Can't forget the bubbles," she muttered as the reflectoire vibrated. She swiped her hand across it and then quickly slid her hand into Conner's as she bit down on her bottom lip. She picked up Seneca's frozen hand and gripped it tightly. At the last moment, her thoughts shifted to another image. She let out a long exhalation as the room faded to black.

CHAPTER SIXTEEN

Wren Issues

J ake tumbled over in a forward roll and landed flat on his back. He opened his eyes and stared at the familiar ceiling. He recognized it. He scrambled to his feet but wobbled. The room was spinning, and he closed his eyes to stop the sensation. He hated the sensation of being dizzy. He grabbed hold of the nearest chair to keep from teetering. He was in the castle library. Shayna was propped on the large ottoman with her legs crossed. She was eating a sandwich. She tilted her head in his direction and grinned. He scanned the rest of the room until he saw Rileau on the far side. Rileau was unmoved by Jake's sudden appearance as he hovered over Seneca. She was listening intently to his instructions as she poured a clear liquid substance from a small vial into her mouth. It suddenly occurred to Jake that she was awake. His attention turned to Conner, who was seated beside Seneca. He wore a concerned expression as he held her hand. They were either speaking quietly, or something had happened to his hearing, because he was unable to pick up on any of the conversation. He felt disoriented and confused.

"What's going on?" Jake asked, searching Shayna's face for a response.

"Why are you yelling?" she replied with her nose turned up.

"I didn't know I was. I couldn't hear anything for a second," Jake said as he stuck his fingers into his ears in an attempt to improve his condition.

"That's nothing. I couldn't hear anything for almost an hour after my first teleporting trip," said Shayna.

"What happened to me?" asked Jake as he leaned against the back of the chair to maintain his balance.

"Oh, you got delayed in the whole teleporting thing," said Shayna. She gave him one of her broadest smiles, which made him a little uneasy. "Rileau explained it all. Evidently, since I changed my mind at the last second, I created some sort of hiccup, and we got here okay, but you were like, um, lost, I guess."

"Lost?" he muttered. "You lost me?" He plopped onto the ottoman next to her and nearly rocked her off. He felt nauseated, and the room hadn't stopped moving.

"More like delayed or misplaced," she replied. "But look—you've arrived!"

"How long was I lost?"

"Oh, I'm guessing an hour or two. Rileau said it could take days, but the trail from my reflectoire would lead you here eventually," she said. "And he was right."

"But it feels like it was only seconds ago. We were just at that shack with the dupelene. Um, weren't we?"

"You're here now, and that's all that matters," she said reassuringly. "My head feels better, Conner is fine, and Seneca is—well, actually, I don't know yet. Rileau's been working on her. The good news is, she's awake and no longer a Popsicle!"

"Yeah, I can see that. What's he giving her?"

"I'm not sure, but she doesn't seem to be resisting any of his treatments," said Shayna.

"What kind of treatments?" Jake asked.

He decided not to wait for a response. He steadied himself and crept slowly across the room. He felt as if he were on a boat and needed to find his sea legs. Seneca's eyes met his as he got closer. She smiled slightly. Conner leaped to his feet and embraced Jake with a hug that lifted him from his feet.

"Ow! A bit tight, dude!" Jake said as he wrestled free.

"Sorry, man. I'm just stoked to see you, being that you were lost and all," Conner said as he gave Jake another quick hug.

"Shayna was telling me all about the getting-lost stuff. Odd, I guess, but at least we're all here now," said Jake.

"Shayna was able to get Seneca and Conner here without incident," Rileau said.

"What he means is that we ended up safely in the library and not plastered in the bookcases." Conner snorted. "Smooth landing—at least I think it was. I was passed out."

"Unfortunately, her focus wavered, and as a result, her hold on you collapsed. The reflectoire yields great strength. As a result, her connection to you kept you tethered. Had this not been the case, you may not have survived the teleportation."

"Thanks, Shayna. I'm still a bit confused, though. My head is foggy, and my stomach is swirling like I was stuck on the teacup ride for too long." Jake moaned and rubbed his head.

"You're welcome!" Shayna said. "You really should perfect your entrance. Your technique with the tuck and roll could use some help. As for the head spinning, that comes with the teleporting thing. Not always, but there's the occasional woozy barf-up-your-lunch thing to deal with too."

"I'm relating to that right about now." Jake closed his eyes to steady himself.

"I'm getting a bit better at controlling it. Just try not to move too quickly. Trust me. I nearly lost it on that flock of sheep. Can you imagine getting the smell out of that sweater?" Shayna shook her head in disgust.

"Huh?"

"Oh, are you having trouble hearing too? That goes away. Don't worry," Shayna said soothingly.

She skipped to Jake's side. He tried his best to laugh and pulled her in for a hug. He stumbled slightly, and Shayna steadied him. He wished she hadn't mentioned the part about getting nauseated; his stomach churned. Beads of sweat formed on his brow just as he was releasing his embrace. He cocked his head as he caught sight of Rileau's expression. He couldn't decide if it was one of worry or disappointment. Jake didn't like either option.

"Rileau, if I was gone for so long, where did I go? I have no memory of it whatsoever," Jake said. He fought back the woozy sensation and grabbed on to an armchair.

Shayna noticed a green tinge rising around his throat and easing up his jaw. "I think Jake needs some of that ambrosia chocolate. Quick!" she snapped.

Before Shayna could turn around, Conner had already retrieved a cup of the concoction and shoved it into Jake's sweaty palm. Without hesitation, Jake raised the sweet-smelling drink to his lips and sipped slowly. The sensation was familiar. He could feel the effects slowly take hold, and his shoulders relaxed. The queasy feeling subsided. The aftertaste of the sweet ambrosia made him feel as if being sick were somehow worth it.

"Thanks, guys. I needed that."

"Yeah, green is not your color," said Shayna. "Thank goodness Keene Ardara hooked us up with that magic chocolate. It works every time."

"Your friends care deeply for you, Jake. It is satisfactory to see you are bonding," said Rileau.

While his words sounded genuine, his expression remained unchanged. Jake read it as a sign they needed to get serious about things quickly. There was much to discuss, and he wasn't sure how much he had already missed.

"Do I need to be concerned about not remembering anything about the teleporting?" Jake asked. "The last time, I didn't feel sick, and I didn't have a gap in my memory."

Before Rileau could utter a word, Shayna leaped in between them and grabbed Jake's hands.

"I can explain! First, I'm sorry, Jake. I really am. It's just that at the last second, I started doubting myself," said Shayna. "It's so unlike me not to feel confident, because I usually am, but anyway, it's just that I've only had to worry about myself, and there I was, having to help all of you, and I guess I kind of freaked. There. I said it!"

"It's okay. I'm okay. Listen, I'm not blaming you. As a matter of fact, you should feel confident. You're awesome! You rocked that reflectoire, and look what you did. You got us all here in one piece. I was just late to the party, but you didn't leave me out. Hanging maybe, but you didn't let go."

"No. I guess I didn't let go. How could I? We're a family!" Shayna beamed. Her perfect smile spread wide, and she hugged Jake and then quickly moved to Conner and Seneca with like embraces. "I really care about all of you. I mean it. You're all my besties!"

"Hey, I told you that you could do it, and you did," Jake said.

"Now, if you are feeling better, please tell me what became of the dupelene," Rileau said. "We can save the discussion about your time away for later."

His voice was low as he stood with his broad shoulders pulled back and his chest out. Jake tried to read his expression but knew it was useless. Jake placed his cup down on an intricately carved oak table. Four Pegasus-like arions were engraved on the legs of it. The artisan had skillfully captured them in flight. They extended away from each table leg in four different directions. Jake hadn't noticed them before, and he made a mental note to look closer at some other time. Sipping the chocolate ambrosia and seeing the arions made him reflect on their time with Keene Ardara. He missed the grumpy cluricaune. He rocked back and forth on his heels and then cranked his neck in a circle to make sure the dizziness was completely gone before speaking. The ambrosia was working. He felt warm and at ease.

"I gave her a send-off on a white-water rafting ride—minus the raft. Just the rapids," Jake said flatly. He raised an eyebrow in contentment and folded his arms across his chest. His mind flashed back to her body being washed across the rocky terrain and dumped over the edge of the cliff.

"You did what?" asked Conner.

"How did you do that?" Shayna asked.

"I'd like to know this as well. Please enlighten us," said Rileau.

Jake couldn't tell if he was being snide or sincere, but he opted not to ask. He explained how he had conjured the whirlpool, and he described the powerful velocity when it had crashed through the wall, as well as the disappearance of the water. He was animated in the retelling of the event. When he was done, he realized he hadn't let it sink in that he had a new gift. It was a powerful one—and it somehow felt familiar.

"Jake, you do realize that this adds yet another gift to your arsenal," said Conner. "I'm trying hard not to be jealous, but seriously, dude! How many powers can one guy have?"

"It's not like I asked for more," Jake said. He didn't want to feel guilty, but he could hear the disappointment in Conner's voice. "I just went with my gut. It was like muscle memory. That's the best way I can explain it."

"It appears Conner is right," said Rileau. "You have harnessed another gift. It is quite impressive, given the circumstances, that you were able to enact it. Dazzling and impressive!"

It was the first time Jake felt he had actually pleased Rileau. He beamed with satisfaction. He caught a glimpse of Conner's glum expression as he turned away. "Do you think I got the water-manipulation thing from when I was in that enchanted rushing river in Kryt na nOg? I had taken the Himalayan crystals and was able to fly, but maybe the water affected me too," he said.

He was trying to work out for himself why this was a new power. He wanted to learn all he could about what it meant. He wondered if he could do it again or if there had to be special circumstances.

"It is not clear, but it is within reasonable probabilities," Rileau said flatly. "It may possibly be innate."

"Humph. The odds are in your favor for sure," said Conner grimly.

Seneca and Shayna exchanged looks of concern. They remained mum, since neither wanted to engage or weigh in on the discussion.

"I'm sure we're all going to discover more powers each time we have to face different attacks," said Jake in an attempt to be reassuring. "How cool is that? I just think it was my turn. I was the last one standing—literally."

He meant his remarks solely for Conner. He waited for a reaction, but none came. Conner sat down and looked off into space. He thought about Jake's words and knew he was right, but he wanted to be of more use and not be a bench warmer. He huffed with crossed arms.

"It is true. Your instincts will always rise to the surface, especially in a crisis," Rileau said. "You must all build up your arsenal of magic. This includes you, Conner."

"Me? What arsenal?" asked Conner. He looked over with a glum expression plastered across his face. He was on the verge of tears. His voice cracked, and his eyes were filled to the brink. "Sure, I can break down a door or lift rocks. Big deal! How's that going to save anyone?"

"You saved me," said Seneca softly. "You took a direct hit, and you survived because of your gift."

Jake was slightly startled when she spoke. He watched as she made her approach and sat next to Conner. Her voice had changed. It was airy and light. Her spunky, deep voice was gone, as were her golden-blonde locks. Her hair was completely white, with silver streaks highlighting it throughout. He had noticed the beginnings of the change before they teleported. The transformation was now complete. Her eyes were a brilliant, majestic blue with flecks of silver that caught the light. She had approached quietly, and her presence made them all listen intently. Even Rileau's shoulders relaxed as he stepped back to allow her to take the lead. Conner obediently got up and stepped into a spot in the circle they'd naturally formed.

"We saved each other, and we did it because we used our gifts together. At least the three of you did," she said. She locked eyes with each of them. "We survived the attack of someone who was able to make the same fiery balls as Brigara. That's a big deal. We beat her, and that makes us an even bigger deal. A force like no other. There's no telling what we can accomplish together, and they know it. I heard firsthand that Brigara's followers are coming at us with all they have. I say let them come. They can't handle the four of us."

"Nice pep talk!" said Shayna.

"The best," added Conner.

"I needed that," said Jake.

"Thank you, Conner," said Seneca. "You too, Shayna and Jake."

"You're obviously feeling better, Seneca, but I've been really dying to ask about your new hair," said Shayna. "Don't get me wrong. It's really cute, especially on you, but what's up?"

The room was silent as all eyes locked on Seneca. She shook her head in search of the right words to say. So much had happened, and she wasn't sure where to begin. Once they had returned to the safety of the castle, Rileau had gone to work on her. She recalled being moved a few times, and several incantations had been recited. She would awake for a brief moment before drifting back under. He'd prepared a potion, described as a nectar of pixie tears and mint, which had worked to fully revive her. He'd explained that it would also bring her temperature to normal levels. However, he hadn't told her that although she was no longer freezing, there were other changes the potion could not fix. Her physical transformation could not be reversed.

If Shayna hadn't pointed her to a mirror, she wouldn't have known her appearance had been altered to such an extreme. She was aware that her outward appearance was not the only change. Most of the alterations had happened internally; she could feel them. It was a knowingness that she couldn't pinpoint or explain, but she would never be the same.

With certainty, she now knew precisely what it meant to be a druid. She embraced it fully.

Seneca eyed Jake and wanted to know what he was thinking, but she resisted reading his mind. She could tell from his expression that he was expecting her to. She watched his nose twitch and his eyes bulge slightly. The way she viewed it, he was practically extending a broadcasted invitation to explore his thoughts. She pretended not to notice and looked away to avoid the temptation.

"Seneca," Rileau said, "perhaps you can begin by telling us exactly what happened once you were forced to cross the portal."

"Okay, I can tell you what I remember, but some of it's hazy," she replied.

"Whatever you are able to recall shall be beneficial," he said.

"Before I get into it, I just want to say that I know it's been crazy, and we're all on edge because of what we've been through, but has anyone seen or heard from Wren?" Seneca asked.

"Great question! Did you guys know that she wasn't at her cottage when we were attacked?" asked Shayna. "The place was trashed too." She had a flash of what they'd seen when they arrived. They'd been attacked before they could investigate. She had been so concerned about Seneca being taken by someone she thought was Brigara that she hadn't bothered to search for Wren. "With all the commotion going on while Seneca was snatched, my only thought was getting back here for help," Shayna said sadly.

"It is understandable, and you responded appropriately," said Rileau. "Your priorities and actions were sound. Now, Seneca, please continue."

"Excuse me, but what about Wren? Do you know if she's okay or not?" Jake said. He wondered why Rileau was brushing the issue aside. He had the impression Rileau and Wren were close allies. To ignore the topic was suspicious. He scanned Rileau's face in search of any sign of distress or concern. He found none.

"Wren is no longer with us," replied Rileau.

"She's dead?" Shayna and Jake asked simultaneously.

"No, she has not passed. She has elected not to reveal her whereabouts or intentions. She may be a willing follower of Brigara. Seneca and Shayna were lured away from this castle without my consent. I am surmising that the plan was to attack and detain Shayna until the dupelene completed her task. Once this took place, then she could return with Shayna under the guise of being Seneca. She could then begin disarming the Dominion of Four until you no longer existed or were a threat. They underestimated your powers."

The four were speechless. The idea that Wren would side with Brigara was something none of them could fathom. They began hurling questions at Rileau and talking over each other. He slammed his tail several times to get their attention and regain composure. The ramblings and convictions of disbelief came to a sudden halt.

"Silence!" Rileau roared. "Let one of you speak without trampling on the words of the other."

They exchanged looks of confusion but complied with his command.

"I can't believe she would turn on us," said Seneca softly.

"Regrettably, it is likely true," Rileau replied. "All those who encounter the dominion are tasked with gaining knowledge of your gifts. In particular, Seneca. They believe this would provide an advantage in your demise."

"Why would they think that?" asked Seneca. "Why would Wren think that?"

"She probably saw you as gullible and anxious to discover what it meant to be a druid," said Jake. "I bet she believed she could lead you directly into their trap."

"If Wren is involved, then she was correct, it would seem," said Rileau.

"I'm not gullible. I just trusted her," said Seneca. "Actually, I trusted you, Rileau. Why wouldn't I? You're the one who said I needed to train with her."

Although her voice was barely raised, her expression didn't match the softened tone. Her eyes flashed a midnight blue before quickly returning to their previous hue. Jake saw it and knew it was a sign of her true emotional state. Her voice masked her actual demeanor, making her sound rational and calm. He knew better and decided to watch her closely for other signs.

"That is true, but I did not tell you to leave the grounds of the castle," Rileau retorted. "You should have solicited any change to your training from me directly!"

"Well, I agree with Seneca," Shayna said. "When Wren told me to train with Seneca, I just figured you asked her to do it. Seems like you're blaming us for having a traitor in your camp. Look at it from our perspective: you introduced us to her. Like my dad always said, 'You are as good as the company you keep.' Or something like that anyway. You know what I'm saying. She was your friend and not ours. I was suspicious of her from the start, with her long legs and staff and all that other stuff. She even refused to show me how to throw my reflectoire into my shadow! And that's not all."

"Shayna! We get it," said Jake. He threw up his hands to get her to halt her rambling. "We were obviously all fooled by her, including Rileau. Am I right?" Jake turned to face Rileau in anticipation of a favorable response, but he received a blank stare instead. Jake rolled his eyes and shook his head. He was baffled by him and kept looking for a reasonable reaction.

Shayna brushed Jake aside and continued her rant. "I wasn't done, Jake! Rileau, we thought you trusted her and that she was your friend!" she huffed. "That's why we took that stupid map and went to her house in the first place."

"Beware of maps. That's what got us here in the first place," said Conner gruffly.

"Valid point," Jake muttered.

Shayna was on the verge of tears, but her blazing temper held them at bay. She thought about all she had learned from Wren in such a short period. Her emotions came boiling forward as she recalled each moment. Wren's treachery cut through her heart like barbed wire. She had never felt such betrayal. "How could she do this to us? Can we even count on any of the stuff she taught us?" Shayna asked as she threw her arms in the air and looked up in search of an answer.

"Her actions were beyond reproach. To my dismay, her quest for power is shared by many," said Rileau. "She, like the others, must desire what has been promised. Those who follow Brigara are swayed by falsehoods and vacant promises. They seek power and believe she is their means for getting it."

"Power? Brigara doesn't strike me as someone who'd want to share that with anyone," said Jake. "Just the opposite, actually. I was under the impression she wanted it all to herself."

"It is not simply power that she desires. She seeks the source of all magic that permeates across all realms. Thus, the highest of power in existence," said Rileau.

"What do you mean the source of magic?" asked Jake.

He hadn't thought about there actually being a source. Seneca, Shayna, and Conner were engrossed in the topic as well. They pressed their bodies close, as if they were discussing a top secret and were concerned about being overheard.

"I don't have to ask why Brigara would want to get to the source, but why would anybody else? Don't most elementals and fairies have some sort of magic already?" asked Jake.

"Most all are born with some essence of magic. There are some who must be remedially taught to access magic. They are usually gifted in using natural methods from the earth to enact spells and potions. It takes longer, but their spells can be quite powerful. Still, there are others who are entirely absent of magic gifts. It is unfortunate, but they are often shunned because of this. As you can assume, this creates fear, resentment, and a blinding zest for having what they lack. Brigara is looking to capitalize on those who believe they are due more. Rejection is not just a mortal phenomenon. It also exists in our Otherworld."

"She's promising they will be powerful if they help get rid of us?" asked Seneca rhetorically. "That's a hard-core recruitment strategy."

She pondered the significance of what Rileau was saying, and it resonated with her. She had been ridiculed about her slight frame. She'd endured teasing about the oversized backpack she lugged around, as well as constant badgering about her lack of friends. She thought about how she had reacted in those moments of being taunted. Would she have agreed to do whatever it took to make the teasing stop? If someone in authority had offered her a way to get back at the offenders, would she have been a willing participant? She was sure she would have been tempted, but she was stronger than that. She knew she would have dealt with the bullies the same way she always had: with wit and avoidance. She actually felt empathy for her tormentors—not then but now. She knew this attitude had to do with the druid influence, which was completely engrained in her now.

"It is an enticing lure indeed. Offering power to those who lack it is a powerful tactic," said Rileau.

"Ah, so she's going after the low-hanging fruit—those who have been bullied and hold a grudge to get back at the offenders. Classic!" said Shayna.

"Those who are most vulnerable," added Seneca. Her voice was solemn. "Those who lack confidence."

"The ones with something to prove too," Conner said. "They've got nothing to lose."

"You are all correct in your summations," said Rileau. "This makes her followers extremely dangerous. The opportunity to face those they consider their oppressors with increased power is an enticing offer."

"The oppressed become the oppressors," Jake mumbled. He looked to Rileau, who bowed in acknowledgment.

"There's a disconnect, though. Why would Wren side with Brigara? It seems to me that she has it all," said Shayna. "I don't get it."

"You mentioned that you were attacked by an elf when you were in Wren's dwelling, correct?" asked Rileau. "Someone you said resembled Wren."

"Yeah, but it wasn't her," said Shayna. "She dressed like her and sort of sounded like her, but it wasn't Wren." Her words came out more as a question than a definitive statement.

"No, it was likely her sister, Lorikeet. She is the younger sister to Wren and was not born with magical abilities. She has always remained in the shadow of Wren, who was quite protective of her. Lorikeet suffered much from the high expectations of the elf clan. They are proud elementals. To experience one of their own without even an echo of magic is not highly regarded. As such, Lorikeet struggled to belong."

"How do you know this?" asked Jake.

"Wren came to me for assistance. She was concerned by the extreme methods Lorikeet was taking to acquire magic. She confided in me that she wanted to give her sister an ancient dragon elixir as a way to help her. She offered a satchel of precious black crystals. It is most rare to acquire crystals of that purity. She believed that if the crystals were mixed with the elixir, her sister's blood would be transformed to contain magic."

"I wondered what was in that bag. These black crystals can give someone magic?" asked Jake. He thought back to when they'd first met Wren. The satchel she'd carried had caught his eye. He wondered if she would have revealed the truth of its contents, had he asked. He knew it was highly unlikely, but it didn't stop him from imagining how she would have explained it.

"I have heard of such things but have never practiced it. I was also wary by the way in which she came into possession of these crystals. I refused to subject her sister to such methods that could potentially end her life. Wren was quite disappointed. I regret to say, she may have sought other means to gain what she was seeking," Rileau said in a concerned tone.

"You mean Brigara," said Conner. "Do you think she contacted Brigara?"

"I have no proof of this, but it is highly probable. She was desperate to give her sister what she desired. Her love for Lorikeet is what drove her to risk so much. Having such a large quantity of black crystals appears to be proof of that," said Rileau. "I've never come across that volume in all my time in the Otherworld."

"How did Wren get the crystals then?" asked Jake. "Did she steal them or something?"

"I do not know, and I did not inquire. She would have been forthcoming if she cared for me to have such information. I can only assume that whatever the origin, the cost was at a great price. If they were taken by force or by farce, the owner may have a desire to reclaim them. They are highly sought. She will likely face threats if it is revealed they are in her possession."

"She's coming after me, isn't she?" said Shayna. Her mouth hung open in a fixed gasp. Her face was colorless, and her eyes bulged. She was rigid and felt she would fall over from the slightest touch. She felt sick and numb.

"What are you talking about?" asked Seneca.

"Wren," said Shayna in an airy whisper. "I killed her sister. She's most definitely coming after me. And if she's on Brigara's side, that's a hundred times worse."

"I cannot speak to her intentions. Wren has always been noble. She has walked with others in harmony to end the war that Brigara has forged. It would be against her nature to side with such evil. But I cannot ignore what has occurred. While I have no proof, it is quite disturbing."

"Yeah, and like you said, she just wanted Lorikeet to have magic and be happy, and now she's dead. Because of me," moaned Shayna. She covered her face and sobbed.

The revelation slammed them hard. They hadn't discussed the fact that Shayna had ended a life or the repercussions of it. They had been so focused on saving Seneca that they hadn't stopped to think about killing anyone. They had been consumed with talking about the changes in their gifts and the discovery of Brigara's goal, but nothing about ending a life had crossed their lips.

Seneca wrapped her arms around Shayna's waist and hugged her gently. Jake eased in and draped his arm across her shoulders. Conner gave her a gentle pat as he joined them.

"It's okay, Shayna. We know you feel bad, but you can't blame yourself," said Jake. "We battled with those annoying acid-spitting fairies, possibly killing a few, and then the murkgoblins, but we had to fight back."

"I know, but this was different. Those others were nameless, faceless enemies," replied Shayna as she pulled away from Seneca and Jake. She dried her tears and smoothed her hair as she regained her composure.

"It's a war of sorrow and potentially revenge now," whispered Seneca. "It's going to get personal."

Shayna thought about Wren's sister's last words. She had willingly provided information that helped them. Shayna wondered if Wren had regrets about the attack and the deception. She had done it all to get what she believed Lorikeet was owed: magic. She had gone to extremes to gain it, yet magic had ended her life.

"You were defending yourself," said Conner. "You were under attack."

"Plus, you were trying to save me. It was a trap, and you did what was needed," Seneca added.

"Maybe, but I'm sure Wren won't see it that way. Remember, her sister didn't have magic to use. I did."

"Then she was a fool to set up that trap and then leave her sister to fight you alone," said Conner. "She's to blame for putting her sister in that situation in the first place. She obviously underestimated how awesomely fierce Shayna is with that sword."

"Conner's got a point, but I agree with Shayna," said Jake. "Wren's going to be on the attack for sure. If she was crazy enough to team up with Brigara, then she'll be out for blood."

"We don't know any of this for sure. You guys are just speculating," said Seneca. "I think we need to stay positive. Maybe there's a good explanation for why Wren wasn't home. Remember, her place was trashed."

"That was a smoke screen to throw you off your game," said Conner. "Good maneuver, if you ask me. On the other hand, if Wren wasn't involved, you'd better believe she will be now."

"What do you think, Rileau?" asked Shayna.

"Seneca has a valid point of view," said Rileau. "Let us consider what we know about the ambush."

They discussed the attack, the change of training sites, and probable motives. The discussion lingered until Shayna stopped contributing to the repetitive theories that were tossed about. She retreated into her own private thoughts. She crossed the room until she reached the window that allowed the most light into the room.

Thick gray clouds moved rapidly across the sky in large, ominous clusters. She wondered if rain would soon follow. The smell of the air and the crisp sensation of the breeze after a heavy storm were some of her favorite sensations. She followed the sway of the branches in a row of large aged trees in the distance. She watched the rhythm the wind created as it lifted dry leaves and twigs. It carried them high and swirled them around before depositing them across the flower garden and lush grass below. She believed it was a way of nature blending the various elements to expose them to new surroundings—much like what had happened with the four of them.

"We're a lot like decorating," Shayna whispered aloud.

Shayna scanned the grounds as the wind continued swirling and redesigning the landscape. She wanted to feel the breeze across her face to dry her tears. She opened the window slightly and took in the fragrance of the rose blossoms. They were losing their petals with each swell of the wind. Shayna wondered if Wren's sister had liked flowers and which would have been her favorite. She was confused by the sorrow she felt for someone she didn't know. This was a person who would have likely ended her life if she had been able. Wasn't that what Lorikeet had been attempting? Shayna knew that Seneca and the others were right about defending themselves. Her intent had not been to kill, but death had been the outcome. She felt a heavy hand upon her shoulder. The familiar scent was unique only to him. She turned and looked up into Rileau's brilliant green eyes. She tried hard to contain herself but buried her face into his chest and cried. Except for her weeping, there were no other sounds in the room. She shuddered slightly and exhaled. The tears subsided. She pulled away and dried her face with her sleeve. Rileau directed her to join the others, and she complied without complaint.

"Sorry, guys. I just feel really bad for what's happened. Not just to Wren's sister but to all of us. Look what we've been through. It's a lot," said Shayna.

"It is, but it's just the beginning," said Jake. He covered her in his arms and gave her a firm embrace before letting go.

"We're going to have to deal with loss. It's a war," said Seneca somberly.

"True," said Jake. "We just need to stick together and end this thing before more families lose the ones they care about."

"Now you know why the Dominion of Four is so critical to our realm and all others. We must end this war and return the Otherworld to harmony," Rileau stated raucously. "We cannot allow Brigara or her followers to gain access to the source of magic, as it will end our way of life and jeopardize the entire world."

Jake felt uneasy, and from the expressions of the others, he could tell he wasn't alone. They were already feeling the pressure of the prophecy. They were being groomed to be the saviors and protectors of the source of all magic.

"You do know this is a lot of pressure to dump on four inexperienced teenagers, right?" Jake said. "I think we would all agree that this is a crazy mess."

"Yeah, like, times five thousand!" said Conner.

"Are we going to let that stop us? Joan of Arcadia was a teenager, and look what she accomplished!" said Shayna.

"You mean Arc," said Jake.

"Who?"

"Joan of Arc. Oh, never mind. You're right; we can do this," replied Jake.

"We most certainly can. We have the magic from the crystals, and the prophecy says we can do it. Plus, we've got Rileau. I bet they don't have a dragon—or do they?" asked Conner.

"No dragons would ever be swayed to follow Brigara," Rileau sneered.

"We have to see this through, because so many are counting on us," said Seneca. "Can we talk about Wren?"

"That is sound," said Rileau. "Yes, we may discuss her."

"In my opinion, Wren probably played a big part in their strategy," said Shayna. "It makes me wonder if we can trust anything she taught us. Can we?"

"Great question!" yelled Conner. "She must have totally set up Seneca and Shayna to get ambushed. What if she trained them in a bunch of bogus stuff?"

"You defeated your attackers. Her training served you well," said Rileau. "It would have been of benefit had you continued on the course of her guidance. The castle was an adequate training ground for you. Taking you away from its protection was not ideal, yet you proved your adaptability. This will serve you well when we are fully engaged in battle."

"It sounds like you're not completely convinced that she betrayed us," said Jake.

"This is true. Her actions are questionable, but I have known her to be noble. We shall uncover her true allegiance, as I am quite sure our paths will cross," said Rileau.

"We thought it was odd that she wasn't at her house and that it was ransacked," said Shayna. "I kept thinking that she was this badass fighter who would never let that happen."

"Seems to me she just wanted to get you alone to play tag team with that other elf and the dupelene," said Conner.

"Lorikeet didn't stand a chance," said Shayna. "Now that I think about it, I'll bet it was Wren she was talking about. They underestimated how good I am with a sword."

"Nope. I'm sure Wren didn't consider that when she was making her plans. But I'm sure she's not too happy about how you handled her sister either," said Conner.

"I am not afraid!" Shayna yelled.

"We have to be careful. Their plan almost worked," said Jake. "I'm glad you mastered your reflectoire and got us there in time to save Seneca, but we can't get cocky."

"Let us continue, as there is much to consider," Rileau said.

A smoke cloud jetted from his nostrils. They knew it was a signal to stay on track. They agreed and began to rehash all they knew and what was still in question. They discussed what Wren had taught them and the areas she had avoided when questioned. The discussion continued for what seemed like hours, and they grew restless.

"It sounds like we're at the stage to launch a plan, Rileau. They obviously have given their attacks some thought," Jake said.

"But we've squashed their plans and tossed them away like yesterday's dog droppings!" said Conner. He kicked up a knee and pumped his fists.

"That's gross," Shayna replied in a perturbed tone. "Use better analogies next time, please."

"Ha! You said *anal*." Conner snorted and laughed loudly.

"I did not!" Shayna huffed.

"Yeah, ya did!"

"Seriously, Conner, cut it out!"

"Hey, don't get mad at me for your potty mouth!" His face turned crimson as he doubled over in laughter. Shayna stormed in his direction, but Jake cut her off and put his arms up to stop her advance.

"You two need to stop!" Jake called out. He wrestled Shayna's arms to her sides as she made futile attempts to swing at Conner. "Enough! We obviously need a break and have been in this room way too long. Leave her alone, Conner; you don't want her pulling out her sword."

Conner eased away in retreat as he smirked with satisfaction. Shayna shook her fist in response as she pulled away from Jake.

"I think you're right, Jake. Maybe we need a break," Seneca said from across the room. She was nestled in a chair with her legs pulled in close. "Those two especially could use a time-out."

"What do you think, Rileau?" Jake asked.

They waited for him to respond, but he remained silent. He remained motionless in front of the wide window that had a view of the lush garden below. Jake slowly approached him and stood by his side. He looked out to see what could have captured his attention, but all Jake could see was the vast landscape.

"Excuse me, Rileau," Jake said. He paused and waited for a response or some sign of being heard, but nothing changed. He cleared his throat and tried again. "We were wondering if we should take a break or something. You know, like leave this room for a while."

"We've gone over everything we can think of, but we keep getting stuck on Wren," said Shayna. "What do we do?"

Rileau spun around and faced her. His green eyes bulged beneath his furrowed brow. She stumbled back in response.

"We must do what is necessary!" he roared. "You are undisciplined, the lot of you! You quibble about nonsense, and your attention wanes quicker than that of a newborn. What do you do, you ask? You do whatever is required to defeat Brigara! You want breaks, reprieves, and rest? Do you think she is resting? Do you think her followers are retreating to bask in leisure? They are not!"

He slammed his fist down on the arion-carved table, and it crumbled into a heap. He yanked the cords that held his cape secure and tossed the garment to the ground. Seneca climbed out of the chair and moved in closer. She tilted her head from one side to the other.

"Rileau, we are young, and because of that, we make more mistakes than we probably should," said Seneca. Her voice was calm, and she smiled slightly. "Perhaps you weren't prepared to train teenagers who have no idea of the Otherworld, but we need each other. We need your help and guidance, but we also need to rest, or we won't be able to help anyone."

"I know what you say is true, Seneca," said Rileau. "However, you must all face the circumstances head-on and forge past the need for rest." He gazed across the meticulous landscape. "Brigara's followers will not rest. Their quest is to destroy the Dominion of Four, as you are all that stand in the way of their leader's return."

"Do you believe Wren is part of their plan?"

"We shall not dwell on Wren for now. Seneca, please continue to share your experience. I do believe there is much we can learn—unless, of course, you desire rest," he said. His voice was matter-of-fact.

He eased away from the window and sat down in one of the wingback chairs. He crossed his legs and positioned his muscular upper limbs atop the armrests. His tail wrapped around his ankle and tapped the carpet. It drummed a beat similar to the tapping of one's fingers in a display of impatience. He leaned back and waited for a reply.

"Sure. I mean, no, I don't need rest. I'm fine," said Seneca. Her voice was airy and didn't show any sign of nervousness.

Jake glanced at her face to see if her eyes changed, but he didn't detect any difference.

Seneca wasn't accustomed to the new sound of her voice and found herself listening as much as the others as the sound lingered in the air.

"Please proceed," Rileau replied.

She had much to tell and decided that jumping right in would be better than fixating on whatever Rileau was hiding about Wren. She climbed onto the large ottoman and immediately understood why Shayna favored it. It was like sitting on an overly stuffed down comforter. She scooted over to make room for Shayna. Jake opted to lean against the wall, and Conner decided to do the same.

Seneca filled them in on the condition of the house when she and Shayna had arrived. They'd thought the house was empty, but they'd decided to look around to be sure. She explained that she'd gone alone to one of the back rooms, while Shayna had searched other parts of the house. They'd worried that if Wren was there, whoever had trashed the place might have hurt her. She explained that she had gone to the rear of the house, and that was where she'd stumbled upon Brigara.

"But now we know it wasn't her," Conner said.

"Sure, but that was my assumption at the time," replied Seneca. "I was startled and about to call for Shayna, but that's when Brigara hurled her first fire sphere at my head."

Seneca explained how she had instinctively shielded herself with her wings, which had acted as a shield of armor and covered her completely. She described how the wings had been able to sustain each hit without any damage. The pride in her voice was evident, and she described the way the experience had felt in detail. While she didn't feel invincible, she was confident in knowing that she couldn't be taken down easily.

"That's awesome!" Conner said excitedly. He caught Rileau's glare and eased back against the wall. "Sorry, Seneca. Keep going. What did the dupelene do next?"

"Dupelene? Yeah, right, but remember, I didn't know at the time. I thought she was Brigara until we got to her shack of a house," said Seneca. While her voice was light, there was intensity in her storytelling. She explained that after several strikes, she could feel the fire sphere's impact waning and the frustration of the dupelene growing. Her muscles tensed as she recalled the encounter and the feelings of being helpless and terrified.

"She was using swear words I'd never heard before. That's when she tackled me and started dragging me across the floor," said Seneca. "I heard Shayna battling someone, but I was too afraid to scream. I thought it would distract Shayna. I also needed to focus on not letting my wings down."

"I tried to reach you in time, but that elf—I mean, Lorikeet—came at me from behind," Shayna said. She shook her head in an attempt to erase the gruesome battle. She didn't want to dwell on it. She knew it was Seneca's time to give her version of the events. Rileau's grimace was also a reminder. "Sorry to interrupt," said Shayna meekly.

Seneca picked up where she'd left off and explained that she'd feared becoming easy prey. "Fighting fire spheres is so out of my comfort zone. At that point, I was still uninjured, but I didn't know what to do. Just when I thought she was out of firepower and I might have a chance to escape, she pulled me into that portal," said Seneca. She leaned her head on Shayna's shoulder. "I'm sorry, but I didn't know how to help you."

"No need to be sorry. You did the right thing. I handled Lorikeet," said Shayna as she wrapped her arms around Seneca. "She actually came in handy when it came to figuring out who'd snatched you."

Seneca smiled and took a deep breath before continuing to recap what had transpired. Jake listened carefully, resisting the temptation to jump in with questions. He was curious about the portal and wondered how difficult portals were to conjure. The notion of moving from one place to another by magic fascinated him.

"The portal led us to that shabby house close to a cliff. It opened just outside of it, and she cursed when she realized she didn't have the strength to drag me inside. She started ranting about her sacrifices and how she was owed for her loyalty. That's when I figured out that she wasn't Brigara. I saw my opening," said Seneca. She raised her head and tightened her fist. Her emotions were connected to that moment.

"Whoa!" Conner shouted. "You actually fought her?"

"Yeah, I sure did," said Seneca. "I kicked her right in the back, and she stumbled. I did a roundhouse kick that knocked her to the ground. I learned that from my Shayna."

"Glad to hear you were paying attention," Shayna said, smiling.

"That's when I spread my wings and sent a gust of wind. It raised her high off the floor and then slammed her to the ground. I thought I had the best of her, until I found myself rising and hitting the ground too. I tried to recover, but before I knew what was happening, I was swirled up in a small hurricane and dumped in a tepid pool of water that reeked of manure."

"Gross! That sounds really nasty," said Shayna. "What did you do?"

"Up until then, I hadn't realized what she was doing."

"You surmised that she was jinxing your gifts by imitating everything you conjured," Rileau said as he rocked in his chair. His tone indicated he was engrossed in every aspect of the story. His nostrils flared, and smoke filled the room. Conner and Jake made futile swipes through the air in an attempt to fan it way.

"That's exactly what happened! She was copying me––uh, I mean jinxing me. At first, I didn't get it, but then I realized that crazy chick was actually trying to look like me."

"Hopefully that's the last time we have to see that freak show!" said Conner.

Seneca described the nuisance of the actual transformation. She spoke of how the dupelene's body had twisted and gelled into her likeness. Most disconcerting had been listening to her own voice being mimicked. Once she'd recovered from the shock and realized what was happening, the first thing that had come to mind was to stop her.

"I started yelling and screaming, and she would just copy whatever sound I made. She wasn't exactly subtle in her plan either," said Seneca. "She bragged about how she was going to take my place and then destroy each of you––one by one. I wasn't about to let that happen!"

Seneca pulled her legs beneath her and sat up straight. She explained that regardless of what happened, she would not reveal her wings. She'd been barraged with pain and ridicule, but she'd remained steadfast. "I just kept slowing my breathing and focused on what Rileau would be serving up for lunch," she said softly. Her mind drifted to the most horrendous parts of the attack. She had never experienced such terror. She took in a deep breath of relief.

"Leave it to Seneca to think about food while she's getting her butt kicked." joked Conner.

"I had to do whatever I could. She made it clear that my wings were the essential thing she needed for her deception to really work."

"I would have been so scared," Shayna said softly. "It's amazing you hung in there."

"I was scared, especially when she tried to persuade me by saying she could end my suffering quickly. Otherwise, my death would be one of slow suffering." Seneca shook from the memory.

"I'm sure, given the circumstances, it was a tempting offer," Rileau said. "Cruel remarks intertwined with physical pain would certainly be a motivation to surrender for most."

"It was tempting until I got a glimpse of her," replied Seneca. "That's when I realized that all her talk was a bunch of nonsense. You saw her, so you know she was definitely suffering. I knew I had to hold on as long as possible. I wasn't about to let her see my wings in full action."

Seneca described how seeing the dupelene had given her a renewed amount of strength to fight harder to keep her wings hidden. She could only hold them tightly for so long, and then she'd have to flex them before she could withdraw them again.

"It was a real workout, worse than doing a hundred crunches!" Seneca said with a smile. "She couldn't keep up or figure out the timing of when I would open and close them. She got really frustrated and started raging like a psycho."

"You were doing the ole fake and bake. The rope-a-dope and the famous snooze-and-you-lose routine," said Conner in an animated voice.

"I guess," Seneca said. She was a bit confused but figured out the point he was trying to make.

"That's probably why she looked like a poor version of you," said Shayna. "At first, I thought you'd been roughed up beyond recognition."

"She couldn't duplicate my wings completely, because even when they would appear to block her attacks, they weren't fully out or lit," replied Seneca. "The most she was able to do was copy my face and body size. She got angrier by the second because I wouldn't give in."

"But what about the ice balls she was hurling at us?" Conner asked.

"That's the strange part, actually," said Seneca. "She had been hitting me with fireballs like the ones Brigara used, but for some reason, when she started turning into me, she wasn't doing it anymore. When I realized they weren't coming anymore, I thought it was my time to retaliate. But before I get into that, I've got to tell you this first. I'm getting ahead of myself."

Seneca stood up to reenact what had happened. She showed how she'd charged across the floor with her wings in full spread, ready to create a wind that would knock down the dupelene. She'd come to an immediate stop once it spun around to face her.

"She was half Brigara and half me!" said Seneca, her voice shrieking slightly. "Way too creepy for me to even begin to explain—totally creepy!"

"That would definitely be on the top of my creep-out list," said Shayna.

"I only got a quick peek before I would retreat back under my wings, but each time, I was just as shocked."

"She obviously saw your wings in full spread," said Jake. "What did you do?"

"You bet she saw them! She was super-spastic excited, but when I realized she was turning into me, I made them disappear. It was like a game—I just had to time it right. She would get furious and then hurl another fireball at me. Thank goodness my wings were faster than she was. At one point, the fiery spheres started sputtering out before they got halfway across the room. That just fueled her wild rage even more," Seneca said. She twitched as she thought about all she had endured. She wiped away a few tears that rolled down her cheeks.

"Is this too much for you?" asked Jake. "You can stop anytime."

"I'm okay. I was just thinking about how desperately I wanted to stop her, but I didn't know how. I knew without a doubt she'd be coming after you guys. I just remember feeling so helpless."

"Please continue, Seneca. It is important for them to hear the rest," said Rileau in a flat tone.

Her eyes sparkled as they caught the light. She whisked away the tears that continued to flow. She tilted her head slightly and took a deep breath before she spoke. "I know you guys found me pretty quickly, but it seemed like I was stuck in that house forever. The dupelene regrouped and started creating fireballs like crazy. My timing sputtered, and she almost took me down a few times. I finally wrapped myself in my wings and kept them dim. She was definitely interested in their light. She said that without the light, they were no better than the wings of a moth."

"That pretty much describes how she looked," said Jake.

"Yeah, a moth that got too close to a flame," added Conner with a snort.

"I was taking hit after hit. Those fireballs were scorching hot. I started telling myself that I needed to stay cool and focus on being cold," said Seneca.

"Why would you want to cool down?" asked Shayna.

"With my wings wrapped around me so tightly, it was like being in a sauna. When it seemed like she was getting her second wind, my priority changed from 'Stay cool' to 'Don't pass out.'"

Seneca elaborated on how she'd begun to imagine anything cold. She'd pictured herself ice-skating, having snowball fights with her brother, getting brain freeze from iced drinks, and biting into frozen carnival snow cones.

"I could feel it working," she said. "At first, I thought it was just my imagination. But then I started to shiver. I relaxed and thought about warming up—and I did! I could actually control my body temperature."

"Wow, so what did you do?" Shayna asked. She was intrigued and fidgeted nervously.

Seneca described how she'd begun timing the assault of the fireballs, and she'd switch to a freezing reaction when they came. Her body had stopped overheating. Her wings had acted as a shield of ice, which had given her enough confidence to make an effort to defend herself.

"Unfortunately, I didn't really think that strategy through very well," said Seneca with a frown. "I hadn't considered her countermoves, which totally went against what Wren spent so much time drilling into my head. Now that I think about it, Wren's training was probably a waste of time."

"I hope not. That training was brutal!" Shayna said. "Sorry to interrupt." She shot a look at Rileau, anticipating a reaction of disappointment. She braced to accept his criticism but received no response. He remained steady and showed no signs of what he was thinking or feeling. She thought she detected a slight release of smoke, but she couldn't be sure.

"What happened next?" Conner asked. "Don't keep us in suspense!" He eased down the wall and flopped onto the floor. He was prepared to probe until he heard every detail.

"What happened? I made a huge blunder. That's what happened! I thought I was being clever. But all I did was give her yet another weapon to use against me."

"That is the way of the dupelene," said Rileau. "Your strategy was flawed."

"What happened?" Conner asked.

"I thought she just wanted to copy my wings or how I looked. I didn't know she could take my powers too, even the powers I didn't know I had. But I fell for it," Seneca said.

"Yeah, Rileau explained that, but of course, you couldn't have known," Jake replied sympathetically.

Seneca explained that she'd been convinced her wings could guard her against the fireballs. She'd believed that if she got close enough, she could take her down. The disfigured dupelene had seen her making an approach and hurled a fireball directly at her. Seneca's wings had responded not as a cocoon but as a sculpted armor of ice. They'd glistened as they wrapped around her tiny frame. The fireball had smashed hard against the frozen wings with a sizzle, dissolving into fragments of ash. Instinctively, Seneca had spread her icy wings behind her. The tips had transformed into daggers that glowed an opaque electric blue. She'd cupped her hands and held them out. As she'd stretched her fingers far apart, an icy, rapidly spinning orb had taken form. She'd glanced at it only for a second before she'd hurled it across the room. The dupelene had hit the floor as it whirled just over her head. The frozen sphere had slammed into the wall. An imprint of a frosty scorch mark had been left behind as melted ice crumbled to the floor.

"Don't ask me how I did it or how I knew I could do it. I just did," said Seneca. "I didn't aim too well, but the orb was magnificent!"

"That explains why the floor was so slippery," Shayna said as she rubbed the bump on her head, which still throbbed.

Seneca described how the dupelene had skillfully avoided being hit and dodged each new sphere of ice that she'd unleashed. The short demonstration of the new power was all the dupelene had needed to duplicate it. The dupelene had begun creating the icy orbs as masterfully as she had the fire spheres. The remaining resemblance of Brigara had vanished, and she'd taken on Seneca's physique and mannerisms. The only thing missing had been the full transformation of her wings.

"I couldn't stop her!" Seneca shouted. "It was a nightmare. She was better at it than I was. I tried to block the orbs, but she was relentless. She kept trying to force me to reveal my wings with their full light. It was all she needed to be completely me."

"She would only have mimicked your looks and abilities," said Rileau. "She could never truly become you."

"That's good to know. But instead of chancing it, I just wrapped my wings around me and took the hits one after another. I hung in there and did whatever I could think of doing to not let her become me," said Seneca.

"She looked super creepy, especially her eyes," added Shayna. "She was most definitely not you."

"There's only one Seneca. No way could she pull that off!" said Conner.

"But that doesn't really explain your new look. It's cute, but I'm not sure if you really want to go with the ice-princess look," said Shayna as she scrunched up her nose. "You're more of an Anna and not Elsa type, if you know what I mean."

"Let it go!" Jake said. "I like the silver streaks; they're cool. I'm not sure if I will still think of you as Gothic Tinkerbell, but it's nice. I'd like to see your new wings. They sound really cool too."

"Enough of the senseless interruptions! Continue Seneca, please," Rileau commanded.

"Maybe I can show them later," said Seneca. She eased back into the seat and rested her head on Shayna's shoulder. She tried to hide her reaction from view as she took in a deep breath and continued with her story. She explained that her reaction to being hit with the ice orbs had been different from her reaction to the fire ones. She'd known fire would do damage, but somehow, the more ice blasts she'd endured, the more relaxed she'd become, and she'd been able to retreat into a dormant state.

"I felt numb but at peace. I knew the ice couldn't harm me as long as I embraced it. That sounds strange, I know, but it was like a safe place for me. I remember the dupelene was hovering over me and screaming like a wild woman. I willed my wings to retract completely, and I collapsed onto the floor."

"Is that the last thing you remember?" Rileau asked.

"Not exactly. It was like I went to sleep—like hibernation—except I was completely aware of my surroundings, as if I were in a capsule or chamber of cold. But strangely, I didn't feel cold at all. I was actually pretty comfortable. I could smell gardenias, and the aroma relaxed me more," said Seneca.

"When I picked you up, you were frozen, and you didn't move," said Conner. His voice was low and serious. "I thought we got there too late."

"I know, Conner, but as you can see, I'm fine," said Seneca. "Rileau explained it to me. I went through a metamorphosis sort of like a butterfly, except by freezing. The hair and the eyes are the new me, and clearly, my voice changed a bit too. It was like my initiation into being a druid. Apparently, it's usually a slower process, but the trauma accelerated things."

"Yeah, your voice is totally different, but it's nice," said Jake.

"We could hear the dupelene screaming at you, but we thought it was you screaming at yourself, because she sounded just like you," said Conner. "I like your new voice, though. It helps me forget she was trying to be you."

"But she looked nothing like you, not really. Well, at first, I thought it was you, but the fake you was holding one of those spinning ice balls, and it was freaky," said Shayna. "I kind of like the new you."

Seneca smiled as her friends urged her to continue retelling the entire experience. They in turn repeated similar comments and observations. They asked countless questions about her powers and transformation.

Conner pleaded for her to create ice orbs. Although tempted, she resisted when she saw Rileau's eyes narrow.

"I'm not so good at it. I'm going to need practice to perfect my aim and increase the velocity," said Seneca, biting her lip slightly. She gathered Rileau was pleased with her response since only a small whiff of smoke escaped his flared nostrils. He brushed past them and headed toward the hallway. Jake caught a glimpse of two shadows in the hall before the door slammed shut. He heard muffled voices but assumed it was the staff. He turned his attention back to Seneca.

"Now, where was I? Oh yeah, those wings! She sure had a tough time copying them."

"Oh, that's so true. They were absolutely hideous!" Shayna exclaimed. "But she definitely had your voice pegged."

They remained enthralled and only interjected when they wanted Seneca to elaborate on aspects of the story. She told them she hadn't tried out her new wings, but she could sense they had changed for the better. The door suddenly swung open. Rileau's large frame filled most of the entrance. The door closed behind him, and he strolled to the center of the room. All eyes were fixed on him. His jaw was tight, and his hands were balled into fists. They knew instantly that something was wrong.

"You have heard enough!" he roared. "The dupelene has been dealt with, and with Seneca's transformation, she is stronger than before. This will serve you well. The battle to protect the source of magic has begun. You must now rely on your gifts without further training. Time is not on our side."

Shayna and Seneca stood up immediately and exchanged worried looks.

"How are we supposed to do that?" asked Conner. "Me especially. Why can't we have more time?"

"There is no other choice. I have been informed that Brigara is in possession of the anointed Book of Grimoire. She has broken its seal of light and forged a bane of dark magic around it," said Rileau sternly.

"Book of what?" asked Conner.

"Yeah, I didn't get that either. Can you tell us what that means in our language?" Shayna asked.

"It means that she holds the book of magic that druids have used to record spells, potions, and incantations since the beginning of our way of life. It holds all known essences of magic derived from the light," he said slowly and deliberately.

"Has she changed it to dark magic?" asked Jake.

"The book cannot be altered. However, the spells and chants it contains can be wrapped in darkness as long as the bane remains fastened to it. It gives her a considerable advantage—one that I did not anticipate. I can only conclude that a spell within the book was used to provide guidance to the dupelene. Brigara masterfully conjured this potent magic without being in the Otherworld. This concerns me greatly."

"Now what do we do?" Seneca asked as the lightness in her voice carried through the room. She tried her best to maintain calm composure, but her knees rattled uncontrollably. She sat down quickly for fear of them giving out.

"This could mean complete devastation! She will use it to destroy all of the Otherworld—and more. We must change our approach now that she has the Grimoire," he said in a graveled voice. "I must take a brief moment to contemplate how to proceed."

Concern was etched across his face; he began to pace in contemplation. His tail was in full swing as it brushed back and forth with each stride. The tip of it caught a few chair legs whenever he turned. He knocked several chairs completely out of the way to create an unobstructed path.

"Brigara doesn't even have to be here to wreak havoc," said Jake, sure to keep his voice close to a whisper. He had waited until Rileau was on the far side of the room and staring out the window.

"I know. We need to get that book back!" said Shayna.

"Yeah, but the only way to do that is to let her back into the Otherworld," said Seneca. She had repeated Jake's thoughts verbatim. He looked at Seneca and nodded. She knew he was thankful she had spoken the words he was too afraid to say aloud.

The door opened only wide enough for two winged creatures no bigger than thimbles to flutter into the room. They moved in unison and hovered inches from Rileau's ear. He nodded slowly as they spoke in a whisper. After a moment, he waved them off, indicating he had heard enough. The winged beings exited quickly, and the door shut upon their exit. He straightened his cloak and turned to face the foursome. From his expression, Seneca thought it best that she remain seated. The others stood at attention in anticipation of an announcement.

CHAPTER SEVENTEEN

She Shall Return

"Let us prepare," declared Rileau as he led them down the quiet halls of the castle. They continued walking through the dimly lit halls until they reached a large brass door. It was located in an area that had remained off limits to them. He pushed back the heavy door, they entered, and their eyes scanned the room in awe.

"This is the place where we shall purge Brigara from the mortal realm," Rileau explained. "Once I receive notice of her position from the arcane sprites, we shall begin the ritual."

"Are you talking about those small winged beings we saw earlier?" Seneca asked.

"Yes, they have the gift to uncover what is hidden. Since Brigara is adept at avoiding detection, she has been quite the challenge. I am sure it was the sprites who assisted your parents in locating her, but that took many mortal years to accomplish. Since she has the Book of Grimoire, she is no longer concerned with renewing her detection-shielding spells."

He gestured for them to enter the chamber. Shayna stepped into the room first, followed by the others. She spun slowly around, taking in the surroundings. She wrapped her arms in a tight self-embrace. "Amazing," she whispered. "Fantastically amazing."

The walls and ceiling were made of crystals in varying sizes. The floor was aged stone slab with various markings carved into it. Seneca recognized one of the symbols. The same engraving had been etched on her druid necklace. It made her wonder if her parents had ever been in the room.

"It's like a prism in here," said Jake. "I've never seen anything like this before."

He moved along with the others to the center of the room. Each of them knew, without uttering a word, that it was the same arrangement used in Brigara's banishment. A total of four chairs were positioned just as the elder druids had done: three on the perimeter and one in the center. They'd held her captive in the center chair as they wielded layers upon layers of magic charms at her. She had fought them with everything she had, but she had finally succumbed to their will. She'd been forcibly cast out of the Otherworld. Yet the plan to trap her in the Inbetween, a realm of suspension, had been unsuccessful. She had been clever enough to counter their spell and cross safely into the mortal realm. Shayna, Jake, Seneca, and Conner were now charged with opening the same gateway to allow her to return to the Otherworld, the realm where she vowed to destroy her enemies on sight.

They continued to survey the room. It was arranged just as they had been told; three ornate gold chairs were arranged just as described. An additional one, not as elaborate, was positioned in the center. The rest of the room was bare.

"I'm confused," Jake said. "Keene Ardara told us that Brigara's banishment happened at her home."

"The ceremony for casting her from the Otherworld happened in the home where she once dwelled," said Rileau. "To bring her back, we shall use this anointed chamber. Our objective is not to abolish but to retrieve. The chamber has been conjured as a means to transport. Unlike a portal, she will be forced to cross over. She will not be able to resist."

"Just to be clear, we're trying not to vanquish her but to trap her here in this little room?" asked Seneca.

"In this gorgeous place, you mean?" Shayna said. "Yeah, I agree—way too nice for her!" Her eyes scanned the room. She noticed a distinct pattern to the alignment of the crystals. Her assumption was that the alignment was created or at least enhanced by magic. Her mind drifted from the conversation as she examined the stones.

"This didn't just happen. This chamber being prepped, I mean," said Jake. "A lot of thought went into this."

"That is true. The Elder Druid Council requested that I allow them to arrange an anointed chamber that would remain a secret," said Rileau. "They anticipated there would be a time when Brigara would be summoned back to the Otherworld. They had the forethought to seek out a place where her magic could be contained upon her reentry."

Shayna walked along the edge of the room. It expanded no more than ten feet in each direction. The room had no windows to allow natural lighting, yet it was well lit. Bright light illuminated the entire room. The source of it came directly from the walls. She ran her hand slowly down the sparkling calcite that formed the cascading walls of undulated stone. The feel of cold limestone sent a tingling sensation down her spine. She lifted her fingers but couldn't resist touching it again. She wondered how the embedded crystals had formed inside the room. She had a fascination for gemstones and knew what it took to form them. She was well versed on calcite and how it formed as deposits in caves.

Every aspect of the room was covered in the light-emitting crystals. They varied in dimension and color. They ranged from nearly colorless to vibrant red, green, yellow, and blue. Some were opaque, while others were translucent, and most appeared to be in hexagonal forms. Each stone, regardless of size, twinkled and shined to contribute to the dazzling cast of light.

"Seneca, come over here," Shayna said, beckoning to her.

"What is it?" Seneca replied.

"See this? These are Iceland spar! This room is covered in them!"

"What's Iceland spar?" Jake asked.

Instead of replying directly to him, Shayna searched Rileau's eyes for confirmation. He nodded, and she continued with even greater enthusiasm.

"Some actually call it sunstone because it can even reflect through fog. I'm right, aren't I? The limestone is full of them. Every tiny inch of the walls is covered," Shayna said exuberantly.

"Your declaration is true. The walls are of Iceland spar," said Rileau. "Walk around and get acclimated before we begin."

She was only partially listening to his response as she resumed the inspection of several larger gems. She noticed they weren't as bright as the smaller ones but still reflected light. The tiniest and most colorless stones were the most brilliant.

"You guys have to check this out. It's fascinating!" said Shayna. "This is like the limestone that was used to make the pyramids in Egypt." She rubbed her hands across the way as she gleamed with a pageant-perfect smile.

"That's cool," said Conner flatly. He was nervous. Being inside the room caused an uneasiness in his stomach. All he could think about was coming face-to-face with Brigara. He shuddered as he worked to remove the image from his mind.

"It's more than just cool, Conner. Iceland spar is like ubertastic perfection! There are no flaws. You know, no impurities," she said, beaming.

Shayna wondered how the pure calcite crystals had formed inside the castle. As she cupped her hand along one of the larger crevices of the wall, she came to a sudden realization. She jerked her head around, her eyes wide with excitement. "Rileau, was the castle built around this limestone? Are we in a cave? They totally seem ancient, like they've been around forever. I mean, it would have to be. Iceland spar is like the gem that retracts light and makes everything look like its double." She rambled without taking a pause. She gently placed her palm on the wall in admiration.

"That is correct. They do polarize light. This castle was built upon mounds of caves filled with these precious stones," he explained. "The shimmering light you see comes from within the stones. It is trapped there and can only be released with the greatest of heat. If that were to happen, the gas the stones emit is lethal."

"They're super cold," said Conner. "I bet it takes a lot to heat them up."

"Would Brigara's fireballs be the right amount of heat?" Jake asked.

"Only if they were separated from the wall. It is fortunate that these Iceland spars are surrounded by specks of crystals from the source of pure magic. As such, no amount of heat will penetrate them," said Rileau. "It is ideal for what we must do."

"They're like billions of sparkling specks! Like a sea of glitter," said Shayna. "It's so beautiful in here."

"Even with their beauty, they yield great power," replied Rileau. "These walls serve as protection and capture any attacks of dark magic. The light of the crystals absorbs it all. In addition, the room has been enchanted to align the essence of the crystals to act in unison."

"That makes sense when you think about it," said Shayna. "Calcite stores carbon dioxide and traps heat like a greenhouse effect. The magic just gives them an extra boost!"

"You sure do know an awful lot about this stuff," said Seneca. She couldn't hide the surprise in her voice and her expression. "How do you know all of this?"

"Hello! Are you kidding? Shiny gems, crystals, rocks. You know—diamonds?" Shayna didn't bother to wait for a response as she continued on her rant. "Anyway, you've gotta know your stuff when it comes to precious gems. You don't want to get fooled when you're shopping for that perfect charm bracelet, and the clerk tells you it's a pearl, and you totally know that it's an opal. Total scam alert!" Shayna snapped her fingers above her head and smirked.

"Okay, got it," said Seneca with a slight snicker. "Good to know you're a resource for all things shiny."

"You seemed to have familiarized yourself with this chamber," Rileau said.

"I'm guessing it's time to talk about the crazy lady," Conner grumbled. He shoved his hands into his pockets and braced for the news.

"Indeed, it is time. We must bring her to this place," said Rileau.

"Rileau, if we do manage to get Brigara in here, will we be safe from her attacks?" asked Jake. The room grew silent as they turned their attention to the dragon.

"She will attempt an attack, but once she realizes she is powerless within these walls, she is likely to seek an escape," he said. "Someone who feels trapped can be quite formidable."

"You mean dangerous," said Seneca.

"There's only one way in and one way out too," said Conner. His voice cracked. He could feel sweat rolling down his back.

"Remember, we've got to keep her in here. We can't let her through that door, no matter what," said Jake. "We need a strategy. We need to know what she might do before she does it."

"Like the elder druids?" Seneca asked. "Look how that turned out. They couldn't outmaneuver her, and that's how she got away."

"I just want to make sure I'm getting this. We have to somehow summon the teacher from hell? Then trap her in this cave with only one way out?" said Conner sarcastically. "I agree with Jake. We definitely need a game plan before we have to deal with her."

"I think we should go over the risks first," said Shayna. "I'm sure there are a ton of them, even if her powers are absorbed in the wall. Hopefully she doesn't affect their beauty."

"Aye, a strategy is necessary, but most of what you will encounter will be based on your gifts and instincts," said Rileau. "You will first enact the spell that will return Brigara to the Otherworld. She will not leave the Book of Grimoire behind, as it is essential to her true quest. Once she appears, you must retrieve it from her. That is imperative!"

"I'm sorry, but I'm still not understanding exactly why we would bring her here. Isn't everyone safer, including the source of magic, if we leave her butt in the mortal realm?" asked Shayna.

"I agree. Plus, what good can the book—the Grimoire—do for her there?" Seneca added.

"I'm struggling with the fact that she's going to know it's a trap," said Jake. "She's going to be prepared right from the start to counter whatever we're trying to pull off."

"You all have valid concerns and perspectives. Her ego will not be able to resist the challenge," replied Rileau. "She is consumed by her desire to possess the source of magic. She will not be dissuaded from achieving what she seeks. She knows not of restraint. The Book of Grimoire will eventually be tasked with returning her to the Otherworld. Its vibrations have been felt across this realm, which means she is making attempts to return. We must not allow her to come without our intervention. By opening the portal, we can summon her within these walls and disarm her."

"In other words, snatch that book right out of the grips of her grubby hangnails!" Shayna said.

"Surprise attack? Cool," said Conner. "I'm ready for that." He attempted to sound confident, but he knew he wasn't fooling anyone.

"All of us are ready," Jake said as he put his arm around Conner.

Seneca walked across the room and stood next to Rileau. She noticed that he had remained next to the door and hadn't fully entered the room. She looked up into his eyes and suddenly felt uneasy. She swallowed hard as she mustered the courage to bring up what had been nagging her.

"We still haven't talked about the risks. I'm sure there are a ton of them," said Seneca. Her voice was airy, but there was no mistaking the seriousness of her tone.

"By opening the gateway from the mortal realm to the Otherworld, we jeopardize the veil that shields and separates all of the realms."

"How many realms are we talking about?" asked Jake.

"As you now know, Arcadrom is the realm where the source of all magic originates," replied Rileau. "It is known that there are four realms that exist. We of the Otherworld know of three. The fourth is beyond our reach and our comprehension."

"Just as I was getting used to the idea of Arcadrom, you throw a mystery one in the mix," said Conner. He folded his arms across his chest and let out an exasperated sigh.

"All realms will be vulnerable to Brigara if she escapes," said Rileau. "Her priority will be to cross to the realm of Arcadrom. She is most obstinate in this mission."

"If we let her escape, it will be like an open invitation to the source of all magic," said Shayna. "There's no way I'm letting that skank get out of this room!"

"She'll act like a kid in a toy store if she gets to Arcadrom," said Conner as he shook his head. "Why isn't she satisfied with the power she already has? I really don't get it."

"I'm sure if she had all the power and magic in the universe, it still wouldn't be enough for her," said Jake. "She's just bad wiring—all misfire and short circuits."

"She's like what Socrates said: 'He who is not contented with what he has would not be contented with what he would like to have,'" said Shayna. "Before any of you fall down in surprise that I just quoted that, my dad made me memorize it when he thought I had gone on way too many shopping sprees."

"I'm done with being surprised by you today," said Seneca. "I'm actually impressed." She smiled and nudged Shayna in the shoulder playfully.

"Seriously, though, now that I think about it, those words kind of sound like a curse or a spell," said Shayna.

"That is because they are just that," said Rileau. "Socrates was quite a prankster in disguising his spells in the mortal realm. Your father likely did not realize this when he caused you to memorize it."

"It makes sense now. I missed all the sales in my favorite department store for the next two seasons after that," said Shayna. Her lips puckered in an exaggerated pout. "It figures that Socrates was from the Otherworld too."

"He was missed while away. He once told me that he wanted mortals to evolve to the level of our kind from the Otherworld. He dismissed that notion and decided he could not teach anyone anything; he could only make them think," said Rileau.

"You must be old if you talked to Socrates," Jake replied with a sly smirk.

"That is enough for now. Our time is being wasted. We must prepare to open the threshold," said Rileau gruffly, sneering at Jake. "The enchantment will force Brigara to cross, at which time we shall seize the Book of Grimoire. She will not be able to cross to Arcadrom without it."

"Nab the book. Got it," Conner said.

"I'm sure it's not going to be that easy, even if she's outnumbered," said Shayna. Jake nodded in agreement.

"Nothing involving Brigara is ever easy," said Rileau. "What have you observed, Seneca?"

"There are only three chairs," she replied. "Who sits where? I know the center one is for Brigara, right?" Seneca agonized over whether or not she really wanted to hear the answer.

"Indeed, Brigara shall be positioned in the center. You, Jake, and Shayna are the closest in your bond and shall take the seats—that is not to dismiss your ties in any way, Conner," said Rileau.

"Hey, I'm not offended at all. Just tell me what to do. I'm all about the team here," said Conner with confidence. He was relieved to have a different responsibility. "Every player has a role, no matter how big or small, as long as we work together." He let out a long sigh of relief.

"Excellent attitude. It is you, Conner, who shall have the greatest responsibility of us all," Rileau said somberly.

Jake watched the color whisk away from Conner's face as he stumbled a few steps back. At that moment, anyone could have knocked him over just by blowing.

"Huh? Me? I have the greatest—um, what did you say?" Conner stammered. He was light-headed and disoriented. He leaned on the wall to steady himself. The crystals felt cool against his heated skin.

"Yes, Conner, it is you who must ensure Brigara does not break through the door that secures this chamber. It is the only way out. To escape will be her first impulse. She will not hesitate to do whatever is possible to exit this chamber," Rileau said. "You must prevent this, and by all means, do not allow her to use the Book of Grimoire."

"Don't let her get out, and guard the book. Okay, so what do I do?" Conner asked. Sweat poured down his hairline as he pulled at the collar of his shirt and craned his neck side to side. Even the crystals were of no assistance in lowering his spiked temperature.

"You will stand guard and not let her pass. No matter what distractions she creates, you must stand firm and righteous. Do you understand?"

"Yeah, I get it. I'd be happier with a suit of armor or at least a breastplate," Conner muttered. He nodded nervously with squinted eyes and a stiff grimace.

"You must be brave and focused on the task you have been assigned. You have the light of the Himalayan crystals within you, as it is buckled around your waist within your very soul," said Rileau. "Tighten it, and call on your power to come forward. You must stand your ground and not let her pass."

Conner relaxed as he wiped the sweat from his palms onto his pants. Rileau's words gave him a sense of calm. He felt confident and reflected back on the strength he had received from the crystals. He surveyed his hands. They had a slight shimmer, something he hadn't noticed before. He pulled his shoulders back and raised his chin. He was ready.

"What about us? What do we have to do?" Seneca asked, wide-eyed. "I don't want to be near her when she gets here." She hoped her place was well beyond the reach of Brigara when she appeared. She fiddled nervously as she thought back to the terror she'd felt in dealing with a mere duplicate of the wicked druid. Anticipating the moment when she would face the real one was terrifying.

"You will do precisely as I tell you. You must remember to seize the Book of Grimoire. Do not become distracted, as she must not be allowed to use it," Rileau warned.

"Got it. Book first, and then we take her down!" Shayna exclaimed. Unlike Conner and Seneca, she was anxious for the confrontation. She held Brigara accountable for all that had happened, from the death of her grandmother Dreya to the encounter that had led to the loss of Wren's sister. She desperately wanted to end the conflict in the Otherworld. She could then reunite with her mother and find a way to return to the mortal realm to see her father.

"You must first take your seats," Rileau instructed.

He ushered them toward the gilded chairs. Without hesitation, they did as they were told. Conner took his place near the door. Jake scanned the room and tried to imagine what must have happened during the ceremony that had ultimately removed her from the Otherworld. He wondered if the elder druids had felt any hesitation or ambivalence toward their mission. He knew they had faltered and hadn't thought everything through. They weren't amateurs and certainly knew more about Brigara, magic, and what ramifications to expect. Jake and his friends were at a disadvantage, and he didn't care for the odds.

"Rileau, maybe we should use all four of us in the ceremony. We're supposed to be a foursome, right?" Jake said. "The dominion should make us stronger."

"It must be three who create the breach. It is the power of three that separates the realms," Rileau said. "Four is a neutral vibration that links all existence together. It will take the off-balance number of three to force the seal between the realms to tilt. This shift is needed to force a fracture and open a gateway."

"What do you think is going to happen? Is there something you're not telling us?" asked Seneca. She could sense that Rileau was still holding back. She had watched his bleak expression. He wasn't being forthcoming, and she knew it.

"I regret that I cannot be present when the gateway opens," he said somberly. "It is you who crossed to our Otherworld, and in keeping this balance, it is you who must open it. It is the only way the magic will take hold."

"What?" Shayna screamed. "We need you!" She jumped from her seat and faced him as tears welled. "You've got to help us! We have absolutely no idea what we're doing!"

"None!" Conner added. He leaned against the door and banged his head, as his legs were begging to collapse.

"I will assist by guiding you in the incantation, but my presence is not allowed. I cannot interfere," said Rileau. "You cannot dwell on what you do not have. You must focus on what is. You all have what is necessary to bring Brigara forth and hold her here until she can be properly dealt with."

"Properly dealt with," Jake repeated slowly. "You mean killed, don't you?"

"It is not for me to make that determination, as the Elder Elf Council will have the say in that matter. They have taken the position of the elder druids in these times. They will decide her fate."

Before he continued, the door opened slightly. Conner dodged as three arcane sprites fluttered inside and swarmed Rileau. Their voices were low hums, and no distinguishable language could be detected by Jake as he leaned in to listen. He sat back when the sprites abruptly retreated. The door closed silently. Rileau turned slowly to face them.

"I'm sure they had plenty to say, and it's etched in their latest edition of the *Prophecy Gazette*," Shayna huffed. She stood up and ran her fingers through her hair in frustration. "Come on. Spit it out! What's the deal?"

"It is time," replied Rileau.

"Let's get on with this," said Seneca flatly. She felt exhausted. She pulled Shayna to her seat; Shayna was despondent and did not resist.

"We can do this. We are meant to do this," Seneca said reassuringly. She rubbed Shayna's back between her shoulder blades until she could feel the tension release as she exhaled.

"Okay. I'm okay," Shayna said. "Just thought we had more firepower, but I'm good to go." She refused to look directly at Rileau, but she could smell smoke filling the room. Her eyes narrowed as she allowed her anger to replace her fear. "I can't wait to see the old bat again. I owe her for what she's done to my family."

"Yeah, I can relate to that," said Seneca softly.

"Tell us what we need to say, Rileau," Jake said as he looked to Shayna and Seneca for confirmation. He shifted nervously in his seat, straddling it like a bull rider in a chute, waiting for the gate to open.

"You will repeat the incantation thrice over and in unison. Remember, you must focus on the Book of Grimoire. Do not be detracted by her cunningness. She will attempt to dissuade you from what you seek," said Rileau grimly. "Conner, once I take my leave, you shall assume guard of the exit. I will remain on the other side. When she is under your control, you must summon me without delay."

"Got it," said Conner. He pushed his back against the wall in preparation. His confidence was returning. He cracked his knuckles and flexed his arms.

"Seneca, it is likely Brigara will focus on you. She is aware that you are a druid. Do not falter. You are a powerful elemental, and she is quite aware, as it was you who held your ground against the dupelene," said Rileau grimly. "And, Jake, Brigara will likely attempt to bait you, as you have the blood of those she truly envies. You, my fair Shayna, shall be the one she tries to lure to her side. You are of the same bloodline, and she will seek to prey upon your familiar connection."

"Not a chance in hell!" said Shayna angrily. "We're not falling for her nonsense!"

Jake was pleased that Shayna had spoken on their behalf. They were all feeling the same. They would not be pawns in Brigara's game. Rileau's words rang in his ears. Why would Brigara envy him? It didn't make sense, but all aspects of the despicable woman were a ball of confusion.

"Let us begin," said Rileau impassively. "Once I take my leave, you will recite the following." He proceeded to reveal the incantation:

Gamma of past, ash of present, dawn of the unforeseen.
Our thoughts, our words, our deeds shall link the realms between.
One shall open whilst another shall close,
hence the jarring of the opening to unfold.

"Do you understand all that I have said?" Rileau asked.

They acknowledged they understood. He hastily left the room, shutting the heavy door behind him. Conner slid in front of it and nodded. His eyes were fixated on the center chair, his chin jutted out, and his lips stretched into a thin line. He was ready. Jake reached out and took hold of Shayna's hand and then Seneca's. His palms were moist with sweat as he held their hands securely. Neither resisted his tight grip.

"Let's get this party started!" Shayna said.

They recited the words Rileau had spoken. Shayna took a deep breath as they began repeating it a second time. They exchanged nervous glances. Seneca clasped Jake's hand tightly as they said the spell for the third and final time.

CHAPTER EIGHTEEN

Family Betrayal

They had failed to ask Rileau what to expect. Without articulating it out loud, each of them had anticipated a grand entrance involving smoke or fire—anything grandiose that would signify the moment Brigara had crossed from the mortal world back into the Otherworld. To their dismay, there was no rumbling or bright flash of light to jolt them into readiness. Brigara simply appeared. There before them, in the center seat, sat the person they despised more than anyone they had ever encountered.

Brigara returned their stares through piercing bloodshot eyes. A lack of sleep was etched across her gaunt, pale skin. She rose slowly to manage her instability. Her spindly fingers stretched wide as she smoothed her clothing into place. Jake, Shayna, and Seneca quickly scrambled to their feet. They slid behind their chairs and formed a line to face her. Brigara shifted her focus and snarled. She tilted her head as if she were listening to something. Her expression changed, and she jerked with a flash of frustration. She scrunched her lips and lifted an eyebrow before tossing her head back. Her nostrils flared as she got a whiff of the air, and then she rolled her eyes and shook her head in disgust.

"I do dread the smell of adolescents," she scoffed. "It would appear you have learned a bit about summoning. I am sure you had assistance, as none of you has an aptitude of any depth. You can be sure I will not be trifled with!"

Shayna opened her mouth slightly but resisted responding. Seneca could feel the heat coming off Shayna. She grabbed hold of her hand in an effort to calm her down. Shayna let out a slow exhalation as she licked her lips. Jake watched Brigara's movements. They were prepared to respond to anything she attempted. Without turning around, he could hear Conner's heavy breathing.

Brigara lifted a hand above her head and waved it back and forth as if she were in a parade procession. The Book of Grimoire was visible. She held it securely in the fold of her arm, pressed firmly to her frail frame. She began to slowly meander around the perimeter of the room, waving her free hand through the air while her eyes scanned the walls. Jake, Shayna, and Seneca turned to follow her movements. She stepped around Conner and smirked. She continued her stroll until she returned to where she'd begun.

All eyes were on Brigara, and she knew it. She cackled in delight. She lowered her hand as a white mist rose from the floor and looped around her feet. The slow-moving mist circled around her several times and then trailed off, creating another circle of mist next to her. Out of the mist rose a duplicate image of Brigara. The trail of mist moved on, looping and circling slowly, until another image rose from it. Another duplicate of Brigara appeared. Three equally jarring replicas of the druid stood menacingly shoulder to shoulder. They were living, breathing, and snarling in exactly the same way.

Together they began lapping the room, the mist creating more bodies every few steps. Their movements were identical, as were their expressions and clothing. Each had a book tucked under her arm. The cackle they made grew louder with each replication.

"What's happening?" Shayna yelled. "How's she doing that? She's not supposed to be able to use dark magic in here!"

Jake didn't answer. He didn't know what to make of it either. His eyes locked on the parade of evil druids. Seneca remained silent as she counted the rapidly multiplying images. *There are seven, now eight, now nine,* she thought as she witnessed the hypnotic process repeat. Her wings emerged and spread wide as she grabbed hold of Jake's arm. Shayna summoned her sword, which materialized and vibrated as she clutched the hilt. They glared in horror as Brigara continued to create more images of herself. They lined the outer edges of the room in a single-file formation.

"I don't get how she's doing this," Seneca whispered. "It should be impossible."

"Maybe the Book of Grimoire gave her extra power that even Rileau was unaware of," said Shayna. Her voice was lowered, but she could tell from the shift of the eyes of the multiple Brigaras that she was overheard.

Jake pulled the girls into a tight huddle. He heard Conner nervously clear his throat. Although he knew it was futile, he gave a hand motion to let Conner know that he needed to relax. Conner's eyes widened in response, but he remained at his post.

"It's not dark magic. That's why it's working," Jake said in a hushed voice.

"She's using light magic?" asked Shayna.

"Yeah, but not in the way you think. She's using science!"

"Science?" asked Seneca and Shayna simultaneously.

"She's using the crystals in the walls. They have that optical-illusion effect, like you were saying, Shayna," Jake explained. "She's creating double images because of how the light is refracting from them. It's all just tricks with the light and crystals."

"Okay, so it's not dark magic. That makes sense, but what do we do about it? I've got no idea which one is the real one or which book to grab," said Shayna.

"We need to put something over the crystals—a barrier of some kind. That should stop the doubling effect," said Jake.

"We need to block them out. Okay, I'm following you," said Seneca. "How?"

"There's nothing in here besides us, a few chairs, and way too many ugly druids. I'm not talking about you, Seneca," said Shayna. She scrunched her nose and shrugged.

"I wasn't worried," Seneca said dryly.

"I've got it!" Jake said with a slight jolt. He struggled to keep his voice low, but it was masked by the increasing volume of Brigara's cackles. "I can throw up a wall of water, and then you know what to do after that, right, Seneca?" Jake asked.

"Oh yeah. I'm going to enjoy it too!" replied Seneca, feeling jubilant with anticipation.

"What about me? What do I do?" asked Shayna as she peeked out from the huddle. She counted at least thirteen Brigaras marching around the room. All of their heads, with the same stringy dark hair, whipped around and glared at her with the same lackluster expression.

"Ew, they're so creepy!" Shayna said. Jake tapped her shoulder to regain her attention. She ducked her head back inside the huddle. "Way too dreadful."

"Shayna, she's trying to intimidate us. We can't let her," said Seneca. "This is just a stall tactic."

"Yeah, but she might come up with something else. What's the plan, Jake?"

"Listen, Shayna, once all of the fake Brigaras are gone, you need to go for the book," said Jake. "She'll probably come up with something clever to stop you, but remember, your sword is of light, so you can use it. Get ready to follow my lead. I will give a signal." Jake stood up straight and raised his hands. Shayna and Seneca stepped back.

A swirling pool of crystal-blue water appeared at his feet. It quickly picked up speed with each revolution. Shayna was mesmerized as she slid to his side and watched the pool expand. Jake caught Seneca's eye, and she gave a nod. She turned her palms upward and allowed two perfect spheres of ice to form. They spun and hovered in midair. Conner watched with fascination until he realized he needed to be prepared. He spread his legs wide and pushed his chest out; he balled his hands to form tight fists. His brow furrowed as he flexed his muscles.

Brigara was preoccupied with the continuous formation of her likeness. Her loud cackling transitioned into screeching laughter that sounded like harsh chirps from a flock of ravens. The expanding pool of water finally captured her attention. The duplicate heads turned in unison with eyes bulged. The entire procession came to a sudden halt, and the laughter ceased. Before the Brigaras had time to react, Jake gave the signal.

"Now!" he shouted.

He shoved his hands downward, spread them wide, and then raised them above his head. The water followed his command and thrust high in the air. Seneca's wings reacted with a blink, and blasts of dagger-like ice shards sprang from the tips. They met the wave of water as it peaked, freezing it upon contact. A solid wall of ice formed from ceiling to floor. Jake turned quickly and shot another wave of water straight into the air. Seneca kept the timing perfect as she sent two more daggers of ice into the targeted water. Without relenting, they continued turning and repeating their movements. One by one, the conjured images of Brigara disappeared. Each wall of ice caused the evaporation of more illusions of Brigara. The crystal walls were completely obscured. They had created a full barrier of ice that encircled them. Shayna, Seneca, and Jake stood on one side. Brigara, now alone, stood on the other. She was stunned as she eyed the icy enclosure.

Shayna lunged and swiped her sword just inches from Brigara's face. Brigara instinctively reacted by raising both hands to block the blade. The Book of Grimoire dropped to the floor. Brigara's eyes narrowed as she became aware that she'd been caught off guard. She scanned the room quickly, and her lips tightened as she returned her glare to meet Shayna's tear-filled eyes. Shayna's hands trembled, and the sword felt heavier than usual. She teetered slightly and blinked hard. Her heart was beating double time and ached in her chest. She gulped and told herself to stay steady. She struggled against the impulse that beckoned her to end the despised druid's life.

"You killed Dreya! You're a miserable piece of trash!" Shayna shouted. Her mouth was dry, and she strained to fight back tears, but they spilled over. She repositioned her sword and aimed it at Brigara's heart.

"I only just arrived. Surely you don't think I had a hand in—what did you say? Ah yes, in killing Dreya," Brigara sneered.

"You did it! You ordered your nasty minions. That's what you did! Who kills her own mother? You're a wretched animal, and you don't deserve to live!" Shayna shouted. "Rot in hell!"

Shayna swung the sword above her head, and the blue blade turned black. Brigara winced in anticipation of the fatal blow, but her eyes remained locked on Shayna. Seneca covered her mouth. Jake jumped in front of Shayna and stopped her in mid-strike. He caught her by the wrist and held it firmly.

"Shayna, no! Stop!" Jake shouted.

"Let go of me, Jake!"

"I can't. You can't do this. You don't want to kill her!" Jake pleaded.

"She killed my grandmother! She's been trying to kill us too!" Shayna shrieked.

"She's not worth it," Jake said softly. "She's nothing, but if you kill her, that will be something. Something you don't want to be. You're not like her, so don't let her ruin who you are. Please," said Jake.

"Jake's right, and we have the book," said Seneca softly. "She can't hurt us in here anyway."

"You're right. She's so not worth it," Shayna said flatly as she allowed her sword to vanish. Jake released his hold and let out a deep exhalation. Shayna kept her eyes locked on Brigara as she scooped up the Book of Grimoire.

Brigara glared with contempt at Shayna. Her eyes zeroed in on Jake and Seneca. She made a deep grumbling sound. Her face turned a fiery red as she stretched her arms wide and let out a bone-chilling screech.

Jake immediately covered his ears. He witnessed Seneca crumple to the floor. "Shield, Seneca! Shield!" he yelled.

He felt blood trickling from his ears. He grimaced, grabbed Seneca around her waist, and pulled her up until she was able to stand, but he had to let go quickly. Shayna grabbed hold of him as he wobbled unsteadily. His head throbbed with excruciating pain. Brigara took in a deep breath and released another round of the piercing screams. The icy walls began to crack on all sides.

"My sword won't appear! What's happening?" Shayna yelled.

"It must be the screaming!" Jake shouted. "Keep trying!" His ears were ringing, and he was sure his hearing would be damaged if the screaming continued much longer. He started to make a run at Brigara, but each step he took in her direction made her intensify the screams. He quickly backed away.

"Stay away from her, Jake!" Shayna shouted as she stretched her hands and flexed her fingers frantically. She repeatedly called for her sword aloud to no avail.

"Get over here!" Seneca shouted. She released her wings and spread them wide. The tips vibrated and glowed in cobalt blue. She reached for Jake and Shayna and pulled them to her chest. She closed her wings high above their heads around them. They were covered completely beneath the illuminated wings. Brigara's screams were muffled.

"Good thinking, Seneca," Jake whispered.

"Thanks," she said softly. "But what now?"

Brigara circled them as she contemplated the barrier they had created. "Awfully clever, children. Or so you think! It appears you are as trapped as I am, but it is I who will succeed. Your demise will be a simple task," she snarled with a venomous tone.

Jake's mind was racing. This was it. They couldn't avoid the inevitable. All of the training, multiple attacks, and near-death experiences had led them to this moment. It would be a showdown with their dreaded teacher. The woman they despised and feared equally was an enemy they could not let win—not now and not ever. They could not allow the feelings of being inferior to take over. They had to stand united as the Dominion of Four and push down all doubt. He needed a strategy. He was confident there was a way to beat her; he just had to figure it out.

Seneca fought back the urge to challenge Brigara telepathically. She had been taught to shield when invading others' thoughts, but she didn't dare risk it now. Shayna's hand began to cramp as she squeezed down tightly on the handle of her sword. She let out a slow exhalation, realizing her sword had reappeared under the safety of Seneca's wings. She straightened her forearm and repositioned her grip. She had withstood the screams and knew it was due to her being a demi-elemental with the same abilities. She hated being related to Brigara and detested her misuse of her gifts.

"Okay, Jake. What's the next move?" Shayna asked. "We can't just stand here. She's going to try to get the book back. I might be able to take her out with my sword, but I don't know if it will vanish again."

"We need Conner," he snapped. His head and ears ached, but he knew he couldn't focus on the discomfort.

"What's he going to do?" asked Seneca. She was breathing shallowly but felt her equilibrium returning to her. She knew she would not be able to withstand another bout of Brigara's screams. She recalled her first encounter with the screaming, when they had first arrived in the Otherworld. Keene Ardara had a remedy that resolved the effects, but that wasn't an option now. She had to force recovery without it.

"He'll have to cover her mouth and hold her arms behind her. Like varsity wrestling on hyperdrive!" Jake said. "Seneca, you have to do your mind-reading thing and tell him."

"Got it. That sounds like a good plan. But do you realize we're in this ice chamber, and he's on the other side of it?" asked Seneca.

"Yeah, that's going to be an issue," said Shayna.

"I didn't forget that part, and he's going to love it!" Jake said, more animated than usual. "You've gotta tell him it's clobbering time!"

"What?" Seneca asked as Shayna's expression reflected the same confusion.

"Just say it to him just like that—same emphasis on *clobber*," Jake said with a smirk. "We've gotta be prepared to move quickly, 'cause this is going to be a spectacular smackdown!"

Seneca closed her eyes and took in a deep breath. She remained still for a moment before her eyes popped open. Her face was strained with worry.

"What's wrong? Can't you do it?" asked Shayna.

"That's not the problem. Conner's easy to read. It's Brigara I'm worried about. She's awfully quiet," said Seneca, her voice barely audible.

"Open your wings enough so we'll have our eyes on her," said Jake. "If she starts screaming, just wrap us up again."

"Okay," said Seneca tentatively. She inhaled as her wings spread slightly apart.

"She's just standing there," Shayna whispered.

Brigara stood rigid. Her eyes were cast downward. Her black cloak, frayed and stained, draped loosely around her frail frame. Her lips were moving quickly, and she was chanting inaudibly.

"What's she doing?" Shayna asked. Her heart raced. She knew this was not a good sign. She despised Brigara, but she was well aware of her talents, and it would have been foolish to underestimate her resolve. Brigara would not give in to anyone, especially them.

"She's like a mad caged animal ready to snap. We'd better act quickly. There's no telling what she's going to do next," said Jake. "Come on, Seneca. Get to Conner!"

"I'm going in," she replied.

Seneca spun around to turn her back to Brigara. She refused to allow any distractions. Jake noticed her swaying and placed his hand gently on her shoulder. She shook it away and focused on reaching Conner. She couldn't help but giggle as she tuned into his thoughts of food and basketball. She interrupted him just as he imagined biting down into a double-decker sandwich.

Conner, it's me—Seneca. I need you to listen to what I'm about to tell you. She waited for his acknowledgment. She could sense his hesitation in communicating back to her. *It really is me, and we need your help. We've got Brigara trapped here, but we're also stuck. Are you listening?*

"Yeah," Conner said. "Seneca?"

He was anxious. He'd heard the screams and feared the worst. He had avoided retrieving Rileau, since he knew they needed the book. No one had confirmed they had it yet. He held his position as instructed. He suddenly realized he didn't need to speak aloud. He slapped his forehead and focused his thoughts to speak internally.

What do I need to do? By the way, this is so cool. You're awesome, Seneca. I mean it! Totally awesome—are you there? Hello, Seneca. Can you hear me? I mean, listen to me?

She replied mentally, *I hear you loud and clear! Now, pay attention, because we're only going to get one chance for this to go right.*

Seneca smiled. She loved her ability. She refocused and began the serious explanation of what was needed from him. She made sure to put emphasis on the necessary actions, as Jake had requested. She could tell from his ecstatic response that he understood what she obviously didn't.

She turned to Jake and Seneca, her eyes wide and anxious. "He's ready. Hit the floor—now!" she screamed.

Shayna tripped. Her foot hooked around Jake's ankle, and they hit the floor hard. Her chin scraped the cold stone, and she bit her lip. She could taste blood as the sound of ice exploding filled the air. She tucked her face into Jake's chest as he pulled her clear of falling spikes of ice.

Seneca covered her head as she rolled clear of crashing ice fragments. She turned and opened her eyes just in time to witness Conner hurdling over her. He plowed squarely into Brigara's chest, slamming her against the frozen barrier. The ice cracked around her stunned frame. Conner took hold of her arm, twisted it around, and pinned it behind her. She spun and jerked, struggling to break free. He grabbed her free arm and pulled it tightly to her side. He wedged her spindly body against his broad shoulders. She stretched her mouth wide to scream. He slapped his open hand across her lips and muffled all sounds. She squirmed and thrashed. She attempted to kick him, but his stance was too broad. He lifted her from the ground as her legs flailed wildly. She began losing her strength beneath his hold, and her stamina waned. He tightened his grip and squeezed until she finally submitted. Brigara stiffened beneath his hold. With little effort, he kept her securely restrained.

"You got her!" Shayna shouted as she looked up while still sprawled on the floor next to Jake.

Seneca scrambled to her feet. Jake helped Shayna up as she wiped away a trickle of blood. Her lip was swelling and stung slightly when she licked it.

"You did it, Conner!" said Jake. "You really know how to make an entrance, dude!"

"Yeah, well, it's the first time I was called for clobbering time. I had to do it right!" Conner boasted excitedly. He tightened his grip around Brigara's trembling arm. He stifled her attempt to wrestle free. She was tenacious, which caused him concern. "Stop wiggling!" Conner demanded.

Brigara growled beneath his sweaty hands. He didn't care for handling her with such force, but he knew that restraint was the only way to guarantee their safety. He hoped her detainment would conclude sooner rather than later.

"What's next, guys?" Conner asked. "She's fighting back so much. I'm afraid if I hold her any tighter, I might crack her in half." Genuine worry was etched across his face.

"Now, that's a delightful image I might be able to live with," Shayna said with a smirk.

"Not funny, Shayna," Seneca said.

"It is a little bit," Shayna scoffed as she glared at Brigara.

"All right, so I'm with Conner. What do we do now? We've got the book," said Seneca.

"We need Rileau. He said he'd be on the other side of the door," said Jake. He darted across the room, sliding and teetering on the broken pieces of ice. "Rileau!" he yelled.

He swung the door open and was taken aback for a moment. Rileau's tall frame filled the doorway. Smoke escaped from his flared nostrils like steam from a screaming tea kettle. Ordinarily, that would have been moderately disconcerting, but what caused Jake to take pause was Rileau's companion. He stepped aside to reveal to the others what he had encountered.

Wren stood stoically by Rileau's side. Her cloak was clasped behind her shoulders, revealing her polished, gleaming armor. Her blade was drawn. She looked past Jake, and her eyes narrowed on their captive.

"What's she doing here?" Jake asked. His stomach sank.

Shayna and Seneca stood motionless as they gazed upon Wren in disbelief.

"Wren has been bestowed the gravely important task of bringing Brigara to the Elder Elf Council," said Rileau. "They have determined that she possesses the proficiencies required to accomplish this." He surveyed the room before making his entry. He brushed past Jake, and Wren followed close behind. The ice crackled loudly beneath their boots.

"So that's it? She betrays us, and all is forgiven because the Elder Elf Council thinks she's a worthy bounty hunter?" said Shayna. "She had us ambushed!"

"Does the council know about what she did?" Seneca added.

"I will not speak on her behalf. It is best she explains to you directly," Rileau replied.

Wren walked around Rileau to face Shayna. Seneca eased in closer. Wren's hair glistened in the light that peered through the shattered and rapidly melting ice dome. Most of the enclosure had been destroyed when Conner made his entrance, and only small traces of it remained. The crystal walls brightened the room as before.

Seneca's wings remained erect; she was on guard. She gleamed under the familiar glow of Shayna's sword, and it was clear Shayna felt the same. Jake hurried across the room to join them. They stood side by side between Wren and their captive. Brigara grumbled incoherently beneath Conner's grasp.

"I can see how you may doubt my intentions," Wren said. "I was summoned by my clan, as the Elder Druid Council has heightened concerns about the increase of elementals joining Brigara. They were aware of my sister's corruption as well as my quest and failure to gain magic for her."

Brigara managed a muffled laugh in spite of Conner's firm clasp over her mouth. Her delight was undeniable. Her eyes danced wildly with satisfaction as she mockingly shook her head.

"What's up with her?" Conner asked. Holding Brigara was making him nervous enough, but her cackling sent chills down his spine.

"She laughs because I failed to dissuade my naive sister. Anyone who knows of Brigara's treachery can attest to her empty pledges to the innocent and desperate. My efforts were of pure heart, whereas hers were lined with deceit for her own gain," Wren said. She stared at Brigara with contempt. "Unfortunately, I failed to return in time to stop my sister. I apologize on behalf of my clan."

Wren walked closer and slid her sword into the sheath that hung low on her hip. Jake, Seneca, and Shayna remained unmoved. Conner took a step back and tightened his hold. Wren observed their reactions, but she only sighed in mild frustration. She turned to Rileau, and he nodded as a prompt for her to continue.

"When I arrived, my home was in disarray, and you were no longer there. When I found my sister, she had already passed on," said Wren, her voice steady and serious. "Her death is not of your doing. It is the result of her actions and the crossroad she willingly chose."

She looked at Seneca and Shayna as she stepped closer. Shayna's sword hummed and glowed a midnight blue. Wren slowly lowered herself down on one knee and bowed her head. Shayna watched her momentarily. She glanced at Jake and Seneca for a reaction. Seneca remained still as Jake shook his head and shrugged in confusion. Rileau was silent.

"I request allowance to join the quest of the Dominion of Four to bring honor to my elf clan. I willfully appeal to you for permission to fulfill the request of the elders," Wren said. She raised her head and looked solely into Jake's eyes.

"What exactly are you asking me?" Jake was bewildered, and his mouth suddenly felt dry.

"I ask for your trust. I give you my solemn word that I will not betray you. I am here to provide what has been asked of me by my clan and the council. This is of my free will and my desire," said Wren.

"Well, okay, I guess," Jake said. He ran his fingers through his sweat-drenched hair. It was clear she was speaking directly to him, and he didn't understand why. He didn't consider himself the leader of the dominion; he actually felt like just the opposite. "I'm not really sure what I'm supposed to say. Is this a ceremony or something?" he asked. "I'm pretty sure everyone should get a vote if it comes to that."

"She has said enough. She was not involved in the attack," Rileau said. "Wren has vowed to align herself with the Dominion of Four. She seeks what we all do—to end the reign of Brigara."

"Sounds good to me. She's got my vote," Conner said. "Ouch!" His voice trembled.

Brigara had jerked hard enough to kick him in the shin. She pushed hard beneath his hold, but he held firm. She tugged at anything she could grab, but he was quick to readjust his grip and bring her back into submission.

"The Elder Elf Council has commanded that Brigara be escorted to them. They will ultimately decide her fate," Rileau said.

Brigara twisted her head wildly. She craned and contorted her neck until she broke free of Conner's hand across her mouth. She snapped at his fingers as he tried to put his hand back. He instinctively pulled away to avoid being bit.

"You are premature, my old friend. I am not in the proper attire to meet the esteemed council," said Brigara in a brittle voice. "Don't be so rude, dear Rileau. Surely this is not how you greet your guests. Have you no offerings of tea or shortbread? It would seem your dragonish manners have not improved whilst I was away. I cannot say I am completely surprised."

"Conner, shut her up!" Jake shouted.

Conner hesitated. He didn't like the idea of losing a finger. He just held her tighter as a compromise. He imagined having the ability to magically create a muzzle that would fit over her entire head. He smirked at the imagery. He squeezed her tighter, which caused her to groan. She spat at his feet in defiance. Wren jumped to her feet and drew her sword to match the tip of Shayna's. Both blades aimed at Brigara. They exchanged quick glances before returning their eyes to their target.

"No need to be rude, Jake. My words might be of interest to you. If I am to be gagged again, you will miss so much," Brigara sneered. "Wouldn't you like to know precisely what tidbits I have acquired?"

"Nothing you have to say will ever interest me unless it's goodbye or farewell," Jake retorted.

"That's quite disconcerting. You were incredibly interested in learning about biology, from what I recall. Though you weren't the brightest, you did seem to have an aptitude for examining all facets of a topic," Brigara said as she pursed her lips and batted her eyes. She was making a great effort to antagonize him. Jake clenched his jaw; his temperature was rising.

"That was before we found out how twisted you are!" Shayna said. She kept her blade steady. Its brilliance glowed brighter.

Brigara ignored the interruption and kept her focus on Jake. "Are you squelching your curiosity? Wren was asking you to sanction her inclusion in your imprudent quest, not the others. Don't you find that quite odd? An even more telling question: Why did Rileau interrupt her plea? Surely your inquisitiveness has not been dampened while trekking through the Otherworld," Brigara said in a deadpan tone.

Jake knew she was baiting him. Rileau had warned them of her tactics. She would do or say anything to gain her freedom. He didn't care for being singled out for her mind games.

"I'm not your student anymore, so I don't have to answer your questions," Jake said. He stared into her bloodshot eyes. He felt uneasiness in his stomach. He swallowed hard.

"Just say the word, Jake, and I can shut her up again!" Conner yelled.

"She has said nothing of importance. Her attempts to delay are a mere ploy. She knows this is the end of her days," Rileau said.

"Perhaps Jake will choose to believe, or perhaps he will remain ignorant. Neither is worth my time," said Brigara as she turned her attention to Shayna. "My dearest niece, your confidence in the handling of your sword has grown since last we met. Your beauty has been enhanced as well. The gift of a reflectoire is quite an improvement over your otherwise common mortal facade. And before you ask of my well-being, you shall be pleased to know that I only twinge in the slightest from the harm you bestowed upon your aunt."

Her voice was exaggeratedly sweet. Shayna cringed as she recalled seeing the distorted image of Brigara vanishing from the portal after she destroyed it. She could still hear the agonizing screams.

"It would seem that you healed just fine. Your attitude, on the other hand, is still as horrid as ever!" snapped Shayna.

"As this may likely be our last meeting, you should know that as family, you shall be the one I endow with my possessions," said Brigara.

"You don't have anything I would ever want," replied Shayna. "For all I care, whatever you have can be destroyed along with all memories of your existence."

"Oh, but I do have something of value," said Brigara slyly. "Something that only a druid possesses. I am willing to offer it to you. Do you want it? Perhaps the day will come when you will want to bequeath it to your own child."

Shayna stared blankly and didn't know how to respond. She contemplated several answers but looked to Rileau for guidance. "What do I do?"

"You must not listen to her tales, as they are laced with deception. Accept none of her offerings," Rileau said flatly. "I will take the Book of Grimoire into my care. The Elder Elf Council is expecting it."

Shayna handed the book to Rileau. She glanced over her shoulder and caught the scowl forming on Brigara's face.

"Well done. You should all be proud today, as this was a wondrous accomplishment," said Rileau He tucked the Book of Grimoire beneath his coat and turned toward the door. "Wren, it is time. Join me in the corridor. We must discuss Brigara's transfer," he said.

Wren lowered her sword and trailed quickly behind Rileau as they exited. The door was left ajar, but their conversation was out of earshot. The room had grown noticeably quiet. Seneca locked on Jake's distraught expression. He was in deep thought, but she resisted invading his private thoughts. She knew that Rileau was holding back from giving them all the information they needed, but the fact that Brigara had knowledge of it was disturbing. Seneca shifted her attention to Shayna. Shayna had lowered her sword and was pacing a few feet away. She noticed sweat streaming down Conner's face as he held fast to his grip around Brigara. As for Brigara, her eyes were closed, and she had an expression of satisfaction plastered across her face. That was worrisome to Seneca. She believed it was probably not a good sign; it was likely the calm before the storm.

She thought about what Brigara had said to Shayna. Seneca knew what Brigara had been referencing. She placed her hand on her chest and felt the necklace and charm. She had kept it close since she was a young child. She had considered it a good-luck piece until Keene Ardara had explained that it was the sign of a druid. While in his home, they'd been shown a photo of Brigara in which she had the same medallion around her neck. The emblem was also engraved on the portal used for crossing between the mortal realm and the Otherworld. Seneca held her breath in anticipation. She wanted Shayna to claim the medallion as her own but hesitated in speaking up. She was suddenly nervous but didn't know why. She felt the urge to get out of the room and move about.

"I'm going to check to see what's keeping them," said Seneca. "The sooner we get her out of here, the better."

"You go do that, little fairy. Run along," sneered Brigara. Her eyes were open, and her expression frightened Seneca.

Seneca elected not to engage as she made her way to the door. Rileau and Wren were at the far end of the long hall, which explained why they couldn't be overheard. Wren was animated with her hands and body language. Seneca could tell she was passionately pleading her case, but Rileau merely shook his head. He was adamant in his response in objecting to whatever she was proposing.

Seneca could tell they hadn't noticed her presence, as they were engrossed in their debate. She observed Rileau's reactions closely. For the first time, she could see worry across his face. His nostrils were absent of smoke, and his tail was still. She hesitated for a moment, and then she did what she had promised herself she would never attempt: she surged deep into his thoughts. She retreated just as quickly as she had gone in. He spun around with eyes narrowed. She had been careless and had been detected.

"I'm sorry, Rileau, but Jake needs to know," Seneca said softly.

Without responding, he turned and began heading her way, taking long strides. His eyes locked on hers. She could feel the disappointment coming off him in waves.

"I'm really sorry. It's just that—" Seneca stopped midsentence, unable to finish her words. A commotion of earsplitting shrieks and riotous yelling filled the corridor. She dashed into the calcite room. Wren and Rileau bolted down the hall in her direction.

Seneca covered her mouth to stifle a scream. Brigara stood in the center of the room. Her arm was pulled tightly around Shayna's neck in a choke hold. In her other hand, she held a shard of ice, its razor-sharp tip aimed between Shayna's collarbone and jaw. It was a standoff. Jake and Conner stood across from them, poised to attack. Seneca tried to assess the situation, baffled by what had happened so quickly.

"Let her go, Brigara!" Rileau bellowed over Seneca's shoulder.

"Step back, Rileau, or she dies right here," Brigara snarled.

Shayna tried to wrestle free, but Brigara scraped the cold shard against her neck to demonstrate that her words were not mere threats. Shayna stiffened as she felt the sting from the fresh cut. It was a minor wound that could easily become fatal if she wasn't careful.

"The castle is charmed, and your forbidden magic will not allow you to escape!" Rileau roared.

"There is always another door that shall open when the obvious is blocked," said Brigara snidely. "You are as foolish as these children, Rileau, which quite disappoints me, actually. Perhaps when we meet again, you might be more willing to offer me that cup of tea."

Without warning, she spun Shayna around to face her. Shayna attempted to raise her sword but halted. Brigara aimed the icy weapon into the hollow of her throat, and their eyes locked. The evil druid's spindly hand fanned across Shayna's face, swiftly brushing across her reflectoire. Brigara vanished. Her screeching laughter echoed against the crystalized walls, and it was all that remained of her presence.

Shayna brandished her sword a split second too late. She screamed in reaction and crumpled to the floor. Conner waved his hands wildly through the air where Brigara had stood only seconds before.

"How did this happen?" Wren asked, slightly winded. "Why was she not restrained?"

"It's my fault. I wanted to see that damn druid necklace," said Shayna. "She kept flaunting it. I thought my mother might want it." She covered her face in shame. She felt foolish and was angry at herself.

Conner said, "I loosened my grip on Brigara's arm so she could show the necklace. Somehow, she slid out of my reach. The next thing you know, she had Shayna by the neck with a sharp piece of ice at her throat."

"She threatened to snap Shayna's neck if we tried to get close. That's when you guys came rushing in," Jake added. "We're all to blame. We underestimated her."

"I thought she was finally trying to do a decent thing by giving me the necklace," said Shayna. "How could I have been so stupid?"

"How she got out of this room is the baffling part," said Seneca. "How was she able to use Shayna's reflectoire?"

"I thought I was the only one who could control it," Shayna said.

"Never disregard the connections of family. Her powerful magic was evidently used as a conduit because of your bloodline," said Rileau. "As such, she harnessed your reflectoire energy."

"You mean she stole it!" Shayna grumbled. She wiped her tears futilely as more streamed down her cheeks.

"We unleashed her to the Otherworld," said Jake. "So much for prophecies about the great Dominion of Four." His tone was cuttingly sarcastic.

"At least we have the book. That's got to count for something, but I don't get why she didn't demand it back. She had the advantage when she grabbed Shayna. It's like it suddenly has no value to her," said Seneca.

"Yeah, it doesn't make sense," Shayna agreed. She attempted to hide her mounting angst.

"Something's off. This whole thing is totally wrong!" said Jake. "There's no way she's going to abandon her grand mission of getting to the source of magic. She must know another way to get to Arcadrom."

"There's merit to what you say, Jake," said Rileau calmly. "I agree with you."

"It figures she'd have a backup plan. That's classic villain strategy," said Conner.

"Do you think my reflectoire took her straight to Arcadrom?" Shayna asked hesitantly.

"No, that is not feasible. There are only two known ways to enter," replied Rileau. "One is by the incantation that can only rise from the Book of Grimoire. The other is with a key."

"A key?" Seneca and Shayna asked.

"What kind of key are you talking about?" asked Jake.

"It is not a key that secures a lock or door. It is the link that allows those from Arcadrom to return if they so desire," replied Rileau.

Jake watched Rileau turn to Wren and exchange a subtle glance. Seneca saw it too. She thought it was the perfect opportunity to speak up and address what she'd picked up from Rileau's thoughts.

"It's time you tell him the truth," said Seneca. "Jake deserves to know!" Her voice rattled nervously.

"Know what?" Jake asked. He stared at Rileau as he waited for a response.

The dragon remained silent as he raised his chin and released a stream of smoke that dissipated as quickly as it had been released. Shayna moved next to Jake and grabbed hold of his hand. Conner placed a hand on his shoulder. Seneca gazed into Jake's eyes, and it was all the confirmation she needed. She couldn't hold back any longer.

"You're from Arcadrom. It's your home," Seneca said slowly. "I just found out."

She bit down on her lip and held her breath. She wasn't sure how he would react. She hadn't thought that far in advance. Jake stared blankly at her. She nodded slowly. He turned to Rileau and then to Wren. He searched their eyes for confirmation. Their lack of denial confirmed it.

"The two of you knew this, and you didn't tell me? Why?" Jake demanded angrily. "Don't you think I deserve to know who I am and where I'm from?" He spun around, searching for something to throw or hit. He settled on kicking over one of the ceremonial chairs, sending it crashing into the crystal wall.

"Calm down, Jake, and let them explain," Conner pleaded. "I'm sure they have a good reason. Back me up, you guys." He looked at Seneca and Shayna, expecting them to speak up.

"I'm guessing they have a great explanation for not telling Jake where he's from," Seneca said unconvincingly. She glared at Wren, and then her eyes drifted to Rileau; she resisted the urge to blink. "I'm sure they have great reasons for keeping you in the dark."

Shayna remained quiet. Her rage had already peaked because of Brigara's escape, and she was still angry about it. She knew if she spoke up, she'd only add to the explosive situation.

"I've only just learned from the Elder Elf Council of your origin," said Wren. "It is why I have been assigned as your griffin."

"What is a griffin? And why do I need one?" asked Jake. His curiosity swiftly replaced his anger.

"I am responsible for your protection. I am tasked with guarding your identity and your life until you can return to Arcadrom. I am told that you were sent to the mortal realm as a precaution," said Wren. "Until it was time for your return, no one knew of your existence."

"Wren the griffin. Perfect," Shayna snarled.

"I'm getting tired of asking this, but why?" asked Jake. His frustration was accented on every word. "Be straight with me!"

"It is not safe for your lineage to be known. Those who seek to raid Arcadrom would surely use you as leverage. Accessing the pure source of magic cannot be resisted by some," said Rileau.

"You mean like Brigara and her followers," Conner said.

"It is precisely the reason for the omission," said Rileau.

"Maybe it was smart to keep Jake and the rest of us in the dark," said Shayna softly.

"Well, Brigara made it clear that she knows something about Jake. It looks like the secret is out!" Seneca exclaimed.

"Why are you guys talking about me as if I'm not here?" Jake shouted. "I have a say in whether or not I'm going to accept a griffin— uh, Wren. Whatever! It's up to me to decide my fate, and no one else gets to decide. Who cares if Brigara knows who I am or where I came from? Apparently, everyone else does!"

He had the urge to continue venting his anger, but he took a deep breath instead. His head hurt from the relentless throbbing at his temples. He knew he was losing it and whispered to himself to settle down and focus.

Shayna could see he was spiraling, but she was unsure what she should do. All except Conner had experienced surprises and well-woven lies about their identities. They had more in common than she'd previously considered.

"Jake, Brigara was hinting about who you were—sort of taunting you. It's obvious she knows something. Who knows how much? It's probably so wrapped up in her crazy brain that we may never know," said Shayna. "And I know what it's like too! She knew who I was, but instead of doing anything about it, she kept it from my mother—her own sister! She made her think I was dead! That's beyond cruel."

"Whatever she knows, she will keep it hidden and use it as a weapon without hesitation," Rileau said flatly.

"We're all in this together, Jake. The truth, lies, and everything in between," said Shayna.

Her soothing tone of empathy eased the tension Jake was feeling. He smiled at her slightly. She was right. He agreed that they'd all been fooled. The stories of their lives continued to unfold like an endless road map.

"I agree it would seem she knows something of your ancestry," said Rileau. "How much is unclear. I do surmise that she may also know the location of a key. It is why the Book of Grimoire was of no further interest," said Rileau. "Again, it is a key meant only for descendants of Arcadrom."

Jake's face lit up. He jerked around and zeroed in on Seneca. Her nose scrunched, and her eyes widened in confusion. Searching his face for a clue, she was baffled by his reaction.

"What's wrong?" she finally asked, shrugging and shaking her head.

"This would've been a perfect opportunity to read my mind," he replied kiddingly. "I know where the key is. I will bet anything that Shayna's reflectoire is taking Brigara there too!"

"Where, Jake?" asked Shayna.

"Remember what the Glactra told me—actually, commanded me to do?" Jake said.

"Get what belongs to you or something like that. Am I right?" Conner asked.

Jake's eyes locked on Seneca. He watched her blank expression slowly turn into a smile.

"Leander. Jake's key is with Leander!" said Seneca. "You saw the key when we were there because it belongs to you."

"It's not a key in the traditional sense, but if I'm right, there are two of them."

"Two keys?" Rileau asked sternly. "Are you sure there are two?"

"Yeah, I'm sure there were two. Why?" Jake asked with bewilderment.

Rileau let out a blast of smoke that filled the room. His tail slammed hard against the floor. The scattered remains of ice popped from the impact. Shayna and Seneca were startled and grabbed on to each other. Jake and Conner barely reacted as they watched the dragon's reaction in awe.

"Brigara's after the key," said Seneca slowly. "That's where she's going, Jake. She's going to Leander."

"No. This can't be happening. Please, no," he moaned.

Jake was being bombarded with reactions from everyone in the room. He couldn't focus; his mind swirled from the chaos. He had a home and possibly a family somewhere, and they had left a key. The images he tried to force wouldn't form; his mind was blank. It finally registered that he needed to protect this home, no matter how foreign or disconnected. He had to explore and find his true path. He could hear Wren yelling, but it took a moment for her words to make sense.

"Huh? What did you say?" he asked, still slightly disoriented.

"She must be stopped!" Wren said. "I will contact the elders; they must know of this." She turned to leave and then turned back to face Jake. "It is an honor to serve you, and I am aligned with you. Arcadrom must be protected. I shall return shortly." She bowed her head slightly before making a quick exit.

"We shall await Wren's return before we take action," said Rileau. "Let us leave this chamber to prepare. Time is not on our side; 'tis a grave enemy."

Chapter Nineteen

Prepare to Fly

The dining hall had been a place of pleasure with the inviting aromas and abundance of offerings, but that day was different. Rileau had insisted they eat while they awaited Wren's return, but eating was by far the last thing on their minds. Waiting for Wren to arrive was torture, and the rack of roasted lamb with rosemary was a waste, as was the leek-and-potato soup. Seneca tried to nibble on a slice of yeast bread with a slather of creamed goat cheese, but it was bland to her unresponsive taste buds. She finally tossed it aside as she noticed she wasn't the only one skipping the feast.

"I can't believe we're going to see Leander again," she said hoarsely. Her throat was dry, and she realized she was parched. She gulped down her goblet of spring water.

"I'm nervous about it," Shayna muttered.

"It's definitely going to be different," said Jake.

Conner, Jake, Seneca, and Shayna discussed Leander and how it felt to be in the presence of the massive tree. Not one of them had conceived of returning; their world and the life-altering events were spinning too quickly. They reminisced about their flight across the vast ocean and the beautiful landscape that surrounded Leander. The memories of retrieving the portal and the rules they had to follow were discussed in great detail. The consequences of not following them had to be avoided.

"Remember, you can't take anything that doesn't belong to you," said Seneca.

"I bet Brigara's going to get around that rule," said Jake in a tight voice.

"You should have grabbed them when we were there," Conner moaned. "I know we've been over it, but it would have saved us a lot of grief."

"Yeah, but if he had, you'd miss out on riding an arion again!" Shayna said.

"If they don't agree to take us, then what do we do?" asked Seneca nervously.

No one wanted to answer. The conversation died out. It had become a pattern since they'd left the crystal room. This had been the most they had spoken since realizing they had to go after Brigara. They'd been instructed to wait and not invoke any magic or attempt leaving the castle. The last instruction had been specifically meant for Jake. He had boisterously declared that he was going to find a way to Leander, even if he had no idea how to get there. Rileau had recognized it as a situation he didn't want to handle. He'd decided that all threats of reckless behavior needed to be managed, and as a result, he'd cast a charm barring their exit from the castle.

"It will be for your protection. You must trust that I know best," Rileau had said.

He'd taken off to gather the arions. He was convinced that Brigara would not have gone straight to Leander. It had been told that she was not allowed to step on hallowed ground. She would have to figure out a way to overcome that barrier, which could potentially buy them some time—but not much. Rileau believed Leander was her ultimate destination. As such, they had to get there before she did. It was a race to the key.

Jake was perplexed by Brigara's knowledge of the key's location. He analyzed various possibilities, but each scenario had the same conclusion: someone was feeding her information. The dilemma was figuring out who and why.

Shayna, Jake, Seneca, and Conner attempted to eat the meal set before them. The offerings were as abundant and well prepared as usual, but their appetites were stunted. Seneca had held the same bowl of beef broth for the entire meal, and most of it still remained. It was now lukewarm, and a thin film had formed on the surface. She rocked the bowl slowly as she stared blankly at the flowered tapestry on the wall. Even Conner was unable to finish more than a few bites of his favorite sandwich. Shayna flicked her fork through her salad. She'd raise a few lettuce leaves to her lips and then ceremoniously let them fall back to her plate. Jake seemed to be the only one who managed to eat at least a partial meal, primarily because he did so absentmindedly. He would take a bite and then drift off into thoughts of his childhood. The multitude of lies he had been fed was mind-numbing. He wondered what would have been different had he been raised in Arcadrom, a land he'd never known existed, in a realm he'd never fathomed. It was a place cut off from the rest of the world, and he was cut off from it.

"We must move quickly!" Rileau interrupted the silence with a voice that bellowed and reverberated off the dining room walls. He had entered without any of them noticing him.

"Is it time to go already?" Shayna asked wearily. She pushed away from the table and rose to her feet. She was tired and knew she needed to get charged, but she felt dejected. Her confidence waned. She dwelled on how she'd created the opportunity for Brigara to escape. No one blamed her, but she felt it was her fault.

"Four arions have agreed to provide transport to Leander. As there are six of us, two must fly," Rileau announced.

"Well, I guess that's me, for one," said Seneca. "I'm going to enjoy this!" She was elated. She hadn't flown much since they'd arrived at the castle. She wanted to master flight and discover more about her wings.

"I haven't tried flying since I escaped from the wild river ride when I first consumed the Himalayan crystals," said Jake. He hadn't a clue whether or not it was even possible.

"You, Jake, will ride by arion," replied Rileau. "Shayna, Conner, and Wren will do the same."

"So that just leaves you. Aren't you coming?" Seneca asked. She felt a sudden jolt of anxiety hit her stomach.

"Naturally, I will be coming," said Rileau.

"But I thought you said there are only four arions," said Conner. "How are you going to get there?"

"Ask Jake about his knowledge of dragons," Rileau replied in a flat tone. "It is affirmative they have the ability to fly. I shall, of course, fly alongside you."

They exchanged looks of surprise and excitement. Jake shook his head in disbelief as Conner's mouth hung open.

"I don't have words to say how totally cool and awesomely spectacular that is!" Shayna exclaimed.

"I think you used all of the right words." Jake laughed. "I can't wait to see this!"

Rileau remained serious and did not engage any further in the banter. His brow furrowed, and he raised one eyebrow as he gazed at them. Both Jake and Conner knew it was a sign to get serious.

"We must make our leave to Leander. Follow me! Wren and the arions await."

They followed Rileau's lead and were cautious not to trip across his tail. It swung briskly back and forth in rhythm with his quickened stride. It was a definitive sign of his anxiousness, along with the trail of smoke that followed. Conner held his breath in anticipation. He had inhaled the sulfur-scented discharge more times than he could count. He deplored the taste it left in his mouth.

"Listen as I tell you the story of Arcadrom, because once the key is retrieved from Leander, we must find our way there," Rileau said as he picked up his pace. The foursome sped up to ensure they heard all he had to say. "We must provide protection to the realm to prevent any breach by Brigara."

"I thought this wasn't allowed," said Seneca. "Going into Arcadrom, I mean."

"There is certainly no other way to protect it from Brigara," said Rileau. "The elders made it absolutely clear. The dominion must take on this dangerous task, even with the risks involved when entering Arcadrom."

"Ah, *risks*, my favorite word," Conner moaned. "It comes in second only to *danger*."

"What can we expect?" asked Jake.

"What you will see first is the black sand beach of Arcadrom. It is the place with no beginning and no end, as it has been present since the beginning of time," said Rileau. His voice deepened the more details he revealed. He continued making his way down the spiral stairs that led to the castle's main floor and exit. His teenage entourage trailed close behind.

"Arcadrom is the origin of nobility, honor, knowledge, and harmony. The Otherworld is a fragment of Arcadrom, as we were cut off and forced to align closer to the mortal realm. As a veil separates our Otherworld from the mortal realm, there is also such a veil that separates us from Arcadrom. We can admire it from afar, but we are forbidden from touching its shores."

"Nobility, you say? Does that mean Jake is a prince?" Shayna asked jubilantly.

"*Noble* isn't the same as *royal*," Seneca said, smirking when she saw the smile disappear from Shayna's expression. Shayna huffed with disappointment.

Seneca latched on to Jake's arm to keep from falling behind. Rileau told them all he knew about the history of Arcadrom. He spoke with pride when he described their way of life and the admirable absence of strife. They were beings of peace.

"The arions are the only beings that can freely cross the threshold that separates us. It has been said that they are from Arcadrom, but this has never been confirmed," Rileau said.

He explained why Arcadrom could not be detected from the Otherworld or the mortal realm. At the conclusion of his lengthy explanation, they finally agreed that Arcadrom existed beyond comprehension.

"Like Leander, no one knows of its actual beginning. It has just always been."

"That's intriguing," Jake said nearly inaudibly.

"As you will learn, discord is the complete polar opposite in Arcadrom. As such, it is also inaccessible to the Otherworld. It was not always so. Greed in harnessing unlimited magical powers ultimately separated us from them. It is known by all that Arcadrom is the birthplace of magic, and to breach its boundaries is a law that we have all accepted."

"Except Brigara!" Shayna snapped. "Tell us about the sand."

"The black sand surrounding its shores is rich in elements necessary to create both light and dark magic. Its essence is untainted and of vivid clarity. Untouched, it is in perfect balance. This sand is said to be the actual remains from the vast sparks that created our earth and all living beings in all realms," Rileau said. His voice was captivating. They were enthralled by the enchanting description.

"The actual source of all magic," Seneca said softly in a modulated tone.

"Yes, the source in its purest state and equally as magnificent as it is deadly," Rileau said.

They made their way into the courtyard of the castle. The sky was lit with a blanket of stars. Jake looked up in contemplation. He was anxious to discover where he'd come from and learn why he'd been raised away from Arcadrom. He felt pride in all Rileau had revealed, as well as a deep desire to protect the sacred realm.

"If Brigara gets there before us, the balance will most definitely be disrupted," said Jake. "I'm not going to let her destroy my home!"

"I'm with you, Jake!" Conner said as he threw a fist in the air.

"Count me and Seneca in too!" Shayna cheered.

"Yeah, what she said," Seneca added with a smile.

"I am pleased to join you in this quest," said Wren as she approached with the four familiar arions flanked on either side. Keene Ardara stepped around her and bowed low as he removed his hat.

"Keene Ardara!" Conner shouted. He grinned and bowed awkwardly in return.

Shayna and Jake waved to the cluricaune and made their way to Wren with Conner trailing close behind. They had already discussed the expectations when approaching the majestic winged arions and the proper greetings required. Seneca hung back to gather her composure. Since she was not assigned to ride an arion, she saw no need to rush. Her focus was on the pint-size fairy.

"You must take along some of my offerings for your journey!" Keene Ardara shouted in his familiar grousing tone.

"Thanks, Keene Ardara!" Jake yelled over his shoulder. "It's great to see you!"

Keene Ardara scratched his massive beard and pulled his hat back into place. He started briskly sorting satchels from a gunnysack. The sack's contents appeared to weigh more than he did. Each satchel was bursting at the seams with supplies. He piled them in a heap as he grumbled incoherently.

Seneca remained motionless and eyed him from a distance. She was so thrilled to see him that she couldn't hold back any longer. She sprinted across the lawn at full speed and threw her arms around him, nearly toppling over upon impact.

"Calm down, indigo child. Calm yourself," he grumbled.

"I missed you, Keene Ardara!" Seneca said joyfully. "I have so much to tell you. So many things have happened!"

"Yes, I am quite aware of how busy you've been since your arrival," said Keene Ardara. "It's been captured quite nicely in the countless scrolls, my dear precious one! The Dominion of Four is keeping me quite busy. I will soon need more shelves to hold the mounds of parchment that are piling up."

"Are you feeling a bit crowded in your home?" Seneca asked teasingly.

"Well, I like it quite cozy. I would change nary a thing! The more shelves the better, I believe. Especially with the most recent release of Cassandra's prophecies."

"You've said that name before. Who is she?" Seneca asked.

"You shall soon find out. Now, my dear, you must listen closely," he said with a tender tone that she was accustomed to hearing. "You will come to a crook in the road that is not normally traveled. It will be your choice to brave it or seek another path."

"You mean this metaphorically, right?" Seneca asked, although she knew the answer.

"I don't know the meaning of your fancy words, but what I do know is that when the time comes, you must choose your way selflessly, as your decision will set the course for the others," he said. The familiar gruffness eased back into his tone.

He rocked back on his heels and twirled his cane in the dirt in contemplation. He rubbed his ruddy beard and sighed. When he raised his head, she saw pools of water gathering in his wide eyes. Seneca was motionless as his words swirled around in her thoughts. She cast her eyes away to avoid the expression of sorrow etched on his broad face. She couldn't look at him for a moment until she gained her composure.

"Oh, Keene Ardara, I will be okay," she whispered. "Don't worry, please."

"Yes, yes, indeed, no worries," he muttered as he wiped his sizable hands across his face.

Seneca hadn't witnessed any tears fall, but the gesture reflected his sadness. Her heart fluttered as she resisted wrapping her arms around him. She knew he wouldn't want consoling. She shoved her hand into her pocket. The stone warmed beneath her fingertips. Her mind flashed to the moment he'd given it to her. He had followed the request of her parents and kept it. It had saved her life once, and she wondered if it would have the same effect when she came to the crossroad Keene Ardara had described.

"It still responds to your touch as it should," he said flatly. "You must call upon it when it is best to do so. You will know when, my dear indigo child. You will know exactly when."

She nodded and forced a smile. She wanted to say something, but the words would not form. She decided to bow, and he returned the gesture.

"I must now do my duty. I am not convinced your friends will be diligent in greeting the arions with their due respect!" he roared, and he marched away. His large feet stomped with authority in the direction of the others.

Seneca smiled demurely. Keene Ardara continued his lecturing and rants to the others while kicking up dust with his well-polished boots. His ruddy beard was braided, which was a vast change from the last time they had met, but his attire was completely unchanged. The large buttons on his jacket were still shiny enough to reflect the sunlight, causing her to squint. She had missed him terribly. A queasy sensation washed over her suddenly as she realized this could be the last time she saw him. As she continued to watch Keene Ardara make his rounds while issuing countless demands and repeated warnings, she realized the ill feeling was more of a knowing. This would definitely be the last time she saw him. She released a slow breath and allowed her wings to appear. She examined their glorious coloring. They were more brilliant and defined since her transformation. They appeared fragile, but she knew that appearance was deceptive and actually added to their beauty.

She could hear her mother's voice whispering sentiments of bravery and love. It made her wonder if they were connected telepathically. Realizing that was possible made her feel connected. A light breeze swept over her face, and with it, the smell of a favorite southwestern dish lingered in the air. The name of it escaped her, but the aroma was unmistakable. She closed her eyes and breathed it in, realizing there was no explanation for the scent, but she allowed it to tease her senses and fill her heart with comfort.

Seneca's gaze turned to Jake, Conner, and Shayna. They were frolicking with the arions and teasing Keene Ardara while he lectured on the dos and don'ts of using the chocolate ambrosia. Wren and Rileau remained solemn as they looked on. As she focused on each of their movements, they seemed to slow down, as if giving her time to see the smallest of details in their smiles, eyes, and gestures. She was able to observe all the various idiosyncrasies that set them apart. Each movement, tone of voice, and laugh would be forever etched in her memory. Her body temperature dropped. She was frigid to her core, but she didn't move or attempt to warm herself. Grief washed over her. A tear trickled slowly down her icy cheek; she allowed it to remain as acceptance of the loss she felt. She shook her head and motioned to wipe away any signs of crying. She was startled to find the tear had frozen into a delicate ice crystal. She looked at it curiously before flicking it away. Seneca took a deep breath and stretched her wings. She admired their beauty as she strolled slowly toward the others. They were ready to take flight.

ABOUT THE AUTHOR

C. Toni Graham is a master storyteller and author of the award-winning *Crossroads and the Himalayan Crystals.* The first installment of the epic Crossroads fantasy series received the Readers Favorite International Book Award for Excellence in Writing and an Honorable Mention Award from the Los Angeles Book Festival for Young Adult Fiction. She lives in California surrounded by family, too many dogs, and a few fairies. To learn more about Toni, visit her website at www.ctonigraham.com.

Printed and bound by PG in the USA